*To my parents, with love*

2008

# Overture

I stood in the darkness backstage, trembling.

Onstage, my singing teacher was making her introductions. I could hear the pride in her voice. Phrases like 'dedicated to his craft' and 'professional accolades' and 'tenor of extraordinary potential' drifted towards me.

She said my name, and there was applause from the auditorium. This was my cue to appear.

My nerves were screaming at me to run, to flee the Conservatoire and keep running until I forgot the whole dreadful scene. But my body had switched to automatic, and a moment later I had slipped out of the shadowed wings and was standing centre stage.

The auditorium loomed in front of me like a vast cavern, cold and dark. It was a modern space, all sharp corners and straight lines, with none of the elaborate decoration present in most older theatres.

Every seat was taken. I couldn't see the faces of the audience, but I knew they were looking at me.

I took a breath. Of *course* they were looking at me. I was onstage. Wasn't this what I wanted?

Somebody giggled. Several coughs echoed off the black walls.

The spotlights burned brighter than any sun, shining on my face. I had only just managed to stop crying, and I knew most of the concealer had been rubbed away. They would be able to see the dark shadows under my eyes, every pore and blemish on my pale skin.

Someone was playing the piano. The sound seemed very far away. I'd missed my cue.

I tried to ignore the taunts inside my head. I nodded at the musical director. The piano started again.

I opened my mouth to sing, but the voice that emerged was quiet and flat. It didn't sound like my voice at all. I cracked a note, and my voice fell silent.

There was no sound from the auditorium.

I looked into the wings. My singing teacher was staring at me in horror.

I ran.

2016

# Prima Donna

It was almost eleven years since I had arrived in London with the following plan:

1. Attend the Conservatoire.
2. Graduate from the Conservatoire.
3. Attend audition for West End show.
4. Get leading role in West End show.
5. Become successful singer on the back of performance in West End show.
6. Solo album.
7. Broadway.

It wasn't the most comprehensive of plans, but I was very young at the time, and the details hadn't seemed particularly important.

Unfortunately, it was almost eight years since my last successful performance, and I was standing in a freezing auditorium, attempting to remove chewing gum from the bottom of a theatre seat.

The gum had been left behind by a school party, to whom I'd delivered a talk on the history of the Moon and Stars Theatre. I had tried my best to make it exciting, telling them the anecdote about the magician who had burned the original building to the ground when a firework had gone awry.

I'd hoped to inspire them with the magic of theatre, but instead I'd been forced to watch as their eyes glazed over.

Chewing gum removal wasn't technically part of my job description, but no one else had volunteered, so it was up to me. I was using a paint scraper I'd borrowed from the workshop. The task would have been satisfying if it wasn't so disgusting.

My mobile rang. I dropped the scraper.

'Hello?'

'Matthew? Is that you?'

It was a woman's voice, musical and strangely familiar in a way which made the back of my neck prickle. 'Who is this?'

'It's Angela.'

Her name conjured up a face, but more importantly a voice, singing across a room from me. There was no audience, just the two of us.

'Are you still there?'

I snapped out of my musical trance. 'Yes. Hello... Angela.'

I couldn't begin to imagine why she was calling me. We hadn't spoken in nearly eight years.

There was a sigh on the other end of the line. 'I'm so glad it's still the right number. How are you?'

'Oh...' I stared at the nearest chewing gum deposit. 'I'm good.'

There was a pause.

'Listen, Matthew. I realise this is totally out of the blue, and I'll completely understand if you're not interested – but I just thought I'd give you a call because I'm about to start recording my next album.'

'That's great.' I was pleased for her, even though she had made it, and I had not. 'Congratulations.'

'We'd like to include a few duets, and we were discussing guest artists when your name came up.'

My hand tightened around the phone. This wasn't real. This couldn't be real. The fact that Angela was recording another album was hardly surprising. What was surprising was that she had thought of me.

'You want me to sing on your album?'

'There's no one else. I really mean that. Your voice is still the best I've ever heard.'

'Right.' I was stunned. I couldn't believe she was paying me this sort of compliment after so many years.

I was tempted to say yes, but then I remembered the competition, the last time we had sung together. And I remembered those words that were always lurking at the back of my mind. For eight years, they had been there every time I had been tempted to sing in front of an audience.

*Angela, you look like a singer. But Matthew, well… you just don't.*

My free hand strayed automatically to my face. 'Are you sure about this, Angela?'

'Of course. The album's classical crossover, mainly musical theatre. You'll be perfect.'

'What would I have to do?'

'Just come along to the studio and sing for my manager. I know I want you, but he insists on hearing any guests. The record label gets the final say.'

Managers and record labels. This was scary stuff, and way beyond my limited experience. And I was still hearing that voice in my head.

*Angela, we can pair you up with someone else. A better match.*

'I'm not sure,' I said. 'I don't think I'm quite in your league. Vocally, I mean. I… haven't sung very much lately.'

'That doesn't matter. Come and audition for us. Then, if you decide it's not for you, that's not a problem.'

I swallowed hard. 'All right. Thank you.'

'Great. Would 9am tomorrow be all right? I'll text you the address…'

It wasn't all right, but I said it was. I would tell work I was going to be late. Pretend to have a dentist appointment, perhaps.

'It's so lovely to talk to you,' said Angela, her voice soft, kind. 'It's been too long. I can't wait to see you again.'

When she'd gone, I slumped into the theatre seat and sat very still for several moments, staring at the phone. I touched my forehead and found it damp with sweat.

Oh, God. What had I done?

I would text her and tell her I'd moved on, that I wasn't interested in singing anymore, that I already had a career I enjoyed.

I stood up, intending to go back to scraping gum, and trod on a half-empty packet of Wotsits, sending a spray of crisp residue across the dark blue carpet. I stared down at the new mess I'd created, and saw my future with terrible, powdery-orange clarity.

I was nearly thirty, practically ancient. I had expected to be a successful performer by now. I knew I couldn't let this opportunity pass me by. I'd already done that too many times. And *Angela* wanted me.

I'd been given another chance, and now I needed to make sure Angela – and her record label – would be impressed enough to hire me.

I couldn't change how I looked. And I couldn't change the past. But at least I could practise until my voice was the best it could be.

It was only 5pm. There was no performance tonight. I had plenty of time to rehearse.

The theatre wasn't quite dark; shows were still performed a few times a week, and an amateur operatic society used it for rehearsal every Sunday afternoon. But on free evenings, the stage was mine.

Just the way I liked it.

I always waited until the other staff had left, to be safe. After six years, the theatre felt like home. But I wasn't supposed to be there after hours. My privileges as manager only extended so far.

I made my way up the centre aisle.

The auditorium had seen better days. There were signs of decay everywhere: peeling paint, chipped plaster. The scent of damp lingered in the air. The blue velvet curtain was faded. The seats were worn. Everything needed repainting, or reupholstering.

I climbed the steps at the side of the stage and stood in my usual position, downstage centre. I stood half in shadow, looking out at an audience of empty seats.

I began with some exercises: scales designed to aid the voice, breath and diaphragm. Then, when I felt that my voice was sufficiently warmed up, I launched into my rehearsal pieces.

I chose 'Being Alive' from *Company*, 'The Impossible Dream' from *Man of La Mancha* and, because I was in the mood for opera, 'The Toreador Song' from *Carmen*.

I was worried my voice was not as fine as it used to be. I had limited time to practise, and a voice can suffer from lack of use. Still, the acoustics in the theatre were good, and gave my voice a pleasing, eerie echo.

If someone had heard me singing, they would have been more than a little startled. But I told myself that by doing this, I was breathing some life back into the old place. It didn't hear enough voices.

When I'd rehearsed all three pieces several times, I was as prepared as I could be. I bowed to the empty auditorium and slipped back into the shadows.

Until next time.

# Audition

Before I went to my audition, I had to attend to my morning routine.

I checked my face in the shower-room mirror. I had to make sure there were no spots or other blemishes on my skin. If I found any, I would rectify the situation by covering the offending patch with a small touch of concealer.

This usually took me around fifteen minutes. Sometimes, if I was attending an important meeting, I would return to the bathroom twice or three times, just to make sure I hadn't missed anything. On the morning of my audition, I checked three times, which could have made me late for my appointment had I not set my alarm half an hour earlier than usual.

The studio was located near Piccadilly, and at 9am I found myself staring at a glass-fronted building with nothing to distinguish it from the offices on either side. I checked the address on my phone for the umpteenth time, in case I was mistaken, but this was definitely the place.

I stepped through the automatic doors into a reception area that looked more like a show floor at Ikea. The walls were painted a pure, glaring white, and low, colourful chairs were arranged around the edges of the room. Everything was ultra-modern, functional and anonymous. The only hint at any sort of musical association was a white bust of Ludwig van Beethoven, which glared at me from the reception desk as if wondering exactly what I was doing there.

I inched towards the reception desk. It was presided over by a young woman who was busy typing something into a computer. Her dark hair was styled in a sharp bob, and her smart appearance made me feel unfashionable in comparison. I smoothed down my suit.

'Excuse me – I'm here to see Angela Nilsson. My name's Matthew Capes.'

She didn't look up from the computer. 'Do you have an appointment?'

'I'm here for an audition.'

She did look up then, and her eyes narrowed sceptically.

'Take a seat. I'll let her know you're here.'

I waited while she made a phone call, my stomach tight with nerves. The previous day's excitement had faded, and even more doubts were starting to crowd in.

Angela hadn't heard me sing for years. What if she was horribly disappointed? I couldn't even be sure my voice was still up to scratch.

And then there was the question of my appearance. As I waited in reception, I began to wonder if I had done enough before leaving the flat. Perhaps I should have checked the mirror one more time. My hand strayed to the tube of concealer in my coat pocket. Maybe I could quickly go to the gents…

The door next to the desk opened.

'Oh my God, *Matthew*!'

Angela hadn't changed. No, that was a lie: she must have changed, but only slightly. Her hair was styled differently. And her face seemed sharper. But she still had the same confident poise of someone who was absolutely sure of her purpose in the world. This was something I'd both admired and envied when we'd first met.

I looked down at the floor, suddenly overcome with shyness. 'Hello, Angela.'

'How are you? You look great.'

I flinched internally at her untruth.

'I'm fine. You do, too.'

We stared at each other for a moment. It was strange, to be confronted by a little piece of my past. Suddenly our time at the Conservatoire felt like yesterday.

Angela grinned at me. 'This is so exciting! I'm so glad you could come. It's just this way...'

I followed her through the door and down a white corridor illuminated by strip lights. I had expected some framed album covers or gold discs, but instead there was just blank wall after blank wall. The blankness heightened my nerves. There was something clinical about it, as if we were in a hospital and not a recording studio.

Angela chuckled. 'Behind the scenes tour. All glamour, huh?'

Finally, we came to a door marked Studio One. Angela opened it, spilling piano music into the corridor.

The music was familiar.

I froze and looked at Angela in confusion. 'That's my song.'

'Yes,' she said, with a soft smile. 'I showed it to my manager. I hope you don't mind.'

The song was a youthful attempt at a love ballad which had felt like a sincere work of genius at the time, but which struck me as gauche and embarrassing now. But I was very touched that she'd kept it all these years.

'Not at all,' I said.

She nodded towards the door. 'Please go in.'

There had been a recording suite at my college which I had used a couple of times for student projects, but this studio was on a different scale entirely. There were rows of electric keyboards and mixing desks, and three separate vocal booths.

At a magnificent grand piano sat a pianist, a man in his fifties with a neatly trimmed beard and stylish glasses. He was playing my song with a focused skill and intensity.

'Hi, Steve,' said Angela.

The man nodded but did not look up.

'Steve's one of our session musicians,' said Angela. 'He's going to play for your audition. We'll have an orchestra for the recording, of course.'

My mouth went dry. I stared at her. 'An *orchestra*?'

'Yes.' She chuckled. 'Please don't look so terrified. I mean a small session orchestra, not a symphony.'

'Right. Good.'

'We just need to wait for Chris – then we can get started.'

'Chris?'

'My manager.'

'Oh, of course.' I kept forgetting how *professional* Angela was. Professional enough to have a manager, a studio and an actual orchestra at her disposal.

Angela gestured at the piano. 'Do you still play?'

'Very occasionally. When I have time.'

'I remember when I first heard you play at college. You were like the next Mozart or something.'

Steve the pianist cleared his throat. I blushed.

'That's a slight exaggeration,' I said. 'I'm nothing special.'

'You always were too modest.' She paused. 'Have you written any new songs recently?'

'Not for a while. I've been quite busy with work and stuff.'

'Ah, I see.' She sounded a little disappointed. 'But you still have all your old material?'

I wondered where this strange line of questioning was heading. Angela had not mentioned my compositions on the phone.

'I've kept the good ones,' I said.

Angela looked ready to say something else, but then the door opened and a man strode into the studio.

'Chris!' said Angela. 'This is Matthew.'

Chris appeared to be about forty. He was dressed in a smart, expensive-looking grey business suit. His dark hair was neatly swept back with gel. He reminded me vaguely of a gangster from my conservatoire's production of *Guys and Dolls*.

He looked at me, and an expression of surprise flashed across his face. But he quickly hid it with a smile and gave me an enthusiastic handshake.

'Matthew, my man! Thanks for coming. I've heard so much about you. This one never stops talking about you.'

'Hello...' I began.

'I know Angela would just hire you right here and now,' Chris continued, still pumping my hand. 'But obviously I'd like to hear you sing in person. Got to make things official, do things properly...'

'I know it's not necessary,' said Angela. 'But Chris insists.'

'No problem,' I said.

'You don't mind singing your own song, do you?'

'Of course not.' I hoped I didn't sound too reluctant. I had practised my audition songs until they were perfect, and I wasn't sure how I felt about singing a song from my past.

'I realise it's a duet,' said Chris, 'but if you could just sing your verse and the chorus to start with, that would be great. Steve?'

Steve nodded and began the introduction. The piano had a beautiful tone; perhaps, if I got the job, I would have the chance to play it myself. But that would never happen, because I could already feel the nerves dancing in my stomach. I was going to fail – my voice would go...

I tried to remember that I was good. Tried to remember that this was what I loved. That this was what I *was*, or had been. And it wasn't as if all the people in the room were strangers. Angela knew that I could sing, which was why she had invited me along.

Gradually, my nerves were soothed by the music, and I became absorbed in song. I sang softly at first, as the song demanded, but then allowed my voice to fill the room with sound.

When I had finished, I looked at Chris. He was staring at me, a slightly stunned expression on his face.

'Well, Chris?' said Angela. 'What do you think?'

'Wow. You weren't exaggerating.' He stepped forward and shook my hand again. 'You, my man, have a great voice.'

I looked at the floor. 'Thank you.'

'When can you start?' Angela's voice was bright with enthusiasm. I looked up again to find her beaming at me.

'You mean I've got the job?'

'Of course you've got the job.'

'Now hold on a sec,' said Chris. 'It's not quite as simple as that.'

'It is as simple as that,' said Angela. 'I want to sing with Matthew.' She turned to me. 'We'd like to start recording as soon as possible. When can you come in?'

'Well, I work full time, so—'

'Can you come in on Saturday?'

I couldn't speak. I just nodded.

'Great. This is going to be so much fun! Chris will sort out all the legal stuff, won't you?'

'Of course.' Chris gave her a forced-looking smile. I was starting to get the impression that he wasn't completely sure about hiring me.

'Great!' She gave me a quick hug. 'Sorry, I must run. I need to get to a magazine interview. I can't wait to sing with you again.'

I was left in the studio with Chris and Steve the pianist.

'Steve, would you leave us alone, please?' said Chris.

Steve rose from the piano stool. As he passed me, he gave me a look which was almost pitying. I wondered what his problem was.

The moment Steve had gone, the smile vanished from Chris's face.

'All right, Matthew, here's the thing. You're here because we need a hit.'

'I'm sorry?' I said, a little startled by his sudden transformation into a businessman. 'Angela has had lots of hits.'

He waved a hand. 'Yes. Classical repertoire. Musical theatre covers. Specialist stuff. It's all a bit *niche*. And there's a danger we're going to start replicating what's already out there. I mean, how many different versions of "You Raise Me Up" does the world actually need?'

'That's one of my favourite songs,' I said defensively.

Chris nodded. 'Mine, too, mate. But that's not the point. We need something *new*, something to appeal to the pop market while still being firmly rooted in classical crossover. Something which will appeal to both mums *and* their teenage daughters.' He smiled. 'I think your song would be perfect. It has hit written all over it.'

'My... song?' I was stunned.

'It's perfect. Romantic, but not soppy. Powerful, but not creepy. We just need to big it up a bit.'

'You're not serious.'

'I'm deadly serious. I want this song, Matthew.' He paused. 'If I had my way, I would buy the rights to this song from you. Then I would call up any of the numerous male singers on my books. They're a great bunch. Polished, experienced, good-looking...'

The nerves fluttered in my stomach.

'But there's one rather big problem,' said Chris. 'Angela wants *you*. She said to me just the other day: "I'll only sing Matthew's song if it's with Matthew."'

'I... see,' I said, both confused and touched.

Chris folded his arms. 'Will you allow me to be blunt?'

I thought Chris had already been sufficiently blunt without asking my permission, but I nodded.

'You're not quite what I expected. Listening to Angela talk about you, she made you sound like this... charismatic star. An absolute pro who could turn his hand to anything. And it painted rather a different picture in my mind.'

I had an awful sense of déjà vu.

But of course it was happening again. What had I expected?

'Well, I'm sorry to disappoint you,' I said.

Chris shook his head. 'I wouldn't go that far. You're a wonderful singer and a wonderful writer. But we really want this album to succeed. I just need some reassurance that you're not going to mess this up. Can I rely on you, Matthew, not to mess this up?'

'Of course. I mean... no, I won't mess it up.'

'Have you ever recorded anything before?'

'Not professionally.'

'But you have plenty of singing experience?'

I hesitated, unable to meet his eye. 'Yes.'

'You sure? Angela tells me it's been a while.'

'I've been having a break, doing other things. But... I still practise every chance I get.'

Chris gave me a long, appraising look, and then seemed to relax. 'Good. I'm glad to hear it.' He crossed to the table and picked up a folder. 'Your other duets. I'm sure you'll be familiar with them.'

'Thank you.'

'If I seem a bit... harsh, it's only because I care passionately about Angela's career. Do you understand?'

I nodded. 'I won't let you down.'

# Ensemble

Later that morning, I stepped through the stage door of the Moon and Stars Theatre and trudged up the three flights of stairs to my office.

There was a Post-it note stuck to my computer screen. It said: *The mice are back. Also: hole in ceiling of Gents toilets.*

I removed it with a scowl. The mice had been a problem for a while. I had called pest control several times, but they were proving elusive (both pest control and the mice). Short of creeping around the theatre with a net, I didn't know what else I was expected to do.

But the hole in the ceiling: that was a new one.

I could already tell that it was going to be one of those days.

I sat down at my desk and eyed my collection of foam stress balls. I had seven of them of varying designs and colours. I had only bought one myself; the rest had been gifted to me in the office Secret Santa. I wondered which one I should use today.

'Afternoon, Matthew.' Jess – the development/marketing/box office assistant – wandered in. Jess was in her mid-twenties and had started working at the theatre two years earlier, as an intern. As usual she looked remarkably relaxed, given that she was doing the jobs of three people.

I smiled. 'Hello, Jess.'

'How did you get on at the dentist?'

'What?'

'The dentist. You said you had toothache?'

'Oh. Yes. I'm fine, thanks. Just needed a filling.'

Jess was great. If I had chosen to tell her about my audition, I was sure she would have been pleased for me. And that was the problem: if I told her, it would lead to lots more questions. Like most of my colleagues at the theatre, Jess had no idea I could sing.

She sat at her desk, which faced mine, our computer monitors almost back-to-back. It was a very small office, tucked away on the top floor of the theatre, above the Grand Circle. The walls were exposed brick, and it was chilly and rather dim, having only one small window. There was also an ever-present musty smell reminiscent of village halls. Jess had tacked posters from past productions to the walls in a futile attempt to cheer the place up.

She peered around her computer screen. 'Just a quick heads-up. We're expecting a royal visit later today.'

'Oh God, no.'

'I'm afraid so. Special emergency meeting. Top secret and all that. Very important, apparently.' Jess grimaced.

'Terrific.' I rubbed my eyes. Yesterday's unscheduled rehearsal session was starting to catch up with me.

'Late night?'

'Something like that.'

'Maybe you should take a holiday.'

'Ha, ha.'

'Did you see my note about the mice?'

'Yes.'

'And the hole?'

'Yes, thank you.'

'What are the chances this place will fall apart by the end of the month?'

I was silent. I didn't want to think about this. Maintenance was becoming a real problem. Every time we found the money to sort something out, a new issue would present itself.

'Maybe Her Ladyship can find us some more cash,' said Jess.

'I wouldn't count on it.' I powered up my computer and opened my work email. Another cancellation – a radical touring production called *Twelfth Night Told Backwards and in the Dark* had pulled out at the last minute due to low ticket sales. This was the third production to cancel in the space of a month, and I was growing increasingly worried about the future of the theatre. I hoped I would be able to persuade the fifty or so customers to swap their tickets for other shows. We needed to avoid issuing refunds if possible.

First on the list: a lady called Rose Anderson.

'Hello, it's Matthew calling from the Moon and Stars Theatre. Am I speaking to Ms Anderson?'

'Yes, hello. We're looking forward to seeing your *Twelfth Night*.'

'Ah, yes, about that. I'm afraid I've got some bad news.'

'Oh?'

'I'm afraid we've had to cancel the show due to unforeseen circumstances.'

'Oh, what a pity.'

'I wondered if you would like to swap your tickets for one of our other exciting shows?'

There was a pause.

'All right,' said Rose. 'That's fine.'

An easy customer! It was a miracle.

'Great. Would you like me to run through the programme with you? Or you could take a look at our website—'

'That's okay. I've already made up my mind.'

'Oh. Great.'

'I would like to see *A Christmas Carol*, please.'

'*A... Christmas Carol*?'

'Yes. I've always wanted to see it at the theatre.'

I rubbed my forehead. 'I'm afraid we're not presenting *A Christmas Carol*.'

'Can't you get some people in to perform it?'

'It doesn't really work like that.'

'Why?'

'Because we can't book shows in just like that. And also it's February, so not really the right time of year.'

'So I can't swap my tickets?'

'Not for a show we're not presenting, no. But I can swap—'

'I can't believe you won't let me swap my tickets. That's appalling.'

'But I can—'

There was the sound of a phone being slammed down, followed by a dial tone. I hung up.

The phone rang again almost immediately.

'Moon and Stars Theatre.'

'Hello. I wish to make a complaint.'

Oh, God. It was definitely going to be one of those days.

Jess caught my eye and held up both our coffee mugs. I nodded in desperation.

'I'm sorry to hear that,' I said. 'What's your complaint regarding, please?'

'The pantomime. I would like a refund.'

'Was there some issue with your seats?'

'No, the seats were fine.'

'...I see?'

'My complaint is about the pantomime horse.'

'Right. What about it, specifically?'

'It terrified my Thomas and made him cry.'

'Okay. And Thomas is...?'

'My son. He's three.'

'I'm very sorry to hear that, madam. It really wasn't intended to be frightening.'

'Yes, well, it had very scary eyes. My Thomas was distraught.'

'As I said, I'm sorry to hear that.'

'Are you going to give me the refund or not?'

I considered this.

'Will it cheer Thomas up if I issue the refund?'

'I beg your pardon?'

Jess placed a coffee on my desk. She looked at me with wide eyes, and drew a finger across her throat, from ear to ear. I ignored her.

'Perhaps I could get Dobbin to send Thomas an apology, and some free tickets to our next children's show?' I was proud of my kind, understanding tone. The customer relations training I had been forced to endure had its uses. Occasionally.

There was a pause.

'I... think I would rather have the refund.'

'Of course, madam. I'm very sorry for the distress caused.' My voice was like honey.

'See that it doesn't happen again. You should really warn people on your publicity, you know.'

'I'll do my best. Thank you for the feedback.'

I hung up.

I sipped my coffee.

The phone rang.

'Moon... and Stars... Theatre...'

'Hello, it's Mrs Anderson again. Would you be able to perform *Cats*?'

*

After my phone calls, I ventured into the toilets to see if I could fix the hole. It was above the sink, about four inches in diameter, and it looked as though the ceiling had simply caved in. I sighed; this was no mere cosmetic job. I would need to cordon off the toilets until someone could assess the damage, and hopefully mend the ceiling. The joys of showbiz.

Unfortunately, my failure to mend the hole meant I would be on time for my meeting with Her Ladyship. Charlotte was an entrepreneur and occasional actress who, together with her business partner, Richard, had bought the Moon and Stars ten years earlier. In the beginning she had cast herself in roles which were way beyond her limited capabilities. She had soon lost interest when the critics had written some less than favourable reviews about her. But she still visited the theatre every few weeks, when she would insist on calling the staff together for an 'emergency meeting'.

The meeting was held in the rehearsal room next door to the office where Jess and I worked. When I arrived, Jess was already there, along with Dave, the head techie. He was in his late fifties, highly experienced, and had little time for Charlotte's whims.

'Darlings!' Charlotte swept into the room in a whirl of pashmina. She smiled at the three of us. 'How are my favourite people? Are we all good?'

Jess and Dave made vaguely positive grunting noises. I didn't say anything. I never knew what to say to Charlotte.

'I have good news, and bad news,' said Charlotte, taking a seat at the head of the table. 'Let's get the bad news out of the way first. As you're no doubt aware, this place needs some help. Both financial and creative. Audience numbers have dwindled, and the place needs some serious TLC.'

'It needs a complete refurb,' muttered Dave.

Charlotte nodded. 'Yes. Quite. But in order to do this, we need something different to bring people through the door.' She smiled. 'That's where the good news comes in.'

We waited. Perhaps Charlotte had been given a generous donation that would solve all our problems.

'This summer, we'll be staging a brand-new production of *The Importance of Being Earnest*.' She clapped her hands together, eyes shining with excitement. 'I shall play Lady Bracknell.'

We all stared at her.

Charlotte beamed at us. 'Well? What do you think?'

There was a long silence, and Charlotte's mouth began to twist.

Jess spotted this and dived in. 'Well, it's a popular play...'

Charlotte nodded. 'That's what I thought.'

'We could probably reuse some old scenery,' said Dave. 'Furniture and whatnot.'

'That should keep the costs down a bit,' said Jess.

Charlotte smiled, and then turned to look at me. 'Matty? You're very quiet, as usual.'

'I don't know what to say.'

'You must have an opinion.'

My palms were starting to sweat. She was staring straight at me, a challenging look in her eye, and I knew she wasn't going to leave until I said something.

I cleared my throat. 'Well. I was just wondering... how exactly is this going to help?'

'What do you mean?'

'I mean... yes, I think it's a good idea. But maybe we need something else, too. More of a draw.'

'But, darling, I will be the draw. This will be my great comeback.' She gave me a condescending smile. 'Really, Matty. You need to buck your ideas up. Think positive. Dream big! Auditions start on Monday. I've left a file on your desk.'

Meeting apparently over, she swept out of the room.

There was another long silence.

'Bloody hell,' said Dave.

'So she's gone completely mad now,' said Jess.

I sighed. 'It would seem so.'

Jess frowned at me. 'Why do you let her call you Matty? No one calls you Matty.'

'That's the least of my worries at the moment.' I stood up. 'I'd better take a look at that file.'

In truth, I didn't want Jess and Dave to see how annoyed I was. Not at the 'Matty' thing, although that was irritating. My sister called me that, too, and it made me wince every time. It was more that Charlotte seemed to exist in a sort of parallel universe, with no real grasp of the difficulties facing the theatre. Apparently, she thought her great comeback would solve all our problems.

In reality, we were dangerously close to losing both the theatre and our jobs.

# Counterpoint

I wanted to go straight home after work, but I had a friendship duty to fulfil. It was Ralph Night.

Ralph was my oldest friend. We had first met at secondary school, where we had been bullied mercilessly: Ralph because he was arty and sensitive, and me because I was 'a weird freak who played the piano all the time'. We had formed an unlikely alliance.

Eleven years ago, on the night before we received our A-level results, we had made a Bacardi Breezer-fuelled pact to look out for each other when we both moved to the big city. Ralph had got a place at a trendy art school whereas I had gone to the more traditional Conservatoire. Since then, we had made a point of meeting on the second Thursday of every other month, first to cheer each other on in our chosen careers, and later to lament our dying dreams. Although, quite frankly, I wasn't sure what Ralph had to complain about. He was a successful model and the most ridiculously handsome man I had ever met.

Ralph was waiting for me at our usual place, a small Indian restaurant near where he lived. I liked the restaurant. It was softly lit, in a way that I think was supposed to be romantic, but in reality was just dim. And it was nearly always quiet, except during happy hour (which I insisted on scrupulously avoiding). Both these characteristics made it the perfect meeting place. And the food was delicious.

I found Ralph already tucking into poppadums.

'Sorry I'm late. I couldn't get away.'

'That's okay.' A waiter arrived, and Ralph picked up the menu. 'Are you having a starter or just a main? Because I'm having both.'

'Just a main for me.'

After we had placed our orders, Ralph looked at me hopefully. 'You know, we don't always have to go out to eat. We could go to the pub.'

I grimaced. 'No.'

'Or we could meet in the West End. There's this great new bar in Soho.'

'Absolutely not.'

Ralph laid aside his menu with a sigh. 'I don't understand you. We're in London, we're young—'

'Not that young.'

'—why can't we go for a proper night out?'

A 'proper night out' with Ralph always involved a visit to a crowded bar. He would spend the entire evening chatting up women, while I would sit in the corner eating crisps. We hadn't had a 'proper night out' in about three years, much to my relief.

I narrowed my eyes at him. 'You know why, Ralph. You'd just spend the whole time talking to other people.'

Ralph smiled. 'If by "people" you mean "women", you might actually get to talk to them, too, if you didn't sit there being all silent and grumpy.'

'I'm not silent or grumpy. That's not the issue here.'

'Hmm.' Ralph took another bite of poppadum. Even when he was chewing, he was still infuriatingly good-looking. People flitted around him like moths around a chandelier. Which was, of course, the problem. If he was a crystal chandelier, I was one of those fluorescent strip lights which buzzed and flickered all the time.

Suddenly, Ralph looked up and flashed a bright, movie-star smile. I heard laughter and looked over my shoulder to see two young women whispering to each other and throwing furtive glances in his direction.

I turned back to face him. 'You see? This happens everywhere we go. People stare at you. It's embarrassing.'

'How do you know they're looking at me? They might be looking at you.'

'I have my back to them, Ralph.'

'Yeah, well, you have a good back. There's nothing wrong with your back.'

I looked over my shoulder again. The women dropped their gazes to their curries.

I raised an eyebrow at Ralph. 'See?'

'That's probably because you glared at them.'

'I did not glare at them.'

'I bet you did.'

Our food arrived, which I hoped would offer me some respite from this embarrassing conversation. But Ralph wouldn't let it go.

'Okay,' he said. 'How about this? If we go to the pub, I'll find you a date.'

'No, thank you. I'm not using you as a matchmaker.'

Ralph was far from cruel, but he tended to run in the opposite direction whenever things got serious. I had no desire to accept romantic advice from him.

He grinned. 'When I introduce you, I'll say: This is my friend Matthew. He's a nice guy, but if he so much as talks to a woman, he might explode, so please be gentle with him.'

I glared at my curry. 'That's not funny.'

'What are you so scared of? Why wouldn't someone want to date you?'

Oh, several reasons.

1. I'm ugly.
2. I'm shy.
3. I'm a professional failure.
4. I hang out in an empty theatre after dark and sing to nobody.

I didn't say this to Ralph. I wished to get through the evening with my dignity still intact.

'Honestly, Ralph, you're obsessed. Anyway...' This was my chance. For once, I actually had some good news to share, and I was determined to enjoy it. 'I'm going to be too busy to go on hypothetical dates.'

'Why? What's going on?'

I leaned forward and lowered my voice conspiratorially. 'I've got a gig.'

'What? You mean you've finally left that dump of a theatre?'

'My theatre is not a dump.'

'Oh, so now it's *your* theatre, is it? Sometimes I think you might as well move in there.'

I closed my eyes briefly. This was why it was a relief we had never become flatmates.

'I haven't left the theatre,' I said. 'But I've been given the opportunity to sing on an album.'

Ralph's eyes widened. 'Wow. That's... wow. But I thought you'd given all that up?'

'Yes, I thought I had, too. But Angela got in touch—'

'Angela? The girl you used to sing with at uni?'

'Yes.'

'Isn't she, like, quite a big deal now?'

'Yes, she is. And she got in touch and asked if I'd duet with her on her new album. It's only in the very early stages. I just had the audition this morning.'

'Mate, that's amazing.' Ralph smiled, then his expression turned wistful. 'I wish I could do something like that.'

'It'll be your turn next.'

'Yeah, right. Says the *actual* opera singer.' He smiled. 'Tell you what: as you're going to be famous, you can pay tonight.'

I felt a flutter of fear in my stomach.

'I'm not going to be famous, Ralph. Don't be ridiculous.'

*

I got home just before ten.

My flat was on the second floor of a converted terraced house, which had thin walls and even thinner carpets. It had three rooms: a living room with a kitchenette, a bedroom and a shower room. Ralph had helped me move in, and his jaw had dropped because, apparently, I had 'loads of space'. The flat needed redecorating: for reasons that were obscure to me, either the landlord or a previous resident had decided to paint all the walls charcoal grey, lending the rooms a certain Gothic feel.

As I was mounting the stairs, I found I could hear music.

Not proper music, but something hideous and heavily metallic – the sort of music which made me want to stick plungers over my ears.

It was louder on the second floor, and I realised with horror that it was coming from behind the door of the neighbouring flat, which had been empty for several weeks.

I sighed. That was all I needed. A new neighbour with terrible taste in music. I hoped they wouldn't be playing it at all hours. If they did, I would need to complain to the landlord.

I locked my door and went into my bedroom, where the racket was at least muffled. I sat at my desk and began to look through the music Chris had given me. The pieces were fairly straightforward, and I had sung them before: 'What I Did for Love' from *A Chorus Line*, 'If I Loved You' from *Carousel*, and – my heart trembled a little – 'Somewhere' from *West Side Story*.

Perhaps Angela had chosen the pieces with my voice in mind. It seemed unlikely, but the thought made me smile.

# Tenor

On Saturday I met Chris and Angela in Studio One. Angela waved at me from a vocal booth. Chris led me inside and talked me through the equipment, testing my headphones and microphone. Then he stepped back outside and took up his position behind the sound desk, alongside the engineer.

I was alone with Angela in a space which resembled a giant fish tank. I realised I was shaking.

She smiled at me. 'Are you ready?'

'Yes.'

'Do you have any questions about the songs?' asked Chris, his voice coming through my headphones.

I didn't. In fact, I was proud of my progress and felt ready to go.

'I thought we might start with your own song,' said Chris. 'Consider this a rehearsal. But we're still going to record you, just so we have some rough tracks to work with. Is that okay?'

I gave him the thumbs-up. I cleared my throat and opened my file of sheet music.

The engineer pressed something on the sound desk, and a backing track began to play.

As soon as Angela sang the first phrase, my heart began to pound. I was nervous: it was just the adrenaline kicking in. It was perfectly normal.

But her voice was soft and full of yearning, and I felt warmth spread from my face and down my limbs. It was the same rush of feeling I used to get when I heard something beautiful and startling, like the day I first heard Tchaikovsky's Piano Concerto No. 1 in B-flat minor, and I knew the piece had been waiting for me to find it.

I was aware how very close she was to me. I focused on my music and avoided catching her eye.

She reached the end of the first verse. I waited for her to continue. And then I realised I had forgotten to sing.

The backing track stopped.

I looked up from my music and found Angela staring at me, her expression somewhere between amused and perplexed.

'Are you all right?' she asked.

'Er... yes.'

'What's wrong?' Chris was peering at me through the window.

'Nothing. Sorry. It's just been a long time since I recorded anything.' I sounded flustered.

'Please concentrate. We haven't got all day.'

I tried to pull myself together. I took several deep breaths and willed myself to stop trembling.

My God, this was a disaster. I was going to get fired.

Angela began again. I forced myself to concentrate on the notes on the page, tracing them with my eyes as Angela followed them with her voice. Soon we had reached the second verse and I was joining her in song. I forgot to look at the sheet music. There was only her voice and mine, and the world disappeared. My nerves vanished. I was lost.

Singing with her was an absolute joy. Our voices complemented each other perfectly. Her voice seemed to reach out to mine, dancing with it, calling out to it, calling out to me.

It was over too soon. I stood gazing at the microphone. Someone tapped on the glass, which startled me so much that I cried out, my body jerking violently. I looked up to find Chris staring at me. He beckoned to us, and we left the vocal booth. I felt like I was floating.

'Was that okay?' I asked tentatively.

'It was… good,' said Chris. 'What do you think, Angie?'

'Matthew,' she said. 'What can I say? That was amazing.'

Warmth flooded my face. I looked down at the floor. 'Thanks.'

'Look at him blushing!' Chris was laughing.

Angela punched him on the arm. 'Don't be mean.'

'It's all right,' I said, although I had hoped neither of them had noticed my embarrassment.

We moved on, singing the musical theatre standards that Chris had chosen. It was the most enjoyable morning of what had passed for my career so far.

At lunchtime, I removed the headphones with great reluctance. Chris had told me that I wouldn't be needed for the afternoon's session, as that would be devoted to Angela's solos.

I was just about to leave when Angela stopped me.

'We've hardly had a chance to talk. Come and have lunch.'

A cold finger of fear ran up my spine. Lunch meant a brightly lit café crowded with people. Lunch meant exposure.

'No, I should get off. Leave you to it…'

'Please. There's something I'd like to ask you.'

I had always found it very hard to say no to Angela. 'All right. But… can we go somewhere quiet?'

She frowned at me for a moment, and then nodded. 'Okay. I think I know a place.'

We went to a small coffee shop a few streets away from the studio. It had framed drawings of West End theatres on the walls, which I would have enjoyed looking at if I hadn't been so nervous. Only three of the tables were currently occupied, and there were no glaring lights. Still, I chose a table in the far corner, for added peace of mind, and sat with my back to the rest of the café.

Angela smiled at me across the table. 'Still shy, I see.'

I picked up the menu in an attempt to hide my embarrassment. 'Sorry.'

'Don't apologise. There's something quite refreshing about a performer who doesn't want to be the centre of attention all the time. It's sweet, really.' She picked up her own menu. 'Shall we?'

Angela ordered a pitta bread filled with vegetables and avocado, and tea made from some sort of obscure fruit, with herbal infusions ('It's great for the voice!'). I was desperate for a bacon sandwich but feared this would look unsophisticated (not to mention unhealthy) alongside Angela's pitta. So I settled for a chicken salad wrap and a cup of black coffee.

'Your voice is great,' said Angela, after we had eaten and chatted about the album for a bit. 'Even better than I remember.'

'Thank you. I was just thinking the same about your voice.'

'What have you been doing all this time?'

'Working in theatres. I'm the general manager at the Moon and Stars at the moment. I've been there for six years.'

'Oh.' She looked surprised. 'But you must have sung a lot, too?'

'Not really. Just little bits here and there.' I spooned sugar into my coffee.

She was quiet for a moment. 'Listen, Matthew, I think I owe you an apology.'

'Whatever for?'

'For what happened at the student showcase.' She stirred her tea, causing little bits of leaf to swirl around the cup. 'You were shaken up, and I should have been more understanding.'

I shook my head. 'It doesn't matter.'

'Really? To be honest I was so nervous about getting in touch with you that I almost didn't make the call. I was worried you wouldn't want to see me again.'

'That's rubbish.' I dared to look at her. 'I always wanted to see you again, but I... think I was embarrassed.'

She laughed lightly. 'What a ridiculous pair we are.'

I tried to smile. 'I suppose so.'

She relaxed, leaning back in her chair. 'I'm glad we're still friends.'

'Yes,' I said, my voice low. 'Me, too.'

We sat quietly for a moment, sipping our drinks. It felt like a companionable silence. At least I hoped it was.

'I've heard all your albums,' I blurted. 'You've done so well.'

She laughed. 'I still can't quite believe it's real.'

'Well, you deserve it.'

'Thank you.' She looked thoughtful for a moment, lowering her gaze to her tea. 'Matthew, I don't know what you'll think of this idea, but I'm doing a concert in a few weeks. This charity gala thing at the Grand. Chris has organised it. And... I was just wondering if you'd sing with me?'

I almost dropped my coffee cup. 'What? You mean for an audience?'

She nodded. 'I wasn't going to ask, but I think it would be lovely.'

My heart was racing; clearly the coffee had been a bad idea. I wanted to say yes, but just the thought of singing onstage, in concert, as myself and not playing a role, caused a knot of anxiety to form in my stomach.

'Are you sure? Remember what happened last time.'

Angela nodded briefly, her face grave, but she carried on. 'I know it's not what you signed up for, and I'll understand if you don't want to. Just give it some thought.'

Her manner had become dismissive. I could feel the opportunity slipping away, and I couldn't let that happen. I was a singer, for heaven's sake. This was my job. I was being offered an opportunity to actually *do my job*, and I was on the brink of turning it down.

'Of course I'll do it,' I said. 'I'd love to. Thank you.'

She clapped her hands together. 'Great! It'll be so much fun.'

There was a lump in my throat. I couldn't tell if it was nerves or coffee grounds or a combination of both.

'Yes. Great. I'm... looking forward to it.'

'Thank you, Matthew.' She gathered up her bag and coat. 'I must run. Chris will want to get started.'

'You're so busy now you're a star.'

'You'll find out what it's like soon enough.' She smiled. 'See you next week.'

She was gone before I had a chance to say anything else.

A part of me was overwhelmed at my luck. I was delighted that she wanted to sing with me, but I also remembered my last public appearance, which had been nothing short of a disaster. Singing in the studio had felt comparatively safe, almost as safe as singing at the Moon and Stars when it was empty. I couldn't quite picture myself standing face to face with Angela on a stage, singing of love, without imagining the audience chuckling away in the background.

But Angela had faith in me. If she thought there was any risk I would fail, she wouldn't have asked me. The idea was comforting and I tried to hold on to it.

I forced down the rest of my coffee, the bitterness of the grounds making me cough, and left to catch the train home.

# Discord

I glided home on staves of music. I'd expected our reunion to be awkward, and I'd been so wrong. Once I'd overcome my initial nervousness, I'd felt entirely comfortable singing with Angela.

There was an independent music shop just around the corner from my flat. It was almost impossible to see through the windows, which seemed to be plastered with posters advertising every gig in East London, but inside was a world of treasures for the serious music enthusiast. They sold vinyl, sheet music and even a selection of second-hand instruments.

Today, I wanted CDs. Ralph had tried to persuade me to download my music, but I wouldn't hear of it. I had patiently explained that buying CDs ensured musicians received fairer royalties, while giving me the pleasure of owning a physical item, complete with sleeve notes. I also made a point about supporting the high street. My arguments must have worked, because Ralph had not questioned my CD ownership again.

I didn't buy them very often – I couldn't really afford it – but today was different. I was, after all, celebrating my first day as a professional recording artist. I deserved a treat.

I went straight to the classical section and found a two-disc compilation called *Songs of Love and Passion: The Greatest Opera Duets of All Time*. It looked perfect.

Once home, I freed the album from its wrapper, inserted the disc into my ancient stereo and pressed play.

The room vibrated with the scream of an electric guitar. I leapt away from the stereo and made a grab for the CD case. Surely there had been some horrible mistake. This couldn't be *Songs of Love and Passion*.

I realised that the noise wasn't coming from my stereo, but from next door. It sounded as though the guitar was being deliberately provocative, raging against all that was musical, while the sounds of the orchestra emitting from my CD player were completely drowned out.

I've always believed that listening to music in one's own home should be a private, intimate experience. If you want to share music, go to a concert where you know others will share your musical taste. I'm also of the opinion that when people play their music loud, their taste in music is invariably awful (this is particularly true of people who drive around with the windows of their cars rolled down).

I glared at the wall.

When this didn't work, I turned my music up, rotating the dial until it was playing at full volume. But it still wasn't enough to drown out the electric guitar, which continued to shout like the wretched extroverted instrument it was.

I turned off the CD player and left my flat. At this point, I realised I couldn't hear any other instruments. This suggested that the poser who lived behind door number two was playing the guitar himself. Marvellous.

I reached Flat Two and knocked.

The guitar continued. I knocked harder.

There was a horrible whine of feedback, followed by a muffled curse.

I folded my arms and waited.

There were footsteps. The door opened a crack. I prepared to give the incompetent instrumentalist a piece of my mind.

The door opened further to reveal a woman with short black hair. She looked about the same age as me, late twenties, and she was wearing a baggy purple jumper. The hint of a tattoo – some sort of flower design – poked out from under her sleeve.

She leaned on the door frame and regarded me with a pair of quizzical dark eyes.

'Yes?'

'Hello,' I said. 'I live next door.'

'Oh, yes?'

'I was just wondering if you might keep it down... just a little.'

'Sorry. I'll be finished in a bit.'

'It's just that I'm trying to listen to opera. It's important.'

Her face softened a little. 'You must be Matthew. The landlord told me about you. I'm Lucy.' She stuck out her hand.

I shook it out of politeness, but my mind was very much on our landlord. Had he gone mad?

'Does he know about the guitar?' I asked, dubious.

'Yes. He said you're a musician, too, so you wouldn't mind.'

I sighed. 'Well, I do mind a bit.'

'I'm sorry. I didn't mean to disturb you.'

'That's all right. Just... would you please keep it down slightly? I'm working.'

'I thought you were listening to opera.'

'Yes. Well. That's part of my work.'

She didn't look convinced. 'What instrument do you play?'

'I'm a singer.' I felt a small thrill at being able to say it and know I was being honest. Until yesterday I had felt like an imposter, even though I had the knowledge and the training.

'An opera singer?'

'Not really. Sort of.'

'You're *sort of* an opera singer?'

'Opera singers perform in operas. I sing classical crossover.'

Lucy raised an eyebrow. 'So you're an opera singer who *doesn't* sing opera?'

'It's a bit more complicated than that.' This was wasting valuable research time. It was also a sore point: under different circumstances, I might well have become an opera singer. 'You wouldn't understand.'

'Oh, really?' Her eyes narrowed. 'Why is that?'

Her expression made me falter. 'Because... well, you obviously enjoy heavy rock music. If you listened to some opera, and then some classical crossover, you would see that there are differences. It's complex. Very different from rock.'

'Are you seriously going to mansplain music genres to me?'

'What's "mansplaining"?'

Lucy rolled her eyes. 'Look, Matthew, it's been a delight, but I've had all the musical education I require. Goodbye.'

She shut the door in my face.

Well, really. How rude.

# Opera

It was Sunday, my day off. Usually, I spent my Sundays listening to music (*Songs of Love and Passion: The Greatest Opera Duets of All Time* was high on my list). Sometimes I would go for a walk in the park or treat myself to a takeaway from the Indian restaurant I visited with Ralph.

Normally, I was quite content with this arrangement. But today I was distracted. I kept wishing I were back in the studio. It was only two weeks since my first recording session, and yet I still felt as if my life had changed beyond recognition. Now, it had Angela and singing in it. The day suddenly felt very long and very empty.

At around 3pm I got a call from my sister. We didn't talk very often, and I was surprised to hear from her.

'Hi, Matthew.'

'Hello, Clara. How are you?'

'Busy. You know how it is…'

I didn't know how it was. Clara was thirty-three, four years older than me. She worked for a bank and organised coffee mornings at her local community centre. She also owned a house with more than one bedroom. Her life was a complete mystery.

'How was the…' I waved my free hand around a bit, trying to think of something my sister had done recently which I should really ask about. 'Sports thing?'

'Sports thing?'

'You know.' I had a sudden flash of inspiration. 'The thing I sponsored you for.'

'Oh. You mean the fun run? It was good, thanks.'

I sagged with relief.

'Julie from the bank gave me fifty pounds.'

I tensed again. This was less good.

'Really? That was very generous of her.'

'Wasn't it? It was great you could send me a tenner, though. Every little bit helps.'

I had an unbidden memory of Clara and I as kids. Every time we visited our grandparents, which was about once a month, they had given us five pounds pocket money each. At the time, this seemed like untold riches. I wondered when a tenner had become 'a little bit' in Clara's world.

'You're very welcome,' I said. 'I wish I could have sent a bit more. But you know how it is...'

'Yes. Yes, I think so.'

A pause.

'I've got something to tell you,' said Clara.

I didn't like her serious tone, and my mind instantly produced an entire montage of potential catastrophes.

'What's happened?'

'Don't worry. It's good news.'

'Oh?'

'Well... you know Ben and I have been together for nearly three years now?'

Ben was Clara's tedious boyfriend. I couldn't imagine a person less interested in music, of any sort. The first time we met, he had tried to talk to me about football, and he told me that he didn't realise 'You'll Never Walk Alone' was from *Carousel*. He also seemed to think I was rich and famous, presumably because all singers are rich and famous.

'Yeeees...'

'Well, we thought it was the right time...' She paused, and gave a short, bright laugh. 'Thing is, we're getting married!'

Silence.

My first thought was to wonder why Clara had thought Julie from the bank giving her fifty pounds was more important than her impending nuptials. But my sister had always been a bit odd, so I let it go.

My next thought was that my sister was doing this huge, scary, grown-up thing, the latest in a long line of huge, scary, grown-up things, while I was still living the life of a semi-student in London.

If there was a race, I was most definitely losing it.

'Matthew? Are you still there?'

'Yes.'

'Aren't you going to congratulate me?'

Oh, God. I was terrible at this.

'Yes. Yes. That's... great news. Congratulations.'

'Thank you.'

'So – when's the wedding?'

'December, the week before Christmas. Won't that be lovely?'

'That seems... quite soon.'

'We were lucky to find a venue. But Ben has a friend at the golf club.' *Of course he does.* 'Another couple split up, you see. So there was a vacancy and we just thought... why wait?'

'How romantic.'

'Isn't it?' She paused. 'There's something I'd like to ask you. About the wedding.'

'Yes?'

'Well, I was wondering if you would sing. At the service.'

The phone slipped out of my hand. I caught it just in time.

'I... don't think I can do that.'

'Why not? It's ages since you had that... problem. It's just the local church. You used to love singing there. I think it would do you good.'

She said this as if singing was like yoga or eating broccoli.

'I... can't.'

There was silence at the other end of the line.

'Clara? Are you still there?'

'Yes. I'm here, Matthew.' There was hurt in her voice. 'I just think it's such a shame you've given up singing.'

I closed my eyes for a couple of seconds. I was glad Clara and I weren't in the same room. I didn't want her to see my expression.

'I haven't,' I said, as patiently as I could. 'In fact, I've been hired to sing on an album.'

Clara went quiet for a moment. Then she gave a shriek. I almost dropped the phone again in alarm.

'What's wrong? Is everything all right?'

'Yes. Sorry. I just got carried away. You mean you're actually going to be on an album? An album we can buy?'

'Yes.'

She made another squealing sound. 'Wait until I tell Ben!'

'I wouldn't bother telling Ben.'

'What's that supposed to mean?'

'I just... I don't think he'll be interested. It's a classical crossover thing. Lots of musical theatre.'

Clara gave a sigh. 'Okay. Have you told Mum and Dad?'

'Not yet, no.'

'You have to tell them. You're coming home at Easter, aren't you?'

Oh, no. The Capes Family Easter Dinner had mercifully slipped my mind.

'Yes, of course.'

'Tell them then. They'll be chuffed to bits.'

'Do you really think so?'

'Oh, Matthew. Of course they will.'

'Okay. I just don't want them to think this is something it's not. I'm only a guest artist.'

'It sounds pretty good to me.' Clara paused for a moment. 'Well done.'

'Thank you.'

'I mean it.'

'I know you do.'

'So… now that you're a professional singer, you should have no problem singing at my wedding. Please? It would mean so much to Ben and me.'

I sighed. I had walked right into that one.

Clara delivered the final blow. 'You wouldn't seriously refuse to sing at your own sister's wedding, would you?'

Bugger.

I took a deep breath. 'All right. I'll sing. But just the one song.'

'Thank you. I'm so pleased. We can discuss it at home. See you in a few weeks.'

'Yes, see you then.'

Clara hung up, presumably before I had a chance to change my mind.

I let my head slump onto my desk.

# Tremolo

The Grand Theatre was currently home to a long-running musical but hosted occasional concerts on Sundays. It seated around 1500 people, making it a fairly small venue compared with most of the other London theatres from a similar era.

I had read up on it online, trying to reassure myself that the venue would not be remotely intimidating. But as I stood staring up at it from the street, it might as well have been Carnegie Hall.

I was only here for a rehearsal, but already this theatre was making me feel very small indeed.

The facade had a cast-iron balcony over the entrance, with posters displayed on either side. One poster had a photo of Angela, with the caption: *Angela Nilsson and Friends*.

I assumed I was one of the friends.

I walked around the side of the building to the stage door, where a young man gave me directions from behind safety glass.

A passage led to some stairs, which took me downwards towards a red curtain. I pulled the curtain aside to reveal the auditorium.

It was like that scene in *The Wizard of Oz* when Dorothy finds herself in a world of vivid Technicolor, and she knows she's not in Kansas anymore. Everywhere I looked there were twists of gleaming gold, offset against red velvet ledges. There was none of the decay that I was used to seeing at the Moon and Stars.

Everything was polished to a dazzling shine. The place smelled of paint and dust and looked like my dreams. I instantly adored it. This was a West End theatre, and I was home.

'Okay, Angie. Ready when you are.' Chris's disembodied voice called out from somewhere above my head. I took a step forward and craned my neck upwards. He was standing at the front of the Royal Circle. 'Can we dim the lights, please?'

The globes on the chandelier dulled, and the gold and red drained away. Then a blue light came up onstage, spilling into the auditorium, giving the large room the quality of twilight. I stood in the side aisle, beneath the glow of an emergency exit sign.

A shadow moved onstage, and a spotlight caught Angela. She was an incongruous figure in rehearsal clothes: jogging bottoms and a T-shirt, her hair pulled back in a messy bun. Somewhere in the orchestra pit, a keyboard began to play. Angela brought a microphone close to her lips.

She sang with a depth I had not heard before. The acoustics in the theatre were different to those in the studio, and her voice seemed to come from all around. The air was charged with sound. The auditorium took on a feeling of unreality, as if I had stepped into a dream. But I was really there, listening to her voice, and I was going to sing with her, and I felt so lucky. A cold shiver ran down the back of my neck.

When the song was over, Chris asked for the lights to be brought up. I blinked several times, cringing in the sudden brightness.

'Thank you,' said Chris. 'That's great.' He disappeared from the Royal Circle.

'Maybe we should try a duet?' Angela shielded her eyes with a hand and peered over the stalls. 'Where's Matthew?'

'Here.' I stepped forward.

She saw me and waved. 'Great. Come on up.'

I climbed the steps at the side of the stage. I set foot on that other world and looked out.

The auditorium leered in front of me, like a huge mouth full of row upon row of red velvet teeth.

The seats whirled before my eyes, and I staggered.

'Are you all right?' asked Angela.

'Yes, I'm fine. It's just... so big.'

There were footsteps on the stage, and Chris appeared at Angela's shoulder. 'Right, Matthew, we're thinking "Some Enchanted Evening" for the concert. Does that sound okay?'

'Yes.'

Chris looked me up and down. I was wearing my smartest work suit, the one I wore for first nights at the Moon and Stars. I felt rather overdressed next to Angela.

'We'll have to get you some better clothes for the concert,' said Chris. 'Something a bit less... job interview. And a more modern hairstyle. I'll have a word with our stylist. She's a miracle worker.' He frowned. 'Hey, are you okay, mate?'

'Yes...'

'You look a bit pale.'

'It's just the heat from the lights,' said Angela. She locked eyes with me. I had a feeling she was trying to cover for me, which made me burn with embarrassment. 'You're fine, aren't you, Matthew?'

I managed to nod.

'Hmm, okay.' Chris didn't look convinced. 'Well, if you're sure, let's get on.'

He left the stage. Somewhere in the orchestra pit, a keyboard began to play.

Angela sang the first verse of 'Some Enchanted Evening', her voice flawless.

I waited for my verse, conscious of the sweat pooling beneath my suit.

I looked up, met Angela's eyes, opened my mouth...

...And the words that I kept buried entered my mind and flew through my thoughts in a confused whirl.

*Not what we're looking for...*

*You don't look that bad...*

*You're just... unusual.*

*At least you've got a lovely voice...*

My first note emerged as a strangled croak.

I brought a hand to my throat, shocked by the sound I had just made.

'Matthew? You okay, mate?' Chris was standing in the centre of the third row of the stalls, arms folded, concern and disapproval written across his face.

I coughed. 'Yes. Sorry. Can I... can I start again?'

Chris nodded to the keyboardist. 'From the second verse, please.'

I felt as if I was glued to the stage, unable to sing properly but unable to run, watching as Angela's expression grew more and more disappointed. My heart raced and my breath became short, anxiety playing havoc with my voice. Where had this come from? I hadn't felt as bad as this since...

Oh, God.

I'd thought things were better now.

I'd thought *I* was better now.

But I was pathetic and everyone was staring and I...

I...

I dropped my gaze to the floor, my voice cut from my throat.

'I'm sorry.' I turned away. 'I can't do this.'

Angela grasped my elbow. 'What's the matter?'

'I just... I need a moment...'

Hurrying from the stage, I made my way unsteadily down the steps, following the glow of the emergency exit sign. I blundered down a gloomy passage until I reached the nearest toilet.

Inside, I ran cold water into the sink and splashed my face, and it was only afterwards that I realised why I had felt the need to do so.

I was crying. 'Some Enchanted Evening' had made me cry.

I stared at my face in the mirror. I was a complete mess; my eyes were red-rimmed and swollen, my skin blotched. The concealer was ruined.

*Angela, you look like a singer. But Matthew, you just... don't.*

I shook my head, trying to chase away the memories.

I decided to wait in the toilets until I had recovered, which was ridiculous, really. I was an adult. There were no teenage boys lying in wait outside, ready to beat up the soft kid. Still, if Chris – or, worse, Angela – saw me and laughed, that would be mortifying. If they asked me if I was all right, that would be worse, because there was a chance I would start to weep again.

I rested my forehead against the cool surface of the mirror and closed my eyes. Strange, that such an unfeeling object should bring comfort in these circumstances. At least mirrors never lie.

I took the tube of concealer from my pocket and reapplied, rubbing it in until my skin tone was even. This made me feel calmer, as it always did. I needed to feel calm to face Angela and Chris.

I took a breath and left the toilets.

Angela was waiting for me in the corridor.

'What's wrong?' she asked. 'What's happened?'

I couldn't look at her, so I looked at the floor instead. 'I'm sorry, Angela. I really can't do this.'

'Can't do what?'

'Sing at the concert. Sing onstage, in front of people.'

'Why?'

'I don't know.' I swallowed. 'It... it was just like at the showcase...'

She was silent. I looked up at her. Her expression was hard.

'Oh, for heaven's sake, Matthew. Not this again.'

'I'm sorry.'

'I thought you'd sorted yourself out.'

'I thought so, too. I don't know what happened.' My eyes stung. I had the horrible feeling I was going to start crying again. 'I'm sorry to let you down.'

'What's going on?' Chris had found us.

'Matthew here is threatening to walk out because he can't cope with his stage fright.'

'What?' Chris stared at me.

'I think he's overreacting,' said Angela.

'I'll still sing on the album,' I said. 'You can find someone else to do the concert, can't you?'

Angela's expression softened. 'I really want to sing with you. Don't you want to sing with me?'

'Of course I do. I just don't want to show you up. I'm sorry. We can still sing together in the studio.'

'I'm afraid it's not that simple, mate,' said Chris.

'What do you mean?'

'This concert doesn't matter, because Angie can just sing another solo. But when the album comes out, there'll be a launch, and more concerts, and other public appearances. I'm afraid you can't do one and not the other. You can't record an album and not publicise it.' He placed a hand on my shoulder. 'Please, Matthew. Don't be hasty. We can't afford passengers. If you can't cope with live appearances, we'll need to find someone else to work on the album.'

'What?' Angela stared at Chris in horror. 'But that's not fair.'

'You know it makes sense, Angie.' Chris sounded aggrieved. He looked at me. 'Go home, sort yourself out, then call me. Let me know what you decide.'

*

I had no idea how to sort myself out.

Back at home, I paced my flat, looking critically at this tiny space that represented how far I had progressed in my life and in my career. It looked like the home of a student, with papers from work scattered across my desk and three dirty coffee mugs lined up next to my laptop. I hadn't even bothered to hang any pictures but had instead resorted to tacking posters to the grey walls: an advert for *Les Misérables*, a blown-up photograph of the Royal Opera House, and a poster from the Conservatoire's production of *West Side Story*.

I wondered what Angela would think of the place, and shuddered.

I was letting her down. Again. I wanted to sing with her. I *had* to sing with her. But I had no idea how.

I had been fine in the studio. It was being onstage, in front of people, that was the problem.

Perhaps I could hide backstage and deliver my performance into a microphone, Angela singing a duet with my disembodied voice.

No. Something told me that she wouldn't go in for that. It lacked the personal touch.

Still, it would be so good – such a perfect solution – to be able to sing without being seen.

I stared at the *West Side Story* poster. Something scratched at my brain.

I froze.

Of course!

Suddenly, I knew what to do. There was a way I could be invisible, but still have the pleasure of performing, and keep my promises to Angela.

I dug around in my pocket for Chris's business card and dialled the number.

'Hello, Chris? I'm really sorry about this afternoon. Um... I've had an idea. It's a bit... unconventional. But I think it just might work.'

# Masque

'Isn't this place *great*?' said Ralph.

The wine bar was a far trendier place than I generally frequented. Everything seemed to be either made from leather or stainless steel. Speakers pumped out intricate jazz music.

I felt like a fraud among the fancy cocktails and pieces of incomprehensible modern art. The bar was crammed with people, and I had been lucky to find a table in the corner. Worst of all, there were mirrors *everywhere*: next to the tables, behind the bar itself, on the door that led to the toilets. Who were all these people who enjoyed looking at themselves all the time?

I hunched my shoulders so my face was partially hidden. My hand strayed into my pocket and clutched the tube of concealer.

'Yes,' I muttered. 'Really great.'

'You hate it, don't you?'

'No, it's fine.'

'We could always go somewhere else.'

'No, no. This is my treat.'

Ralph folded his arms. 'Okay, Matthew, what's going on? Because I don't think you've come here for the fun of it.'

I took a sip of my wine to buy myself more time. This was it. I would have to tread carefully.

'You know I'm recording an album with Angela?'

'Yes?'

'Well, the thing is, she also wants someone to help with publicity. Sing at concerts, that sort of thing.' I stared into my glass.

'And that's a problem because...?'

'You remember the last time I tried to sing at a concert? When I had that... episode?'

'That was years ago.'

'It happened again. When I was rehearsing with Angela.' I shook my head. 'I just can't sing in front of people anymore.'

Ralph frowned. 'I'm sorry to hear that. But what do you want me to do?'

'You've seen *West Side Story*, haven't you? The film?'

'I think so.'

'Did you know that Maria was dubbed?'

'Who?'

'Maria. The main character? The actress you see playing the part isn't doing the singing. Someone else is. It's the same in *My Fair Lady* and *The King and I*.'

Ralph rubbed his eyes. 'If you've asked me here just so you can talk about musicals, I'm afraid I'm going to have to go home. It's been a long day.'

'No, no... what I mean is, I think I need someone like Maria.'

'Okay, now you've really lost me.'

'The record label needs someone to appear in the publicity, who's used to being in the public eye. Who'll look good onstage. A model, for example.'

Ralph's eyes widened. 'But I can't sing. Not like you, anyway.'

I took a strengthening gulp of wine. This was it.

'You wouldn't have to. I'd be doing the singing.'

Ralph stared at me, and I saw understanding dawn in his eyes. 'Oh, no. No way.'

'Ralph, please, just hear me out.'

'You've actually gone mad now.'

'Is it so mad? As I said, they did it all the time in old musicals.'

'But this isn't a musical. It's just... weird.'

'Is it any weirder than you parading around pretending to be the lord of the manor in those ridiculous clothes?'

He glared at me. 'They're not ridiculous.'

'It would just be modelling, with a bit of miming thrown in. You've worked on music videos, haven't you? You've mimed before?'

'That's different.' He didn't sound too sure. Perhaps I could convince him after all.

'You say you're getting sick of fashion. This could be a way of getting into something else.'

'Like what?'

'I know Angela's manager. Maybe we could convince him to have a listen to some of your songs?'

For the first time, Ralph looked intrigued. 'Do you think he would do that?'

'He's already recording one of mine, so he's obviously not averse to new talent.'

He looked thoughtful. 'It would just be for the one album, right?'

'Yes. We can see how it goes.'

Ralph was quiet for a moment. Then he put down his glass with a resolute *clunk*. 'What the hell. Let's try it.'

'Really? You're up for it?' It seemed such an odd request that I was surprised he had agreed.

'Sure, why not? As you say, it can't be any worse than pretending to be a bridegroom for the millionth time.' He smiled. 'When do we start?'

# Trio

'Come on, Matthew. Concentrate.'

'What exactly am I doing wrong, Chris?'

'You're singing "Oh, What a Beautiful Mornin'" as if it's some bleak folk ballad or something.'

I was at the studio to start work on the final versions of the tracks. But Angela was at a photo shoot, so I had spent the last half hour singing the duets with myself. 'Oh, What a Beautiful Mornin'' was going to be the bonus track, and the new arrangement wasn't easy. To make matters worse, Chris had dispensed with the services of the studio engineer and was now recording the vocals himself, so as not to compromise his 'artistic vision'. Angela had raised her eyebrows at this but had not argued.

'Sorry,' I said.

'What's up?'

'Nothing. It's just difficult to do this without Angela.'

'I'm sure they won't keep her much longer.' Chris glanced at his watch. 'What time did you say your friend was coming?'

'Twelve.'

'Right.' Chris frowned. 'Are you sure about this?'

'It was my idea, wasn't it?' In truth, the thought of watching Ralph mime to my voice was making me feel slightly queasy. I tried not to dwell on this too much. 'Can we try the song one more time?'

We began again. After the first two lines, Chris decided he had had enough. He took off his headphones and dropped them onto his desk chair.

'Right,' he said. 'This isn't working.'

'What's wrong with it?'

Chris sighed and gave me a look which said: *You know what's wrong with it*, even though I really didn't. 'I'm going to get coffee. Do you want some?'

'Yes, please.'

He left the studio, shaking his head.

In the absence of anything else to do, I returned to the vocal booth and looked through the song again, trying to ascertain where I was going wrong. I sang the chorus several times, attempting to sound enthusiastic, but there was definitely something missing. I would just have to keep trying...

The door swung open. I looked up, surprised that Chris was back so soon.

'Hey, Matthew.' Ralph stood in the doorway, carrying his guitar case and wearing a big grin.

'You're early,' I said.

He frowned. 'Sorry. Would you like me to come back later?'

'No, I'm sorry. I didn't mean to snap. It's been a frustrating morning.'

Ralph looked around the studio, a star-struck gleam in his eyes. 'Wow. This place is amazing.'

'It's okay,' I said.

'Just okay? You're living the dream! Aren't you excited?'

Fortunately, I was saved from having to answer that question by the arrival of Angela. She hurried in, a picture of harassed glamour.

'I'm so sorry. That took longer than expected...' She noticed Ralph. 'Oh. Hi.'

'This is Ralph,' I said.

'Nice to meet you. I'm Angela.'

Ralph grinned at her in a gawky sort of way that was quite different from his usual smooth, winning smile. Something twisted in my stomach.

Chris burst into the studio, bearing a tray of takeaway coffee cups. He smiled when he saw Ralph and shot me an approving look before introducing himself. 'Hi – you must be Ralph. Good you could make it. I'm Chris. Here, have a coffee.'

'Thanks,' said Ralph. He glanced at his guitar. 'Actually, there was something I wanted to ask you. I've got this new song.'

'Good, good.' Chris passed one of the other coffees to Angela.

'It's called "Noodles on Toast". It's about first love and, er... living in a flat share.'

'Sounds great. Maybe later. We really need to get on.'

Ralph glanced at me, as if hoping I would say something. I shrugged.

Chris turned to Angela. 'We've been running through "Oh, What a Beautiful Mornin'", but I think we should leave that for the moment.'

'It's afternoon now, anyway,' quipped Ralph.

Angela chuckled. I rolled my eyes.

'Is that okay with you, Matthew?' said Chris.

'Fine,' I said. 'Is there a coffee left for me?'

Chris looked at the tray and frowned. 'I only bought three.'

Ralph stepped forward, offering me his cup. 'Sorry, mate. This must be yours. Here.'

'No. It's fine. I'm sure I'll survive without it.'

Chris shot me a long-suffering look. 'I was thinking we could sing your song, for Ralph's sake, just because it's the single. It'll give you both a chance to rehearse. Does that sound okay?'

'Sounds great,' said Ralph.

'Matthew, can you sing from the booth? Ralph and Angela can stand near the piano, just for the benefit of the rehearsal.'

'Fine by me,' I muttered, turning towards the booth.

The backing track started to play. I told myself that this was exactly like any other time I had sung with Angela. I was standing in exactly the same place, singing words I had already sung on multiple occasions.

It would be fine.

It was all about being professional.

*

Ralph was everything I'd hoped he'd be. He was charming, relaxed and conscientious, and responded to all of Chris's instructions. By the end of the rehearsal, I knew I couldn't ask for a better public persona.

So why did I feel so irritated?

'Cheers, Ralph, that was great,' said Chris.

'No worries,' said Ralph, picking up his guitar case. 'Maybe I could play you my song next time?'

'Yes, yes, sure.' Chris left the studio.

Ralph hesitated for a moment, waved at me, and then hurried after Chris.

I was left alone with Angela.

She smiled. 'That went well.'

'Yes, I suppose it did.'

'Your friend's lovely.'

A sheet of music slid out of my hand. I bent to pick it up.

'Yes, he's great.'

'Where did you meet?'

'School.'

'Gosh, a very old friend. So he's a songwriter?'

'Yes, well, sort of. He's not a professional or anything. He didn't study music, so his stuff's very rough and ready.'

Angela grimaced. 'Don't be like that.'

'Like what?'

'Arrogant.'

The twisting feeling was back in my stomach. 'I'm not arrogant.'

Angela quirked an eyebrow. Then she sighed. 'Okay. You're not arrogant. But I'd like to hear Ralph's stuff.'

'I'm sure he'll play for you if you ask him.' I was tired of talking about Ralph. I tried to order my thoughts into a series of clear, assertive questions. *Angela, do you fancy going for a drink tomorrow? Angela, what are you doing on Friday?*

'Angela...'

'See you later, Matthew.'

'Yes. Yes. See you soon.'

I watched her leave.

I sighed.

Sometimes, I think characters in the world of musical theatre have it so much easier. They can sing about their feelings, loudly and at great length, and no one ever bats an eyelid.

If only we could do that in real life.

If only...

I started to smile.

Maybe I *could* do it in real life. I could write something for Angela to sing in concert: a new love song, just for her voice. It would be a gesture, if nothing else.

# Piano

There was one obvious flaw in my new plan.

I didn't have anything to write music *on*.

Technically, I still owned a piano, but it was at my parents' house. I hadn't played it for years, and there was no room for it in my flat.

So on the way home, I called into the music shop, which I was visiting more frequently since starting my unconventional singing career. I liked James, the owner. He was a quiet, intense-looking man in his early forties, with long brown hair greying slightly at the temples, and the most tasteful sort of nose stud. He left me alone to browse, and never sneered at my purchases. He seemed oblivious to most of the goings-on in his shop and spent most of his time reading – either a magazine or a thick classic novel. On the occasions when I did speak to him, however, I found that he had an almost unnervingly encyclopaedic knowledge of the stock.

That afternoon, he had his nose buried in a copy of *NME*.

'Do you have any keyboards?' I asked. 'Second-hand ones?'

He laid his magazine aside and looked thoughtful. 'Someone brought one in a few days ago. It seems pretty good. I'll show you.'

I followed him to the back of the shop, where several electric keyboards were balanced on stands. He pointed to a basic model, all brown plastic. I was assailed by a sudden memory of sitting onstage at college, trying hard to ignore the laughter as I coaxed an intense cacophony out of a very similar instrument.

I shuddered, and James must have noticed my expression of distaste. 'Not for you? What about this one?'

He pointed to a long, sleek, black keyboard with enough buttons to pilot a small spacecraft. I looked at the price tag and winced.

'You can try it, if you like.'

I hesitated, not entirely sure I wanted an audience. James seemed to understand, because he nodded towards the counter. 'Just give us a shout if you need any help.'

He returned to the front of the shop. I sat down at the keyboard.

Its default setting was Grand Piano, and it had a surprisingly rich tone. I played one of the Gymnopédies by Erik Satie.

James cleared his throat. I glanced around and saw that he was still engrossed in his magazine.

I moved on to a bit of Gershwin's 'Rhapsody in Blue'. Finally, I played Queen's 'Love of My Life', singing the lyrics softly under my breath.

I paused, flexing my fingers, wondering if I could get away with playing a fourth piece.

'Wow. You're *good*, aren't you?'

I almost fell off the piano stool.

James was standing a couple of feet behind me. His pale face had broken into a shy smile.

'Sorry,' he said. 'I didn't mean to startle you.'

I stood up. 'I'm just going...'

'Have you ever played with a band?'

'No. I tend to play classical. Why do you ask?'

James pushed his long hair out of his face. 'I'm in a bit of a fix. I'm in a band, and our keyboardist has walked out on us.'

'Oh. I'm sorry to hear that.'

He shrugged. 'It was going to happen. He's been behaving like a prat for a while, to be honest. Would you be interested in stepping in?'

I stared at him. 'You're asking me to join your band?'

'Yes. Well, not join, exactly. Just stand in and see how it goes.'

'But I'm a stranger.'

'You seem okay. I mean, you buy some crap music sometimes, but you buy some good stuff, too. And you play really well.'

'Thank you... I think. But I'm not really into rock.'

'How do you know we play rock?'

I pointed to his faded Nirvana T-shirt and raised my eyebrows. 'Wild guess?'

'Okay,' he said. 'Point taken. But you were playing Queen just now.'

'Yes, well. It's very melodic.'

'We need someone melodic. God, do we need someone melodic.' James passed a hand over his eyes. He looked a bit tired. 'Listen, er...?'

'Matthew.'

'Matthew. You would be doing us a huge favour. Tell you what – come along to our rehearsal next Tuesday. If you do, I'll lend you that fancy keyboard.'

'You'll lend it to me? Are you allowed to do that?'

'I'm the owner. I can do whatever I like. Just don't spill tea on it or anything.'

I looked at the keyboard. It really was an excellent instrument. 'I don't know, James...'

'Come on. You might even enjoy it.'

'What about the other members? Will they mind?'

'No. They'll be cool with it. They don't have two heads or anything.'

I took a breath. 'Okay. Where's the rehearsal?'

'Right here. Upstairs. 7pm.'

*

I set the keyboard up on the desk in my living room, adjusting my office chair so I could play it comfortably.

I had always considered keyboards to be a little soulless, without the subtlety of tone present in a piano. But there was something quite satisfying about being able to change the sound from that of a piano to an organ to a passable violin, and everything in between.

Once I had run through half a dozen items in my repertoire, I thought it was time to begin my serious composition work. I sat up straighter and flexed my fingers.

My mind went completely blank.

What kind of song would Angela enjoy? She seemed to like singing the standards, so a ballad might be best. But what should it be about? Did Angela like sunsets? Could I write a song about sunsets without sounding sentimental? How about an eclipse? Could meeting her be like an eclipse? A total eclipse... No, that had already been done.

Inspiration would come. I just had to give it time.

# Intermezzo

It was Sunday afternoon, and I was at the theatre. The singing hordes were about to descend for the first rehearsal of *Kiss Me, Kate*.

The Moon and Stars Operatic Society was Charlotte's pet project. Every year she would direct a 'community musical' (two words which, quite frankly, do not belong in the same sentence). For six years I had managed to avoid having anything to do with these theatrical abominations, but this time Charlotte had roped me in to assist.

'But why me?' was my perfectly reasonable question.

Charlotte had given me an enigmatic smile. 'Because you know your musicals, darling. And I could do with some help.'

It was up to me to get the place ready, be on hand during the rehearsal for whatever Charlotte needed, and then lock up afterwards.

It was quite an inconvenience, as I was eager to get back to work on Angela's song.

I sat at the front of the auditorium to await the arrival of 'the stars', as Charlotte liked to call them. It didn't take long. Soon I heard chattering voices and the odd snatch of song, mixed with laughter. Then they started to file in.

There were about twenty-five members of varying ages, predominantly women; I only counted six men. Some of them were wearing red sweatshirts with the group logo embroidered on them.

Charlotte stood onstage, greeting them all one by one. I retreated to the shadows at the back of the auditorium and took out my laptop. I was planning to catch up on some work. The group were rehearsing for three hours, so it would be a good opportunity.

'You're not going to spend the whole rehearsal hiding back here, are you, darling?'

I looked up to see Charlotte smiling at me.

'What would you like me to do?'

'Don't you want to join in?'

I grimaced. 'No, thank you. I've got work to do. Let me know if you need anything.'

She narrowed her eyes but did not argue. Then she glided back up the aisle, clapping her hands together to get the company's attention.

I fired up my laptop and began to read emails.

But the music was distracting – they had a good accompanist, even if the old upright piano had seen better days – and I found myself repeatedly glancing up from my computer screen to watch the action onstage. I couldn't deny that both the leads had excellent voices.

I was pleasantly surprised. It was not nearly as awful as it could have been.

Everything was in the chaotic early stages which I remembered well from my brief teenage am-dram career. The chorus didn't know where to stand, there were no props, and more than once Charlotte had to bring proceedings to a halt to correct something or other.

Everyone seemed to be having a whale of a time.

I forced myself to look at my computer screen. I opened a spectacularly boring email about the theatre accounts.

Within minutes, my gaze was dragged back to the stage. The company had started to choreograph 'Too Darn Hot'. There was a lot of giggling.

I closed my laptop. I had to go somewhere quieter and less... *stagey.*

I went to my office, where I could still hear the music, but at least I was one step removed from it. I managed to deal with the awful accounts email and moved on to my next task.

The office lights flickered and went out.

There was a chorus of shrieks from the auditorium. I swore and fumbled around on the desk for my torch.

Two minutes later I had reached the auditorium. I threw open the door to more shrieking and shone my torch towards the stage.

The singers were standing in a huddle. The faces I could see were either startled or contorted with nervous laughter.

'Oh, for heaven's sake! It's just a power cut.' This was Charlotte's voice. A moment later she was standing right in my torch beam.

'Is everything all right?' I asked.

'Apart from it being dark? Yes. Can you do something?'

'Give me a few minutes. I'll sort it out.'

The main fuse box was in the passage that led to the stage door. I opened the small cupboard, shining my torch inside. It looked like a switch had tripped, but even when I pushed it back into place, the lights didn't come back on. Beyond that, I couldn't see what the problem was. I would need to call Dave, who knew more about the technical workings of the theatre.

I made my way back to the auditorium. The operatic society were sitting in the velvet seats, using their mobile phones to provide some light.

I found Charlotte, who was standing by the piano, chatting to the accompanist.

'Sorry,' I said. 'I can't fix it. I need to get Dave in.'

'So we have to stop?'

'I'm afraid so. I don't think I'll get the lights back on until later. I'm really sorry.'

'It's not your fault.' She raised her voice above the chatter. 'Sorry, darlings. We're going to have to call it a day.'

There were murmurs of disappointment from the singers. I used my torch to light their way out of the auditorium and up the stairs. I stood with Charlotte at the stage door while she made sure everyone was accounted for.

'I really am sorry,' I said.

'Don't worry. We were ready for a break, anyway.' She paused. 'Did you think they were good, darling?'

'They weren't bad.'

Charlotte smiled. 'If you ever fancy joining in…'

'I'm happy to watch. Thanks.'

When Charlotte had gone, I returned to my office. I tried to call Dave but got no answer. I left a message – 'It's happened again,' or words to that effect – and locked up the office.

I was just about to lock the auditorium when the lights came back on.

I sighed. That was wonderful timing. Ah, well. There was nothing I could do about it. I'd lock up and go home.

I stared at the empty stage.

It seemed a shame to waste this unexpected chance.

I spent the next hour singing.

# Maestro

I hesitated at the door of the music shop, clutching a plastic carrier bag. The sound of something approximating music thrummed from the first floor, where a lighted window showed me the location of the rehearsal.

If I rang the doorbell, I would be joining a rock band, which was ridiculous. I was too old to join a rock band with any hope of success, and too young to join one for recreational purposes. Surely there were more productive things I could be doing with my time?

But James and I had a deal: a keyboard in return for a small amount of musical torture.

I rang the bell and wondered if it was too late to run away. But a moment later there was the sound of footsteps thumping down a staircase. The door opened and James appeared.

'Hi, Matthew – thanks for coming. I thought you might have chickened out on us.'

'I wouldn't dream of it.'

I followed James upstairs. As we ascended, the music grew increasingly loud. An electric guitar roared aggressively, accompanied by the *dum-dum-du-dum* of that most dreaded of not-quite-instruments: a drum kit.

James pushed open a door. The music stopped abruptly, and the guitarist turned to look at me.

Oh, no.

James stepped forward. 'Guys, this is Matthew. He's here to play the keyboard.'

'Yes,' said Lucy, with a tight smile. 'We've met.'

*

'Beer?' said the drummer, whose name was Dan. He appeared to be in his early thirties, and was broad, with a deep, gravelly voice, a beard and blonde hair down to his shoulders. His arms were covered with some terrifying tattoos. But his tone was gentle, and he was the only person to offer me any sort of hospitality. For some reason, he made me think of a relaxed pirate.

'Thanks.'

'Beer, Luce?'

Lucy walked over, took the can from him, turned and caught my eye. I tried to smile at her. She didn't smile back.

There was a long silence.

I stood nervously in the doorway, clutching my beer. I looked around at the room. Once, it had probably been a living room in a flat similar to mine, complete with a small kitchenette. But now it had been taken over by instruments. A drum kit occupied a third of the floor space, with a keyboard next to it. Much of the floor was a mess of cables and guitars and amps, but there was a small sitting area, with a saggy black leather sofa and a squashed blue beanbag.

'Well,' said James. 'Isn't this nice?'

'Yeah,' said Lucy, sitting on the sofa. 'Great.'

'What's in the bag, Matt?' asked Dan.

'Um...' I had forgotten all about the carrier bag. I held it up. 'I didn't know if I was supposed to bring anything, so I brought some mini quiches.'

All three of them stared at me. Lucy gave a stifled laugh and hid her mouth with her hand.

I glanced down at the bag, now convinced I had committed some quiche-based faux pas.

'Sorry, sorry,' said Lucy. 'I didn't mean to laugh.'

I looked around at them. They were all so... *edgy*, with their Dr Martens and black clothes and angry music. I didn't belong here.

'I should go,' I said.

'What?' said James. 'No! You owe me at least one rehearsal.'

'I don't think this is for me...'

'Why?' asked Lucy, eyes still glinting with amusement. 'Because rock is terrible and classical music is vastly superior?'

I sighed. 'Sorry, I didn't mean to come across as rude.'

Lucy raised an eyebrow. 'The word I would have chosen is "pretentious". But I'm happy to let it go.' She reached for her guitar.

'Is anyone going to eat those quiches?' said Dan. 'Because I'm starving.'

'Here.' I handed the bag to him.

'Magic.'

There was a moment of silence, broken only by the sound of Dan munching.

'I heard Matthew playing in the shop,' said James, a little too brightly. 'And I thought: here's a man who can play *anything*.'

'That's a slight exaggeration,' I said.

'Have you played in a band before?' asked Lucy.

'Not exactly.'

'Not exactly?'

'I've accompanied other singers on the piano. And... I've been in several choirs.'

'Right. Well, that'll come in handy when we do our death metal version of "Silent Night".'

I looked at her worriedly.

James clicked his tongue. 'Ignore her, Matthew. She's only joking.'

'Oh. Right. Good. Because I'm really not familiar with this sort of thing.'

James's face lit up. 'Oh, you'll love it! And it's not death metal. It's more like hard rock.'

'With melancholic influences,' said Dan, between mouthfuls of quiche.

'...Okay,' I said.

'We should really get started,' said James. 'Dan?'

'What's the hurry?' Dan held up his half-eaten quiche. 'Can't I finish this first?'

'It's just we've got a lot to get through tonight, a lot to show Matthew...'

Dan offered James the carrier bag. 'You should try one. They're good.'

'No, thank you.' James looked at me. 'You see what I'm up against? This is why I tried to ban snacks from the rehearsal room.'

'Yeah, you tried and you failed,' said Dan cheerfully.

'We seem to spend all our time eating and drinking and talking.' James paced across the floor. 'If we're going to make this work, we need to start approaching things with a bit more discipline—'

'Careful, James,' said Lucy. 'You're starting to sound like Mark.'

James folded his arms. 'I am not. I just... I want to get started, that's all.'

Dan sighed. 'It's okay, Luce – I know when I'm beaten.'

He stood up, leaving the bag of quiches on his chair, and took his place at the drum kit.

'Finally,' said James. 'That's your keyboard, Matthew.' He gestured towards it helpfully.

I sat down at the instrument, which was just as impressive as the keyboard James had loaned me. I decided that the best course of action, under the circumstances, was to keep my head down, do exactly what they asked, and try not to antagonise Lucy, who clearly thought I should not be there. It was just one rehearsal, after all. How bad could it possibly be?

'This is what we're playing first,' said James, handing me two pages of music.

I read it and felt an unexpected pang of disappointment. It was more or less the same three chords, played in sequence over and over again, with a short phrase of melody at the very end. Ah, well. I hadn't been expecting very much.

'Ready?' said James. 'One, two, three, four...'

I found myself engulfed in the most dreadful cacophony I had ever heard. Lucy's guitar screamed, Dan pummelled away at the drums as if he was trying to drown all other sound out and James's bass underscored the whole thing with a soulless, eardrum-melting *thrum-thrum-thrum*.

I could barely hear myself think, let alone play.

The noise swelled, and just when I thought things couldn't get any worse, Lucy began to sing.

Except it wasn't really singing. It was more like a series of shrill howls, like a particularly irritated werewolf. I couldn't make out any words, even though her voice was so loud.

I winced; the pain was almost physical. Was it *supposed* to be as bad as this? Was it just the style of the music, or was it genuinely terrible?

Her howls reached a crescendo.

I struck the wrong keys and stopped playing abruptly. The other three instruments crashed to a halt behind me. Mercifully, so did Lucy's voice.

There was a moment of blissful silence. Or there would have been, if my ears hadn't been ringing.

'Everything okay?' asked James. 'Why did you stop?'

'I played the wrong chord.'

Dan shrugged. 'Sounded okay to me.'

'Not to me,' I said.

'Does it matter?' asked Lucy. 'We can hardly hear you anyway.'

*Yes. I wonder why that is?* I thought.

Lucy narrowed her eyes at me. 'What's wrong?'

'Can't we tone it down a bit?'

James looked as if I had just suggested playing a gig on the moon. 'Tone it down?'

'Not this again,' groaned Lucy. 'This is what he was like when I was practising at home.'

'It's just... it's a bit *intense*,' I said.

James blinked. 'It's supposed to sound intense. It's a particular aesthetic. It needs a rawness.'

I swallowed. 'Yes, but surely it needs to sound as if we're doing it deliberately, not that it's actually *bad*.'

James inhaled sharply. I looked down at the keyboard.

'Sorry,' I said, standing up. 'I should be going...'

Dan laid aside his drumsticks. 'Can I make an observation?'

'What?' asked James.

'I think Matthew has a point.'

'I'm sorry?'

'It's that song. It's... well, it's a bit crap, isn't it?'

'Helpful, as ever,' said James.

'Sorry, but it needs to be said. Mark's not in the band anymore, so why are we still playing crap songs from the Mark era?'

There was a long, thoughtful silence.

'That's actually a good point,' said Lucy.

'We wrote that song together,' said James, a tense note in his voice. 'People expect us to play it.'

'Which explains why no one comes to our gigs,' said Dan. He looked at Lucy. 'You've written some great songs. Why can't we play those?'

'I'm saving those for when I embark on my solo career and move to New York,' said Lucy, deadpan.

'What do you think, Matthew?' asked Dan.

I hesitated, fearing that anything I said would turn out to be wrong.

'Come on,' said Lucy. 'You were only too eager to give your opinion before.'

'I'm not keen on that song,' I said.

'*Thank you*,' said Dan.

'I think I'd like to hear Lucy's,' I added, attempting to smile at her.

Lucy was quiet for a moment. Then she sighed. 'Okay. Fine. We'll try that new one from last week. It'll give the maestro here something to get his teeth into.'

James passed around more music. I looked at my pages and frowned. It wasn't even printed: it was just a series of messy notes, scribbled on stave paper.

'Problem?' asked Lucy. I noticed she had dispensed with her guitar.

'Not at all.'

We began, and I went back to keeping my head down. In contrast to the last cacophony, this song began with a gently melancholic piano melody. The drums and bass were pared right back, and when Lucy began to sing, the sound was more natural. She actually had a half-decent alto, and I wondered why she felt the need to shout and scream so much.

The song built gradually, the piano line surprisingly complex. My fingers danced across the keys. This was more like it. I could prove myself now. I dared to raise my head, and saw that Lucy was looking at me with apparent surprise, as if she had not thought me capable of really playing. I wasn't sure whether to be pleased or insulted.

The song ended with the same gentle note of melancholy.

There was a moment of almost reverent silence.

'Well, maestro? Was that better?'

Lucy's words should have sounded contemptuous, but they didn't. They sounded like a genuine question.

'Yes. Thank you.'

Dan looked at James. 'He's bloody good, isn't he?'

James nodded. 'What do you think, Lucy?'

She had turned away and was gathering up the scribbled sheets of music. 'He's okay.'

Some of the tension seemed to drain out of the room.

We moved on to the next song. This was another eardrum-shredder, which sounded very like a guitar and bass having a fight with a drum kit. The keyboard provided a strange, discordant counterpoint that might have been interesting, if only it were audible.

Most of the songs followed this same pattern.

After an hour, Lucy unplugged her guitar. 'I'd better call it a night. Early start tomorrow.'

'How's the new job?' asked James.

'Fine, I think. Intense.' She slung her guitar case over her shoulder and smiled, but when she looked at me, the expression did not quite meet her eyes. 'Bye, maestro. Have fun.'

She left the room. I heard her footsteps on the stairs.

'I don't think she likes me very much,' I said.

'You're new, that's all,' said James. 'It's just because she cares about the band.'

'Right.' I wasn't entirely convinced. Surely a person who cared about music wouldn't make such horrible noises with her voice, especially given she could actually sing. Did she not know that a voice was a valuable, delicate instrument?

And yet her song had been good.

Dan gave me another beer, and James showed me some of the other songs in their repertoire. I was starting to think that James and this Mark, whoever he was, had basically written the same song over and over again, with slightly different lyrics.

'Do you have any more of Lucy's songs?' I asked.

James shook his head. 'She guards those with her life. She hasn't even let me have copies. It took a lot of persuasion to let us play that one.'

'I see.'

'But maybe, now that we've got a decent keyboardist, she'll want to play more,' said James. 'Will we see you next week?'

I hesitated. Lucy made me nervous, but her music intrigued me. Perhaps I would come back, just one more time.

'Yes.'

'Excellent!' James smiled. 'Welcome to Shattered Chandelier.'

'What?'

'That's the name of the band.'

'Why?'

'Because we couldn't think of a better one,' said Dan.

'We've been through this.' James glared at him, then turned to me. 'Because our music is so powerful it can shatter glass.'

'Oh. Right.' I couldn't argue with that, although 'powerful' wasn't the word I would have chosen.

'I told you it was a crap name,' mumbled Dan.

*

Later, back in my flat, I sat down at the keyboard. Out of curiosity, I tried to remember the songs from the rehearsal, but the melodies were difficult to recall. This was probably because there hadn't actually been much melody. Or maybe I just wasn't cut out to be a rock musician.

Never mind. I needed to write Angela's song. And I thought I finally had an idea.

My hands found a chord, and then another. For the first time in years, I heard unfamiliar music in my mind's ear. Music which belonged to me.

An hour later, I had a full melody worked out.

It was just a simple tune. But it was a start.

# Da Capo

Easter arrived. I wanted to spend the long weekend working on Angela's song, but instead I had been summoned to my parents' house for the traditional family get-together. This was one of only two extended annual visits I now made to my family home, the other being at Christmas.

As the train drew out of King's Cross, I found that I was almost looking forward to the weekend. Things were different this year. I had made definite progress in my career: I was recording an album. For once, I would be the sibling with news to share.

My journey took me by train to central Newcastle, where I had to catch another train, followed by a bus. It was early evening when I reached my family home: a semi-detached house on a sprawling, leafy estate.

I rang the doorbell.

A moment later, the door was thrown open and my mother appeared. She was wearing her dark blue party dress, the one she always wore for special occasions, and she looked mildly surprised to see me, as if she hadn't quite believed I would turn up. I felt a rush of affection and guilt.

'Hi, Mum.'

'Happy Easter, Matthew.' She gave me a quick hug. 'You're a little late.'

'The train was delayed. Then I missed the bus...'

'Well, you should have taken an earlier train. Clara's already here.'

*Of course she is.*

'Come in.' Her eyes narrowed. 'Are you all right? You look a bit flushed.'

'It's nothing. I'm fine.' I reached into my coat pocket and touched the tube of concealer. 'Can I just have a minute to freshen up?'

'Don't be too long. Dinner's nearly ready.'

I trudged upstairs to my teenage bedroom, which was still exactly as I had left it, down to the *Les Misérables* and *Blood Brothers* posters on the walls, and the glow-in-the-dark *Cats* mug on my desk.

I threw my suitcase onto my former bed, and changed into a fresh shirt, trousers and pullover. For a moment I considered looking in the wardrobe to see if any of my adolescent fashion disasters were still lurking in there, but quickly decided against it.

I went into the bathroom and inspected my face in the mirror. I did look flushed: some of the concealer had rubbed away, creating uneven pink patches. I splashed my face and reapplied. Then I went back downstairs and approached the dining room. The rich tones of Pavarotti drifted from the half-open door. They always put opera on when I came to visit.

I took a deep breath and opened the door. My family was already gathered around the polished dining table.

'Hi, Matt,' said my dad, peering at me shyly from behind an enormous bowl of steamed vegetables. Dad was a quiet architect who preferred studying building plans in his office to almost any social occasion. He had met Mum at university, where she was the world's most extroverted drama student. Their paths had crossed when he had been bullied into building the set for a production of *Anything Goes*. Even now, my dad barely got a word in edgeways. He sometimes looked a little bewildered, as if he had stumbled into a house filled with mad theatre people and was unable to find the exit.

'Hi, Dad.'

'How was your journey?'

'Fine.'

'Good.'

My dad was a man of few words. This was one of the things we had in common.

Clara stood up to embrace me. She was wearing a smart trouser suit, as if she had just come from the office. This was entirely possible, even though it was Saturday. Her light brown hair was styled in careful waves. 'Happy Easter, Matty.'

'You, too.' I glanced around the room. 'Is Ben not joining us?'

'He's coming tomorrow in time for lunch.'

'Great. I'll look forward to that.'

Clara prodded my arm gently. 'Promise you'll be nice.'

I gave her my most innocent look. 'I'm always nice.'

'Hmm.'

'Well!' said Mum, sitting down. 'Shall we eat?'

I took the last empty chair, across the table from Clara. It was also opposite my old upright piano, which I had not played for years. My parents had hung my framed degree certificate on the wall above it, along with various music grade certificates. And, worst of all, my graduation photo, in which I was pale and unsmiling and wishing I was far away.

It was a little Museum of Matthew's Achievements, none of which were dated beyond 2008.

'I wish you would take those down and hang something else,' I said.

'Why would I want to do that?' asked Mum. 'What would I hang instead?'

'I don't know. A Monet reproduction? A picture of the Queen? Anything would do.'

'They're not going anywhere. We're proud of your achievements. You should be, too.'

'It's all a long time ago now, Mum...'

'Rubbish. It's just a few years. Come on, eat up.'

As well as the steamed vegetables, dinner consisted of a vegetable lasagne and a side salad.

'Have you all become vegetarians in my absence?' I asked, skewering a green bean with my fork.

'This will do you good,' said Mum. 'I know what you're like. I hope you're not living on takeaways down there.'

I sighed. It was Parental Advice Time. I shot a pleading glance at Clara, hoping she would come to my aid, but she just smiled at me sweetly and reached for more steamed carrots.

'Can we please change the subject?' I asked.

'Good idea,' said Dad.

'Oh, *fine*,' said Mum. 'How's your singing going?'

My heart was beating fast. This was the moment. My moment of triumph.

'Really good,' I said. 'In fact...'

'I hope you still practise every day,' said Mum.

An image of the empty auditorium of the Moon and Stars flashed in my mind. 'Most days. When I have time.'

'Have you found a nice teacher to work with?'

'I don't have a teacher at the moment.'

'You should find someone to coach you. You don't want to be a theatre manager forever, do you?'

My throat tightened. 'Well, actually—'

'A voice like yours... it's such a waste.'

I dropped my fork. It hit my plate with a clatter.

'Mum,' said Clara, warningly.

Mum gave a tight smile. 'Well, I'm glad you're singing at Clara's wedding. It's good to see you getting back into it.'

I stared at my congealing lasagne. This was why I didn't come home very often. Every time I did, I was reminded of all I should have been. It was like I was letting them down all over again.

'Actually, Matthew has some big news,' prompted Clara. 'Don't you?'

'Yes,' I said softly, still looking at my plate.

There was a pause.

'Well?' said Mum.

'I'm... recording an album. As a guest artist. It's out this summer.'

Another pause. Perhaps they had been expecting more. A solo concert at the Royal Opera House, possibly.

'Oh, Matthew, that's wonderful!' said Mum. 'Isn't that wonderful, Eric?'

'Brilliant,' said Dad.

I raised my head and saw that Mum was smiling, but her eyes had gone misty.

'Please don't cry, Mum. It's no big deal.'

'Sorry! I'm just so *pleased* for you, darling. Well done.'

'I'm just a guest artist...'

'Stop putting yourself down. You're always putting yourself down – isn't he, Eric?'

'He is,' said Dad.

'We should have a toast. Clara? Get that champagne left over from Christmas, would you?'

My cheeks were burning. 'No, Mum, that's too much...'

'Nonsense.'

I looked at Clara for help, but she just smiled and stood up.

'So,' said Mum, beaming. 'Tell me everything. What sort of album is it?'

'Well, it's mainly musical theatre...'

'How lovely! And who's the star? Have we heard of her?'

'Well, actually, yes... it's Angela Nilsson.'

There was a *clunk* as Clara put down the champagne bottle a little too heavily. Then there was silence. The smiles had fallen from the faces of my family.

'You never said it was Angela,' said Clara.

'Angela?' said Mum. 'The Angela you knew at the Conservatoire?'

'Yes,' I said. I frowned. 'What's the matter?'

'The Angela who refused to sing with you at the showcase?' asked Mum.

'Well... yes.'

Clara shook her head. 'Oh, Matthew.'

'What's wrong? Why do you all look so shocked?'

'Don't tell me you've forgotten what you were *like* after the showcase?' said Clara.

'Well, I was upset. Obviously.'

'You shut yourself in your room,' said Mum. 'For two weeks.'

'You barely ate,' said Clara.

I folded my arms. 'You're exaggerating.'

'Hardly!' snapped Clara.

'It wasn't all about Angela. Anyway, it was so long ago... things are different now.'

'Are they?' asked Clara. Her eyes had narrowed.

'She wants to sing with me. Our voices sound great together... We're friends again.'

'And you're happy with that?' asked Clara.

I was silent. The opening bars of Angela's new song drifted through my mind.

'Well, I hope you know what you're doing.' Clara picked up the champagne.

'I'm quite capable of managing my own life, thank you.'

Clara opened her mouth again, but Mum held up a hand.

'Of course you are, Matthew,' she said. 'We just don't want you to get hurt, that's all.'

'I won't. I'm fine. Honestly.'

Clara poured the champagne and sat down.

Everyone was quiet for a long moment.

Dad raised his glass and smiled weakly. 'I think we should have a toast. To Matthew and his first album.'

Mum looked relieved. She raised her own glass. 'Cheers! Congratulations, darling.'

Clara was silent. She didn't smile when we clinked glasses.

'So,' said Mum. 'Do you have any concerts lined up with Angela?'

A cold prickle ran up my spine. I had been so keen to share my news about the album that I had failed to consider how I was going to deal with the more awkward follow-up questions.

'I'm not sure yet,' I said, picking at my lasagne.

'But surely they'll want to promote it? Angela's given concerts before. Hasn't she asked you to sing with her?'

'It's early days. I think they're still working out the... er... marketing plan. I don't suppose they've booked any venues yet.'

I reached for my wine glass and caught Clara's gaze across the table. The familiar look of suspicion was back in her eyes. I had seen this look before, usually when I had returned home from college as a teenager and told everyone I was fine. My sister had never believed me.

'If you do give any concerts, you'll tell us, won't you?' asked Mum. 'We'd love to come and see you.'

I looked back down at my plate.

'Of course I will.'

*

We spent the rest of the evening talking about Clara's wedding. Or rather, Clara talked about Clara's wedding, and the rest of us nodded and made affirmative noises.

She wanted me to sing 'Some Enchanted Evening' at the service, which struck me as an interesting choice. I'd never had her down as a musical theatre fan. At school, she'd liked whatever her friends had liked. In practice, this had meant a Spice Girls phase, followed by an Evanescence phase. There was also a brief flirtation with experimental jazz while she was at university. Bearing all this in mind, I was relieved she had chosen a song I knew well – although it did bring back an unpleasant memory of hiding in the toilets at the Grand Theatre.

I was relieved there was no more talk of concerts, or of Angela. The longer the evening went on, the more I was convinced everything was fine.

I was wrong.

The moment our parents went up to bed and were safely out of earshot, Clara turned to me.

'Okay, what aren't you telling us?'

I blinked at her. I was tired, I'd had three glasses of wine, and I really wasn't in the mood. 'Sorry, what?'

'This Angela stuff.'

'What Angela stuff?'

'You looked really shifty when Mum asked you about giving concerts.' Her expression was serious. 'Has something been said?'

'By who?'

She shrugged. 'I don't know. Angela? Her label?'

I shook my head rather too forcefully. 'No.'

'You're not struggling with stage fright again, are you?'

I looked away. 'No, no… nothing like that.'

'Hmm.' Clara didn't sound convinced. 'I'm glad to hear it.'

I stood up, putting my wine glass on the coffee table. 'I'm going to bed.'

I had reached the living-room door when Clara spoke again.

'Matthew?'

'Yes?'

'Just… take care, won't you?'

I sighed. 'Goodnight, Clara.'

# Notation

It was the end of our last day of recording. The album – or mine and Angela's part in it, at least – was almost complete.

We were performing a version of 'What I Did for Love' from *A Chorus Line*. It was the worst possible choice for a final recording session. A beautiful song, but rather more introspective about a career in the performing arts than I wished to be at that moment.

I hadn't allowed myself to think beyond finishing the album. Finishing the album meant I would go back to my everyday life. It meant singing alone, and in secret. Unless I could persuade Angela to see me again.

We came to the end of the final chorus. There was a moment of silence. Then Chris gave a thumbs-up and rose from his chair with a big grin on his face.

'That's it,' he said. 'Vocals done.'

'Oh, thank God for that!' Angela sighed, but she was smiling.

'But... it can't be finished,' I said. 'Not yet.'

'I'm happy with it,' said Angela.

'But that last verse... I think I cracked a note...'

Chris rolled his eyes. 'Matthew, it's finished. It was fine. It was perfect. We're done here.' He turned to Angela and smiled. 'Congratulations, Angie.'

Angela gave Chris a hug. 'Thanks for everything.'

'You're welcome. This is just the beginning. We're starting work on the music video next week.' Chris's smile widened. 'Be sure to pack an overnight bag.'

Angela looked confused. 'Why?'

'Because we'll be filming the video on location in Venice.'

Although this sounded a bit excessive, I liked the thought of going to Venice. It was a place I had always wanted to visit. I imagined sitting outside Florian's with a mug of very good hot chocolate, listening to the pleasant sound of a string quartet drifting across St Mark's Square. Later, I would ask Angela if she wanted to go to a nice restaurant with me. We would dine by candlelight at a table overlooking a canal, gondolas sliding by tranquilly. I would have the risotto, or maybe a nice piece of fish. The next day, we could go for an historic walk around the city. Ralph could go swimming on the Lido; he wouldn't appreciate Venice the way I would.

'Do you need me for that?' I asked.

'I don't think so. We just need Ralph and Angela for the filming.'

'Oh. Right.'

'Matthew *is* the guest artist,' said Angela.

'Yes. And he's done a brilliant job,' said Chris. 'But we only need the performers for the video. The folk in finance will kill me if I take anyone else.'

'But shouldn't we have Matthew there? Just in case?'

'There's really no need,' said Chris. He looked at me. 'I'm sorry you can't go.'

I shrugged. 'Can't be helped, can it?'

'If it's any consolation, it'll be really boring. We'll fly out late at night, film for the whole of the next day, and fly back early the next morning. It's not like we're going on holiday.' He turned to Angela. 'I've got to run. See you soon.'

Angela and I were left alone. She started putting on her coat. I felt I should say something. I'd only regret it if I didn't.

'I just wanted to thank you. It's been a pleasure... To sing with you again, I mean.'

'Likewise.' Angela frowned. 'Are you okay? You sound a bit choked up.'

'I'm fine. Just a bit tired.'

'You've been working hard. You should rest your voice for a bit.'

I nodded. 'I hope we can sing together again soon.'

'There'll be the launch.'

It seemed a long way off. 'Yes, I suppose... Maybe I can come and see you. Sing, I mean. Are you performing in London?'

She shook her head. 'I'm doing a workshop for a new musical. I don't know if it'll be staged or not. And then I'm off on holiday. It's been a busy few months.'

'Oh,' I said, trying once again to crush my disappointment. 'Well, have a good time.'

'Thank you.' She patted my arm. 'You take care of yourself. Keep that gorgeous voice in top condition.'

'I will.' I paused. 'Angela...'

'Yes?'

I hesitated for a little too long.

'What is it, Matthew?'

'I just wanted to say... good luck. With the show, I mean.'

'Thank you. I'll see you soon.'

'Yes. See you soon.'

*

Someone had slipped a folded sheet of paper under my door.

I bent to retrieve it and found that it was actually two thin sheets of music stapled together. Across the top of the first page, there was a message scrawled in red biro: *Learn me by tomorrow please. L.*

I scowled. If Lucy thought I was going to start practising her music in my free time, she thought wrong. I had far more important things to do.

The first phrase caught my eye. I hummed it, softly, under my breath.

Interesting.

I went to the keyboard and played the song through. It had the same complex chord sequences, the same gentle, melancholic tone, as Lucy's other song. But she had only taken the melody so far. At the end, she had drawn a big question mark, and scribbled the words: *Needs more here???*

It was an invitation. As I played, I could see how the song could be developed further.

I took an extra sheet of paper from my desk drawer and picked up a pen.

The next morning, as I was leaving for work, I pushed the sheets of music back under Lucy's door, together with an extra page of notation.

*

'Have you heard the latest?' asked Jess.

I looked up from my sandwich. As usual, I was eating at my desk. I didn't like to leave it to take a lunch break; there were too many things that could go wrong in my absence.

'What's that?'

Jess grinned. 'They're saying this place is haunted.'

'But of course. Aren't all theatres haunted?'

'Yes, but apparently people have *heard things*.' Jess said this in an ominous horror-film voice.

'What sort of things?'

'Well, the other night, Dave came back to get something he'd left backstage, and he heard someone singing.'

I dropped my sandwich, then tried to look nonchalant by arranging it neatly on its napkin.

'Really?'

I cursed inwardly. I had thought I was being so careful, but I had been so wrapped up in my music that I hadn't even been aware of Dave's presence in the theatre.

'Creepy, huh?' said Jess. She was clearly enjoying every second of this.

'Very. Did Dave actually see anything?'

'Nah. He said he was going to investigate, but he got cold feet before he reached the auditorium. I think the whole thing freaked him out a bit.'

'Oh dear.'

'You haven't heard anything, have you?'

I coughed. 'I can't say that I have.'

'I was thinking of staying late tonight. Just to see if anything happens. Want to come?'

I had hoped to stay by myself and sing, but due to my own carelessness and Jess's ambition to turn ghost hunter, it seemed that would no longer be possible. It would have to wait until tomorrow.

'No, thanks. I don't believe in ghosts.'

'Aw, come on! Don't be such a spoilsport.'

I was about to refuse a second time when Dave walked in. Jess immediately spun to face him. 'Dave! I was just telling Matthew about our ghost.'

Dave gave a long-suffering sigh. 'There's no such thing. But I definitely heard *something*.'

'I'm sure it was nothing,' I said.

'I know what I heard.' Dave fixed me with a penetrating stare. 'I think someone's playing silly buggers.'

'How do you mean?' asked Jess.

'I think someone's sneaking in here after dark and using the stage. They're nicking our sweets, too. I've been talking to the bar staff. Five packets of Haribo have gone missing in the last month alone.'

I felt my face grow warm. I hoped the blush wasn't visible.

'Well?' said Dave. 'What are we going to do?'

'I don't think we have to do anything,' I said. 'I mean... no one else has a key, and there are no signs of a break-in, so—'

'It has to be a ghost!' finished Jess. She smiled wickedly at Dave and wiggled her fingers in his face. 'Woooooo!'

Dave tried to look dignified. 'Whoever it is, I'm not going back in there on my own. Not until I know what's going on.' He turned to me. 'I want you to take a look tonight.'

'That's exactly what I've been saying,' said Jess. 'If you don't come with us, we'll report you to an employment tribunal.'

I stared at her. 'On what grounds?'

'Adverse working conditions,' said Dave.

'Cowardice,' said Jess.

I knew they were teasing me. But I also knew I wouldn't get any peace until I played along.

'Oh, *fine*,' I said.

*

At 5pm I followed Jess and Dave to the 'haunted' auditorium.

I reached for the lights, but Jess grabbed my hand.

'No, don't. If there's anyone here, you'll frighten them away.'

Muttering under my breath, I went back to the office for my torch.

When I returned, Jess and Dave had walked halfway up the aisle. I thought about creeping up on them, but decided I was above such things. Instead, I switched on the torch and allowed the beam to fan across the seats. The light danced over the walls, illuminating the faded frescoes representing constellations. The painted shapes of a swan, a lion and Pegasus the winged horse glowed ghoulishly against their own private night sky.

'There doesn't seem to be anything amiss,' I said.

'The singing was coming from the stage,' said Dave. 'I'm sure of it.'

I sighed and stomped up the steps, until I was standing in the spot where I normally sang. Jess and Dave joined me and started to poke about in the wings.

I made a big show of shining my torch into every corner of the stage. 'Hello? Anybody there?'

Naturally, the ghost didn't answer.

Jess emerged from the wings. 'I've found something.'

My heart leapt into my throat. Had I left something behind? A song sheet? My staff ID? I waited for Jess to reveal the incriminating evidence.

She held out a half-empty pack of Haribo.

'I told you they were nicking stuff,' said Dave.

Jess chuckled. 'Maybe we could send it off for DNA testing.'

'So we've established it's not a ghost,' I said. 'Can we go now?'

'I definitely heard something,' said Dave, clearly determined to stretch out our very own episode of *Scooby Doo* for as long as possible.

I forced a laugh. 'Why would anyone sneak in here at night and sing?'

'I don't know,' said Dave, narrowing his eyes. 'You tell me.'

There was a long silence. I took a small, instinctive step backwards.

He knew.

I didn't know how he knew, but somehow he did.

'I need to go,' I said.

We left the theatre together, Jess looking disappointed that our ghost hunt had been abandoned.

I tried to reassure myself. It was just a packet of Haribo. Dave could prove nothing.

When we reached the stage door, his hand fell on my arm.

'By the way, Matthew. I forgot to mention. We need a new spotlight. For *Earnest*. Do you think the budget could stretch to it? I would have asked sooner, but I know you've been busy...' He smiled.

'Yes, yes. I think so.'

I walked home with the strangest feeling that I'd just been gently blackmailed.

A new spotlight in return for Dave's silence.

# Melodrama

'What's this?' Lucy dropped three familiar sheets of paper onto the keyboard.

I shrank back in my seat, staring at the music. 'What?'

'This.' Lucy tapped the top sheet of music with a finger. My heart began to pound. I didn't know exactly what I had done wrong, but I knew I'd messed up. Again.

James appeared in the doorway, looked at Lucy and frowned. 'What's going on?'

Lucy shrugged. 'Oh, nothing. I only gave Chopin here one of my songs to learn, and he's written these... these twiddly little piano bits all over it.'

James gasped. 'Did you *really*?'

I looked down at the keyboard. 'Um. Yes.'

Lucy turned back to face me. Her eyes glittered. 'May I ask why you've *improvised* all over my music, Matthew?'

'It was only because I liked it,' I spluttered. 'I really liked it, and I thought it could be even better...'

'Ooh, did you hear that, James? He thought he could make it better.'

I held up my hands. 'I was only trying to help. You wrote *needs more here* on it, and I just thought...' I tailed off, hunching my shoulders. I had wanted to impress the band, to prove that I was a good musician. That's what I had been thinking.

'I'm sorry,' I said finally, not daring to look at Lucy. 'I should have asked first.'

'You should have.'

There was a stomping noise on the stairs, and Dan appeared holding two bulging plastic bags. 'Chips are here.' He glanced around at us. 'Everything okay?'

'Yeah, apart from my work being *Matthewed*,' said Lucy, taking one of the bags from him.

I waited by the keyboard, keeping my distance while they stood in the kitchenette, passing around takeaway containers. I wondered again if I should leave.

'Are you joining us?' asked James, bringing his chips into the sitting area.

I glanced at Lucy, who had her back to me. 'I'm not sure that's a good idea...'

'Just come and eat,' said Dan. 'You can argue afterwards.'

I perched hesitantly on the one remaining seat, which happened to be the sagging beanbag. Dan dropped a polystyrene carton into my lap. 'I didn't know what you'd like, so I just got you fish and chips, but there's curry sauce, and you can have a bit of my deep-fried Mars bar if you like.'

'No, I'm good, thanks.'

I ate in silence. I avoided Lucy's eye, which wasn't difficult, because she also seemed to be avoiding mine. It was ages since I had eaten fish and chips, and I was struck by how decadently delicious they were. Over the last few months I had done my best to avoid anything so obviously unhealthy.

I reached for the curry sauce.

Forty minutes later, we were finally ready to start rehearsing. The abundance of carbohydrates seemed to have mellowed everybody, much to my relief.

'Okay,' said Lucy. 'We'll try my song. And no shenanigans.'

Her eyes flicked towards me.

We played it through, and again I was struck by the song's melodic beauty, the way it cried out for me to improvise, to take it further. But I resisted the temptation and played the notes I was allotted.

'What do you think?' asked James, afterwards.

Lucy bit her lip. It was a moment before she spoke.

'I still think it needs something more,' she said.

'Maybe some "twiddly little piano bits" could work?' said James, winking at me.

'No. I'm not going down that route. It's too... bright.'

My fingers twitched on the keys. I found that I knew what Lucy meant, and I thought I knew how to resolve it.

'I could do a drum solo,' suggested Dan.

Lucy grimaced. 'No.'

I half-raised a hand. 'I...'

'A bit more bass?' said James. 'Or you could repeat the final verse and sort of fade it out.'

Lucy shook her head. 'No, it needs to go in another direction. It needs something... unexpected.'

'Er...' I said.

Lucy turned to me. 'Go on then, maestro. You'd better spit it out.'

'Er, well, I thought... for the end, we could try taking the first verse and sort of... turning it on its head. Musically speaking, that is. So it's a bit like in a musical when you have two characters singing in counterpoint.'

They all looked at me blankly.

'I mean so the song has a twist. Like this...'

I pressed a key experimentally, and picked up from the last verse, trying to illustrate what I meant.

'Something like that,' I said.

The band exchanged glances.

'That could actually work,' said James.

'I like it,' said Dan.

'I don't know,' said Lucy. 'Isn't it a little bit sentimental?'

'I could play it on the organ setting,' I said. 'That might make it darker.'

She wrinkled her nose. 'Too Hammer Horror.'

'Then maybe you could contrast it with the guitar?'

'Hmm...' Lucy strummed a few chords. 'Okay, let's try that.'

*

Two hours later, I was exhausted, but also strangely satisfied. We had settled on an ending for Lucy's song and experimented a little with the heavier songs in the repertoire. Lucy wasn't making so many of the howling noises, instead using her rich, smoky alto. I thought I would like to hear her voice with just a simple piano accompaniment, but of course I didn't dare suggest such a thing.

'Great rehearsal tonight, Matthew,' said James, as I stood up to leave. 'Well done on that song.'

'Yeah, cheers, mate,' said Dan.

I glanced at Lucy, but she was packing her guitar away and didn't look at me.

'Bye, then,' I said, heading for the door.

'Matthew, wait,' said Lucy.

I turned to face her, bracing myself for some critical feedback, or possibly another telling off.

'Will you stay for a drink?'

'Er...'

Lucy tucked a strand of hair behind her ear. 'Please? Consider it a peace offering.'

'Erm... okay.'

She caught James's eye. 'James, weren't you going to give Dan a first look at your new stock?'

James looked momentarily confused. 'Was I?'

'Were you?' asked Dan.

'I think you mentioned it earlier,' said Lucy. She flicked her gaze towards me.

There was a pause. Lucy glanced at me a second time.

'Oh!' said James. 'Yes, so I did. Come on, Dan, let's go.'

'Can I have a beer first?'

James patted him on the back. 'Let's go, Dan.'

'Okay. If I buy something, do I get a discount?'

The door closed behind them.

Lucy went to the kitchenette and opened the fridge. She returned with two bottles of beer. She handed one to me and sat down on the sofa.

'Peace at last,' she said, with a small smile.

'Yes,' I said.

We sat in silence for a moment.

'Listen, Matthew. I asked the others to go downstairs because I wanted a... private word with you.'

'Oh?' My heart began to race again. Maybe things were even worse than I feared. Maybe I had offended Lucy so thoroughly that she was going to dismiss me from the band.

'I'm sorry,' said Lucy, 'if I've been a bit... weird with you. A bit harsh, I mean.'

I blinked. 'Oh. Right.'

'It's not about you – it's all the stuff with Mark.'

'Your old keyboardist?'

Lucy nodded.

'James said he'd behaved like a prat.'

Lucy laughed. 'I suppose that's one way of putting it. He always took things far too seriously. He kept talking about becoming professionals, giving up our jobs. And the rest of us just wanted to do it in our free time, for fun, you know?'

I nodded. 'He does sound a little... pretentious.'

'He started writing these new songs, without James, and they didn't suit my voice at all. He dropped hints that we needed a second vocalist, that maybe we'd done all we could with just the four of us.'

'I see.'

Lucy sighed. 'The thing is, I sort of agreed. I'm not a particularly great singer. You know that. You've heard me.'

I hesitated. It was true that Lucy's voice wouldn't be to everyone's taste, but I couldn't exactly say that to her. And this Mark person did sound awful.

'Well... at least you're nice and loud.'

She rolled her eyes. 'Gee, thanks, Matthew. The next time I need a compliment, I know who to call.'

I squirmed in my seat. 'Sorry. It's just that your voice is untrained—'

'Keep digging.'

'Those other singers probably all trained at the Royal College or something.'

'Would you like a bigger shovel, or are you happy with the one you've got?'

'Sorry. I didn't mean it like that.'

Her face softened. 'I'm just kidding.'

'Oh.' I cleared my throat. 'So what happened? With Mark?'

'Well, one night he was going on and on about how much better one of our songs needed to be. Dan lost his temper and told him to shut up.'

'Dan?' I couldn't imagine easy-going Dan losing his temper with anyone.

'He's like me. He's in this for fun. He doesn't like drama. Anyway, Mark called us all amateurs and stormed off. We haven't seen him since.'

'Wow,' I said.

Lucy sipped her beer.

'So, I hope you understand my... reaction... when you turned up. None of us want to go through all that rubbish again.'

'Yes. I can understand that.'

Lucy met my eyes. 'Can you promise me something, Matthew? Can you promise you're not a pretentious, hyper-critical snob?'

'I—'

'Because this band thing is a hobby for me. I want to enjoy it.'

'I'll... do my best not to be. A snob, I mean.'

'Good.'

'I'm sorry about your music. I was only trying to help.'

'That's okay.'

We sat for a few moments, drinking our beers in what I dared hope was a companionable silence.

'So, maestro, do you sing professionally?'

'I'm a theatre manager. I... do a bit of singing on the side.' I paused, not wishing to go into details about my arrangement with Ralph. 'Dan said you had a new job?'

'I'm a music therapist.'

I had vaguely heard of music therapy at the Conservatoire. It had something to do with using music to help people express themselves.

'Are they any good?' I asked. 'Your patients?'

'Any good at what?'

'At music.'

Lucy stared at me for a moment. Then she laughed. 'Matthew, that's not the point. It's to help people feel better. I'm not training my clients for Carnegie Hall.'

'You think music helps people feel better?'

'Well... yes.' She frowned. 'Why? Don't you?'

I thought of all the time I had spent practising alone, either at my parents' house or the Conservatoire. I thought of my nerves, and the unkind voice that whispered in my head when I tried to sing in front of anyone.

'I'm not sure,' I said. 'I mean, it can be hard work.'

There was a moment of silence. Lucy was looking at me in an odd, searching way which I couldn't quite understand, but which made me blush.

I stood up. 'I'd better be going.'

Lucy stood up, too. 'Matthew, I just want to say...' She broke off, her eyes meeting mine. 'You did well tonight.'

I stared at her in astonishment. I felt a little like I had just been awarded a gold star for my homework.

'Thanks, Lucy.' I reached for the door. 'See you next week.'

'Yeah.' She gave a quick smile. 'Just don't go getting ideas above your station.'

'I wouldn't dream of it.'

# Quartet

My phone pinged. It was Angela, on Messenger.

*Angela: Hi! How are you?*

What could I say? It's only been a week, and I already miss you terribly? Can we meet up and sing all day long?

*Me: Fine thanks. You?*
*Angela: Fine. Bored. Still filming the music video. Think it's going to take longer than two days. You had a lucky escape. Chris thinks he's the new Spielberg.*

I bit my lip. So much for the flying visit to Venice. I might have had time to do some sightseeing after all.

*Me: LOL.*
*Angela: I thought you might like to hear this.*

She had attached an audio file. My heart gave a little leap.

*Me: Is that what I think it is?*
*Angela: Yep. Our album. Don't tell Chris. I'm not supposed to share it. It's not the finished version.*

*Me: Thank you!*
*Angela: No probs.*

The audio file stared at me from the screen. I stared back. I only had to click on it, and I would hear our songs.

My hand hovered over the file. But it was no good. This was an important moment. I needed to do things properly.

I walked around my flat, making sure all the windows were closed and the door was locked. I didn't want anyone to overhear our music. I wanted to listen to it by myself, just for now. I made myself a cup of tea and opened Angela's message on my laptop, knowing I would get better sound quality that way. Then I clicked play, lay back on the sofa and closed my eyes.

It began with our cover of 'If I Loved You'. Angela sang the first verse, and I had forgotten how good she was. It was like audio sunlight, warm and bright, sparkling on water.

And then my own voice, dark and rich, smoother than I had anticipated. I had expected some harshness. Had I been auto tuned? No. It was me. It was definitely me and I could hardly believe it.

The song came to an end. My eyes had filled with tears, but I laughed.

I had done it! I had proven that I could still sing, that I could make a career out of my voice.

I had reached the third track when there was a knock on the door.

I ignored it. I was too wrapped up in the music.

There was another knock, and a voice said, 'Matthew? Are you there?'

Sighing heavily, I left the sofa. I opened the door to reveal Lucy in full Goth regalia: thick eye makeup, black lipstick, a long purple velvet dress trimmed with black lace, and Victorian-style ankle boots. She was holding her guitar case.

'Hello, Lucy.'

'Hi, Matthew. Are you doing anything tonight?'

'Well, I...' In truth, I had big plans which involved listening to my album at least three times, while drinking wine and eating Haribo. But I didn't want to share this information with Lucy. 'No. Not really.'

Lucy smiled. The expression was a bit disconcerting. 'Good. We need you.'

'Need me for what?'

'We're playing a gig at Ye Olde Inne. This other band had to drop out. The landlord phoned James and asked if we wanted to play instead. You up for it?'

A gig. A completely unexpected gig, tonight. I couldn't. I wasn't ready.

'I don't know.' The strains of Angela's voice caught my attention again, drifting from the laptop. 'I'm a bit busy. I've got work stuff...'

Lucy raised an eyebrow. 'Listening to opera again?'

'Not exactly. Sorry, Lucy.'

I started to close the door, but Lucy grabbed the handle. 'Please. Just for one gig. It's ages since we've been invited to play anywhere. It'll be fun.'

Her expression was hopeful, her eyes holding mine, and suddenly I felt like a complete killjoy.

'It's very short notice. I don't know if I'm ready.'

Lucy sighed. 'Give it a try. It's only for an hour. You might even enjoy it. Please.'

It was only for an hour. And as it was a pub, it would be dimly lit. I could wear my concealer and sit at the back, behind the rest of the band. And it wasn't as if they were a well-known band. Probably no one would turn up anyway.

'Okay.'

'Thank you!' Lucy grinned. Then she looked me up and down. 'You'll need to get changed.'

I glanced at my clothes. I was wearing jeans, a white shirt, and a burgundy pullover. 'Why?'

'Because we're a rock band, and you look like my Year Eight English teacher.'

'I don't think I have anything... er... rocky?'

'Just put on the darkest things you own.' She glanced over my shoulder. 'Can I come in and wait?'

I hesitated. I wasn't keen on the idea of Lucy being in my flat. I was sure she would find it distinctly uncool. But I couldn't think of a reason to refuse.

I nodded. She stepped across the threshold and sat down on the sofa.

'Thanks.' She wrinkled her nose. 'What's that, anyway?'

Oh, God. Maybe my flat smelled. Maybe there was a pair of old socks under the sofa or something. 'What?'

'That music.'

My album was still playing away to itself in the background. It was on the tip of my tongue to tell Lucy all about it. But then I remembered Chris's embargo.

'Oh. She's called Angela Nilsson. Isn't she brilliant?'

She shook her head. 'Oh, Matthew. I thought you had *some* taste.'

'What's wrong with it?'

'It's so... I don't know... *syrupy.*'

'It's a classic Rodgers and Hammerstein song. She's a trained soprano.'

'I see. It's not really my sort of...' Lucy stopped. Her eyes went wide. 'Oh my God. Who. Is. *That?*'

Angela's verse had ended and now it was my turn. I suddenly found myself overcome with shyness.

'Nobody. Just some tenor.'

I reached for the laptop with the intention of turning it off.

'No,' said Lucy. 'Leave him on. Wow. His voice is gorgeous.'

I blinked. 'Do you really think so?'

'Yeah. It kind of sounds like dark chocolate if dark chocolate could sing. Quite sexy, really.' She grinned, then frowned. 'Hey, are you okay?'

'Yes. Why?'

'Your face has gone really pink.'

'I'm fine.' I coughed. 'I'm surprised you like him.'

'I like a good voice. It's still a soppy song, though.' She paused. 'Are you going to get ready, then?'

'I'll just be a few minutes.'

I went into the bedroom and rifled through my wardrobe. I found exactly what I had expected: shirts and pullovers of various colours, jeans and several pairs of identical dark suit trousers. At least the trousers would be okay. But what else?

My hand rested on something black. *Yes.*

I got changed, and then headed for the shower room.

'Are you going to be long?' called Lucy.

'Just a minute.'

'It's just that I'm getting seriously tortured by the operatics out here.'

'I'm coming.'

I had been in all day, so I wasn't wearing the concealer. Lucy hadn't passed comment on my appearance, but the pub would be different. I would be performing for people I didn't know.

I applied a generous amount, my fingers moving in quick circles. Then I inspected my face. The makeup wasn't perfect – there were a number of uneven patches – but it would have to do. Hopefully it would be hardly noticeable in the low light of a pub.

Resisting the urge to look in the mirror a second time, I returned to the living room.

I found Lucy sitting on the sofa with her hands clapped over her ears. 'Can't... take... it... anymore!'

I switched off the laptop, and she turned to look at me, her gaze resting on my jacket.

She burst out laughing.

I stared at her in horror.

'What on earth are you wearing?' asked Lucy.

'Er... it's a tailcoat.'

'Yes, I can see it's a tailcoat.' She wiped her eyes.

'You asked me to wear something dark.'

'That's not exactly what I had in mind.'

'Shall I go and change again?'

She shook her head. 'No, no. I guess it sort of works.' She smiled. 'Come on, maestro. Let's go and play some real music.'

*

Pubs weren't exactly my natural habitat, and my heart sank as soon as I stepped into the lounge. It wasn't much larger than the room above the music shop, and the stage was a tiny raised platform with nothing to separate us from where the audience would be sitting.

The pub was also neither particularly 'olde', nor really an 'inne'. I had imagined open fires and paintings of horses, but instead the place was a time warp to the 1970s, with hideous yellow wallpaper and whirring ceiling fans.

When I arrived, the band were already onstage, getting their equipment ready.

Dan saw me first and laughed. 'The Royal Albert Hall gig's next weekend.'

I glowered at him. 'Very funny.'

'I'm only having a laugh. You're over here.'

The keyboard had been placed directly beneath the glass dome of a light. So much for my plan to remain inconspicuous. I switched it on and played a few chords, trying to distract myself.

As we carried out our soundcheck, I was aware of the room filling up. I heard loud voices, the clink of glasses, raucous laughter. I made the mistake of looking up and saw that the place was suddenly packed.

'Big crowd tonight,' said James, sounding pleased.

'Maybe they heard Mark wasn't coming,' said Dan.

Lucy started to test her microphone. 'One two, one two...'

I looked at the audience. They looked back at me. Heat rushed to my face, and beads of sweat broke out on my forehead. My heart raced, and I took a deep breath, trying to calm myself. The scent of stale beer and chip fat flew up my nostrils.

I gagged. Even above the pub noise, my retching sounded embarrassingly loud.

'You all right, mate?' asked Dan.

'Yes. Excuse me... just need some fresh air...' I hurried off the stage and through the pub, staying as close to the edge of the room as I could.

I burst out of the front door and leaned against the brick wall. Feeling sick and shaky, I closed my eyes. This had been a horrible mistake.

The voice whirled around my mind: *You don't look right. You don't look right. You don't look right.*

'Matthew?'

*Ugly. Ugly. UGLY.*

'Matthew?' Someone touched my arm. It was a gentle touch, but I jumped. My eyes flew open, and I saw Lucy staring at me.

*UGLY...*

'Hey,' she said. 'Are you okay?'

I managed to shake my head. It had happened again. I had let them all down, let Lucy down, and now she was going to kick me out of the band. Which was only to be expected, because I didn't look right.

'Matthew, what's wrong? You look terrible.'

I tried to answer her, to agree that yes, I did look terrible, and that was the problem, but suddenly it was very hard to breathe, let alone speak. I braced my hands against the wall in case I fell. I was aware that the pub door had opened again, spilling light onto the pavement, and now James and Dan were staring at me, too.

'What's up?' asked James.

'I can't... can't go back in there,' I managed, my voice harsh. 'I... can't... play...'

Lucy's eyes went wide. 'Okay. James, go and get Matthew a chair. Dan? Get some water.'

James hesitated. 'But...'

'Chair. Water. Now.'

Her bandmates scarpered.

I closed my eyes again and waited for Lucy to tell me to snap out of it, to pull myself together.

But she didn't.

Instead, she placed a hand on my back. 'Has this happened before?'

'Yes...'

James came back with a chair, and Lucy gently pushed me into it.

'What's wrong with him?' asked James.

'I think it's a panic attack.' Lucy began to rub my back, between my shoulder blades. 'It's okay. Deep breaths, now.'

In the confused fug of my brain, I wondered why she was helping when she didn't like me.

I took a deep, shuddering breath.

'Good,' said Lucy. 'That's good.'

'I'm sorry.'

'There's no need to be sorry. Just breathe.'

I focused on my breathing, and on the light, rhythmic pressure of Lucy's hand. The shaking began to subside.

Dan reappeared and pushed a glass of water into my hand. I lifted it and drank deeply.

I sat like that for five minutes, until my breath became more natural and my heart slowed. I took the occasional sip of water.

'Feeling better?' asked Lucy.

'Yes.' Now the panic was passing, I was embarrassed, and I suddenly had an urgent need to make things right. 'We should get started.'

Lucy frowned. 'Do you really think you can go on? If you're not feeling well, you probably shouldn't...'

'I'm fine now.' This wasn't entirely true. I still felt nauseous and weak, but I couldn't imagine walking away from the gig. Not after everyone had been so understanding. 'I want to play.'

Lucy looked ready to protest. But she must have seen something in my expression that changed her mind, because she nodded.

'Okay, Dan? Will you get Matthew a beer? Leave it onstage.'

Dan gave her a long-suffering look and shuffled back into the pub. James followed him.

Lucy patted me on the shoulder. 'All right, maestro. Up you get.'

I shakily rose to my feet, and we went back inside. Somehow, I managed to walk past the crowd and take my place at the keyboard. Dan had left a pint of beer just next to the stand.

Lucy walked up to the mic and introduced us. Just before we started to play, she threw a brief look in my direction, and smiled.

I looked down at the keyboard and focused on the music.

And somehow, I made it through the set.

*

Dan had bought three bags of the smelliest crisps he could find – cheese and onion, barbecue beef and prawn cocktail. He tore them wide open, put them in the middle of the table and cheerfully pushed them all together to make a crisp smorgasbord.

'Dig in,' he said.

I've never been one for sharing food. I stared at the crisp pile and removed one tentatively from the edge.

'Crisps, Luce?'

Lucy grimaced. 'I think I'll pass.'

'Are you all right now?' asked James. 'You had us worried there for a minute.'

I nodded. 'I'm fine.'

James helped himself to a cautious crisp. 'So what did you think of Shattered Chandelier in action?'

I considered this. 'Well, I was pleasantly surprised. It went much better than I thought it would.'

Lucy almost choked on her drink. James and Dan stared at me, their expressions somewhere between amused and offended.

I really wished, in that moment, that I was some sort of crustacean. A snail, maybe. I think coming out of your shell is a highly overrated concept.

'I'm... sorry,' I stammered. 'I didn't mean it like that.'

Lucy laughed. 'Maestro's an opera fan. I don't think this is really his scene.' She touched my shoulder again. She seemed to be doing that a lot. 'It's okay. These guys have endured worse.'

James nodded. 'Much worse. Someone threw a hotdog at me once. It had onions on it.'

They began to recount a series of horror stories from past gigs. I listened and sipped my pint. I didn't have much to contribute to the discussion, but no one seemed to mind, and I began to relax.

'Anyone for another drink?' Dan said. He looked at me. 'Martini, Matthew? Shaken, not stirred?'

'All right, all right.' I glared down at my jacket.

'Okay, sorry. What would you like?'

'It's my round,' I said, without thinking. Another round meant I would have to stay longer, but I realised with surprise that I wanted to.

When I came back from the bar, I found the three of them leaning over the table, their heads together, conversing in whispers. I had a sudden cold back-at-school feeling. A walking-down-the-street-without-concealer feeling. Whispers always had this effect on me.

I put the tray of drinks down. 'Is everything all right?'

James and Dan exchanged a glance.

'We have a suggestion to make,' said James.

'What?'

'I know I just asked you to fill in on keyboard for a bit. But we were wondering if you'd like to join us on a more permanent basis?'

I was silent. This was not what I had expected. Not after I had shown myself up.

'You're asking me to be in the band?' My voice was soft.

'Yes,' said Lucy.

I wish I could say that being in a band was a childhood dream, but it wasn't. My musical ambitions had always been of a vocal nature, in opera or musical theatre. The thought of sitting in the corner of a dark pub and playing the keyboard had never held any appeal to me, never even crossed my mind up until a few hours earlier. I still wasn't sure it was really for me, but I was touched by their invitation.

I smiled. 'I'd like that.'

*

Later, I walked home with Lucy.

We were going in exactly the same direction, so I didn't have much choice in the matter. We walked in silence for most of the way, but it wasn't the awkward silence I had expected. It was almost... companionable.

We reached the house. Lucy paused outside the door to her flat. 'Matthew?'

'Yes?'

'Don't worry about what happened tonight, yeah? It's not a big deal.'

'Thank you.' I dropped my gaze to the carpet. 'And thanks for... what you did.'

'It was nothing.' Then Lucy stepped forward and did something completely unexpected. She hugged me.

It was just a friendly hug, but that didn't matter. It was as if someone had struck a particularly evocative chord on a piano, a chord that went straight to my nerves. I went absolutely still.

Lucy pulled away. 'Are you okay?'

I nodded, once, a tiny movement in my overall stillness. 'Yes.'

'I thought you'd turned to stone or something.'

'No, no. I'm fine.'

She didn't hug me again, much to my relief.

'Take care of yourself, yeah?'

She disappeared into her flat. I stared at the closed door.

'You, too,' I said.

Back in my own flat, I felt too full of adrenaline to even think about going to bed. So I sat down at the keyboard and turned my attention to Angela's song. I had decided to write it as a duet for soprano and tenor.

The music came to me easily. Perhaps it was because I had been playing something different and felt liberated as a result. I closed my eyes and brought Angela's voice into my mind. I wove our two voices together in harmony, listening to them both in my mind's ear and transcribing what I heard.

Shortly after midnight, I laid my pen down with a smile. The song was finished.

Angela was going to love it.

My phone gave a ping, and my heart leapt when I realised it was probably Angela again, with another update from Venice. How very serendipitous that she should text me just as I had finished her song.

I reached for the phone.

*Ralph: Hey! Look what we did today!*

There was a photo with the message. Ralph and Angela were sitting together in a gondola, arms around each other's shoulders. Both were wearing sunglasses and big smiles.

Invisible cold fingers dug into my chest. I tried to ignore them.

*Me: How's Venice?*
*Ralph: Amazing! You'd love it. Filming went on a bit, but we've finally managed to escape from Chris. Look where we are!*

I noted the 'we'.

Another photo appeared. This time it showed St Mark's Square, the Basilica aglow with lights.

*Me: Amazing.*
*Ralph: We thought we might stay for a few extra days and explore!*

'We' again.

*Ralph: I've put some nice pics on Facebook.*

I clicked on Ralph's Facebook profile. He fancied himself as something of an amateur photographer.

He had posted an album that afternoon and called it: *Venice with Angela 2016.* There was another photo of him with his arm around Angela's shoulders. This time they were posing with the Campanile in the background. There was also a picture of them both tucking into enormous ice creams, and then a photo of a big bowl of risotto.

Ralph was eating my risotto.

*Ralph: U ok, mate?*
*Me: Fine.*
*Ralph: There's a lot of mask shops here. Would you like a mask?*
*Me: Not really, no.*

Time for bed.

I had just emerged from the bathroom and was changing into my pyjamas when my phone pinged once again.

*Ralph: Ok. Serious question. Do u think Angela would like*
    *a mask?*

I stared at the message for a long moment.

*Me: Why???*
*Ralph: I'd like to buy her a present. To say thanks for the trip.*
    *Masks are very Venetian. Do u think she'd like one?*
*Me: I've no idea.*
*Ralph: Come on. You're friends. You must know if she'd like*
    *a mask.*
*Me: The topic's never come up, believe it or not.*
*Ralph: Do u think she'd prefer chocolates?*
*Ralph: Matthew?*
*Ralph: U still there?*

*Me: Why don't you compromise and buy her a chocolate mask?*
*Ralph: Great idea!*
*Ralph: Does she like dark or milk chocolate?*

I decided to switch off my phone.

# Debut

It had been a long two months, with only my job and the band rehearsals to distract me. But now the day that would change my life was finally here.

The day of the launch.

I had marked it on my desk calendar, adding a big, scribbled star and the words *ALBUM RELEASED*.

It was going to be spectacular. I would be able to sing with Angela without being forced to deal with any stage fright. Everyone would praise my voice, and my original song would prove a huge hit. And after the show, I would have champagne with Angela and present her with her new song.

My first errand of the day was to go to the music shop. I arrived at 9.30am, just as it was opening.

I found James unpacking CDs.

'You're eager today,' he said.

'It's a special occasion.'

'Looking for anything in particular?' He glanced up. 'Let me guess: electronic-techno-grunge?'

'What's that?'

'I don't know. I made it up.' He looked uncertain for a moment. 'I think.'

'I'm here for classical.'

'I thought you might be. What's it today?'

'I'm looking for Angela Nilsson's album.'

'Angela who?'

'Nilsson. It's songs from the musicals.'

He rubbed his chin. 'I think I just put a copy in Easy Listening. Would you like me to look?'

'No. It's fine, I'm sure I'll find it.'

I went to the Easy Listening section, flicked through to 'N' for Nilsson, and there it was.

I stared at it. On the cover there was a black and white photo of Ralph and Angela posing in front of a gondola.

My heart gave a little lurch. The album was here. It existed. And it was mine. Well, partially mine. I couldn't quite believe it was real.

I laid it reverently on the counter.

James's lip curled in apparent distaste. Then he shook his head sadly. 'All those rehearsals, and we still haven't managed to wean you off this stuff. I give up, I really do.'

I tried to glare at him, but I couldn't bring myself to be annoyed. Not today. 'I'd like to order two more copies, please.'

\*

Once home, I freed my new album from its cellophane wrapper.

My phone pinged with a message.

*Angela: Congratulations! Also, music video up!*

She had included a link to YouTube. I clicked on it and regretted it instantly.

The first shot was of Ralph, staring across the Grand Canal. He spent the entire video pouting and brooding and smouldering and generally overacting. But I had to hand it to the studio: the production was flawless. There was no sign at all that he was miming.

The video featured a strange gondola ride during which there was a dramatic rainstorm (neither Ralph nor Angela got wet), before culminating in a dance in St Mark's Square. Everyone was masked, because apparently it was now the carnival. Angela and Ralph both wore masks. Angela's mask had big white feathers and Ralph's mask was very small, barely surrounding his eyes. Presumably this was so we weren't deprived of the sight of him.

At the end of the song, Ralph leaned towards Angela, and they gazed into each other's eyes, as if they were about to share a kiss.

I was saved by the phone ringing.

'Matthew, it's Clara.'

'Oh. Hello.' I tried to drag my mind away from the nightmarish Venetian visions I had just witnessed.

'Are you okay? You sound a bit... strange.'

'I'm fine.' I swallowed. 'Have you heard the album yet?'

'Not just yet.'

'Did you manage to get a copy?'

'Of course I've got a copy. It arrived this morning.' There was a pause. 'That's why I'm calling, actually. I'm a little confused.'

'In what way?'

'Why aren't you on the cover? Who's the random guy with Angela?'

'It's Ralph. You remember Ralph? My friend from school?'

'That's *Ralph* on the cover?'

'Yes. He's a model now.'

'What's that all about, then?'

I took a deep breath and tried to calm my racing heart. Of course, I'd known this conversation was going to happen eventually. I just wished it wasn't on my much-anticipated launch day.

'You know how I get nervous onstage sometimes?'

'Yes?'

'Well, we decided to use Ralph as a sort of... stand-in.'

'A stand-in?'

'Yes. I sing backstage and he mimes to my voice, so I don't have to go onstage, and I don't get nervous.'

There was a long silence.

'Clara? Are you still there?'

'I *knew* there was something weird going on.' Her voice had risen by several decibels. 'Is this why you're not giving any concerts?'

'I *am* giving concerts. I'm just not *appearing* in them.'

'And Ralph's happy to go along with this? I thought he was your friend.'

'He is my friend. I asked him to do this. I thought it would be for the best.'

'So you're really okay with this? With them using your voice without giving you proper credit?'

'They are giving me proper credit.'

'Really? I checked the sleeve notes, and there's no mention of your name anywhere.'

The back of my neck prickled. 'No. That can't be right...'

'It just says "Angela with guests". No names.'

'Just a minute...' I reached for the CD and took out the sleeve notes. I scanned the minuscule text and saw that my sister was right. Then I looked at the track list and saw there was no writing credit next to my song.

'It... it must just be an oversight.' My voice was hoarse. 'I'll have to talk to Chris. Maybe it's because it's a first printing?'

I wasn't convinced by this theory even as I voiced it.

'Clara,' I said. 'Please could you keep all this to yourself for the time being?'

'What do you mean?'

'Don't tell Mum and Dad. I don't think they'd understand.'

'Matthew, *I* don't understand.'

'I'd just rather talk to them myself.'

She sighed. 'Okay. Fine.'

'Thank you.'

There was a pause.

'Did she put you up to this?' Clara's voice sounded strained.

'Who?'

'Angela!'

'What? No! What makes you say that?'

'Oh, I don't know. Maybe because of the way she treated you at music school.'

'Angela's my friend.'

'Matthew, she threw you away like a piece of rubbish the moment you started having difficulties. What kind of friend does that?'

My hand shook against the phone. 'Yes, well, it was a long time ago.'

'And that makes it okay?'

I sighed. 'Listen. I'm just being realistic. I've finally found a way I can sing. It's wonderful. Can't you just let me enjoy it?'

A silence.

'All right, Matthew.' Clara sounded tired. 'As long as you're happy.'

'I am, thank you. I'm very happy.'

*

'The mic's all rigged up,' said Chris. 'I hope you'll be comfortable here. The chair was the best I could find, but we might be able to get a cushion from somewhere...'

We were back at the Grand Theatre, just behind the proscenium arch, in the corner of the wings where the prompt would sit during a play. But the corner had been curtained off with two black drapes, forming a sort of booth. There was a folding metal chair inside the booth, and a shelf jutting from one of the solid walls. The shelf had a microphone on it, and a desk lamp.

So this was it. I would quite literally be singing behind a curtain. There was something pathetic about it, now that it was actually happening.

'Thanks.' I swallowed the lump which seemed to be blocking my throat. 'Chris, there's something I need to check with you. About the album's sleeve notes...'

'Fire away.'

'Why isn't my name mentioned anywhere?'

'Ah.' Chris tried to lean casually against a wall, before realising the wall was actually a curtain, and straightening up. 'I probably should have explained about that...'

'You probably should have.'

'Well, the record execs... they thought it would be best if we left your name off the album, just for the sake of consistency. So we've just put you down as a "guest". That way, we're not lying to anybody. You'll notice we haven't mentioned Ralph, either. So the album's a true collaborative effort.'

'Right. So no one will know I'm the one doing the singing? Or that I've written the single?'

Chris ran a hand through his hair. 'Mate, with respect, you can't have your cake and eat it. Most people are just going to assume Ralph's doing the singing, anyway. And as for your song... that was an oversight.'

I thought this was a lie, but I didn't quite have the courage to say so.

'So, no one will know I've made any contribution to this album at all.'

'I wouldn't say that,' said Chris. 'All the important people know. I know, you know, Angela knows... Come on, why can't you just enjoy this? I mean, what other chance are you realistically going to get?'

It was those words that made me shrink into my seat. He was right. I took a deep breath. 'Okay.'

Chris patted me on the back. 'Good man! Just sit tight. We'll make a start as soon as Ralph gets here.' He disappeared through the curtains.

I picked up the microphone. I wanted to stand up. Singing while seated placed too many restrictions on the voice. It meant I couldn't use my diaphragm properly. If I thought about the technicalities of singing, focused on the professional aspects, I could forget the strange situation in which I now found myself. I could make the decision to treat this as a job, and just a job. But of course it was more than that, which was why I was still here. Perhaps this was the sacrifice I had to make in order to be heard.

Voices onstage alerted me that Ralph had arrived, and we ran through the single. I closed my eyes as I sang, trying to imagine myself back in the studio, standing in front of Angela, looking into her eyes – no, not looking into her eyes. If I did that, I would blush. Instead, I imagined looking at a spot just beyond her shoulder. But this wasn't the same as being in the studio. The sound of her voice was too far away, muffled by curtains and side flats. It was like listening to someone singing under water or rehearsing in the next room.

After the song, I emerged from the booth and stepped onto the stage. Angela and Ralph were frozen in a pose, staring at each other, bathed in blue light, and for a moment I thought this picture had been plucked from my imagination. It was all there, except that Ralph was actually able to make eye contact and not look remotely shy about it.

'Right,' said Chris's voice, from the front the stalls. 'That's great.'

The lights came up, and Ralph and Angela moved apart.

'I don't know,' said Angela. 'I think it's a bit cheesy.'

'Rubbish. It's just the effect I wanted. Matthew? What are you doing?'

I had been standing to one side, waiting for a chance to speak.

'I want some headphones,' I said.

'Why do you need headphones?'

'I can't hear the music properly. Or Angela. It's like listening from behind a brick wall.'

'Does it matter?'

'If you want me to be accurate, and not come in too soon, then yes.'

This wasn't strictly true: I could hear my cues well enough. There was just no sense of involvement. I felt like I was singing with a recording, not another person, but something told me Chris would not understand this.

Chris raised his hands. 'Fine, fine. Get Matthew some headphones.'

This order seemed to be directed at the theatre in general, because when I returned to the booth a moment or two later, someone had already placed a pair of headphones on the shelf.

We rehearsed 'If I Loved You', and it was much better with the headphones. I could almost imagine I was back in the studio again. Angela's voice was much clearer, and I sang better as a result.

After the rehearsal, Chris called me on to the stage. The three of us – myself, Ralph and Angela – stood in a row while he addressed us.

'You're going to be great,' he said. 'Ralph, your lip-syncing is perfect. I wish you could see it, Matthew.'

I didn't want to see it. I'd had enough of watching him miming at the studio.

'The concert is going to be brilliant. Just do exactly what you did in rehearsal, and they'll love you.' He gave a broad smile. 'Now go and get some rest. Grab a bite to eat.'

Ralph and Angela left the stage. I started to follow them.

'Not you, Matthew.'

'Why?'

'I just think it would be better if you stayed back here. Then you're in position before the audience arrives.'

'But no one will know who I am even if they can see me.'

'Still, best be on the safe side.'

'Don't be ridiculous, Chris,' said Angela, glaring at him. 'He can eat wherever he likes.'

I shook my head, determined not to show my hurt in front of Angela. 'No. It's fine. I wouldn't mind some time on my own. I can warm up a bit more.'

'Perfect,' said Chris. 'I'll bring you a sandwich. Let me show you to the green room.'

Half an hour later I was sitting on an old sofa in a room that was part sitting room, part kitchen. It smelled of burnt toast and baked beans. Chris had brought me the promised sandwich (grated cheese, no mayo). He told me that I was welcome to make a cup of tea, and he pointed to the kettle, as if I would be unable to work out the method for tea-making by myself.

After I had eaten, I stood in the middle of the room and began my warm-up. I sang up and down the scale, from chest voice to head voice, and practised my vowel sounds and pronunciation. I would sing well tonight. I was damned if Chris and his stupid sleeve notes were going to stop me from doing my best.

After my warm-up, I went to wait backstage. There I found another world carefully folded and stacked away behind the curtains. A fountain, a sofa, a pot plant; pieces of set from the current production.

I found myself thinking of my old town hall, where I had appeared in several amateur musicals as a teenager. Sceptical though I was about Charlotte's am-dram group, I missed my teenage productions. As a professional I could look back and see these shows were flawed, and yet there had been *joy*. Camaraderie.

I had loved waiting backstage among the set pieces and props; they had a self-contained magic all of their own. Perhaps I had been too quick to judge Charlotte and her 'stars'.

I forced the memories away. After wanting to sing for as long as I could remember, now I was doing it. I was a real, professional performer. This hiding behind a curtain thing was just another performance.

'Pssst, mate!'

The voice made me jump. I spun around to see Ralph standing in the wings, half in shadow. He stepped forward, and I saw that he was holding an enormous bouquet of red roses.

He smiled. 'Would you do me a favour?'

'What?'

'Could you hide these in your booth thing during the show?'

He waved the roses at me.

I eyed them suspiciously. 'What are they for?'

'They're for Angela. A sort of congratulations present.' His gaze slid down to the floor.

I raised an eyebrow. 'Red roses?'

'Well... yeah. Do you think it's too much? I just thought I should get her something.'

He waved the roses at me again.

I sighed. 'Okay. Fine.'

'Thank you! I'll grab them from you during curtain call.' He smiled. 'Have a good show!'

I was left alone, holding the contents of a small florist in my arms.

Returning to my curtained booth, I placed the roses on the floor by my feet.

There was a peculiar, hollow feeling in my chest. I hoped I wasn't coming down with something just before the show.

Why roses? Surely they were a romantic gesture, not a congratulatory one?

Unless Ralph...

I thought of the messages we had exchanged when he was in Venice. The photos of him with his arms around Angela. Their smiles.

Oh, no.

He *couldn't*.

I was aware of movement outside, footsteps and muffled voices – probably the stage manager and assistants getting the stage ready, and Angela and Ralph getting into position. Something caught against the curtains of my booth, causing the desk lamp to send distorted shadows dancing across the wall.

I could hear a rumble of voices coming from the auditorium. I wondered what sort of crowd we had. It sounded like a big one.

Grateful for the distraction, I put on my headphones and waited for the show to begin.

Whatever happened, it was important to remain professional. I looked at the roses. They would be my rocket fuel. My reminder to sing well and prove myself to Angela.

The lights faded, and for a moment there was great darkness and stillness.

Perhaps I could have performed onstage in this darkness. It seemed an unequal relationship, to have a singer illuminated by bright lights, while the audience could hide in shadow. If I could sing in the dark, the audience could listen to my voice, with no other distractions. Then, if I was feeling brave, I might ask the lighting technician to bring up the lights at the end, just for a moment, so the audience could see I was a real person and not a recording.

Instead I had Ralph, which was perhaps not so different.

The music began, the gentle sound of a keyboard from the orchestra pit, the introduction to 'Some Enchanted Evening'. My heart began to pound. My palms were sweating as I reached for the microphone. I rose to my feet and waited as Angela began to sing.

I could hear her voice both through my headphones and from the stage. It was a strange effect, like hearing a voice and its echo at the same time. But this did nothing to detract from its beauty.

My turn. My verse. I took a breath and sang. I closed my eyes and sang to the voice in the headphones, the voice on the stage. And again, I tried to imagine myself in Ralph's place. The acoustics in the little booth were surprisingly good. I wondered how my voice sounded through the speakers, through Ralph.

Angela and I finished the last chorus together, and this was followed by a very long silence. I shivered, feeling the skin on my arms coming up in goosebumps. Fear seized my heart. Something was wrong. Maybe the speakers had failed. Maybe Angela had just sung a duet with herself, or a duet with Ralph, who could not sing.

Just as I was thinking our careers were over, that I would never sing again, the applause began.

Even through the headphones and curtains, I could tell it was loud. I removed my headphones so I could hear it better, and my ears were greeted with a joyous roar of percussive sound. It lasted for quite some time, and I sat very still, and listened.

Finally, I heard Angela's soft 'Thank you' from the stage, and the audience quieted. She then sang a couple of songs on her own, and I leaned back in the chair and listened.

This wasn't so bad. This was okay.

Every one of Angela's solos got an enthusiastic response from the audience, but the applause seemed to reach a crescendo after each of our duets. I told myself that this was my imagination, that I wanted to hear a stronger reaction because I was singing, too. But each time we sang together there was that same moment of rapt silence, followed by a slowly cresting wave of applause.

The single, my own song, was our final number. My voice was soft, the first words whispered close to the mic. Then I allowed it to build. I closed my eyes and the curtained walls of the booth fell away, and in my mind's eye I was standing on the stage, the audience an indistinct mass, the stage lights shining in my eyes. My voice reached across the space separating me from Angela.

And then it was over, and I was back in the booth, surrounded by curtains. Again there was that silence, and again the applause, and I tore off the headphones so as not to miss a single part of it.

Now they had heard me, truly heard me, perhaps they would accept me? Next time I would sing out there, as myself.

There was the sound of thumping footsteps, and a hand shot through the curtains, into the booth. A face appeared above it.

'Roses! Quick!' said Ralph.

I handed him the bouquet.

He smiled at me. His eyes were shining.

'Thanks!' He vanished.

A moment later, there was a loud, bright laugh and a 'Thank you' from Angela.

Gradually the applause faded, and the band started up again, playing us out. The lights came up and I heard a cacophony of voices signalling that the audience was leaving. They would be collecting their coats, tripping over the feet of those who stayed for the last taste of music, pushing through the aisles to the exits.

I waited for someone to pull aside the curtains and congratulate me, to call me out into the open. I imagined Chris opening the curtain with a flourish, like a stage magician. *Ta dah! This is the real singer! This is Matthew Capes!*

But nothing of that sort happened, so I switched off the desk lamp and left the booth.

Angela wasn't in the star's dressing room, and the backstage corridors were empty. Maybe she'd already left or was greeting people in the theatre bar.

I reached the stage door office and signed myself out.

Then I pushed open the door and stepped right into a huge crowd of people. Several of them turned to look at me, holding out programmes.

It was actually happening.

I was being stage-doored.

I tried to remember what I was supposed to do. Smile. Offer my autograph.

I stepped forward.

The eyes slid away from me.

Of course. They didn't know who I was.

'Matthew! Over here!' Angela waved at me from within the crowd. I began to weave my way between the fans. Angela looked tired, but she was smiling, and I waited while she posed for a selfie with a teenage girl.

'OH MY GOD! IT'S HIM!'

The crowd seemed to turn, as one, towards the stage door.

Ralph was surrounded by a group of concert-goers. They held up their phones, taking photos, and some of them surged forwards.

Ralph blinked in apparent confusion, his eyes meeting mine. For a moment I thought he would flee or confess that he was not the one who had been singing. But then he smiled his flawless smile. He stepped into the crowd, posing for photos and signing programmes with a flourish.

'Can I have a selfie?'

'You were amazing!'

I looked for Angela, but Chris was ushering her through the crowd to Ralph's side. Angela caught my eye and gave an apologetic smile. And then Ralph had his arm around her shoulders, and both of them were smiling, and they looked like something off the cover of a showbiz magazine. The crowd held up their mobile phones.

Ralph leaned forward and kissed Angela on the cheek.

I'd seen enough.

# Diminuendo

My morning had been carefully planned out: I would go for a run, eat a healthy breakfast of cereal and a banana, shower and dress, then go to the empty Moon and Stars and practise.

Now, I thought a better plan would be to stay in bed all morning, get up briefly to make some instant noodles, and then go back to bed.

My phone buzzed on the bedside table. I reached for it.

Angela.

I wasn't ready to speak to her. An image of Ralph kissing her cheek flashed through my mind.

I forced myself to answer.

'Hi, Matthew.'

I was silent.

Angela continued: 'I've just heard about the sleeve notes. I'm really, really sorry.'

'It wasn't your fault.'

'I feel terrible. I had no idea Chris was going to do that.'

'It's okay, really.'

'Are you free on Tuesday night?'

'Why?'

'Chris has called a meeting. He says he has a great idea.' I could hear the excitement in her voice.

I tried to imagine what this 'great idea' could be, but I had no doubt it would involve me hiding behind a curtain again.

'I don't know, Angela.'

'I want to make things right. Please come to the meeting.'

A part of me wanted to stay in my flat forever, but I had only just rebuilt my friendship with Angela. I didn't want to risk losing her again. 'Okay. I'll come.'

'Great! Thank you so much, Matthew. It means so much to be able to sing with you again.'

'Thanks. It… means a lot to me, too.'

'I'll see you at the studios. Looking forward to it!'

I spent the rest of the day wondering if I was doing the right thing. I wanted so much to be able to sing with Angela as myself, in front of an audience, without my nerves getting in the way. But then I would remember the contest back in 2008, and I knew in my heart that such a thing was impossible.

\*

The contest was called Dynamic Duets. It was specifically for duos, and Angela had persuaded me to enter with her. We were in our third and final year at the Conservatoire, and I couldn't deny that the contest offered an excellent opportunity to showcase our voices. The later rounds would be televised, and the prize was a recording contract.

The first round of auditions was held at a theatre in the West End. We had rehearsed every day for a fortnight and were as confident as we could be.

It was a scorching hot day, and I was wearing my smart concert suit. Angela had been more practical and was wearing a summer dress printed with big blue flowers.

Inside the foyer, we were given matching numbered stickers, and told to wait in the auditorium until our number was called. Then we would appear onstage, where we would have five minutes to impress the judges.

I slid into a red velvet seat and looked around. The auditorium had maybe three hundred people in it, spread out across the stalls, sitting in pairs or small groups. Onstage, there were two microphones standing in front of a plain black backdrop.

I was nervous, but I had been to auditions before. And Angela had been to dozens. We would be fine.

We sat back and watched the endless parade of duet partners. They were mainly men and women, but there were also tenors singing with baritones, and altos singing with sopranos, and teenage girls and boys imitating their favourite pop stars.

They were all frighteningly good.

The audience was respectful. There was polite applause after each audition, and no one laughed or jeered or shouted anything. The judges were also very low-key. They sat in the front row of the stalls, slightly to one side, quietly scribbling notes.

I whispered in Angela's ear. 'This isn't what I was expecting.'

'What were you expecting?'

'I don't know. A bit more drama, I guess. Singers and judges flouncing around, shouting at each other.'

Angela smiled. 'I think they're saving that for the cameras.'

I hoped this wasn't the case.

Then, two hours into proceedings, our number was called.

The stage lights hit me full in the face. I blinked. When my eyes adjusted, I found myself looking out at the biggest theatre I had ever performed in. It hadn't looked so massive when I was sitting in it. But it was beautiful, too: all green art deco lights and decorative white and gold panels.

We introduced ourselves.

'We're going to sing an original composition,' said Angela.

I heard the first note of my song, looked at Angela, and felt my nervousness evaporate.

The next few minutes were wonderful. Our voices echoed in the vast auditorium, making the hairs on the back of my neck stand on end. The atmosphere had that silent, rapt chill which managed to be warm at the same time. The judges leaned forward in their seats. We had them.

This was what we had worked for.

Afterwards, there was a round of applause. I looked at the judges, trying to read their faces, but they just exchanged a few muttered words and scribbled in their notepads.

'What happens now?' I asked when we were back in our seats.

'We wait and see if we get called back to a second round of auditions.'

So we waited. And waited. Another hour went by. Then, at a little after 2pm, one of the judges got up onstage and spoke into a microphone.

'Thanks so much for your patience, ladies and gentlemen. The standard of singing today has been exceptionally high, but unfortunately we can only take twenty acts through to the next round. Please stay if we say your number...'

\*

'I can't believe we did it,' said Angela.

We sat in the theatre bar, where the production company behind Dynamic Duets had laid on sandwiches for the contestants.

I could barely eat. Angela didn't seem to eat much, either; she nibbled a sandwich while chatting excitedly about the next round, and about how great it would be if we ended up on television. Her enthusiasm was infectious, and I found myself smiling along with her.

Apparently the next stage was an 'informal chat' about the show. We were called into a small function room, where two producers – a man and a woman – greeted us.

'We were very impressed with your audition,' said the woman. She gave us an encouraging smile.

I blushed and looked down at my shoes.

'Thank you so much,' said Angela.

'We'd love to send you both through.' Her smile faltered; she looked almost uncomfortable. 'But we're not sure it would be fair. You were both brilliant. But together... we don't think it quite works.'

I looked at Angela, who had gone pale.

'I beg to differ,' she said. 'I think our voices go very well together.'

The male producer waved a hand dismissively. 'We're not talking about your voices.'

'Then what are you talking about?' There was an odd tone to Angela's voice. A dark, challenging tone that I had never heard before.

'You just don't look right together.'

'What do you mean?' My voice was very small and distant even to my own ears.

The producer sighed. 'All right. I'll explain if I have to. Angela, you look like a singer. A star.' He turned to me. 'But Matthew... well...' He shook his head. 'You just *don't*. I'm sorry.'

There was a moment of silence. Angela had gone very still next to me. I tried to find an appropriate response.

'Is there anything I can do?' I asked.

'Well, short of plastic surgery...' The producer tailed off with a shrug. His colleague looked at him in horror.

I stared at them both, too shocked and embarrassed to speak.

'*I beg your pardon?*' said Angela, her voice full of fury.

'Just a joke,' he said, in a tone that convinced me it was nothing of the sort. 'But if I can offer you some advice – that hair...' He mimed opening and closing a pair of scissors. 'Snip snip.'

The producer sat up straight in his chair and looked at Angela. He gave a thin smile. 'We'd be happy to send you through, Angela. We can pair you up with someone else. A better match.'

Angela hesitated, and for a moment I thought she was considering it. I wondered if I should encourage her. *Go for it, Angela. Follow your dream, don't worry about me*, etc. But the shock had taken my voice away.

'No,' said Angela, her voice like ice. 'I don't think so.'

Then she turned and left without another word. I shuffled after her, head down.

Angela didn't stop until we were outside the theatre. She turned onto a quiet street down the side of the building and stopped abruptly.

'What an arsehole.' She was trembling. I was, too. But mainly I felt sick, and ashamed. She looked at me properly for the first time. 'Oh, Matthew. Are you okay?'

'I'm so sorry, Angela.'

'What?' Her eyes narrowed. 'What have you got to be sorry about? That total... I've never been so angry.'

'You could have gone through.' The horrible truth was starting to dawn on me. Angela had given up the chance of a recording contract and who knew what other opportunities because of me. Because the judges didn't think I looked right.

'You really think I want to work with someone like that? Give me some credit.'

'But you could have been on television...'

'So bloody what? Come on, let's get a drink.' Angela nodded towards the theatre. 'We don't need them.'

# Pitch

I arrived at the studio on Tuesday evening to find Ralph waiting in reception.

He waved at me as I stepped through the automatic doors.

'Hi, Matthew. Great show the other night.'

'Yes,' I said. 'Great.'

'Angela was wonderful, wasn't she?'

I didn't reply. I had no desire to make small talk with Ralph.

The receptionist buzzed me through the interior door.

Ralph followed me. 'What's up?'

'Nothing's up.'

'Have I done something to upset you?'

'No.'

'Then why are you in a bad mood?'

'I'm not. I just don't want to talk about the other night.'

'Why?'

I carried on walking.

Angela smiled at me as I reached the studio office. I attempted to smile back. Ralph entered just behind me and took a seat beside Angela. He looked a bit sheepish and didn't meet my eye, which was fine by me.

Chris leapt to his feet. He appeared suspiciously alert for an overworked music manager. This may or may not have had something to do with the large mug of sludgy black coffee on the table in front of him.

'Matthew! The man of the hour! Do sit down! Coffee?'

'No, thank you.'

'I've invited you all here today because I wanted to congratulate you. Last weekend's concert was truly the highlight of my career. The single is shooting up the charts, and the album is already doing extraordinarily well.'

'That's wonderful news,' said Angela.

Chris's eyes gleamed. 'The other reason you're here is that we can't afford to let the grass grow under our feet. We need to strike while the iron's hot. The record label wants more, the public wants more, and I think you'll probably want more, yes?'

A silence. Chris placed both hands palm down on the long white table and leaned towards us. 'We need to start planning the next album right away. And this time, I want more original material.'

Ralph sat up straighter in his chair.

Chris looked at me. 'And I want you, Matthew, my man, to write it.'

Ralph sagged back into his chair.

'What?' I said. 'Me?'

Chris smiled. 'Who better? Your music is perfect. Romantic, melodic, easy listening, wholesome. It's the musical equivalent of a giant ice cream sundae. Everyone loves it.'

I wasn't sure how I felt about being an ice cream sundae – particularly an anonymous, uncredited sundae.

'Will my name be on it this time?' I asked.

Chris waved a hand. 'Of course, of course. Awful oversight with the sleeve notes. We'll get it right this time, give you the credit you deserve.' His smile widened. 'And then, of course, there's the tour.'

Angela stared at Chris. 'Tour?'

'Yes. The label is arranging a tour for you guys. It should take a few months. All major UK cities.'

'By "you guys", do you mean all three of us?' asked Ralph.

'Of course. Why mess with a winning formula?'

'So I'll be miming again?'

'I prefer to think of it as choreography. And maybe we can look at recording some of your songs at a later date.'

Ralph looked a bit glum. I didn't understand why he was so bothered. I would be the one hiding behind a curtain for weeks on end.

And yet... I would be writing music and singing with Angela. It was what I'd always wanted. Wasn't it?

'So, Matthew,' said Chris, 'are you in?'

I hesitated, then nodded. 'Yes.'

'Ralph?'

He sighed. 'I suppose so.'

'Angela?'

She beamed at him. 'Absolutely!'

Chris clapped his hands together. 'Marvellous! The dream team! Just you wait. We're going to have so much fun.'

*

By the time I got home, I was feeling much more positive. Although I still wasn't happy about hiding behind a curtain or going on the road with Ralph, it occurred to me that there were certain advantages to the tour:

1. I would get to spend more time with Angela.
2. We would be visiting lots of different cities, so there would be plenty of romantic and/or cultural places for us to explore.
3. Travelling to new places would be inspiring, giving me raw material for new songs.
4. Angela would be on hand to help me try out the new songs.

I had not anticipated Ralph's overtures towards Angela, but didn't every romantic musical have a love triangle? Perhaps real life wasn't so different. Ralph was the handsome one with the red roses, but Angela and I had a shared history and a musical connection. Surely talent would win the day.

There was one major disadvantage, of course. Going on tour meant time away from both the theatre and the band. Shattered Chandelier was a recent commitment, and I knew I couldn't sacrifice the opportunity to sing professionally so I could play the keyboard at the odd pub gig. But the theatre was *work*. I would have to handle this carefully.

\*

'You can't reduce your hours,' said Charlotte. 'Darling, I need you here. *Earnest* opens next month.'

I stared at my clasped hands. 'It would mainly be weekends. Saturdays, and the occasional Friday. Not for very long. A few months, that's all. And I am owed some leave.'

'You could just take two weeks' holiday, like a normal person,' grumbled Richard.

The three of us were sitting in his office, which was significantly larger than the office I shared with Jess. It had its own fridge, and a coffee machine, and an exercise bike.

Charlotte didn't have an office ('Why would I need one of those, darling?'), and I wished I could have had this conversation with her alone, somewhere informal.

'Why do you need all these weekends off?' asked Charlotte.

'I have to look after my sister's dog,' I said.

I had lain awake for most of the previous night, trying to think of a plausible excuse. This had been the best I could come up with. I was starting to think imagination was not my strong point.

Charlotte raised a perfectly manicured eyebrow.

'Your sister's dog,' repeated Richard, in a flat tone.

'Yes. My sister has to work weekends for the next few months, and I'm the only member of the family who isn't allergic.'

'Right,' said Richard.

'So it's a family thing,' I said. 'But only temporary.'

'You're seriously asking us to change your hours just so you can look after some scruffy mutt?' asked Richard.

'Well... he's not exactly scruffy. They're entering him into Crufts next year.'

I thought a certain amount of detail might make my lie more convincing.

'Oh!' said Charlotte. 'How exciting! Which category?'

I hesitated. My research hadn't extended that far.

'Er... tiny dogs?'

'You mean toy dogs,' said Charlotte.

'Yes. That's the one.'

Richard didn't look convinced. 'Well, she'll have to find another dog-sitter.'

'Oh,' I said, staring at the floor. 'Right.'

'Hang on a moment, Richard,' said Charlotte. 'Matty is fully entitled to holidays.'

'Certainly, and I'm happy to grant him two weeks. Together.' Richard turned towards the coffee machine. 'If you'll excuse me, I have real work to do.'

I stood up, tried to think of a way to argue my case, failed and left the room.

I had almost reached my own office when I heard Richard's door close. I turned to see Charlotte walking towards me.

'Matthew, what's going on?'

'Nothing.'

'*Tiny dogs?*' Charlotte's eyes were sharp. 'Do you think I was born yesterday?'

'Sorry, I don't know what you mean.'

'Why do you really want all these days off? Why don't you just take a proper holiday?' Her eyes searched my face, and her voice became gentle. 'What's wrong, darling?'

I hesitated, weighing up the possible consequences of confiding in Charlotte.

'Can I talk to you for a minute?' I asked. 'Alone?'

'Of course.'

I poked my head into the office to see if Jess was there, but the room was empty. I held the door open for Charlotte, and then closed it behind her.

'So I take it the dog situation was a lie?' said Charlotte.

'Yes. Sorry.' I plucked a stress ball from the collection on my desk and rolled it between my palms. 'I don't suppose you remember from my interview, but I used to sing.'

Charlotte smiled. 'Actually, I do remember. The London Conservatoire, wasn't it? I was just disappointed that you wouldn't give us a blast of *HMS Pinafore*.'

'Yes, well... an opportunity has come up. I've been invited to go on tour, supporting a classical crossover star.'

'You mean singing?'

'Yes.'

'Who's the star?'

'I'm afraid I can't say yet. But I'm doing some backing singing, choruses, that sort of thing.'

'That sounds like a good opportunity, darling.'

'Yes. At least... I hope so. The first date's next month. But I realise *Earnest* opens just afterwards, so if you want me to say no...'

Charlotte was silent for a moment. Her searching gaze was starting to make me feel uncomfortable.

'I'll say no,' I said.

Charlotte sighed. 'You should say yes. We get so few chances in life. Particularly in this industry. Do you think I don't know that?'

'But Richard said—'

'It's my decision as well as his. I'll talk him round. Don't worry.'

'But the theatre—'

'The theatre will be fine. We'll just have to juggle things around a bit.' She leaned forward slightly, looking into my eyes. 'But I need you to promise me something.'

'What?'

'You'll be here for the opening night of *Earnest*. And the final show. And you won't neglect the theatre in between your concerts. This is a difficult time, and we need all the help we can get. Do you promise me that?'

I nodded, a little startled by the intensity of her words. 'I promise.'

Charlotte smiled. 'Thank you, darling.'

# Aria

Our first concert was in Manchester.

Chris drove us there in his 'tour bus', which wasn't a bus at all, but an impressively large car. Angela sat in the front, next to Chris, which disappointed me slightly, because it meant I was in the back with Ralph.

'Wine gum?' said Ralph, offering a packet to me.

'Thanks.'

'This is like a school trip, isn't it?'

'I hope not.'

If Ralph thought he could spend the journey making small talk, then he was destined to be disappointed. I had done the calculations, and the journey to Manchester was long enough for me to listen to the entire original cast recording of *Les Misérables* and three quarters of *Chess*. I was going to make good use of the time.

I put my earphones in, leaned back and closed my eyes.

Several musical fatalities, a number of broken hearts and a dash of international politics later, the car slowed to a halt.

Chris had booked us into a surprisingly nice hotel, just across the street from the theatre.

'I'll let you all get freshened up,' he said. 'Soundcheck's at four.'

We were checked into rooms next door to each other on the third floor.

Within minutes, I was lying back on the largest, comfiest bed I had ever encountered, sipping a cup of tea. I decided I could get used to the touring life.

I had been in my room for no more than twenty minutes when there was a knock on the door.

Sighing, I slipped off the bed and padded over to answer. I was convinced it would be Chris, here to present me with yet another one of his great ideas.

But it was Angela.

'Hey, Matthew.'

'Oh,' I said. 'Hi.'

She smiled. 'I'm not disturbing you, am I?'

'No, no.'

'Could I borrow you for a while? I'm a bit worried about one of the songs.'

A musical conundrum. Excellent. This was exactly what I had hoped for: the chance to spend more time with Angela. I hoped the problem would prove complicated.

I followed Angela to the theatre, through the stage door, and up some stairs to a rehearsal studio. It was clearly used for dance, as the walls were covered with mirrors, and I tried to ignore my reflection as I stepped inside.

There was a piano in one corner. It was well used, the varnish scratched in places and the keys yellowed.

Angela opened a file and handed me some sheet music. It was 'Song to the Moon' from *Rusalka*.

'I recorded this on my first album,' she said.

'Yes. I remember.'

'I've had a special request from a fan on Twitter. They want me to sing it for some anniversary or other.' Her mouth twisted.

'But you don't want to,' I said.

'I do, but I'm worried about it.'

'It's beautiful. Your version's beautiful. You should definitely sing it.'

She shook her head. 'I haven't sung it in over three years. Chris... he's been so focused on the lighter, more popular stuff. Opera's gone out of the window a bit. I'm afraid I'm going to be horribly rusty.'

'That won't happen. You sing everything perfectly.'

Angela gave a short laugh. 'That's not true.'

'It is.' I was suddenly unable to meet her eye. I looked at the music instead. 'You've got nothing to worry about.'

She sighed. 'I'm not so sure. I don't think my voice is as strong as it used to be. Don't you think it sounds tired sometimes?'

'No,' I said. 'Never.'

'So you think I should sing the aria?'

'Absolutely.'

'Will you accompany me?'

I was already sitting at the piano. 'Of course.'

'Promise you won't laugh?'

'I could never laugh at your voice.'

I began to play.

Angela did not sound remotely rusty. I honestly had no idea what she was worried about. My heart leapt at every high note. I wanted to close my eyes and fall into her voice, to let it sweep me away completely.

I remembered all the times we had spent together at the Conservatoire, singing in a room much like this. The first time, I had been sitting alone in the corner of the lecture hall. We had been asked to find duet partners. It was only our third week, and I had barely spoken to anyone. I felt as though most of the other students already had their cliques and friendship groups, while I had fallen through the cracks. I was sure I would be the odd one out. And then Angela had slipped into the seat in front of me and said those magic words: 'Do you want to pair up?'

From that moment, we were a musical team. And now, listening to her sing while I played the piano, it felt just like old times. We were a team again.

'Was it okay?' she asked afterwards.

'Yes,' I murmured. 'Yes, it was beautiful.'

'Are you sure?'

'Quite sure.'

'Thank you.' She propped one elbow on the piano. 'You know, I've really missed this. Just you and me, making music.'

'I was just thinking the same thing.'

'We should do it more often.'

'I'd like that.'

She checked her watch. 'Oh, crap, I'd better go. Soundcheck's soon.' She paused at the door. 'Fancy a drink after the show?'

For a moment I didn't answer. I just stared at her while a voice in my head said *Oh God Oh God Oh God this is it*, accompanied by Beethoven's 'Ode to Joy'.

'Matthew? Are you okay?'

'Yes. You're lov— I mean... that would be lovely.'

She smiled. 'Great. Meet you in the hotel bar?'

'Bar. Yes. Good.'

The triumphant symphony continued to play in my head throughout the soundcheck and the performance. I managed to channel it into my voice, performing each duet with warm, romantic fervour. Angela's rendition of 'Song to the Moon' was glorious, and this time I allowed myself to close my eyes and lose myself in the music.

When the show was over, I didn't wait for the curtain. I hurried back to the hotel, hoping to buy myself time to freshen up and get changed. I also wanted to collect Angela's song, which I had tucked into the side pocket of my bag just in case this exact scenario presented itself.

Dressed in my smartest suit jacket, concealer carefully in place, I headed down to the bar.

'Matthew!' Angela waved at me from a table in a booth. It was in a corner, set slightly apart from the other guests, the wooden partitions providing some privacy. I was touched by her thoughtfulness.

'Hey,' she said, as I walked over.

My hands were shaking. I hid them behind my back. 'Er... hi.'

She smiled. 'Aren't you going to sit down?'

'Would you like a drink first?'

'I've ordered a bottle of wine. Fancy sharing?'

'Yes. Great.'

I slipped into the seat opposite her.

'I thought it went well tonight,' she said. 'Thanks for helping me out with that song.'

'You're welcome.' My hand strayed to the song in my pocket. Perhaps this would be a good moment. 'Angela...'

'Hi guys.' I turned to see Ralph, also wearing a smart suit jacket. Trust him to turn up and interrupt our date.

'Hey, Ralph,' said Angela. 'I've ordered some wine.'

'Great.'

Ralph sat down next to me.

'Er...' I said.

Ralph gave me a funny look. 'Are you all right, Matthew?'

My shoulders slumped. 'Yes. Fine.'

'I thought it would be nice, just the three of us, without the management,' said Angela.

'You didn't invite Chris?' Ralph smiled. 'You're mean.'

'Chris is fine in small doses,' said Angela.

So my romantic evening with Angela was actually an anti-Chris group-bonding exercise. Wonderful.

The wine arrived.

I stared at my full glass and tried to think of a reason to excuse myself.

'Matthew tells me you knew each other at school,' said Angela.

Oh, God. Could this evening get any worse?

'Yeah,' said Ralph cheerfully. 'Mainly sixth form.'

'Did you ever sing together?'

Ralph laughed. 'He wouldn't be seen dead singing with me, would you, mate? But I played the guitar for him sometimes.'

I locked eyes with him. *Please*, I thought. *Please, Ralph. Don't tell Angela what I was like at college.*

'Matthew was a total legend at college,' said Ralph. 'He always wore black, and he had this amazing long hair and black nail varnish.'

'I remember the hair,' said Angela.

Ralph nodded. 'And he gave off this... *vibe*. Like he gave zero fucks what anyone else thought of him.'

I closed my eyes. *Please, Ralph, please just shut up...*

'There were these horrible students on our music course. Total bullies. You remember them?'

'Yes,' I said, staring at my glass.

Ralph nudged me. 'Tell Angela what happened at the concert.'

I was silent.

Angela smiled at me. 'Go on. What happened?'

'They ruined our song, but Matthew turned the tables on them. It was hilarious.'

I drained my glass and stood up. 'I think I'll go to bed.'

Angela frowned. 'Are you all right?'

'Have I said something wrong?' asked Ralph.

I stared at him. His expression was entirely innocent. Maybe these were fond memories for him. I wished I felt the same way.

I shook my head. 'Just a bit tired. I'll see you tomorrow.'

'Oh, okay,' said Ralph. 'Night, mate.'

As I walked up to my room, it occurred to me that Ralph did not know how much I had suffered at college. No one did.

*

The ringleader of my sixth-form bullies was called Robert. We had been to the same secondary school, where I had usurped him at a school concert, diving in and taking over his solo when he had forgotten the words.

Robert's campaign was relentless. And with the clinical precision of bullies, he chose to focus on the thing I was at that point most self-conscious about: my acne.

'Should you really be doing that?' This question was directed at a girl with whom I was about to share a stage kiss, during a scene from *West Side Story*.

The girl drew back. 'What?'

'Kissing Matthew. You might hurt his skin.' Robert looked worried. 'Or catch something.'

And once, during lunch: 'Hey, Matthew? You know what you should sing at the next concert?'

'What?'

'A medley of songs from *The Phantom of the Opera*. It would just suit your voice so well, and you'd get to wear a mask. Everybody wins.'

And: 'Hey, Matthew? I know Photoshop. Would you like me to airbrush your photo in the *Godspell* programme?'

He 'borrowed' my music books and scrawled messages across the pages: *Matthew Capes is a freak. Matthew Capes is ugly.*

He left spot removal cream on my desk.

Once, when I was alone, he walked up to me and said there was no point in my auditioning for music school, because no one wanted to see my ugly mug onstage.

I didn't dare tell anyone I was being bullied. Bullying was something that happened to little kids, not seventeen-year-old boys.

So I did the only thing I could. I threw myself into my music.

Music provided an escape. When I sang or played the piano, I forgot about the way I looked, forgot my shyness, forgot Robert. I knew I was coming into my own as a singer, finding my true voice, which could be perfect for either opera or musical theatre.

I wanted to go to the Conservatoire with all of my being. And to my delight, after two auditions in London, I got in. I would be leaving in September.

But first there was the end-of-term show to enjoy.

I was looking forward to it. I would be performing one of my own compositions, singing and accompanying myself on the keyboard. I hoped the piece had a David Bowie-esque combination of rock and theatricality, and I'd asked Ralph to help with the rock part by playing his electric guitar.

I'd included lots of riffs. I liked riffs back then.

I waited in the wings, wearing my outfit of choice: a long black leather trench coat I had found in a local charity shop, and a pair of heavy black boots with big steel buckles. I wanted to look edgy. I had a vague idea that this was what Mozart would wear if he had been born in Newcastle in the era of mosh pits. I had grown my dark hair long, so it hung halfway down my back. This was mainly so I could swish it about dramatically like I'd seen rock stars do in music videos.

When my turn came, I stepped onto the stage. My entrance was supposed to be silent, but instead I was greeted by a blast of a novelty song which I vaguely recognised – it had been in the pop charts a few years ago. A song which called the listener 'ugly' repeatedly.

U.G.L.Y.

I froze and stared out at the audience. Robert and some of my fellow music students were sitting in the front row, bent double with laughter.

I looked at Ralph, who was standing at the other side of the stage, guitar at the ready, his expression frozen in a mask of horror.

I glared at the tech booth.

The music wasn't stopping.

My drama teachers were always saying the show must go on, and as a teenager I believed it with an almost maniacal fervour.

I looked at the hysterical bullies, and I knew there was only one thing for it.

I opened my mouth and sang along, bashing the keyboard in time to the tune.

I risked a glance at Robert. The laughter had fallen from his face, and he was staring at me in disbelief.

I whipped my hair forward and began to headbang.

The other students clapped and sang along.

I sensed the song was nearing its conclusion. Leaping up from the piano stool, I whirled to face Robert and howled the final lines at his astonished face.

The hall exploded into cheers.

Robert had gone pale. He jumped up from his own seat, face twisting with fury.

'What are you doing?' he hissed. 'Freak!'

'Shut up!' I howled. 'Just shut up and leave me alone!'

Mr Williams, my favourite teacher, stepped out from the wings. 'That's enough, Matthew.'

I glared at him. 'He ruined my song!'

'I know, and I'm going to talk to him... Just leave the stage and calm down, okay?'

Ralph's hand fell on my shoulder. 'Come on, mate, let's go.'

We walked up the aisle. Various students thumped me on the back and called me a legend.

Some of them were still singing the song.

I was trembling with anger and adrenaline.

Ralph was laughing. 'You really don't care what anyone thinks of you, do you?'

But Ralph was wrong. I did care what other people thought of me. When I got home, I ran upstairs, shut myself in my room, and cried.

# Operetta

'Matthew?'

I was in my office, trying to make sense of the spreadsheet on my computer screen. But the data kept swimming in front of my eyes.

'Matthew!'

God, I was tired. I never slept well in hotels, even when I wasn't reliving memories of my good old college days. Thanks for that, Ralph.

A yellow stress ball flew past my head. I looked up to see Jess scowling at me.

'Earth to Matthew! Are you reading me?'

'Sorry, what?'

Jess sighed. 'I asked if you'd seen the sales data. For *Earnest*.'

'Yes. I'm looking at it now.'

'It's not good.'

'Isn't it?'

'No. It's not.'

I managed to focus on the spreadsheet. Oh God, Jess was right. The sales were not good at all. And it was only another three weeks to opening night. It was as I'd feared: Charlotte's production wasn't the draw she had anticipated.

I grabbed a stress ball and squeezed it. What if sales didn't pick up and the theatre closed? We would all lose our jobs. I would have nowhere to sing.

'What should we do?' asked Jess.

I forced a smile. 'It'll be fine. We still have enough time. I'll ring round our VIPs, invite them personally.'

'Okay,' said Jess. 'If you're sure that's all it'll take?'

'Maybe you could contact the papers again?'

'I'll get on it.' Jess's expression brightened. 'By the way, I wanted to show you this.'

She passed me a sheet of paper. I looked down at it and saw that it was a poster.

*Late-Night Ghost Tours at the Moon and Stars: England's Most Haunted Theatre*
*Dare you take a night-time tour of the spookiest theatre in the land? Become a ghost hunter as your guide shares stories of the theatre's chilling, blood-soaked past. Explore this historic building from its creepy cellars to its shadowy attics. And listen out for the theatre's very own Phantom Tenor, a ghost with a voice so beautiful it will make you cry... with terror!*

It had been printed in that gooey Hallowe'en font, and the text was surrounded by drawings of ghosts, bats and – somewhat incongruously – musical notes. Down one side of the page there was a picture of what could only be our Phantom Tenor: a figure in a long black cloak and broad-brimmed hat, with a pair of glowing yellow eyes.

So that was supposed to be me, then. Brilliant.

'What do you think?' asked Jess.

'What is it?'

'It's my new fundraising idea.' She smiled. 'Ghost walks. I went on one in York once. It was ace. And genuinely scary. Look at this.'

She passed me her mobile phone.

'What am I looking at?'

'I gave the Ghost his own Twitter account.'

I stared at the screen. The Ghost's icon was the same little drawing from the poster, and his name was @PhantomOfTheMoonAndStars. I scrolled through the tweets.

@PhantomOfTheMoonAndStars: *Boo!*

*Just stole some Haribo.*

*Going to sing at midnight.*

*My theatre is full of actors. I might complain to the management.*

*If the management does not send 20,000 packets of Haribo to the Phantom Tenor, there will be severe, music-based consequences.*

*Found another ghost. I'm not impressed. He can't sing.*

*If only there were a beautiful lady ghost who I could sing duets with. *sigh**

I looked up at Jess, baffled. 'Why would you do this?'

'For fun. And to advertise the tours. Look, he's already got more than a hundred followers.'

My heart sank. If Jess started using our free nights to run ghost tours, I would have fewer opportunities to sing. There was also a higher chance that my secret would be discovered, particularly if Jess and Dave continued with their mission to discover the identity of the Ghost. I would be exposed and humiliated. No, it was out of the question. I would have to put a stop to this.

'It's ridiculous,' I said. 'We're a theatre, not some haunted-house theme-park ride.'

Jess looked crestfallen. 'I just thought it might, you know, spark people's imaginations...'

'We're a serious theatre. I don't want us to become a laughing stock.'

The door opened again, and Charlotte appeared. 'Hello, darlings.' She looked at Jess's poster. 'What's this?'

'It's an idea I've had for a fundraiser,' said Jess. 'A ghost tour.'

'I've tried to tell her it's ridiculous,' I said. 'But she won't listen.'

Charlotte's face broke into a grin. 'But, darling, I *love* this.'

I blinked. 'You... do?'

'Yes! It looks such fun. We could get a few people to dress up as the ghosts along the tour. You'd be up for that, wouldn't you, Matty?'

I thought of the last time I'd had to wear a costume in the name of marketing. I'd been the rear end of a pantomime horse. If you've never been out leafleting around the East End dressed as half a horse, you've never lived.

'I... guess so,' I said weakly.

'Wonderful!' Charlotte clapped her hands together. 'Jessica, darling, how are the *Earnest* tickets going?'

'Oh. Okay. Not many yet, but it's early days...'

Charlotte seemed oblivious to Jess's evasive tone. 'That's excellent news.' She tapped me on the shoulder. 'Wake up, Matty. It's a big day today! First rehearsal! Aren't you excited?'

'Yes.'

'Come on, then. We need to set up. They'll start arriving soon.'

I followed Charlotte to the auditorium. She came up onstage and watched while I moved furniture around to give an approximation of the set.

'I'm so looking forward to this,' said Charlotte, as I pushed a heavy chaise longue on from the wings.

'Yes?'

'It's been years – literally decades since I've trodden the boards. I can't wait to bring this old place back to life. It'll be just like it was in the old days.'

I glanced up at Charlotte and felt a pang of sadness.

'Do you really think so?'

'Why, of course! I know there's lots of work to do, but we have to stay positive.' She frowned. 'Are you all right, darling? You look a bit pale.'

'It's nothing. Just a bit of a headache.'

'I'm glad to hear it.' She indicated the remaining set pieces. 'Now, where shall we put the aspidistra?'

# Fortissimo

*From the Love Song Blog*

*This week I'm very excited to talk to Angela Nilsson.*

*Since her latest album was released two months ago, Angela's star has continued to rise. Two tracks from the album have remained in the top five of the classical download charts, with the swooningly romantic single reaching number one a fortnight after release.*

*At the time of writing, Angela is already planning another album with her self-effacing duet partner, Ralph. I chatted to them both ahead of their latest concert performance.*

*Love Song Blog: What can you tell us about your next album?*

*Angela: We're still in the early planning stages, but I'm hoping it will be a mix of original material and more operatic and musical theatre standards. A wonderful songwriter is working on the new songs. We're looking at Christmas next year for the release.*

*Love Song Blog: What's it like working with Angela, Ralph?*

*Ralph: It's like a dream come true. Sometimes I think it can't be real. (He laughs.)*

*Love Song Blog: What are your plans for the future?*

*Angela: We've got a few more concerts planned around the country. And then, who knows? I'd just like to keep performing.*

*Love Song Blog: What about you, Ralph?*

*Ralph: I'd love to record some of my own material. I'm a song-writer, too, and I play guitar. It would be nice if that opportunity came up. But I'm very happy for the moment, of course.*

*Angela: I'd like to thank my duet partner. He does so much and takes so little credit.*

I closed the webpage with a glare and tucked the phone into my pocket. Of course Ralph was self-effacing. He wasn't actually doing anything.

But at least Angela had called me a 'wonderful songwriter'. I supposed that was something.

It was a month into the tour, and we were in Liverpool. I knew the routine by now. I was in disguise: Matthew Capes, Sound Technician. I had a lanyard with my name and role, so no one at the venue suspected that I shouldn't be there.

I was in my booth in the wings, which had turned out to be conveniently tour-able.

My phone buzzed with a text.

*I need u in dressing room 3. Pls come. Urgent!!! R.*

My heart lurched. What if he was ill and couldn't go on tonight? Or what if it was Angela? What if she'd had an accident?

Various horrible scenarios flashed through my mind as I rushed along the corridors that led to the dressing rooms.

Panting for breath, I knocked on the door of number three. 'Angela? Ralph?'

'Come in!' Ralph's voice sounded remarkably bright, considering some sort of disaster had occurred.

I opened the door to find him sitting at his dressing table, wearing his smart grey concert suit, hair impeccably styled. He smiled shyly. He didn't look like a man with an urgent problem, but he certainly looked nervous.

'Hiya, mate.'

'I got your text,' I said. 'Is everything all right?'

'Fine. I just wanted a word.'

'Can't it wait until after the show?'

'I'd rather ask you now.'

Ralph was wringing his hands, which made me nervous. Was he getting cold feet?

'Okay,' I said. 'We'll have to be quick.'

'There's something I need to... run by you. It's a bit awkward.'

'Right.'

He ran a hand through his hair, messing up the style slightly. 'I just wanted to check that things were okay between us. As far as Angela is concerned.'

My throat felt tight. 'What do you mean?'

'Angela and I... we've been getting closer. And the thing is, I really want her to be my girlfriend.'

No. No, no, no. This couldn't be happening.

'Girlfriend?'

'Well, yes.' Ralph blushed. 'I know you used to like her. Back at music school, I mean. You're my oldest friend, and I don't want to make things difficult between us. I was just wondering if you felt okay about it?'

I was silent.

'So... do you feel okay about it?'

Oldest friend, indeed. How could he do this to me?

Ralph was starting to look worried. 'Please say something, Matthew.'

I turned away. 'I have to go.'

'Mate, please—'

I shot him a glare over my shoulder. 'Don't you "mate" me!'

Ignoring his spluttered protests, I marched out of the dressing room. I returned to my booth and sat seething in the dark.

The curtains twitched and opened a crack, revealing Chris's face.

'Five minutes,' he said. 'Are you ready?'

'Yes.'

'Big crowd tonight.'

'Good.'

'Don't let us down.'

'I won't.'

He started to duck back through the curtains, then changed his mind. 'Oh, and Matthew?'

'Yes?'

'Tone it down a bit during "If I Loved You", will you? There's no need to be so loud. It's distracting.'

He vanished.

I waited while the orchestra tuned up and the lights dimmed. I barely heard Angela's first solo. Instead, I thought about my talk with Ralph, and Chris's words. My hands were clenched by my sides, and my breath was shallow. There were tears in my eyes, but I was determined not to cry. Not this time.

A cheer went up as Ralph stepped onstage, ready for my first duet with Angela.

Oh, I would tone it down, all right. I would tone it *right* down.

Angela sang her verse. There was a bar of music.

I clamped my mouth shut.

The band played on for a few bars, and then stuttered into silence. I could picture the scene: Ralph opening and closing his mouth like a goldfish, with no sound coming out.

I could hear mutterings coming from the audience, and I thought I heard Angela say something, laughing nervously as she tried to keep things together...

Oh my God. Angela. She would be humiliated. What was I doing?

I leaned towards the mic and prepared to come in with the next verse. I was late, but the band and Ralph would catch up. It would look like a mistake. A failure of the mics.

But before I could even open my mouth, a familiar voice began to sing.

It was my voice.

My voice, captured.

They were playing a pre-recorded track.

I stood frozen in horror as my voice sang on without me. Angela joined in, and it sounded like she was still singing live. The tracks were being mixed in real time.

Applause.

I sank into my chair. Of course, Chris had prepared for this eventuality. It made sense.

At the interval, he wrenched the curtains apart and marched into my booth, furious.

'What do you think you're playing at?'

I glared at him. 'I could ask you the same thing. How dare you record me without my permission?'

'The tracks were recorded in the studio, *with* your permission. A good thing, too. You almost ruined everything.'

'Yes, well. You did ask me to tone it down.'

He leaned towards me until his face was a mere two inches away from mine. 'You know, Matthew, you could just stay at home. I have the recordings. Ralph is miming. You don't even need to be here. If you're going to be a liability, maybe you should stay away. We don't actually need you. And I can soon find another writer.'

We stared at each other. I was trembling with anger.

Chris straightened up. But his sneer remained in place.

'Just something to bear in mind,' he said. 'Word soon gets around in this business. We don't want people to think you're incompetent, now, do we? It's so tough to get a break these days.'

\*

Somehow, I managed to get through the rest of the concert. I was careful to sing my part in the two remaining duets. I didn't want to hear my captured voice again.

After the concert, I tried to sneak away, but Angela caught me in the corridor before I could reach the stage door.

'What happened in Act One?'

I was still shaking after my encounter with Chris, and I wanted to throw my arms around her. Or, to be more accurate, I wanted her to put her arms around me.

'Nothing. I just lost concentration for a second. Sorry.'

'And what about Act Two? Was that another lapse in concentration?'

'I... don't know what you mean.'

'You sounded really rough. Your voice kept shaking.'

I looked down at the floor. 'Just a bit tired.'

'It wasn't good enough, Matthew. I'm sorry, but it wasn't.'

I met her eyes. She was looking at me coldly, and I realised how badly I'd messed up. What had I been thinking?

'I'm sorry. It... won't happen again.'

'That's good to hear.' Her expression softened. 'Would you like to come for a drink with me and Ralph?'

'I don't think he'd want me there.'

'Why? What's wrong?'

I turned towards the stage door. 'Nothing. I'd just rather be alone.'

*

Later, in my hotel room, I was awoken by a man and a woman laughing. The laughter grew closer, then a door banged. I glanced at the digital clock on the bedside table: it was nearly 2am.

I rolled over and closed my eyes.

Someone started to strum an acoustic guitar. Then a voice joined in: a whiny, angsty voice which could only belong to Ralph. The song was followed by one person clapping, and then more laughter.

There was a moment of blissful silence.

And then Ralph launched into an acoustic cover of 'Hey Jude'.

This improvised concert went on for a very, very, very long time.

I pulled the duvet over my head.

# Sotto

I couldn't face Angela and Ralph at breakfast. And I couldn't stand the thought of a long car journey with Chris. So I checked out of the hotel early, before any of them were up, and took the train back to London, my thoughts whirling with Angela and Ralph's laughter and Chris's words: *We don't actually need you.*

My head was no clearer when I got home. I was in such a hurry to reach my flat that I almost ran straight into Lucy, who was coming downstairs, her guitar on her back and a rucksack in her hand.

'Hi, Matthew...'

I stomped past her without a word. I couldn't face a conversation with anyone. I just wanted to be on my own. But she turned and followed me back up the stairs.

'Hey, wait! What's the matter?'

'Nothing. I'm fine.'

I had reached my door. Flustered, I searched in my pocket for the key, and promptly dropped it. It bounced off the skirting board and landed at Lucy's feet.

She bent to retrieve it. 'Are you coming today?'

'What?'

She frowned. 'James has been trying to reach you.'

'Sorry. I had my phone turned off.'

'He's called an extra rehearsal. Something's come up.'

I finally managed to open the door. 'I can't.'

'Look, Matthew, if I've said something to upset you—'

'It's not that.'

'Then why are you avoiding me?'

'I'm not. It's just work stuff.'

She leaned against the wall.

'Every time I see you lately, you seem… upset. Then you make a dash for it.'

I thought of the gig at Ye Olde Inne, and how she had been sympathetic when I'd had my… episode. Maybe she would understand.

'I'm sorry, Lucy. Do you have time for a coffee?'

'Is the reclusive Maestro Capes offering me hospitality?'

'Only instant coffee, I'm afraid.'

'Oh, go on, then.'

Lucy sat on the sofa while I went to the kitchenette.

'So,' she said. 'What's up?'

I couldn't tell her everything, of course. But I could give her some sense of my predicament.

'I was threatened with dismissal yesterday,' I said, spooning coffee into mugs.

'You mean at the theatre?'

'No, as a singer. I have a problem with my voice.'

'What do you mean?'

'I… can't sing in front of people.' This was the truth, whichever way you looked at it. 'I went to a rehearsal for a concert a few months ago. I tried to sing and nothing came out. It was like my voice just… seized up. It's happened a few times before.'

'Oh, I see. I'm sorry.'

'Thank you.' I handed her a coffee.

'Have you been to the doctor?'

I sat on the edge of the sofa. 'Yes, years ago. She thought it was psychological. Stage fright, or something.'

'What happened?'

'She suggested I talk to someone about it. It... didn't go very well.'

It had actually gone terribly. I had spent the session tearing up paper handkerchiefs. The counsellor had noticed this and given me my first stress ball. Apparently this was supposed to be the answer to my problems.

'What did they say?' asked Lucy.

'She told me to be kind to myself. What does that even mean? Kindness has nothing to do with it.'

Lucy gave me a strange, sad look. Then her expression turned thoughtful. 'There was this girl I knew at college. A violinist. She had no problems at all during rehearsals. But one night, before a concert, she found she just couldn't go onstage. Her hands were shaking so badly she could barely hold the bow. She didn't go on, in the end.'

'What's your point?'

Lucy shrugged. 'Well, she was good. So I guess it... happens.'

'She was a student. Not exactly what I'd call experienced.'

She raised an eyebrow. 'No? I suppose not. But she'd just broken up with her boyfriend a couple of days before, and I don't think she realised how much it had upset her until she found herself under pressure.'

'Are you saying she couldn't play because of... matters of the heart?'

Lucy laughed. 'I wouldn't put it exactly like that. I don't think it was a grand romance or anything. But yeah, kind of. She'd put all this pressure on herself to play perfectly at a cost to other parts of her life. It was like she was trying to prove something, and in the end she just couldn't handle the stress.'

'Why are you telling me this?'

'Maybe you need to stop trying so hard.'

'It's a competitive world. I need to be at my best, otherwise I won't get the work.'

'Do you enjoy singing?'

'What?'

'Do you enjoy singing?'

'What are you talking about? Of course I enjoy singing.'

'Do you really?'

'Yes, I do.' I wondered where she could possibly be going with this.

'Do you sing in the shower?'

'What's that got to do with it?'

'I do. I sing in the shower. I sing along to the radio.'

I winced. 'Yes. I think I've heard you.'

'You see, that's odd.'

'What is?'

'You say you're a singer. We live in the same house with, I think you'll agree, thin walls. You can hear me singing and playing the guitar.'

This conversation was making me uneasy. I couldn't pinpoint why.

'Yes, well, it is rather loud—'

'I've never heard you sing. Not once since I moved here.'

'I do sing sometimes. I need to rehearse.' I hesitated, reluctant to mention the theatre. 'There's... a room I use at work.'

'So you basically just sing when no one else is around?'

'Yes. What's your point?'

'You say you love singing more than anything, but you never do it just for fun. I think you're worried you'll show yourself up.'

'That's rubbish. I'm a trained singer. A professional singer—'

'Then sing.'

I stared at her in horror. 'Here? Now?'

'Yes.' She leaned back against the sofa cushions, as if preparing to watch TV. 'Go on.'

'I can't.'

'Why not?'

'I told you. I can't... not with you watching. I'll sound awful.'

She rolled her eyes. 'Matthew, this is *me* you're talking to. Come on. Sing anything. Sing "Mary Had a Little Lamb".'

'I am not singing "Mary Had a Little Lamb". Not ever.'

'Then sing "Nessun Dorma". It's all good.'

'It really isn't, you know. And that might be a bit of a stretch, under the circumstances.'

'Just sing whatever you like, then.'

'No.'

She folded her arms. 'I won't shut up until you do.'

'Why do you care so much?'

'Because I'm sick of you mooning around the place. Go on, maestro.'

I glowered at her. 'Fine.'

'Right.'

'I'll sing.'

'Good.'

I took a breath.

Looked at Lucy.

And realised I couldn't. I closed my mouth and allowed my gaze to drop to the floor.

'I'm sorry,' I said. 'I can't. I... don't know why.'

'Okay,' said Lucy. She stood up. 'Right.'

'You're off, then?' I felt an unreasonable irritation at the fact she was going after only one attempt. So much for 'I won't shut up until you do.'

'I have to go. We both do. Rehearsal, remember?'

'Oh. Right.'

'You *are* coming?'

The alternative was an afternoon alone in my flat. I had been intending to work on the new album, but I found I was no longer in the mood to write songs for Chris. Not after our confrontation at the concert.

'I suppose so.'

'*Such* enthusiasm.'

'All right. I'll come for a bit.'

\*

'So, maestro: Florence and the Machine. What are your thoughts?'

Lucy and I were walking to the music shop together. We had done this several times, and she seemed to view our walks as an opportunity to educate me about the music she liked. I was having none of it. I did not need educating.

'I don't know. I've never listened to them.'

She made a loud tutting noise. 'Okay. R.E.M. Thoughts?'

'I don't know.'

We walked on, passing Ye Olde Inne, which threatened us with *Karaoke Every Friday!*

'So what bands do you like, maestro?'

'I don't know.'

'Led Zeppelin? The Darkness? Joy Division? *The Beatles?*' She looked at me sideways. 'Do I have to keep saying names?'

'I don't listen to many bands,' I said.

Lucy laughed. 'Of course. You're all about the op-er-aaa, aren't you?'

'Well. It's more melodic.'

'No, it's not. We really need to get you listening to more bands. Have you ever asked James for a recommendation? It's an experience.'

We had reached the music shop. Lucy rang the doorbell.

'Come on up.' James's voice crackled over the intercom. He sounded unusually sharp. Almost angry.

Lucy and I exchanged a glance.

'Odd,' she said.

'Yes.'

As we climbed the stairs, we heard raised voices. Or one raised voice, which belonged to James. Dan's voice was softer, so I couldn't make out the words.

'What were you thinking?' said James.

*Mumble*, said Dan.

'Yeah, well, you should have talked to me first.'

Lucy glanced over her shoulder at me. 'Oh, no. This isn't good.'

*Mumble mumble-mumble*, said Dan.

'*Pleased?* She's going to kill you.'

*Mumble… mumble…?* said Dan, sounding a bit apprehensive now.

Lucy opened the door.

James paused mid-pace, his arms folded. Dan was lounging on the sofa, his expression contrite.

'All right,' said Lucy. 'What's going on?'

There was a long pause.

'Well, I'm not going to tell them,' snarled James.

Dan rubbed the back of his neck. 'Yeah, well, thing is… I've sort of got us a gig. It's a good gig, and I thought it sounded fun, but James thinks it's a bad idea. Dunno why.'

'Dan has a friend at the University of London. He was talking to him about the band, and the upshot is we've been invited to play at the Student Union's Hallowe'en ball.'

'So what's the problem?' said Lucy.

'They want us to perform for a full two hours,' said James. He glared at Dan. 'He knows we don't have enough material, especially now we're not playing Mark's stuff anymore. But he went ahead and said yes anyway. And now we have, like, two months to put an entire concert together. And we're totally going to show ourselves up.'

'Oh,' said Lucy. 'Is that all?'

James stared at her. 'You're not mad?'

'Are you kidding? That sounds amazing!'

Dan gave a slow, lazy smile. 'I told you she'd be pleased.'

'But... we don't have enough songs,' said James.

'I may be able to help there,' said Lucy. She reached into her rucksack and brought out a thick stack of sheet music. She dropped it on the coffee table.

'Whoa,' said Dan.

'It's mainly new stuff,' said Lucy.

'You've been busy,' said James. 'Muse strike, did it?'

Lucy glanced at me, then shrugged. 'Yeah, something like that.'

Dan, James and I all reached into the pile.

I looked at the song in my hand. I could see it had a strong melody, and a beautiful, haunting keyboard track.

'The keyboard's quite prominent,' I said.

'Yes,' said Lucy. 'I just thought, now that we have a proper pianist...'

'This one's great.' Dan grinned and waved his song in James's face. 'It's like epic seventies rock with a modern melancholic feel. Like... Meat Loaf meets millennial angst.'

James stared at him. 'What are you talking about?'

Dan shrugged and sank back onto the sofa. 'It's just the vibe I get.'

'What do you know about vibes?' James stared at his own song. 'What's this? A duet?'

Lucy nodded. 'Yes. I thought it would be a bit different.'

James frowned. 'This other voice. Is it a tenor? You know I can't sing that high, right?'

'I didn't think you could sing at all,' said Dan, his face hidden behind his song sheet.

'Shut up.'

Lucy smiled. 'I'm going to let you into a secret. We have an actual real life opera singer in our midst.'

There was a moment of silence. Dan and James stared at me.

'Who?' I said. 'Me?'

'*Of course* you.'

'Really?' said James. 'You sing?'

'Matthew's a classically trained singer,' said Lucy. 'He sings opera that isn't really opera.'

I sighed. 'That's not quite what I do.'

'Wow,' said Dan. 'You don't look like an opera singer.'

My shoulders tensed. 'What do you mean?'

Lucy rolled her eyes. 'Ignore him. He means you're not wearing a helmet with horns on it.'

Dan and James looked at me expectantly.

'Give us a song, then,' said Dan.

I looked down at the keyboard. 'Maybe later.'

'You're among friends,' said Lucy. 'Why not give it a shot?'

'You're not going to let this go, are you?'

'No, I'm not. What's the worst that could happen?'

I turned away. She really had no idea.

'What's going on?' asked James.

'Matthew can't sing because he's nervous, so I'm trying to create a supportive singing environment.' Lucy's tone was irritatingly reasonable.

I folded my arms. 'Yes. Very supportive, Lucy. Thank you.'

'So you don't want to sing,' said James.

'I do. It's just... it's complicated.' I picked up another of Lucy's songs. 'Can we try the music first?'

'Maybe he's not a very good opera singer,' said Dan.

I looked up from the music and caught Lucy's eye. Her expression had softened.

'All right, maestro, let's try the music first.' She smiled. 'But one day, very soon, we want to hear this amazing voice of yours. No excuses. Okay?'

My gaze slid back to the music. 'Okay.'

# Opus

It was opening night of *The Importance of Being Earnest*. I had a horrible feeling that tonight would decide the fate of the Moon and Stars Theatre. After the performance, we would know if we had a success on our hands that could help secure the venue's future, or a flop that would hasten its demise. I didn't think I could bear to watch.

Angela and I had given a concert in Cardiff the previous night. I'd caught an early train back to London and had barely found time to eat a slice of toast before changing into my smartest suit and hurrying to the theatre.

The entrance was plastered with copies of the poster, which resembled a vintage railway advertisement. As I approached, I saw the sign saying *Tickets available* had been put on display near the doors. My heart sank.

I walked through the foyer and into the auditorium, where I was immediately confronted by Jess.

She looked angry. Jess *never* looked angry.

'What's wrong?' I asked.

'Where have you been? I've been trying to ring you all afternoon.'

'I was away last night. I've only just got back.'

'You could've answered your bloody phone.'

'Sorry – I had other things on my mind.'

She shook her head. 'You had other things on your mind? Matthew, what's wrong with you lately?'

'Please calm down, Jess.'

She put her hands on her hips. 'Don't tell me to calm down! This is a disaster.'

'What's happened?'

'We're less than a quarter full, that's what's happened.'

I stared at her. 'No – that's not possible.'

'Well, apparently it is.' Jess's voice quivered. She sank into a blue velvet seat. 'I don't understand. We did everything we could. I sent the press release; you invited the VIPs.'

I was silent.

Oh, no.

Jess looked up at me and narrowed her eyes. 'Matthew, you *did* invite the VIPs, didn't you?'

I twisted my hands together. 'I... think I forgot.'

'You *forgot*? How could you forget?'

I drew back a step. Jess had never spoken to me like this before.

'I don't know. I've had a lot on my mind.'

'God, Matthew, what have you done?' Jess closed her eyes. 'The theatre's going to close. We'll all lose our jobs.'

'I'm sorry—'

'I don't think sorry quite covers it, do you? We were already struggling, and now this.'

'It'll be all right,' I said, my voice trembling. 'You invited the critics, didn't you? We'll get some reviews. That'll bring people in.'

'I bloody hope so,' said Jess. 'What are we going to tell Charlotte?'

'It's okay. I'll talk to her.'

I found Charlotte onstage, behind the closed curtains, giving a pep talk to her fellow actors. She was in her element, practically glowing with excitement.

'Matty!' She swooped towards me, and I found myself encircled in a suffocating hug. She released me and looked me up and down. 'You're looking very swish tonight.'

'Thank you.' My throat was dry. I swallowed. 'Charlotte—'

'How are we? Are we good? How are the ticket sales? Is it very full? I'm so nervous!' She tugged at her pearl necklace.

And I realised I couldn't tell her. 'I'm fine. We're good. Ticket sales are... okay. I'm sure you'll be great.'

I wasn't sure she would be great, and we weren't good, but what else could I say? It was the first night and I didn't want to spoil things. She had theatre critics for that. And Richard.

Richard was going to be furious.

Charlotte grasped my hand and smiled. 'Thank you for all your help.'

'You're welcome.' Tears pricked my eyes. I stepped away. 'Enjoy it.'

I took my usual seat in the back row of the auditorium, so I could make a quick exit if I was needed elsewhere. Or if I just wanted to get away from any hurled tomatoes.

The auditorium slowly filled to around twenty-five per cent capacity. A minute before curtain-up, Richard took his seat directly across the aisle from me. He looked at me, and then gestured at the empty seats. I bowed my head.

The lights dimmed, and the performance began.

What followed was a perfectly acceptable staging of *The Importance of Being Earnest*. The show was good, but nothing special. Nothing to write home about, but certainly nothing to be ashamed of either. If I hadn't been so worried about the theatre, I would have been pleasantly entertained. I was also concerned about Charlotte. What if the tiny audience put her off, and she gave a dreadful performance? What if she gave a bad performance anyway? A critic from the *Daily Telegraph* was sitting front-row centre. *The Stage* and *Time Out* were in attendance, too. It would not be good.

It was a while before Lady Bracknell made her entrance, and when she did, I found myself holding my breath.

The theatre was quite small, so even from the back row, I thought I saw a dismayed expression cross Charlotte's face when she peered out and was greeted by rows of empty seats. Her speech faltered – she seemed to have forgotten the words.

I glanced across at Richard and saw that his face was frozen in an expression of horror.

*Come on*, I thought, turning my attention back to Charlotte. *Get it together. Please.*

Charlotte's gaze travelled to the back of the auditorium. Even though she wouldn't be able to see me, I tried to smile.

Then something changed. Charlotte seemed to snap back into character. She found her voice; her lines came back to her.

As her performance progressed, I realised she was genuinely good. More than good. I had never seen her as a serious actress before. Now I thought about it, I had never actually *seen* her perform at all. Everything I had heard about her acting prowess was second hand. Maybe jealousy had played a large part in skewing the facts.

What I was seeing surprised me so much that I leaned forward until I was literally on the edge of my seat. The atmosphere seemed to spark, and a rapt attentiveness settled across the audience. Laughter rippled around the auditorium.

Yes. She was more than good. She was excellent.

When the play ended, I stood up. The small audience joined in the ovation. I glanced at Richard's seat and saw he had gone.

I went upstairs to wait in the rehearsal room. It was a bright, cheerful space, with a large noticeboard covered with posters from past productions. This was where the company always gathered after shows, where congratulations or words of commiseration were exchanged. I usually avoided these gatherings, but tonight I wanted to be there.

They began to file in. I congratulated them all in turn. Charlotte arrived last, grinning and carrying a bottle of champagne.

'Darlings! I'm so, so proud of you all.'

'You were truly excellent,' I said. 'Well done.'

'Oh, piffle – it was nothing.' Charlotte began to pour the champagne into plastic cups.

The rehearsal room was soon filled with chatter and laughter. I smiled; I remembered this well from my am-dram days. The conviviality. The natural high that came with a successful opening night. Best of all, no one mentioned the small audience. Maybe they didn't care.

The festive atmosphere lasted approximately ten minutes. Then the door banged open, and Richard strode into the room. Everyone froze and turned to look at him. In contrast to Charlotte, he only ever mixed with the company when something was wrong.

I remembered the look on his face at the beginning of the play and felt cold.

'Richard! Darling, have a drink.' Charlotte glided forward with the last of the champagne.

Richard held up a hand. 'No, thank you. I need to speak to you.' He turned to me. 'And you, Matthew.'

We followed him to his office. Richard sat down and fixed me with his most penetrating stare.

'What the hell happened tonight?'

'What do you mean?' I tried to keep my voice level.

'The empty theatre. That's what I mean.'

'Be reasonable,' said Charlotte. 'It wasn't quite empty.'

'It might as well have been,' said Richard. 'So what went wrong?'

I was silent, looking at them both in turn. And I realised that although I could make my excuses to Richard, I couldn't lie to Charlotte. Not anymore.

'I guess there's just too much competition,' I said. 'And I may have forgotten to do the VIP mailing.'

'How could you forget a thing like that?' snapped Richard.

'I... don't know. I'm not sure what I was thinking. I'm sorry.'

'That's just not good enough. Have you any idea how much trouble this place is in?'

Charlotte had gone pale. 'Come on, Richard, it's not so bad—'

'But it is.' Richard got to his feet. 'I think it might be time to cut our losses. Sell up.'

A horrible series of images flashed through my mind: the theatre dark and empty and shuttered.

No. It couldn't happen.

'But you can't do that!' I gasped.

'We may not have any choice,' said Richard.

I clenched my hands into fists. 'You can't sell my theatre! I won't let you!"

'I beg your pardon?' Richard frowned. '*Your* theatre?'

Heat rushed to my face. 'I mean *the* theatre. This theatre.'

'We can't just give up,' said Charlotte. She looked at me. 'You've got lots of great ideas to raise funds, haven't you?'

I stared at her. Had I? 'Yes... yes, of course. Loads of ideas.'

'Hmm.' Richard narrowed his eyes at me. 'All right. But we need to turn this place around urgently. I want these "ideas" on my desk on Monday.'

*

Everyone had gone. I was alone in the auditorium, black bin liner in hand, doing a last check for rubbish between the seats. I had hoped this task would distract me from the fact I had managed to mess things up so completely. It didn't.

'A *handbag*?'

The voice echoed around the auditorium, making me start. I spun around in time to see Charlotte sink onto the chaise longue. She looked pale, and it was obvious she hadn't noticed me.

'A handbag!'

I wondered briefly if she was drunk. I coughed.

'A HAND-baaag?!'

I stepped into the aisle.

'Oh!' Charlotte jumped, her hand going to her heart. 'Darling, you startled me.'

'Charlotte,' I said, making my way cautiously towards the stage. 'What are you doing?'

'I love that line. There are so many ways you can say it.'

'Yes. Yes, I suppose there are.'

She patted the chaise longue. 'Come and sit with me for a minute? I'd like to talk to you.'

I hesitantly joined her onstage and sat down.

She regarded me with sharp eyes. 'You promised me something, Matthew.'

I squirmed.

'Yes,' I murmured.

'You promised you wouldn't let your tour distract you from the theatre.'

'I know. I'm so sorry, Charlotte.'

We sat in silence. I fully expected her to be angry, and justifiably so. My heart raced as I waited for her to dismiss me, probably permanently.

Instead, she sighed. 'Matty, darling, if I asked you a question, would you answer me truthfully?'

I looked up at her. Her eyes were red. 'Of course.'

'Do you think this is all my fault? Have I ruined this place?'

'No. Of course not.'

She sniffed. 'I just wanted a chance to play a great role. And Lady Bracknell was my dream. Do you think I'm a foolish old woman?'

'No,' I said. 'Not a bit.'

'Performing for no audience,' said Charlotte, shaking her head. 'How pathetic.'

'You did have an audience. A small one, but it was there.'

Charlotte scoffed. 'Hardly. Maybe Richard's right. Maybe it's time I recognised that I'm no longer relevant. That this place' – she gestured around the auditorium – 'is no longer relevant.'

I found myself thinking of the concert in Liverpool, of Chris's words when I heard my recorded voice. *We don't actually need you...*

My throat felt tight. I coughed.

'No,' I said. 'You're not irrelevant, and neither is this place.'

Charlotte pulled a handkerchief from her pocket and dabbed her eyes. 'Do you really think so?'

'Yes.' I stood up and looked out at the decayed beauty of the auditorium. The soft glow of the chandelier bathed the frescoed walls in a gentle twilight, blurring the colours into each other like the strokes of an impressionist painting. The occasional gold star winked at me. 'We're going to fix this.'

We had to.

# Allegro

The knock on my door came on Sunday night, just before seven.

I wasn't in the mood to see anyone. I was curled up on the sofa with a cup of tea, staring straight ahead. A notebook was open in my lap, filled with theatre-saving ideas:

1. Giant raffle.
2. Black tie dinner.
3. Variety show.
4. Sponsor an actor.
5. Actor auction (win an actor for the day).
6. Sponsored silence.
7. Pantomime horse race, with betting.
8. Sponsor a pantomime horse.
9. Sponsor a brick.
10. Sponsored throw-wet-sponges-at-Dave.

Everything felt too expensive, or too impractical, or too frivolous.

'Matthew?' Lucy's voice was insistent.

I forced myself up from the sofa and went to the door.

Lucy was holding a cardboard box. It had wires spilling out of it. 'I've had an amazing idea.'

'What?'

'I've thought of a way to help you sing again.'

I eyed the box suspiciously. Lucy laughed.

'Don't worry, you're going to love it. Can I come in?'

I stepped to one side. She put the box on the coffee table and started to unpack it. There were more wires, and a thin plastic white thing which looked like some sort of games console.

'What's that?'

'It's my old Wii.' She gave me the end of a cable. 'Plug that into the back of the telly, would you?'

'What for? What are you doing?'

'You'll have to wait and see.' She smiled. 'It's all part of the plan.'

It took a moment to locate the port at the back of the television. When I'd connected the console, I turned around to see Lucy holding two plastic games cases.

'Right. I've got *You Can Sing!* and *Pop Factor*. Which would you prefer?'

'You must be joking.'

'Come on. Look. I've got microphones.'

She held up two little white plastic mics.

I stared at her. '*This* is your amazing idea?'

'Yes. I thought it might help you.'

'How on earth is this going to help me?'

'It's pressure-free singing. All you have to do is follow the words. Like karaoke.'

'I've never tried karaoke.'

'Are you serious?'

'Yes. Which is why I've never tried karaoke.'

She rolled her eyes. 'Come on. Give it a go. At least it'll get you singing again.'

'Is this what you do in your music therapy sessions?'

She grinned. 'No, this is just for you.'

I looked at the microphones and sighed. 'You're not going to take no for an answer, are you?'

'No, I'm not. Do you have any snacks? Anything to drink?'

'Why?'

'I think it'll help. Or it'll help me, anyway.'

'I've got some apple juice. There might be some peanuts, too.'

'Wow. You really know how to party.'

'If you disapprove of my catering facilities, we could always do this in your flat.'

'I don't think so.'

'Why not?'

'Because I don't want to give you an excuse to run away, that's why.'

I frowned. 'Is it really that bad?'

'No, it's fun.' She headed for the door. 'I'll just be a sec.'

While Lucy was gone, I looked at the games. They both had photographs of good-looking, dancing people on the covers. *You Can Sing!* promised fun for all the family, guaranteed.

I sighed. It was going to be a very long evening.

Lucy returned a few minutes later with a bottle of white wine and a huge packet of cheese nachos.

'Have you chosen one?' she asked.

I held up *You Can Sing!* I feared that *Pop Factor* would bring back bad memories.

'Cool. You pour the wine; I'll sort the game.'

I only had one wine glass, so I poured my own wine into the glass I normally used for my fruit juice and gave the proper one to Lucy. If she noticed, she didn't comment.

'Right,' she said, opening the nachos and releasing an odour that was somewhere between cheddar and old socks. 'We're all set.'

I didn't understand why the nachos were necessary, but their opening seemed to have an almost ceremonial significance, so I wasn't going to ask any questions.

The game's menu screen appeared on the TV. It was accompanied by a repetitive tinkling soundtrack and offered a range of options.

'Okay. We've got solo, duet, and head-to-head. How should we start?'

I considered the options. I assumed 'head-to-head' was the competitive option, and I really didn't want to compete. A duet would make me think of Angela, and I couldn't face that right then.

'Solo,' I said.

'Not duets?'

'I'd prefer solos. You go first.'

'Why me? You're the professional.'

'This was your idea.'

'Okay. Fair enough.' She selected 'Solo' and began to scroll through a range of songs. I was waiting for her to choose something dark and intense and was quite surprised when she chose 'Waterloo'.

I looked at her incredulously. 'You like ABBA?'

'I love ABBA.'

'That surprises me.'

'I like a lot of different music. Not just the heavy stuff.' She lifted the microphone to her lips. 'Here we go.'

I had to hand it to Lucy, she was certainly a trier. Her rendition of 'Waterloo' wasn't the best rendition of 'Waterloo' I had ever heard, but it was delivered with gusto. Meanwhile, messages popped up on screen, telling her she was *Amazing!* and *Fabulous!* and *Wow!*, which had apparently become an adjective.

I hoped the song wouldn't end. This wasn't because I was particularly enjoying listening to it, but because I wanted my own attempt at singing to be indefinitely postponed.

But end it did, and Lucy handed me a microphone with a big grin on her face.

'Your turn.'

I scrolled slowly through the songs.

Lucy nudged me. 'Come on.'

'I'm looking at the songs.'

'You're procrastinating.'

'I'm not.'

'There's a good one.' And Lucy used her own remote to select 'Summer Nights' from *Grease*.

'That's not even a solo...'

But it was too late. John Travolta was already informing us about summer loving, and the game was disappointed that I hadn't bothered to sing along. It declared that I *could do better*.

'Go on,' said Lucy.

I waited until Olivia Newton-John had sung her next line, and then lifted the microphone.

My voice was barely more than a whisper. And I was shaking, which was ridiculous. I mean, it was *Grease*, the musical I had been forced to listen to at the school disco. And here I was, afraid of singing it. I would not be defeated by *Grease*, of all things.

So I took a breath, and went for it.

'Summer Nights' was hardly the best showcase for my talents, but somehow I began to sing along. I cringed; my voice was quiet and thin and reedy, a shadow of its usual self.

About halfway through, Lucy came in with Sandy's part. And our voices sounded so incongruous, so unlike either of the voices on the video, that it was a struggle not to start laughing.

I was enjoying myself, despite my weak voice.

Maybe Lucy was right. Maybe this *was* a good idea.

When the song was over, I looked at Lucy. She was shaking with laughter.

I glared at her.

'What's so funny?'

'You. The way you enunciate everything.'

'What do you mean?'

'You're so... *posh.*'

'I am *not* posh.'

'You are. You're posh.'

'Shut up,' I said, but by now I was laughing, too.

Lucy wiped her eyes. 'I told you it would be fun.'

I shrugged and looked away. 'It was okay, I suppose.'

'Come on. You enjoyed it. Admit it.'

'It was... liberating, in an odd sort of way. How was my voice?'

'Okay. A little on the quiet side.' She flicked through the songs. 'Maybe you could try something like the sort of thing you usually sing?'

I was going to protest, but what harm could it do? And for the first time in weeks, I was actually enjoying singing.

'How about this one?'

Lucy had found 'Love Changes Everything'. I cringed. I had expected less of a challenge.

'I'll give it a go. But it might be awful.'

Lucy raised her glass of wine. 'I'm more than prepared.'

I clicked on the song, grasped the toy microphone with a shaking hand, and closed my eyes.

The music began. I sang softly, tentatively, but then the melody built, becoming more powerful, and I closed my eyes. I tried to absorb myself in the music, to think of nothing but the song. I forgot about Ralph and Chris and the album. The London flat and the television and the Wii console vanished. And suddenly I was...

*...back in my town hall, at home. The spotlights were hot, and they made me squint, so I couldn't see anyone, but I knew they were there. And I felt excited and thrilled at being up there, but not anxious. I didn't want to rush offstage, or hide, because this was singing, and I loved it.*

The song ended. I opened my eyes.

Lucy was staring at me. All trace of laughter had disappeared from her face. I wondered if I had been truly awful.

'Wow,' she said.

'Did it work?'

'Yes.' She laughed. 'Yes, it was amazing.'

I looked at the floor. 'Thank you.'

'You know, when you said you could sing opera, I didn't quite believe you.'

I swallowed. 'Well, that wasn't opera—'

'No, but you could sing opera, if you wanted to. Have you ever recorded anything?'

I winced internally at the question. I couldn't tell her the truth. That would be far too humiliating.

'No.'

Lucy frowned. 'Are you sure?'

'I think I'd remember if I had.'

'It's just I'm sure I've heard your voice before.'

'I suppose quite a few singers sound like me.'

'No.' She shook her head. 'I don't think so. For a start, I don't listen to much opera or whatever.'

'I haven't recorded anything, Lucy.'

'You haven't been on *The X Factor* or anything? Er... not that I ever watch it.'

'Definitely not.'

Lucy gave me a puzzled look. She was obviously searching her memory for something, and I hoped she hadn't seen Ralph's music video.

Then I remembered that she *had* heard me before, on the night of our first gig. She had come in while I was playing the album.

'Thank you for the game,' I said, attempting to change the subject, but also because I was genuinely grateful. 'I didn't think it would help.'

'Weird, huh?'

'Yes.' I met her eyes and smiled. 'Thank you, Lucy.'

'I'll leave it here so you can practise.'

'Thanks.'

Lucy picked up her microphone. 'Fancy another go?'

*

I decided to show my list of theatre-saving ideas to Jess before presenting them to Richard.

'Hmm,' she said. 'As much as I'm in favour of throwing wet sponges at Dave, I think the variety show's a better idea.'

'I was thinking we could present highlights from the theatre's past,' I said. 'Extracts from famous plays and operettas, that sort of thing.'

Jess frowned. 'I'd be tempted to make it more like a modern gala night. Get various local acts. Singers, dancers, bands, that sort of thing. Maybe some stand-up?'

I smiled, relieved that she liked at least one of my ideas. 'That could work.'

'Know anyone famous?'

The only slightly famous people I knew were Angela and Ralph, and I had no desire to go there. I wasn't going to hide in the wings of my own theatre.

'No. Sorry.'

'I'll do some research, see who's performed here in the past,' said Jess. 'Charlotte might know some people.'

'Good idea.'

I was drinking my mid-morning coffee when it occurred to me that I could ask Lucy and the band. They were far from famous, but they had the advantage of being musicians I actually knew. I had no idea if a variety show would be their thing – Lucy probably considered herself too edgy – but there was no harm in asking.

Maybe I could bribe them with pizza.

# Serenade

There was a knock on the door. I opened it to find Lucy, looking glum.

'Rehearsal's off,' she said.

'What?'

'Somebody complained about the noise.'

'Oh dear.' This wasn't exactly surprising: James's shop was next door to some flats, and not everyone would be happy about a rock band rehearsing in such close proximity to them. Secretly, I thought we were lucky we'd got away with it for as long as we had. 'What are we going to do?'

Lucy shrugged. 'We'll need to find somewhere else, but it might take a while. This place is too small, and Dan's neighbours wouldn't be happy. It looks like we'll have to stop rehearsing, at least for a little while.'

'But we can't do that. We need all the practice we can get.'

She grimaced. 'Thanks for that vote of confidence, Matthew.'

'That's not what I meant… We've got the university gig coming up soon. We need to rehearse.'

'Yes, well. It can't be helped, can it?' She folded her arms. 'Unless you know somewhere.'

I was silent. My hand strayed to the key in my pocket.

I couldn't do it. It was stupid, and impossible.

Lucy had noticed my hesitation. 'Matthew? Do you know somewhere?'

I answered before I could overthink it.

'Yes. I think I do.'

*

Fifteen minutes later, we were standing at the stage door of the theatre. It was in a little cobbled alley, illuminated by an old-fashioned streetlamp. Some of the blue paint was peeling away from the door to reveal black underneath. It would need repainting before the gala night.

I struggled with the lock, which needed oiling.

'All the times I've passed this place, and I've never been inside,' said Lucy.

'Yes, well. That makes you and the rest of the world.' I was starting to think this was a particularly bad idea. I had never brought anyone else back here on an evening when the theatre was closed. It had always been my private space, and an extra person meant a greater chance of discovery.

The lock gave a click. We were in.

'So, this is where you work,' said Lucy, as I turned on my torch and led our way down the stairs. Even in the dim light, I could see her dubious expression.

'Yes. I'm the manager.'

'And we're allowed to be in here?'

'Well, no. Not technically. I'm supposed to have a good reason to come in out of hours, and I'm meant to sign in at the stage door. It's mainly for health and safety. Careful – the stairs are a bit steep here.'

Offering her my hand, I guided her down the last few steps. I pushed open the door that led to the auditorium.

'Are you sure about this?' asked Lucy. 'I wouldn't want to get you in trouble.'

'You won't,' I said, although in all honesty I couldn't be certain of that.

I knew my way around the auditorium with only the safety lights to help me, but Lucy didn't. I realised it was very dark for anyone who wasn't used to it.

'Hang on,' I said. 'Let me just get the lights…'

There was an electric hum, and the auditorium burst into full colour.

I looked at Lucy. For some reason, I found that I wanted her to like the theatre. It felt more personal, somehow, than showing her my flat.

Her eyes were wide.

'Wow,' she said.

'Do you like it?' My voice was small.

'I had no idea.' Her face broke into a grin. 'It's beautiful!'

I smiled as she hurried down the aisle, brushing a hand against the backs of the worn velvet chairs, and examining the frescoes representing constellations on the walls.

'These are lovely,' she said, turning to me. 'Are they meant to be like that?'

'Like what?'

'All distressed? Like, shabby chic?'

I laughed. 'No. It's because we have no money and we can't afford to restore them.'

'I kind of like it the way it is,' said Lucy, tracing the shape of a plaster star. 'It's atmospheric. It's cool.'

I felt suddenly warm. 'I'm glad you like it.'

She peered up at the painted ceiling. I followed her gaze.

The ceiling was, in my opinion, the most beautiful part of the theatre. The inside of the dome was painted to resemble the night sky, with the patterns of constellations picked out in gold against a dark blue background. The chandelier was shaped like a crescent moon and hung with tiny crystal stars. When it was lit, the whole ceiling glinted.

'Amazing,' said Lucy. 'I can't believe I didn't know about this place.'

I felt a pang of sadness and turned away. Lucy was right; the theatre was amazing. It was too awful to imagine it closed. I would try not to think of that tonight.

'Can we really rehearse in here?'

'Well, yes, if we're...' I was about to say 'quiet', but this seemed a stupid thing to say about a rock band. 'If we're careful.'

'I don't want you to get into trouble.'

'Well, I do it all the time, and it's been fine so far.'

'You mean you come here at night? Why?'

I cringed. 'Okay. I'll tell you, but please don't laugh... I actually come here to sing.'

Lucy did laugh. I blushed. 'What? You mean you stand on the stage and sing to an empty theatre?'

'See? You're laughing.'

'Do you do anything else?'

'Well, sometimes I sit for a bit. Catch up on work. Have a snack...' I glared at her. 'You're still laughing.'

'Sorry, sorry – but it is kind of funny. I mean, my ex-boyfriend had a man cave, but this takes things to a whole new level.' I folded my arms. She tapped me just below the elbow. 'Oh, don't look so tragic.'

'It's just that I've never told anyone. I don't know what would happen if the theatre owners found out.'

Lucy's expression turned serious. 'Why? You're only singing... and eating snacks. You're not doing any harm.'

'Yes. Well. I don't think Richard likes me very much.'

'But you don't think anyone's overheard you?'

'Dave has – our techie. I think he knows it's me, but he hasn't told anyone. The first time he heard me, he thought I was a ghost.'

Lucy's mouth twitched again. 'An opera-singing ghost?'

'Well, yes. Apparently.'

'Matthew, you lead a strange life.'

I sighed. 'Do you want to rehearse in here or not?'

'I'd love to, but what about the instruments? The keyboard and the drum kit. They're a lot to drag in here just for a rehearsal.'

'I could manage the keyboard. I think we've got an old drum kit in the props store. Would Dan mind?'

'No. He's pretty easy going.'

'Then it's settled.' I smiled. The thought of having the band in my theatre was quite exciting.

At least, it would be exciting as long as no one overheard us.

'Thanks, Matthew.' Lucy encircled me in a hug. This time I hugged her back. She pulled away and looked at me. 'Well?'

'Well, what?'

She pointed to the stage. 'Are you going to sing?'

'What? Now?'

'Yes.' She took a seat in the front row. 'I'd like to hear what the acoustics are like.'

'Yes. Well, I suppose acoustics are important.'

'Uh-huh. Very.'

I took my place on the stage and looked at Lucy. For the very first time, I had an audience in my theatre. True, it was an audience of one, but it was still very different from what I was used to.

She caught my eye and smiled. I told myself it was no different from karaoke.

I decided to try something different, a ballad I had found in the 'Rock' category of Lucy's game.

I began to sing.

# Lacrimoso

'I'm going to be honest with you, Matthew,' said Chris, frowning at me from his position next to Steve the pianist. 'I'm a little concerned.'

I had arrived at the studio to rehearse for our next concert, only to find that Angela and Ralph had been delayed while giving an interview for a talk show. I had spent the last half hour running through my parts of the repertoire, and it soon became clear that Chris was in a bad mood. He kept stopping proceedings to inform me that I was too loud, or too intense, or too romantic (whatever that meant). He also snapped at the pianist, telling him he was slow or had played the wrong verse. I could almost see Steve gritting his teeth.

'Concerned about what?' I tried to keep the tremor out of my voice.

'About the new songs. You must have finished at least one of them by now. We have deadlines, you know.'

'Oh. Yes.' Relief washed over me. I opened my briefcase, took out several sheets of music, and passed them to Chris. I had worked on this song for hours, over lunch and after work, and I was quite proud of it. 'Here.'

Chris looked at the music, then up at me. 'What the hell is this?'

'Er... it's a new song.'

'No, it isn't.'

'I thought it might be an interesting addition to the next album. Or maybe we could even release it as a single.'

Chris grimaced. 'It's horrible. Morbid.'

'It's supposed to be melancholic. Poignant.'

'It's not. It's just depressing. And what's this part?'

I looked down at my clasped hands and spoke quietly. 'It's a guitar solo.'

Chris laughed. 'Guitar solo? Do people still like those?'

I didn't reply.

'Look,' said Chris. 'We need something commercial, something mainstream.'

'I don't see what's so unusual about a guitar solo.'

'Matthew, we need our songs to appeal to a wider audience. We need rousing ballads, not this dark shit.'

'It's not shit,' I muttered.

'I beg your pardon?'

I was getting tired of Chris talking down to me. His criticism was constant, and I was no longer sure I deserved it.

I met his eye. 'It's not shit. It's good.'

'Oh, well if *you* think it's good, then it *must* be,' said Chris. 'Because you're obviously the very epitome of fine taste.'

We stared at each other. I tried to think of a way to defend my music, but any reply withered in the face of Chris's glacial glare.

The door burst open.

'Sorry I'm late.' Angela hurried in. She looked a little harried, pushing her long hair out of her face.

Chris's icy expression melted. He smiled. 'Hi, Angie.'

Angela glanced at me and frowned. 'Is everything okay?'

'Of course, of course,' said Chris. 'Matthew and I were just having a little chat about music.'

'Oh. That's... good.' Angela sank into a spare chair. I realised how tired she looked.

'Are you okay?' I asked.

'Yes. Fine.'

'We should crack on,' said Chris. 'Where's Ralph?'

'He's gone to buy sandwiches,' said Angela.

Chris blinked. 'Why?'

Angela's eyes glittered. 'Because it's nearly 3pm, neither of us have had lunch yet, and I'm bloody starving.'

Chris flinched slightly at her tone, but quickly recovered. 'Well, while he's waiting for overpriced avocado or whatever, maybe we could make good use of the time?'

'I could really do with a break, Chris.'

'Come on. The next concert's in a week. We need to work on "If I Loved You", after what happened *last time*.' He gave me a pointed look.

Angela sighed. 'Okay, fine.'

Steve began to play.

Angela sang well, if not as strongly as she usually did. She was obviously exhausted. I tried to catch her eye, but she looked away each time.

I opened my mouth, ready to join her in song.

'Okay, stop,' said Chris. He looked at Angela with raised eyebrows. 'Let's just try that again, Angela, shall we?'

She rubbed her temples. 'I could really use a rest.'

'It won't take long.' Chris glanced at the pianist. 'Steve, take it from the top.'

Angela reached the second line of the song, but then her voice cracked. She shook her head. Her face was pale, and for the first time, I noticed dark shadows beneath her eyes.

My heart contracted. 'Angela?'

'What's the matter now?' asked Chris. 'Come on. We need to get this right.'

'I told you. I. Need. A. Break! For God's sake. Why is that so hard to understand?'

Chris was on his feet. 'We need to rehearse. We're wasting studio time.'

'Well, tough!' Angela headed for the door.

'The label won't be happy...'

Angela marched out of the studio.

I started to follow her. Chris glared at me. 'Where do you think you're going?'

Ignoring him, I hurried after Angela. I found her a little way down the corridor, leaning against the wall, her eyes closed.

I approached cautiously. 'Are you okay?'

Her eyes opened. 'Fine. I just needed a moment away from Chris.'

'He's not easy to work with, is he?'

'That's the understatement of the year. He just doesn't seem to get that I'm a human being.' Angela rubbed her eyes. 'Do you know *why* I was an hour late today?'

'No.'

'They wanted me to sing. On TV. And Chris hadn't told me, and I had nothing prepared. They sprang it on me, just like that.'

'What did you do?'

Angela gave a hoarse laugh. 'What do you think? I sang for them, of course. How could I say no?'

I was silent, uncomfortable in the knowledge that Angela was far more professional than me. If I had been in that position, I would have fled.

'I sometimes wonder why I do this to myself,' said Angela. 'I feel like I don't have a life.'

'What do you mean?'

'I'm running myself ragged. I haven't seen my parents in six months. I don't even have time to go out with my friends.' Her eyes were red. She wiped them on her sleeve.

I stared at her in astonishment. 'I had no idea you felt like this.'

'Yes, well, I try to get on with things.'

'Maybe you should tell Chris.'

She narrowed her eyes. 'Do you really think he'd listen?'

'I'll go with you if you like. Maybe it would be harder for him to ignore both of us?'

'We'd be wasting our time. The man's impossible.' She smiled weakly. 'But thanks for the offer.'

I felt a rush of warmth. Perhaps now would be a good moment to retrieve her song from my briefcase and give it to her. It might cheer her up.

I heard feet pounding down the corridor and turned to see Ralph.

'There you are,' he panted, holding out a sandwich bag.

'Oh, thank God.' Angela snatched the bag from him, opened it, and peered inside. 'My hero.'

'Me, or the panini?' asked Ralph.

'It's a tough call, isn't it?' said Angela.

I turned away, unable to resist rolling my eyes, and left them to it. My song, the thing I had laboured over, had been usurped by Ralph and his sandwich. It was typical, really.

I returned to the studio to find Chris seated behind the sound desk, glaring at the pages of my new song. Retreating to a corner, I looked through my music until Angela and Ralph reappeared fifteen minutes later.

'Are you finally ready?' asked Chris, not looking up from the pages.

'I'm feeling much better. Thanks for asking.' There was a hard edge to Angela's voice.

'I'm very glad to hear it.' Chris tossed my song onto the desk and stood up. 'Let's start with "What I Did for Love".'

Angela and Ralph took their places beside the piano, and I stood several paces away, to represent the distance between my booth in the wings and the stage. Chris nodded to Steve the pianist.

Angela's voice sounded much stronger this time. I joined her for the second verse. My secret karaoke sessions seemed to be paying off. I was pleased with how I sounded.

'Stop!' yelled Chris.

The piano stumbled jarringly to a halt.

Chris marched up to me. 'What's wrong with you?'

'What... what do you mean?' My voice shook.

'You're practically yelling. And your voice has this really rough edge on the lower notes.'

'I thought it would suit the song. I thought it would sound more... I don't know... passionate.'

'Well, it doesn't. You just sound like an angry geezer with a sore throat. You need to up your game.'

'Sorry.'

'Chris, what exactly is your problem with Matthew?'

I turned to look at Ralph, who had kept his head down throughout this exchange. He was leaning against the piano. The Heroic Bringer of Sandwiches had vanished. He looked tired, and – I realised for the first time – thin. He never challenged Chris, so his words took me completely by surprise.

'I beg your pardon?' asked Chris.

'You seem to do nothing but goad him,' said Ralph. 'So what's up?'

'Nothing's up,' said Chris. 'I just want us to give the best performance we possibly can.'

'That's difficult, considering the pressure you're putting us all under,' said Ralph. His arm reached protectively around Angela's shoulders. I felt a sharp twinge of jealousy.

Chris snorted. 'Pressure? What do you know about pressure? All you need to do is stand there and look good.'

Ralph glanced at me as if hoping I would back him up, but frankly I lacked the energy to do so. He turned back to Chris, opening his mouth in readiness to say something else.

Angela touched his arm. 'Let's just finish the song, shall we?'

Ralph met her eyes and gave a strained smile. 'All right.'

The rest of the rehearsal was a muted affair. I sang as well as I could, but I was aware of Chris glowering at me every few minutes, and Angela throwing questioning glances in his direction. The tension in the room was palpable, and I found myself asking the same question as Ralph: what exactly was Chris's problem with me? With everyone?

The atmosphere was distracting, and my voice was growing tired. I cracked the last note of our duet.

Chris glowered even more.

I left the studio without a word to Ralph and Angela. I knew Chris was obnoxious, but that didn't stop his words getting to me. Maybe he was right after all; maybe the song was no good. And maybe my voice wasn't at its best.

Perhaps I needed more rehearsal.

I went to the Moon and Stars and spent the rest of the evening singing on the empty stage. Instead of my usual musical theatre songs, I revisited the rock ballads I had performed for Lucy, trying to smooth away the rough edges on the low notes.

At one point, I thought I saw a movement in the control booth and stopped mid-verse. But when I crept up the aisle to look, there was no one there.

# Harmony

'Wow,' said James, as he stepped onto the stage of the Moon and Stars and looked out at the auditorium. 'You told me it was beautiful, but I had no idea it would be like this.'

'Isn't it great?' Lucy was grinning. 'Have you seen the ceiling?'

Dan peered into the darkness of the wings. 'Please tell me it's haunted.'

Lucy winked at me. 'Well, it's funny you should say that...'

I nudged her. 'Here, let me show you the drum kit.'

I had lugged the kit piece by piece out of the props store, a claustrophobic space beneath the stage filled with fluff, cobwebs, and rather too many plastic flowers and fake swords. The kit was covered in a thick layer of dust. I had wiped the worst of it away, but it still wasn't the most pristine of instruments.

Dan leaned over to examine it, scratching the back of his neck.

'I hope it's okay,' I said.

'As long as I can bash it with a stick and it makes a noise, we're good.'

I smiled. 'If only the same philosophy could be applied to the piano.'

'Well, as angry as I am with the neighbours, this is pretty cool,' said James. His eyes lit up. 'We should play a gig here. Maybe we could get together with some other bands. What about next summer?'

There was suddenly a lump in my throat.

'This place might not be open next summer,' I said.

'What do you mean?' asked Lucy.

All three of them were looking at me, expressions serious. I hadn't meant to share my fears about the theatre, but it was too late to stop now.

'The owners are thinking of selling,' I said. 'At best, the place is going to be shuttered for years.'

'That sucks,' said Dan. 'Sorry.'

The happy, relaxed atmosphere evaporated. Everyone looked grim.

'Well, that's a cheery thought,' said James.

Lucy stood up. 'We have to do something. A campaign, or a protest, or... *something*.'

'We have a few ideas. We're holding a fundraising gala.' I hesitated, then told myself that the worst they could do was say no. 'Would you like to play at that?'

'A gala?' said Dan. 'You mean, like, the Royal Variety Performance?'

'A bit, but not as posh,' I said. 'We could really do with more performers.'

The band exchanged glances.

'I'm working on some new songs,' said Lucy. 'We could debut them on the night.'

'We could sell some merch and give half the money to the theatre,' said James.

'We have merch?' I asked.

'Yeah,' said Dan. 'We have mugs, T-shirts and umbrellas. Not much demand for the umbrellas, so we could always donate a few as raffle prizes.'

'Thanks, guys.' My eyes were suddenly watering. It was probably just the dust. 'Shall we get started?'

We began to run through Lucy's new songs for the university gig. The first song began with a piano introduction which then segued into a rock number, incorporating the guitar and Lucy's vocals. I struck my chords with a new emphasis and energy, my fingers dancing across the keys. I was getting used to the style of music. I was even enjoying it.

'I think it needs another voice,' said Lucy, when we had finished. She looked at me and smiled. 'What do you think, maestro? Your time to shine?'

I shifted nervously in my seat, looking at Dan and James. 'I don't know…'

'Guys?' said Lucy. 'Could you leave us alone for five minutes?'

Dan and James looked at each other, then sloped off into the wings. Lucy placed both hands on my keyboard and peered down at me.

'Are you okay?'

'Yes.'

'You're in your theatre, the theatre where you've sung a million times. You're with friends.'

'I…'

'If it helps, imagine we're singing karaoke in your flat. Okay?'

I swallowed hard and nodded. 'Okay.'

Lucy patted my hand. Then she turned towards the wings. 'All right, guys. You can come back now.'

Dan and James reappeared from the wings and took their places.

We started again. I tried to focus on the keyboard, pushing the thought of singing to the back of my mind. We reached the chorus, and Lucy raised a hand, signalling for me to come in.

I improvised, singing beneath her, and then echoing her words. I kept it soft, but it sounded good, so for the next chorus I raised my voice. Lucy caught my eye and smiled again.

And then I was lost, swept away by a tide of music. It was as if something had clicked into place. The music made sense now, and I let it course through me. As the song reached a crescendo, I finally unleashed the full power of my voice in one long, perfect, rich note. It echoed, bell-like, around the theatre.

I struck the keyboard in a final chord and was silent.

I looked up to find the band staring at me.

'Was that okay?' I asked.

'Whoa,' said Dan. His eyes had gone very wide. 'Where have you been hiding?'

Lucy patted my shoulder. 'Does it matter? We've found him now.'

'Did the harmonies work?' I asked.

She laughed. 'Yes, they really worked.'

James shook his head. 'I don't get it. You're classically trained, right? Why aren't you singing professionally?'

As if it were that easy.

'I've been having some vocal problems recently,' I said softly.

'Well, you could've fooled me. You should be singing alongside Lucy. No offence, Luce.'

'None taken,' said Lucy.

'You have to rehearse that duet for the concert. It'll be amazing.'

'The concert?' I murmured.

'It'll be class,' said Dan.

All three of them were staring at me with hunger in their eyes. A shiver ran down my spine.

And suddenly it all crashed in on me, like a wave inside my head.

*U.G.L.Y.*

The student showcase.

And worst of all, the words of the producer at the competition.

*Angela, you look like a singer. But Matthew, you just... don't.*

I leapt up from the keyboard, almost knocking over the stool.

'No! I... can't...'

'Why?' asked Dan.

'I can't sing in front of people. Not properly.'

'You sing karaoke with me,' said Lucy.

I shook my head. 'That's different. I couldn't sing in a band.'

'Why not?' asked James.

'Can't you see?'

'Huh?' said Dan.

I gestured at my face.

'I don't understand,' said Lucy. 'What are we supposed to be looking at?'

'I'm *ugly*!' I blurted. 'That's the reason I'm not a singer. Are you all satisfied now?'

They looked at me blankly.

There was a long silence.

I felt a sob rise and tremble in my throat. It came out as a choked gasp.

Lucy stepped forward. 'Oh, Matthew...'

She reached for my arm. I recoiled. 'I don't want your pity.'

'Pity?' She looked confused, and slightly hurt.

'I'm sorry...' My hand closed around the tube of concealer in my trouser pocket. 'Excuse me.'

'Matthew?'

I turned and hurried into the wings.

I went to the toilets, stood beneath the stark white lights, braced myself against the sink and looked in the mirror.

My skin was as bad as it had been when I was a teenager. I took out the concealer, and applied it to my cheeks, to the tip of my nose, to my chin.

I turned towards the door. Stopped.

I turned back to the mirror and saw that I had missed a blemish on my jaw. I took the concealer out again. Covered the spot.

Turned towards the door...

Stopped.

Turned back to the mirror.

Checked.

Found an unsightly red mark beneath my left eye.

Took out the concealer...

Covered.

Turned.

Door.

Mirror.

Concealer.

Door... pause... turn... mirror...

I gave a sob of frustration, threw the concealer into the sink and covered my face with my hands. It was clear I wasn't going anywhere for a while.

There was a soft knock on the door, and Lucy's voice said, 'Matthew?'

'Yes?'

'Are you all right in there?'

'I'm fine.' I did my best to keep my tone light and reassuring.

'You've been ages.'

'I... won't be long.' My voice shook.

'What's going on?'

'Nothing.'

'You don't sound well.'

'I'm fine.'

God. Could my voice sound any weaker?

A pause.

'I'm coming in,' said Lucy.

'What? No, you can't...'

The door creaked open.

Lucy's gaze went to my face, to the mirror, to the tube of concealer in the sink, and back to my face.

'What's wrong?' she asked, softly.

'Nothing... I just needed to apply some concealer.'

'...Okay...'

'But I don't think I can stop.'

'Right.'

I gripped the sink. 'I'm sorry... sorry I walked out like that.'

'There's no need to be sorry.' She moved closer. I looked up and saw her reflected face next to mine in the mirror. 'Why do you use the concealer?'

I flinched, lowering my eyes so I didn't have to look at my reflection anymore.

'My skin is awful. I had acne as a teenager, and it's been bad ever since.'

Lucy peered at my face. I fought an urge to turn away.

'Matthew, your skin is great. You don't need the concealer.'

I shook my head. 'That's not true.'

'You look fine. Honest.' I was still gripping the rim of the sink. Lucy slid her hand over and placed it on top of my own. 'Why on earth do you think you're ugly? And don't tell me it's obvious, because that's simply not true.'

I shuddered, my gaze flicking to the squashed tube of concealer.

'I suppose... when you hear something so many times, you start to believe it.'

'People have *called* you ugly?'

'Yes. Well, not always *directly*—'

'I may have to hunt these people down.'

I chuckled weakly.

'Ah!' said Lucy. 'He laughs! That's a start, I suppose. Who? Come on. Tell me.'

I shrugged. 'Music industry people. Casting directors, producers...'

'Well, they're wrong. This industry has its share of bullies. They probably talk to everyone like that.'

I sniffed. 'Yes, but they have a point, don't they? I don't look like a singer.'

'And what does a singer look like? Beauty standards are rubbish. Meaningless.'

'That's easy for you to say.'

Lucy laughed. 'It really isn't. You think I haven't experienced it?'

I stared at her. 'You?'

'Of course. But then I stopped caring what other people thought of me. It took a while, but I got there.'

I sighed. 'That must be nice.'

She squeezed my fingers. 'Do you do this a lot? Check your face in the mirror, I mean.'

I cringed. 'Quite a lot. It's... very tiring.'

'Maybe you should talk to someone about it.'

I tensed. 'It's embarrassing.'

'It's not. Just think about it. Okay?'

'Okay.'

She patted my hand. 'Do you think you can come back into the theatre now?'

I glanced down at my fingers, which were smeared with concealer. 'Can you just give me a few minutes to get cleaned up?'

'Sure.' Lucy locked eyes with me. She raised her hand and cupped my cheek. My breath caught in my throat. 'You're not ugly at all.'

I stood very still, frozen beneath her touch. 'I... okay?'

She smiled. 'See you in a minute.'

Her hand left my face.

The door swung shut behind her, breaking my trance. I took paper towels from the dispenser and wiped my hands and face. Thoughts danced through my head.

*Lucy touched my face. She touched it. She doesn't think I'm ugly. Maybe she's right?*

I had worn the word 'ugly' like a heavy cloak for a long time. I had never seriously considered that it might not fit me.

The tube of concealer was almost empty. Trembling, I slipped it back into my pocket, and went to join the band.

# Fantasia

It was the first night of Jess's bonkers Ghost Tour.

I had been bullied into playing the part of one of the ghosts. Jess had also managed to rope in several of the front-of-house staff, and they had a great time covering themselves with stage makeup and fake blood.

Inevitably, Jess had cast me as the Phantom Tenor and presented me with a long black cloak and a black top hat from wardrobe. Although I wasn't entirely happy with the situation, at least it provided me with a distraction from thinking about my last rehearsal with Shattered Chandelier. While Lucy and the band had been sympathetic, the memory of my behaviour still made me cringe.

The Ghost Tour would start at the stage door. At 10pm, I poked my head out of the door and saw a crowd of perhaps a dozen people gathered around Jess in the little cobbled alleyway. My eyes widened in surprise. This wasn't at all bad for a first attempt. Maybe there was mileage in the idea after all.

I slipped back inside the theatre and took up my position in the wings. The stage and house lights were down, leaving the ghost light – a tall lamp centre stage – to provide most of the illumination. Its round, cage-like shade cast strange, barred shadows across the blue backdrop.

The safety lights would guide the tour group up the aisle. When they arrived, I would slip out of the wings and cross the stage, while Jess told the appropriate ghost story. For some reason, this was the end of the tour. I was the headline act.

I was unexpectedly nervous as I waited in the wings, trying to distract myself by scrolling through my phone.

Fifty minutes later, I heard footsteps and the murmur of voices in the auditorium, then the creak of theatre seats as the group sat down.

I tried to remember the class on method acting I had taken at the Conservatoire.

Okay. You're a ghost. Think *ghostly*. What would Stanislavsky do?

Jess began her story, her strong, clear voice full of mysterious menace.

This was my cue. I slipped out of the wings and started to cross the stage in what I hoped was a ghostly manner.

A dry ice machine had sputtered into life in the opposite wing, and I found myself walking through clouds of white smoke.

There were a few *ooohs* from the audience.

I stifled a cough and paused next to the ghost light. I swirled my cloak a bit for good measure, and to waft away some of the dry ice, which was rather excessive.

Jess was in full flow: 'And so, the poor tenor was rejected by the beautiful actress. He went into a decline and died of a broken heart. Sometimes, in the dead of night, when the theatre is dark and empty, you can still hear him singing, pining for his lost love...'

That was when I heard the voice.

I jumped, and then froze.

It was *my* voice.

My tenor echoed around the theatre, singing a rock ballad with surprising power. There were several gasps from the audience, and I would have been flattered if I hadn't been so shocked.

How had they done this?

What was going on?

Then I remembered the last time I had rehearsed alone in the theatre, and I had thought I'd seen someone in the control booth. And I realised there could only be one possible explanation.

*Dave.*

*

I found Dave and Jess in the office, drinking tea and laughing. Jess was wearing her 'ghost hunter' costume – full Victorian mourning dress, including a hat with black feathers – while Dave was still in his uniform of jeans and a T-shirt. The effect was rather incongruous.

I marched over to them. 'Where did that recording come from?'

'What?' asked Jess. Then she smiled. 'Oh, you mean the singing! Dave recorded the Ghost.'

'Is that a problem?' asked Dave, all innocence. But by now I was quite certain he knew it was me.

'I wasn't expecting it,' I said. 'It scared me half to death.'

'Good, isn't it? He got it on video, too,' said Jess. She clicked her computer mouse. 'Look.'

I stared at the screen. My voice began to sing, and I could just make out a dark shape on the screen, a silhouette backlit by the ghost light.

'How did you get this?' I asked.

'I filmed it from the control booth the other week,' said Dave. 'I was working late again.'

*The hell you were*, I thought.

'He's got a gorgeous voice, hasn't he?' said Jess, dreamily.

'Hmm,' I said.

'I wonder who he is?'

'I've no idea.'

'I put it on YouTube, too.'

'You've *what*?'

'I've linked it to the Ghost's Twitter account. Look.'

She opened Twitter, and I read the latest post.

@PhantomOfTheMoonAndStars: *Very pleased with my performance tonight. Might even sing at the gala! What do you think?*

'It's gone viral,' said Jess.

'It's… what?'

'It's trending. People are loving it. They're trying to guess who the Ghost is. They think it's someone famous.'

I stared at the screen in disbelieving horror. The video had dozens of comments, most of them suggesting the names of various well-known singers.

One comment in particular caught my eye.

*He sounds like Ralph!*

I suddenly felt cold. What if people matched the Ghost's voice to the voice on Angela's album? They might realise Ralph wasn't doing the singing. And then it would only be a matter of time before I was exposed. Ralph's fans would be so disappointed when they saw me, and I would be too humiliated ever to sing again.

'Take it down,' I said.

'Why?'

'Because we're trying to run a theatre here, and this makes a joke of the whole thing. Please just take it down.'

Jess frowned. 'Matthew, you're being weird. What's wrong?'

I realised my hands were shaking. I hid them behind my back. 'I'm not being weird.'

'You are. You've been against this whole Ghost thing from the beginning. What's your problem?'

I said nothing.

'It seems my original suspicions were correct,' said Dave.

'You don't mean...' Jess's eyes had grown very wide. 'You're the Ghost!'

I took a step backwards. 'I am not. Why would you think that?'

'It has to be a member of the theatre staff,' said Jess. 'You have a spare key. And you look shifty every time we mention the Ghost. It's you, isn't it?'

Her eyes were boring into mine. I sighed. It appeared the game was up.

I stared at my feet. 'I just wanted to rehearse.'

'Ha!' Dave clapped his hands together. 'I knew it.'

'I don't understand,' said Jess. 'Why didn't you tell us about this?'

'I wanted to rehearse in private. And I know using the stage after hours isn't strictly allowed. Also, it's embarrassing.'

'I don't see what's so embarrassing about it,' said Jess. 'You have a beautiful voice. Here, let me show you more of the comments—'

'I don't want to see them. I just want you to delete it.'

Jess looked uncomfortable. 'I don't think I can.'

'Why not?'

'It's just... you know how I wrote that the Ghost might sing at the gala night? It was meant to be a joke, but... well, we've already sold most of the tickets. People actually want to come because of the Ghost.'

'Let me get this straight. The gala is nearly sold out because people want to see who this Ghost is?'

'Yeah, pretty much,' said Jess. 'And people are asking us if we'll livestream the event on YouTube. They're offering to make donations if the Ghost sings. I thought I might set up a crowdfunding campaign and link it to the video.' She met my eyes. 'People really want to hear you, Matthew. I think we could actually raise a lot of money for the theatre.'

I felt lightheaded and put both hands on the desk to steady myself. Out of the corner of my eye, I could see Dave smiling.

'No,' I said.

'But—'

'I can't do it.' I took a shuddering breath. 'Look. Imagine if you turned up at the concert expecting – I don't know – Josh Groban or someone. And instead you got me. Wouldn't you be a bit disappointed?'

'Yes, but then we'd play up the whole *A Star is Born*, *X Factor* hopeful, came-from-nowhere angle.' Her eyes shone with what looked distressingly like unshed tears. 'Please, Matthew. This could really help the theatre. You could save our jobs.'

# Presto

I spent the day after the Ghost Tour avoiding Jess. I threw myself into various housekeeping jobs around the foyers and auditorium – anything that would keep me out of the office and away from talk of the Phantom.

I took an inventory of the bar supplies and ordered some Prosecco for the gala, and sweets to replace those that the Ghost had eaten. Then, after lunch, I repainted both the stage door and the auditorium door. I was determined that the theatre would look its best for the concert.

When I got home, my clothes were spattered with blue paint. I was just making myself a cup of tea when the doorbell buzzed.

I went downstairs to find Dan on the doorstep.

'You need to come with me,' he said.

I hesitated. Dan was bigger than me, and for a moment I was concerned that he was going to frog-march me out of the building.

'Where? Why?'

Dan sighed, the sound emanating from the dark depths of his rocker soul.

'James wants to show you something.'

I glanced down at my clothes. 'Can I at least get changed?'

'No time. Sorry.'

Dan led me to the music shop and rang the bell. James opened the door a crack. 'Did you bring him?'

'Yes, he's right here.'

'Good. You may enter.'

We went upstairs.

'Did you order the Chinese?' said Dan. 'Because that's the only reason I'm here.'

James rolled his eyes. 'Yes, I ordered the Chinese.'

'Did you remember the spring rolls?'

'Why am I here?' I asked.

James smiled broadly, an odd expression on his usually intense face. I wasn't sure I liked it. 'All will soon become clear. Sit down.'

He pushed me onto the sofa and left the room. Dan padded over to the kitchenette.

A horrible thought occurred to me. I had not spoken to James or Dan since our last rehearsal at the Moon and Stars. Perhaps they had brought me here to tell me I was no longer welcome in the band. My mind whirled with possible reasons for my impending dismissal:

1. My refusal to sing at the gig.
2. Too ugly.
3. Too intense/sensitive/weird.
4. Not trendy enough.
5. Not talented enough.

I waited, my stomach twisting itself into knots.

Presently, James returned, and placed a laptop on the coffee table in front of the sofa. He opened it to reveal a screensaver: stars swirling in a galaxy. Maybe he and Dan intended to hypnotise me first, so I wouldn't be able to defend myself against the horrible, inevitable rejection that was coming my way.

Dan padded back into the living area, flopped down beside me on the sofa, and tossed me a can of beer. This was, at least, a reassuringly familiar thing to hold on to.

James stood smartly beside the laptop, hands clasped behind his back. 'We've brought you here tonight,' he said, starting to pace the floor like a detective in a whodunnit, 'because we're worried about you.'

'I'm sorry,' I said. 'I know I haven't been at my best lately—'

'No, you haven't. And something needs to be done.'

God, this was worse than school.

'Sorry... I'll do better. I just need time...' I was perspiring as if I was in a job interview.

'Just shut up and listen,' said James.

'This is a whatsit,' said Dan. 'An intervention.'

I blinked. 'A... what?'

'This whole "I'm too ugly for music" thing has got to stop,' said James.

'It's insane,' said Dan.

'Yes, thank you, Dan.' James peered down at me. 'You seem convinced that you have to be good-looking to be a singer. We're going to show you otherwise.'

'We're going to show you the Truth,' said Dan. 'And it's going to blow. Your. Mind.'

'Tonight' – James clicked the mouse on the laptop – 'we give you... Aesthetically Challenged Blokes in Rock: an illustrated PowerPoint presentation.'

I stared at the screen, at the photo of the man with wild hair, forehead pouring with sweat, mouth wide, yelling into a microphone.

'I... see?' I said.

'All the blokes you'll see tonight have had massive careers in rock, despite being...' He hesitated, as if searching for the right words.

'Butt ugly?' suggested Dan.

James glared at him. 'I thought we'd decided to avoid the U word.' He pointed to the screen. 'Recognise Exhibit A?'

'Of course,' I said.

'Have you any idea how many albums Exhibit A has sold? How many millions of dollars he's worth? Here are some stats—'

'James likes stats,' said Dan, darkly.

'I *love* stats.' He clicked the mouse again. 'Exhibit B. Truly hideous. Five platinum albums. Sold-out stadiums, all over the world.'

'Voice of an angel,' said Dan.

'Yes, that, too. Exhibit C... I mean, come on, look at him! He's not going to win any beauty contests, is he? But just look at that crowd! He's got them in the palm of his hand! Here's a video...' James looked on with dewy-eyed reverence as the singer howled into the mic, the huge audience jumping up and down.

After a moment, he paused the video and turned to look at me. 'Are we getting through to you at all?'

I stared at the frozen singer on the screen. 'Listen, guys, I get what you're trying to do, and I'm really touched, it's just...'

'Just what?' asked James.

'I can't be a rock singer. I only really know classical.'

'You and I both know that's a blatant lie. Besides, quite a lot of rock musicians are classically trained.'

'Okay, but I'm not cool, I'm not spontaneous, I'd look rubbish in the clothes—'

'Mate,' said Dan, 'you were *born* to be a rock star. You're intense, troubled and weird-looking.'

I glared at him. 'Thank you.'

'And you're a great musician,' said James. 'We've played with you, remember? I've seen the way you attack that keyboard, and I can tell you're dying to sing.' He sat down next to me. 'Look, I'll be honest: I wasn't sure it would work when you first joined. But now I think we're on to something great.'

'Because you can actually play an instrument,' said Dan.

James rolled his eyes. 'Yes, and not just that... You add interest. *Presence.* It works. You just need to stop holding back. Really go for it.'

I looked down at the floor for a moment. 'Okay. Let's say you're right, and I'm secretly a natural rock star. What should I do to... really go for it?'

'You should stop talking like that,' said Dan.

'You need to relax, and not worry that you're "really going for it",' said James.

'Relax. Right.' I dug my fingernails into the leather sofa cushion.

James sighed. 'Okay, we'll take a more methodical approach, if you like. What are you going to wear for the next gig?'

I glanced down at my clothes. 'Something like this. But... er... without the paint.'

James shook his head. 'No.'

'No? But Lucy said I should wear black.'

'Lucy's right. In principle. But you need something *more*. Something' – James's eyes glittered – 'spectacular.'

Oh God.

James looked me up and down. 'You're about my size. Bit taller, maybe. Give me a minute.'

He disappeared into the next room.

'You okay, mate?' asked Dan. 'You look a bit scared.'

'Yes, I am a bit.'

'Don't worry. James knows about these things.'

James returned a few minutes later, carrying a huge pile of dark fabric. He dumped it on the sofa.

I eyed it suspiciously. 'What's that?'

'Your gig outfit. Well, one of them is. You've got a choice.' James pulled a hideous black leather trench coat from the top of the pile. It was studded with an excess of buttons. Apparently it had also been attacked by a stationery cupboard at some point, because the shoulders were covered in staples and paperclips. 'What do you think of this one?'

I stared at the coat, which was quite possibly the ugliest garment I had ever seen. 'I think you've gone mad.'

James laughed and tossed the coat aside. 'Okay. We'll add that one to the "possible" pile.'

'No, we won't.'

Undeterred, he continued to search through the coats. 'Ah-ha! What about this one?'

I braced myself for what would surely be another buttoned, stapled horror.

Instead, James held up a black coat. It had a high, stiff collar, and was decorated with twists of brocade on the shoulders and cuffs. A self-respecting Victorian might have worn something similar at some point.

'That's not half bad,' I said.

He handed it to me. 'Try it on.'

I wrapped myself in the coat and fastened the unobtrusive silver buttons. It was warm and an excellent fit. It was also deliberately long and voluminous, falling around my ankles like a cloak.

James smiled. 'That looks great. What do you think, Dan?'

'Cool. You look like a modern Dracula.'

'And that's a good thing because…?'

'There's a mirror in the hall,' said James. 'See for yourself.'

I proceeded cautiously into the hall. Mirrors were a necessary evil, a tool I used to check that the concealer was right. I didn't normally enjoy unexpected confrontations with them. But now I found that I wanted to see my reflection.

I stared at myself in the mirror.

My younger self stared back at me. The self with black clothes and long hair. The self who loved loud music, and *theatre*.

The coat was dramatic and ridiculous.

I loved it.

I walked back into the rehearsal room with a smile on my face.

'What do you think?' asked James.

I attempted a nonchalant shrug but was unable to hide my smile. 'It's all right, I suppose.'

'Just mess up your hair a little, wear black boots, bit of silver jewellery, maybe, and you're good to go.'

'Er... okay.' I looked down at the floor, suddenly feeling a bit choked up. 'Thanks, guys.'

'Don't mention it.'

A phone buzzed. Dan smiled. 'Chinese is here.'

# Flat

Next stop on our Grand Tour of Musical Deception: Newcastle.

Nerves danced in my stomach as we arrived at the theatre, an imposing building with neoclassical columns around its facade. This was my local theatre, where I had seen my first musicals as a teenager. I had always longed to perform here, and tonight's concert should have been a magical occasion. I wished I could appear onstage like a normal singer, wished my parents could see me perform. After my last discussion with Clara, I hadn't dared tell them about my arrangement with Ralph, or even that I was singing in Newcastle. I was pretty sure they wouldn't approve of my circumstances. But I still missed them.

Soon I was sitting in my booth backstage, waiting for the concert to begin. As had become my habit before concerts, I took out my notebook and began to scribble a tune to distract myself.

I was still working on Angela's next album, but I found myself unable to focus on the gentle classical crossover material favoured by Chris. Instead, I had continued down the rock ballad route. I now had several compositions which I thought I might develop into a song cycle if Chris didn't want them. Maybe I could even turn them into a short musical. I couldn't help imagining the premiere at the Moon and Stars, with Angela in the lead role.

One could always dream.

A gigantic box of chocolates shot through the gap in the curtains. 'Want one?'

I leapt from my chair, dropping the notebook. A face appeared above the chocolates.

'For God's sake, Ralph!'

Ralph gave an apologetic smile. 'Sorry. Didn't mean to startle you.'

'What are you doing here?'

'Angela's doing this meet-and-greet press thingy. Mind if I hang out here for a while?'

He glanced over his shoulder. He looked nervous.

'Don't they want you there?' I asked.

'Well, yeah. But when I said "hang out", I actually meant "hide".'

I sighed. 'Okay.'

Ralph leaned against the only solid wall and ran a hand through his hair. 'I hate talking to the press. I hate lying.'

'Yes, well. This is what you signed up for.'

'Aren't you afraid someone we know might show up here?'

I stared at him. 'Like who?'

'I don't know – people from college? Teachers? What if they recognise your voice? They'll know I'm faking it.'

An image of Robert and his minions laughing in the front row of the theatre flashed into my mind. I suppressed a shudder.

'I doubt they'd make the connection,' I said, trying to convince myself as much as Ralph.

'I suppose you're right.' Ralph offered me the chocolates again.

'Thanks.' I took one without meeting his eye. If he wanted to be friends again, it was going to take more than chocolate to win me over.

'The record label sent them. Isn't that nice?'

I nodded, while simultaneously wondering where *my* chocolates were.

'Shame I'm off chocolate, really.' He closed the box with a regretful look.

Since the album launch, Ralph had acquired his own fan base. I might have found this flattering, but I suspected it had less to do with my voice and more to do with his appearance in the music video, particularly during the masked carnival scene. He even had his own hashtag: #HotMaskedTenor.

The irony of this was not lost on me.

I'd expected him to be over the moon. But #HotMaskedTenor seemed subdued of late. This wasn't the first time he had come backstage early to hide from the press.

I wondered if his sullen state had anything to do with his romance with Angela. Perhaps things had fizzled out. Ralph's crushes generally ended like this.

I bent to retrieve my notebook.

Ralph squinted at the music. 'What are you writing?'

'Songs for the new album.'

'Good for you. I keep trying to show my stuff to Chris, but he doesn't seem to care.'

I felt a twinge of guilt. I knew this was one of the reasons Ralph had agreed to help me. 'I'll have a word with Chris.'

'No offence, but he never seems to listen to you either.'

'True.'

He looked straight at me. 'Aren't you getting tired of this?'

I stared back at him. 'Are you?'

'You didn't answer my question.'

'Well... at least I get to perform. It's a job.'

He forced a laugh. 'You know, it's the silliest thing, but I really miss busking.'

'You used to busk?'

'Yes. Covent Garden. Trafalgar Square. I wish I was there right now. It seemed rough at the time, but at least it was my voice, my songs.'

'Well, just wait until the tour's over, and you'll be able to busk all you want.'

Ralph laughed again. It was an oddly humourless sound. 'Do you really think it'll work like that?'

'What do you mean?'

'If we make this second album, we'll have to promote it. That might mean another tour. And then what? We could be doing this for years.'

'Surely not?'

Ralph just shrugged.

'I'd better get ready,' he said. 'It's nearly showtime.'

He left the chocolates behind.

*

Ralph's words haunted me throughout the concert. I hadn't been thinking about the future. Not in any serious way. I'd been thinking about Angela, about the next time I'd be able to record with her. It had simply not occurred to me that this situation could go on indefinitely.

When the show was over, I waited backstage for twenty minutes, hoping to avoid the crush of fans at the stage door. But as I approached the exit, a voice drifted in from the street. It was painfully familiar and raised in outrage.

Oh, no...

'How could you?' screeched the voice. 'How could you stand up there and... and *nick* our Matthew's voice?'

I poked my head around the stage door. My sister was standing in the middle of the pavement, jabbing a finger at Ralph, who looked a little scared. Angela stood a couple of feet away, her features creased with anger. A small group of fans looked on in puzzled fascination.

'I don't know what you're talking about,' said Ralph.

'Don't lie,' said Clara. 'I saw you! You were miming! To Matthew's voice. It's... it's fraudulent!'

Angela stepped forward. She spoke calmly and coldly. 'If you don't leave immediately, I'll call security.'

Clara glared at her. 'And you! You're the one who broke our Matthew's heart. You think it's acceptable to use him like this?'

It was time to intervene. I took a breath and slipped out of the stage door. 'Clara...'

She whirled around. 'Matthew! Are you all right? I was just telling these so-called friends of yours that what they're doing is unacceptable.'

I looked at Angela and Ralph. They were both a bit pale. 'I'm so sorry. This is my sister. Come on, Clara. I think we need to have a talk.'

I draped my arm around Clara's shoulders and led her away, not daring to look back.

'Could you be any more embarrassing?' I groaned.

'I was trying to stick up for you.'

'We're not in the playground anymore. I'm no longer six.'

'Yes, well. You're no better at sticking up for yourself now than you were back then.'

I sighed. 'Let's get a drink.'

There was a wine bar just across the road from the theatre, with Saturday night revellers gathered around tables on the pavement. I ushered Clara inside, and she sat at a table in a quiet corner, looking fierce.

'What would you like?'

'Coffee. I'm driving.'

I went to the bar to order. When I returned, her angry expression had vanished, and she looked disappointed, which was far worse.

I slipped into the chair opposite and waited for the inevitable lecture.

My sister was silent.

'Well?' I prompted. 'What exactly did you hope to achieve by coming here tonight?'

'Believe it or not, I wanted to hear you sing,' said Clara.

'Rubbish. You wanted to have it out with my friends. God, Clara, can't you just leave me alone?'

She sighed, closing her eyes briefly. 'Matthew, I don't know why you always insist on making me the enemy.'

'Because you're always sticking your nose into my business. And you never approve of anything I do. You're worse than Mum and Dad.'

'How can you say that? We've always been there for you. All three of us. Even when we were kids, it was all: Matthew this, Matthew that. We must make sure Matthew gets to his piano lesson. And then that stupid bloody conservatoire. The *cost* of that, while us mere ungifted mortals had to *work* for a living, and then sit back and watch you throw it all away because of some ridiculous... *complex*. And now *this*. I mean... for God's sake!'

There was a horrible, frozen moment in which all the air seemed to have been sucked out of the room.

I blinked. 'Are you done? Because, honestly, you can't make me feel any more of a loser than I already do.'

There was a moment of silence. Then Clara leaned back in her seat and shook her head. 'Oh, Matty.'

This was her typical 'big sister' voice. The way she had spoken to me when I was still a teenager. I felt like a teenager in that moment, and it annoyed me.

'What do you mean, "Oh, Matty"?'

'I just... thought you had more sense than this. Someone of your talent, selling yourself short.'

'How am I selling myself short?'

She frowned. 'I think you know the answer to that. All those years of hard work, and you're just going to waste your talent like this.'

'I'm not wasting my talent. It's a... it's a job.'

'Why aren't you singing in a musical somewhere?'

'I don't know. Why aren't you an Olympic athlete?'

'Oh, now you're just being silly.'

'Am I? Have you any idea how hard it is to make it as a singer?'

Clara picked up her coffee cup. 'Yes, Matthew. I do. Which is why this makes me so sad. I could almost understand this if I thought you were enjoying it. But you're not, are you? When I heard you tonight, your voice sounded... flat.' I bristled at this, and she raised a hand. 'Not in the *musical* sense. Just sort of joyless. Someone going through the motions. As if you didn't really want to be there.'

I stared at my hands, folded on the table. 'It must be great to be like you.'

'What's that supposed to mean?'

'You've done everything you're supposed to do at the exact time you're supposed to do it. Great job, nice house, now a fiancé. You've got it all figured out. No wonder I'm such a disappointment.'

Clara held up a hand again. 'Just stop right there. Listen to me. No one thinks you're a disappointment.'

'But I've messed everything up...' There was a catch in my voice.

She looked me straight in the eye – something that always made me a little nervous.

'Okay, Matthew. Let's say you're right, and I have this wonderful life. Which I don't. If you had the chance, would you swap places with me? Would you buy my house? Get married?'

'Would it have to be at the golf club?'

She rolled her eyes. 'We all just want you to be happy. Does music still make you happy? Because if it doesn't, there's nothing wrong with giving it up and doing something else. You wouldn't be letting anyone down, least of all me.' She held my gaze. 'What do you want, Matthew?'

I was quiet for a moment. I *wanted* to want the things that Clara had. But the truth was, I didn't.

'I want to be a musician,' I said softly.

She smiled. 'Well, that's good news, because you already are a musician.'

'A *successful* musician. One who doesn't have to hide behind a curtain.'

'Okay. So are you doing anything else, other than... whatever *this* is?'

I shifted in my seat. 'I've... sort of joined a rock band. I'm playing the keyboard.'

She stared at me for a moment, and then she actually laughed. 'Ah! So that's why you're growing your hair again. You're trying to look like a rocker.'

'I'm not growing my...' I pushed a lock of hair back behind my ear. I tried to remember the last time I'd been to the hairdresser and drew a blank. 'All right, maybe I am. But it's got nothing to do with the band.'

'Whatever you say. So, this band. Do they play actual gigs?'

'Yes, I've played one. We've got another one on Hallowe'en, a university thing. And then we're hoping to appear at a fundraising concert at the Moon and Stars.'

'That's wonderful.' She was looking a little happier, for some reason. 'Would you send me the date? I'd love to come and watch you.'

'Yes, of course. But it's nothing really. I'm just the keyboardist.'

'There you go again. Never say you're "just the keyboardist".'

I recalled her outburst, and shame curled around my heart.

'Clara...'

'Yes, Matty?'

'I'm sorry. I... didn't realise you felt that way about the Conservatoire.'

'It's all right.' She reached for my hand, squeezed it. 'So, have you practised my wedding song yet?'

# Bravura

'Okay,' said James. 'Welcome to "How to Perform Like a Rock Star 101".'

It was our penultimate rehearsal before the Hallowe'en gig, and we were at the Moon and Stars. I was sitting at the keyboard and wearing my new coat, because, apparently, it would help me get into character.

Lucy peered up at us from her seat on the front row of the stalls. 'Are you sure you're qualified to teach Matthew this course, James?'

'Yes, thank you, I'm very experienced.'

'So what's first? How to smash a guitar? Crowd-surfing techniques? Smouldering looks?'

'Stage presence.'

Dan looked up from the takeaway pizza box which he was resting on the drum kit. 'Isn't stage presence, like, intrinsic by its very nature?'

James looked at him blankly. 'What?'

'I mean, can it actually be taught?'

'Shut up and eat your pizza.' James turned to me. 'So, Matthew, what do you normally do when you're performing?'

'I normally sit here. At the keyboard,' I said uncertainly.

'Correct.' James walked over to where I was sitting. 'Stand up.'

I stood up.

James kicked over the stool. It landed on its side with a heavy *thud*.

I stared at it. 'What did you do that for?'

'I want you to come out from behind the keyboard. Don't take this the wrong way, but you always look a bit... *formal* when you sit there.'

'Does that matter?' I asked.

'Does it matter?' James stalked downstage and spread his arms wide, as if addressing the auditorium. '*Does it matter?* We're a rock band! Where's the passion? Where's the rage?'

'I don't have any rage,' I said. 'I'm a professional.'

'I don't have any either,' said Dan, taking another bite of pizza.

James sighed. 'You need to stop using the keyboard as a prop.'

'So how am I supposed to play?'

'Good point,' said Dan.

James massaged the bridge of his nose. 'Just... trust me, will you?'

'I'm sorry,' I said.

'And stop apologising! Rock stars don't apologise.'

'Sorry. I mean—'

'Lucy, would you play the keyboard for us?'

Lucy joined us onstage. She winked as she walked past me.

'Okay,' said James. 'Do you know "Boulevard of Broken Dreams" by Green Day?'

'Um... yes. But I've never sung it.'

'Well, this is a night for new experiences. Lucy?'

Lucy began to play.

This song had always been one of Ralph's favourites. He played a good acoustic version. I couldn't shake the thought that he would be a much more effective rock singer than I was.

I stood very still, my arms straight by my sides, and began to sing. James paced around me, shouting instructions.

'Louder! Where's the *swagger*? Loosen up! Raise your head, sing out at the audience. Don't be afraid to *move*. It needs more intensity.'

I tried. I really did. But I didn't have swagger or sound intense. I just sounded a bit scared.

'Okay, stop.' James shook his head. 'That was... a different take, I suppose.'

'It was stripped back,' said Dan. 'Minimalist.'

James glared at him. 'You're really not helping.'

'I'm not very good at this,' I said. My flair for stating the obvious was truly unequalled.

'Rubbish,' said James. 'You just need practice. Let's go again, and try not to look so bloody terrified this time.'

I didn't want to go again. I wanted a trapdoor to open onstage and swallow me whole.

'Matthew,' said Lucy. 'I don't think this music is really you, is it?'

'Er... no. I like it, but I can't do this whole angry, swagger... thing.'

'Neither can I,' said Dan.

'Yes, well, you're a lost cause,' said James. 'So laid back you're practically horizontal, you are.'

'Will you two knock it off?' Lucy sighed. 'Matthew, you don't need to sound angry. You just need confidence. What's a rock song you've always wanted to sing, but have never dared?'

'Um.' I looked down at the floor. '"I Would Do Anything for Love"?'

Dan grinned. 'Brilliant!'

James slapped his palm to his face.

Lucy glared at him, then turned back to me. 'That's good. It's theatrical and passionate, just like...' She trailed off and looked at the keyboard. 'Er, shall we?'

James ran a hand through his hair. 'Okay, but let's go with the condensed version, or we'll be here all night.'

'Philistine,' muttered Dan.

'Eat your pizza.'

We began again.

I sang softly at first, but then gradually raised my voice as I grew more confident.

'Look at the audience,' said James.

I straightened my shoulders and raised my head. I felt my body loosen. My fists unclenched, and I raised my hands for emphasis.

And then I was no longer scared. I was flying, and my voice was soaring, and I was singing as myself.

Afterwards, I stared out, stunned and breathless, at the empty auditorium.

Dan began to clap.

Lucy put her arms around me. 'Well done.'

'Thank you.'

'Well,' said James. He looked a bit dazed. 'That was all right, I suppose.'

'You think you can sing at the gig?' asked Lucy. 'Just harmonies, and see how it goes?'

Her eyes were shining, and I thought: *Maybe I can actually do this.*

# Nocturne

The University of London's Hallowe'en Ball was, by all accounts, going to be a big event. We were actually getting paid to play our music, which I couldn't deny was a huge plus.

I found myself feeling increasingly nervous on the day of the gig. Apart from anything else, it marked the public debut of the Goth coat, which no longer felt like such a good idea.

At 5pm, it was still hanging on the front of my wardrobe. I stared at it.

I had already dressed as close to the Gothic theme as I could, and was wearing all black: black work trousers, black shirt and black waistcoat. A visit to Spitalfields Market had yielded a pair of chunky black lace-up boots that reached past my ankles, and a silver ring with a stone of black onyx.

Now there was just the coat to go.

I would have to make the first move. The coat wasn't going to do that for me.

I swept it from the hanger and draped it around my shoulders. I instantly felt better. There was something about the voluminous coat that made me feel confident. Bigger, but at the same time more likely to blend into the background.

I combed out my hair, allowing it to brush against the collar of the coat. Finally, I applied the concealer.

Then I took a deep breath, left the flat...

...and almost collided with Lucy on the landing.

'Matthew!' Her eyes went wide. Then she grinned. 'Wow! You look amazing!'

I stared down at my boots. That wasn't exactly a compliment I was used to hearing.

'Thank you.'

'That coat's gorgeous.'

I tried to smile. 'Hands off. It's mine.'

She laughed. 'Are you ready for this, then?'

'As I'll ever be.'

'Great.' She linked her arm through mine. 'Shall we?'

\*

The university had really gone to town with the Hallowe'en theme. Upon arrival, we found that we would be competing for attention with a fancy dress competition, a professional fire-eater, a bouncy Dracula's castle and a range of spooky cocktails.

We were on at the early time of 8pm, but by 7pm the Students Union was already quite full. There must have been at least three hundred students in the hall.

After a quick soundcheck, Lucy, James and Dan went off to the bar. I was too nervous to mingle. An instinct for self-preservation drove me into the 'backstage' area, which was a narrow passage between the walls and the black drapes which formed the rear of the temporary stage. It reminded me of the booth I used when I was on tour with Angela, and I found this oddly comforting.

I leaned back against the wall, closed my eyes, and took a breath to calm my nerves.

'Hey.'

I jumped and opened my eyes to find Lucy holding a cocktail glass. The liquid inside it was a lurid red, and it was steaming dramatically.

'Why are you hiding back here?' she asked.

'I just... needed a moment to prepare.'

Lucy smiled. 'Here. I've brought you something to get you in the mood.'

She held out the cocktail.

'Er... what is it?'

'It's called a Steamy Vampire.'

'It looks dangerous.'

'I've already had one. They're actually quite nice.'

I took the glass from her. 'Thanks... I think.'

I sipped the cocktail. I detected delicate fruity notes, a hint of raspberry perhaps... and then a huge hit of bitter alcohol that made my tongue want to crawl out of my mouth and hide.

'*GAAAAH!*' I said, making a face. 'What the hell's in it?'

Lucy shrugged. 'I don't know. I just thought it was interesting.'

'It's definitely that.'

She smiled. 'So, maestro. Here we are – the biggest gig of our careers. How do you feel?'

'Apart from afraid you're trying to poison me? Fine.'

'You sure?'

'Yes...' I took another sip of the cocktail, which was growing on me. 'A bit nervous.'

'Just do exactly what you did in rehearsal. It'll be great.'

'Thanks.'

Her hand brushed my arm. 'Good luck.'

*

We began the set with two of James's new songs, which had Shattered Chandelier's traditional trademark of instruments fighting to the death with Lucy yelling over the cacophony. I sat at the back and did what was required of me, which was to play the same three chords over and over again at maximum volume on the pipe organ setting.

The response from the audience of students could best be described as 'mildly distracted'. So after the second song, we knew a change of direction was in order.

I began the delicate piano introduction. Lucy leaned closer to the mic. And when she began the song, she was no longer shouting.

Her dark alto still had a rawness and edge which was entirely hers, but there was also a melodic plaintiveness which was quite entrancing. The students seemed to think so, too, because soon more people had gathered around to watch, and a hush fell over the hall.

The song built, guitar and bass and drums lifting Lucy's voice, contrasting the beauty with danger. The atmosphere crackled into life.

And I knew then that this was working. This was good.

Twenty minutes later, we ended our first set on an electrifying wave of applause.

Lucy caught my eye and smiled.

'Drink?' I asked, as we left the stage.

'Please.'

I went in search of more Steamy Vampires. James and Dan were chatting to a group of people at the other end of the bar, and they already seemed to have acquired drinks, so I headed back towards the stage, cocktails in hand.

Lucy was leaning against the wall. A man stood next to her. He was mid-thirties, with sandy-coloured hair, and he was dressed smartly in dark trousers and a grey polo-neck sweater.

He was smiling at her, laughing, and something twisted in my gut. I hung back, wondering if I should walk over to them or return to the bar. But then I noticed the expression on Lucy's face.

She looked annoyed.

'I already *said* I'm not interested!' Lucy's tone was sharp.

'Are you sure?' The man had a very posh voice, and he sounded slightly stunned by Lucy's reaction.

I walked over. 'Is everything okay?'

Lucy blushed. I'd never seen her do that before. 'Everything's fine.'

Handsome Guy turned to me and smiled. 'Ah! You're the pianist. I was just having a chat with Lucy. She has a stunning voice.'

'Yes,' I said. 'She does.'

Lucy glared at Handsome Guy. 'We don't have time for this. We need to get ready for our next set.'

'Oh. Of course.' He looked a bit disappointed. But then he reached into his pocket and produced a white rectangle. 'Here's my card, just in case you change your mind.'

Lucy hesitated for a moment, then took it. 'Yeah. Cheers. I won't.'

Handsome Guy wandered away.

'Are you okay?' I asked.

'Yes, fine.' She didn't look fine. She looked a little shaken.

'Was he bothering you?'

She shook her head. 'No, no. Not like that.'

'Why did he give you his card?'

'He was weird. Please can we just drop it?' She reached for the cocktail. 'Oh, great! Another Vampire!'

She took a long swig.

'Are you sure you're okay?'

'Yes, Matthew. I'm fine.' She frowned. 'Where are the others? Did they see any of that?'

'I don't think so. I think they're still at the bar.'

'We'd better go and fetch them. We're back on in five minutes.'

*

There was something haunted about Lucy's expression when we took to the stage for our second set of the evening. I noticed her eyes scanning the crowd. I wondered if she was searching for Handsome Guy, and why she was so nervous of him.

Her nerves didn't last. Two songs in, and she was singing with even more strength and power than in the first half.

But it was more than that. She sounded angry. Angry, and defiant.

The hall had filled up, and the larger audience heightened the electric atmosphere.

We ran through Lucy's songs, and I heard the shift, the moment when the anger died and the passion returned. The odd episode with Handsome Guy was forgotten, and we were just enjoying making music. My hands danced across the keys, striking chords at full volume. Lucy didn't hold back, so neither did I.

We came to the end of our penultimate song. During the applause, Lucy turned to look at me, eyebrows raised in a question.

'Ready?' she said, the word almost lost in the din.

My heart was racing, but I nodded.

Lucy turned back to the audience, raising her hands for quiet.

'Thanks so much, everyone. We're Shattered Chandelier, and you've been awesome. For our final song, I would like to introduce our newest member, Matthew, on harmonies for the first time.'

Oh God. This was it.

I began to play. I was still seated at the keyboard, towards the back of the stage, away from the full glare of the lights. I had insisted on some shadow.

Lucy began to sing. Her song was soft and melancholic, the keyboard and her voice the primary instruments, with a stripped-back guitar and drums on the chorus.

She reached the chorus, and I began to harmonise, my voice weaving softly beneath and around hers, a gentle, ethereal echo.

The audience fell away, and for a moment all I could see and hear was Lucy, and our voices entwined.

I was brought back down to earth by a cheer from the crowd. Our song was finished. The room snapped back to reality, and I saw the students clapping, their arms raised above their heads. Some were stomping their feet.

I brushed my hair from my forehead and found my skin clammy with sweat. But it wasn't from nerves this time.

I felt invigorated.

I felt alive.

I looked around at my bandmates and knew a moment of intense, uncomplicated happiness. Dan was grinning, James was laughing and Lucy, not usually given to theatrical displays of gratitude, threw both her hands up in the air and bowed.

# Cadence

'I can't believe I did it,' I said. I kept smiling. I couldn't help it.

'It was so cool!' Lucy grinned. 'We'll try the duet next time.'

We were back in my flat, which Lucy had entered without invitation. Dan and James had stayed on at the uni ball for another drink, but Lucy said that she was tired and wanted to get home, so I had gone with her.

She had apparently been lying, but I didn't care. This was a good night, and I was enjoying sharing our triumph.

I had poured us both a glass of wine, and we were sitting on the sofa.

Lucy nodded towards the pile of sheet music next to the keyboard. 'What's that?'

'Oh. I write songs sometimes.'

'Can I see?'

'Er... well, they're not very interesting...'

But Lucy had already reached the keyboard.

'You've been busy.' She picked up the first sheet, examined it briefly, and laid it aside. She did the same with the next sheet. 'What is this? It looks like a big project.'

I squirmed in my seat. I felt as if she'd stumbled across my private diaries. 'It's... er... well, they're sort of... rock songs.'

'You're *writing* rock now?'

'I'm afraid so.'

'Don't be daft. That's awesome.'

'It's not the sort of rock we play. It's more... melodic. Rock ballads, I guess.'

Lucy laughed, and I looked away. This situation was already excruciatingly embarrassing, and she hadn't even got to Angela's song yet.

'Oh my God! This is... wow. There's a lot of references to stars in this. A *lot*.'

I blushed. She'd found it. 'Yes.'

'And love. And the moon.'

'Yes. I'm not very good at lyrics.'

She continued to turn the pages. 'Will you play it for me?'

'Oh, I don't know—'

'Please? You've heard my songs. It's only fair.'

I sighed. I had really wanted Angela to be the first person to hear it, but perhaps getting another musician to listen would be no bad thing. And there didn't seem to be any way of getting out of it without sounding churlish.

'All right. But it's still a bit rough.'

Lucy made herself comfortable on the sofa. I perched uncomfortably on my desk chair.

The introduction was sweet and soft, and then my voice joined the music. It was a stereotypical rock ballad, three verses and a chorus which slowly built to a crescendo.

But as I played it, I found myself pulling back, making it gentler and more quietly rueful. It had occurred to me that it did not need bombast.

A soft voice joined mine for the final verse, and I turned to see Lucy leaning over my shoulder. Her hair brushed against my cheek. She ignored the separate parts for soprano and tenor, and instead sang in counterpoint, creating a melody of her own which seemed such an improvement on my written music, so much more subtle.

We finished the final chorus together, my voice high, her voice low.

We sat in silence for a moment. I turned to look at her. She smiled.

'My way is better,' she whispered.

Her eyes were soft.

I had seen that look before. It was the same look Ralph gave Angela in the Venetian music video.

Which was ridiculous. I must be mistaken.

I coughed and reached for a pen. 'Yes. You're right. I'll change it.'

'You'd better,' said Lucy. I kept my eyes focused on the music, but I could still feel her looking at me. She gave a low chuckle.

This made me turn around. 'What?'

'I just can't get over how good you look in that coat.'

'Oh.' I blushed and looked back at the music. 'Thanks.'

'It just seems so… incongruous. After all the pullovers.'

'I like my pullovers.'

Lucy laughed.

I grinned at her. 'I'll have you know I was a bit of a Goth at college. I used to wear things like this all the time.'

'Really? What changed?'

I was quiet for a moment.

'Nothing,' I said finally. 'Just my tastes.'

'Full of surprises, aren't you?' She gave an almost evil grin. 'Any other dark secrets I should know about?'

I squirmed a little in my seat.

Wait a minute… was she *flirting* with me?

'Um.' I swallowed hard.

'Come on, maestro. Out with it.'

'Well, if you must know, I have a tattoo.'

Lucy's eyes went wide. Then she gave a squeal of laugher. 'You're kidding me!'

I blushed. 'It's true.'

'You're having me on.'

'Why would I lie?'

'Okay, prove it.' She folded her arms. 'Show me.'

'Absolutely not.'

'Why? Is it somewhere private?'

'No!' I blushed even hotter. 'It's on my upper arm.'

'I'll never believe you unless you show me.' She held my gaze.

'Oh, fine,' I said. 'Anything to end this appalling conversation.'

I rolled up my sleeve as far as it would go.

Lucy was silent for a moment. Then she laughed again, as I'd known she would.

'A treble clef,' she said. 'Of course.'

I glowered at her. 'See? This is why I didn't want to show you.'

'May I ask why you got a treble clef tattooed on your arm? I mean, at what stage did that seem like a positive life choice?'

I sighed. 'I was eighteen and going off to the Conservatoire. I... guess I wanted it to remind me who I was and why I was going. Or something.' This was getting a little too embarrassing for comfort. 'Look, it was a summer of regret, fuelled by alcopops. What more can I say? It was also bloody painful.'

Lucy reached out and lightly traced the symbol with her finger. My arm came up in goosebumps, and I shivered.

'I like it,' she said. 'It's simultaneously cool and nerdy – a bit like you.'

She met my eyes again, and I saw that the soft look was back.

'I'm not nerdy.' My mouth had gone very dry.

She laughed gently. 'You're the biggest nerd I know.'

And then she was leaning forward. And then her lips were brushing against mine.

I jerked backwards as if I'd had an electric shock, arms flailing, knocking the sheet music from the keyboard and creating a musical avalanche.

Lucy stared at me. She looked surprised, even a little offended. 'Hey, I'm sorry—'

'No, no... I'm sorry...' Flustered, I bent down and gathered up the sheet music. 'I'm sorry, Lucy. I didn't mean to... do that.'

'What's wrong?' The soft look had gone from her eyes. 'Is there someone else?'

I was silent. I honestly had no answer to that.

'Er... kind of. I'm sorry.'

'No, no...' Lucy was on her feet, grabbing her coat and bag and guitar case. 'It was me. I made an assumption. Very stupid.'

She hurried over to the door, a mess of coat and bags, not looking at me.

'Lucy, wait. Please.'

'I think I should go.'

'I just—'

'It's fine. Night, Matthew.'

The door clicked shut behind her.

The sudden silence was as overpowering as any symphony.

Something caught my eye. Lying on the carpet, just in front of the door, was a small white card. Lucy had evidently dropped it.

I picked it up and turned it over. The words *Artists and Repertoire* were followed by some contact details.

My heart started racing.

Handsome Guy.

He was an A&R man.

A talent scout.

# Virtuoso

'The tickets are still going well,' said Jess, while I was looking over a possible running order for the concert.

'Good.'

She leaned forward in her chair and peered around the computer screens at me. 'The television people have emailed me again. They've asked if the Ghost's going to make an appearance.' She paused. 'Is he going to make an appearance?'

'I haven't decided yet.'

'Don't leave it too long, or they'll lose interest.'

'Hmm.'

My mind had been elsewhere for the last few days. I was worried that I had ruined my friendship with Lucy. My thoughts kept returning to our awkward kiss. I tried to reassure myself that it was nothing, that we were both a bit drunk and happy after our successful gig, that she would never have made such a move under normal circumstances.

Unfortunately, this train of thought didn't make me feel any better.

That evening, when everyone else had left the theatre, I went to the stage door to wait for the band.

Lucy was first to arrive. She looked tired: there were dark smudges under her eyes. I thought of the business card in my coat pocket. 'Hey, Matthew.'

I clasped my hands together. I couldn't quite meet her eyes.

'Lucy, I just wanted to say… I'm sorry again about the other night.'

She looked at me strangely. 'Why?'

I shuffled from foot to foot. 'I'm just worried I did something to upset you.'

Lucy sighed. 'Don't worry, Mr Dramatic. We're good.'

'We are?'

'Yes.'

'Right.' So it hadn't meant anything after all. 'That's... good.' I reached into my pocket and held out the business card. 'You dropped this in my flat.'

Lucy stared at the card. Her cheeks turned pink. 'Oh.'

'So, that man you were talking to... he was from a record label?'

Lucy took the card and pocketed it without looking at me. 'Yes.'

'He seemed very impressed with your voice. Did he... did he want to sign you?'

She did look at me then. There was desperation in her eyes. 'Please don't tell the others.'

'Why? You're not going to leave, are you?' I was surprised by how much this thought distressed me.

Lucy looked horrified. 'No, of course not.'

'Then why all the secrecy?'

She sighed. 'Because he wasn't just interested in me. He was only talking to me because I'm the lead singer. He's interested in the band. He was inviting us to an audition.'

I was silent. Our little band had label interest.

And Lucy looked appalled by the idea.

'But... isn't that good news? James and Dan will be over the moon.'

'You can't tell them.'

'Surely it's their decision, too?'

Lucy shook her head violently. 'You don't understand. I can't do it...'

Oh.

*Oh.*

Was it possible that Lucy also suffered from stage fright, as I did?

'It sounds like a great opportunity,' I said carefully. 'Maybe you shouldn't be so quick to throw it away.'

She scowled at me. 'That's a bit rich coming from you.'

I flinched.

Lucy's expression softened. 'Sorry. Sorry, Matthew – I shouldn't have said that.'

I shook my head. 'It's okay. It's just... you love performing. You always look so happy up there. I don't understand why you won't at least consider it.'

'Because I've been there before. I've done it all before, and it almost ruined music for me. That's why.'

I stared at her. 'What happened?'

Lucy looked conflicted, as if she was trying to decide whether to answer me or not. But then we saw Dan and James ambling down the street towards us.

Lucy gripped my arm. 'Please, Matthew. Please don't tell them.'

Her grip was tight. I looked at her pale, pleading face. 'All right. I won't tell them.'

She let out a sigh. 'Thank you.'

*

We began our rehearsal, but I couldn't concentrate. I kept glancing at Lucy, trying to fathom why the opportunity to audition the band had frightened her so much. She was a seasoned performer, far more confident than me.

And there was something else, too. Something born out of our almost-kiss, and her dismissal of it. A strange sort of emptiness.

I clumsily bashed my way through three songs. Lucy provided an unusually lacklustre vocal.

In short, neither of us sounded great.

'God, what's wrong with you both?' asked James, when we finally stopped for a break. 'It's like you're sleepwalking or something.'

'Sorry,' I said.

Lucy just shrugged.

'I don't understand,' said James. 'You were both on fire the other night. We all were.'

Lucy glared at him. 'Maybe we're just tired, James. Had you thought of that?'

James held up his hands. 'Sorry. Don't take it out on me.'

There was an awkward silence.

'How's the gala going, Matthew?' asked Dan, in an obvious attempt to change the subject.

'Fine. It's nearly sold out.'

Lucy looked up from her guitar. 'What?'

'It's nearly sold out.'

'Yeah, I heard that. But... how?'

'Because of this Ghost thing,' I mumbled.

'Ghost thing?' Lucy smiled for the first time that night. 'You mean *your* Ghost thing?'

James looked puzzled. 'What are you talking about?'

'Matthew's been using this place to practise his singing,' said Lucy. 'But one of the techies overheard him and thought he was a ghost. The Ghost's become a celebrity, hasn't he, Matthew? He has his own Twitter account and everything.'

James and Dan laughed.

I glared at Lucy. 'Yes. Thank you. Dave – the techie – recorded me while I was singing, and they've put my voice on YouTube...'

'This I must see,' said Dan.

A moment later, all three of them were peering at James's mobile, listening to the Ghost sing. I stood a few feet away, arms folded, glowering.

'Wow,' said James. 'You really can sing, can't you?'

'Yes,' I said. 'But now everyone's expecting the Ghost to reveal his identity at the gala. Do you see the problem here?'

'Not really. You're a singer, and they're giving you a chance to sing. It sounds amazing.'

'You were great the other night,' said Lucy.

'Thanks, but that was just harmonies. It's not the same as singing alone in a spotlight.'

'We could perform with you. Back you up.'

I shook my head. 'Thanks. But... it's not that simple.'

We packed away the instruments in silence. Dan and James said their goodbyes and left the auditorium.

Lucy laid a hand on my arm. 'What's wrong?'

'Nothing.' I swallowed the lump in my throat.

'You're upset.'

'I'm fine.' I zipped up the keyboard case. 'We should go.'

The chandelier flickered. There was a strange hum from the stage lights. Then the entire theatre was plunged into darkness.

'What?!' squeaked Lucy.

I reached out and found her arm. 'Are you okay?'

'Yes. What's happened?'

I sighed. 'It happens every few weeks. Sorry.'

A tiny but very bright torch beam hit me in the face. I realised it was coming from Lucy's phone.

'What should we do?' she asked.

'I'll have a look in the fuse box. It's sometimes a tripped switch... Could you bring your phone?'

Lucy followed me backstage, her phone torch lighting the way.

'Could you hold your torch up a bit?' I asked. 'Thanks.'

I peered into the fuse box. Lucy shone the torch inside.

'Matthew?'

'Yes?'

'Why don't you want to sing with us?'

'It's not you.'

'What is it, then?'

I frowned at the fuses. 'It's no good.'

'What?'

'I can't see the problem. I'm going to have to ring Dave.'

We went back to the auditorium, where I tried Dave from my own phone. As usual, there was no answer. I left a message.

'This could take a while,' I said. 'I can walk home with you and come back later if you like.'

'No, I'll stay.' The theatre seat creaked as she sat down. 'I'd like to talk to you.'

I sat down next to her. 'What about?'

'About what's going on with you. You're hiding something from us.'

I hesitated. Perhaps it would be good to confide in someone.

'If I tell you, will you promise to keep it to yourself?' I said.

'You know I will. Come on, maestro. Spill the beans.'

'You know you asked me if I'd ever recorded anything, and I said I hadn't?'

She nodded.

'Well, I wasn't entirely honest.'

'I knew it! Sorry... Go on.'

I sighed. 'It's probably easier if I show you.'

I brought up YouTube on my phone and searched for Angela's music video.

It came up straight away. I noticed it had had another 4000 views in the last three days.

I glanced at Lucy, still wondering if this was really such a good idea. But I was tired of lying to her. I was tired of lying, full stop.

I pressed play and handed her the phone.

She watched the video in silence for a moment, frowning in the glow from the screen. 'I don't understand. What am I looking at?'

'It's Angela, the singer I told you about. The other singer's my friend Ralph. He's miming.'

On the screen, Ralph started to 'sing'. Lucy looked up at me, her eyes wide in the torchlight. 'Wait... that's *you*.'

I nodded.

'But... this song's a big hit.'

'Yes.'

'Why is he miming to your voice?'

'When Angela invited me to be on the album, I thought I'd got over it—'

'Got over what?'

'When I was in my last year at the Conservatoire, I entered this singing competition with Angela. As a duo. The judges liked Angela, but they didn't like me. One of them said I looked wrong – that I should try plastic surgery.'

'What the actual hell? That's messed up.'

'It made me nervous about performing for years. I thought I'd finally conquered it, but I panicked during a rehearsal with Angela. So I asked Ralph if he would mime for me at concerts. And that's what we've been doing ever since.'

Lucy grimaced. 'But it's not fair. You're not getting any credit for it. Have you told anyone about this?'

'My sister knows. She may have told my parents – I'm not sure. I can't tell anyone else.'

'Why?'

I hesitated. 'This is the first time my voice has ever had this sort of exposure. I've just been too nervous. At least this way I'm being heard. It'll damage my career if I start telling people.'

'Why can't you just walk away? You've got us now.'

'Thanks, Lucy, but it's not that simple.'

'I don't understand...'

I shook my head. 'It's Angela. I want to sing with her.'

'I see.'

There was a moment of silence.

'I know it sounds mad,' I said.

'Yes. It does a bit. What does Angela think?'

'I think she... disapproves.'

'But she's going along with it?'

'It's not like that.' I swallowed. 'At the contest, the judges offered to put Angela through on her own, but she refused. She could have been famous years ago if it wasn't for me.'

'I'm sure that's not true.'

'So I can't sing at the theatre, as a soloist. Harmonies might be okay, but anything else is too risky. It might give the game away. Ralph's my oldest friend, and Angela... I just don't want to wreck things for them.' I glared at my phone. 'Where the bloody hell is Dave?'

'It sounds like they're taking advantage of you.'

'I'm sorry?'

'Angela and Ralph, and the record label. It sounds like you're being exploited.'

I shook my head. 'It was my idea. They gave me a chance... My only chance.'

'That's rubbish, and you know it.' Her expression was fierce in the wan light. 'I think you're too scared to do what you really want to do, which is sing as yourself, and you're just making excuses.'

'That's not true.'

Lucy was quiet for a moment. 'I'd like to show you something.'

'What?'

'Just give me a minute.' She began to scroll around on her phone. A moment later, music started to play.

It was violin music, and I recognised it immediately as Paganini's Caprice No. 24. Lucy thrust the phone into my hands. 'Here.'

It was another YouTube video. A teenage girl, no older than sixteen, stood on a candlelit stage, playing a violin with virtuosic skill. She sounded wonderful, but I had no idea why Lucy was showing her to me.

'I don't understand,' I said.

'That's me.' Lucy's voice was soft, and her face was partly turned away.

Since when did Lucy play the violin? Why had she never mentioned it before?

'You were amazing,' I said, transfixed by the music.

'You're missing the point. I was fifteen, Matthew. Have you any idea how much effort, how much practice it takes to get that good by the age of fifteen?'

I had always considered myself something of a talent on the piano, but listening to this video made me realise that Lucy's talent was in a different league entirely.

'No.'

'Lots, Matthew. Lots of practice. I loved my violin, but it took over my life. Stole my teenage years from me. I had a contract with a record label, and they insisted on sending me on this ridiculous concert tour. My life revolved around playing the violin. I had no time for anything else. No time for rest, no time for friendships, or my boyfriend. My schoolwork suffered.'

I thought back to our earlier conversation. 'So that's what you meant when you said you'd done it all before.'

'Yeah. When I was eighteen, I was due to go to a conservatoire, but by that time I'd had enough. I was exhausted, having panic attacks before concerts. So I walked away from it all. The contract, classical music, the violin... everything.'

I stared at her. 'That's so sad.'

'It's not. It's not sad. I gave it up so I could do something that would make me happy. I went to uni, and then I joined a rock band. And I found a way I could use music to help people.'

'But… don't you ever worry that you're wasting your talent?'

Lucy gave a short laugh. 'I did, sometimes, at first. But that's the thing. It's *my* talent. I can do what I like with it, or not. Yes, music is valuable. Yes, it's important and therapeutic. But, personally, I also think it's meant to be *fun*. If singing with Angela is making you unhappy, you should walk away.'

'What did your family think? About you giving up the violin.'

'My parents hit the roof. They didn't understand why I wanted to give it all up. Told me I was being silly.'

'Don't you think they were just worried about you?'

'They just didn't get it.' Her voice was hoarse. 'We barely speak.'

'Oh.' I thought of my own parents, at home in Newcastle. They had always encouraged me, and I knew my mum hoped that I would return to singing, but they had never been openly critical. 'I'm sorry.'

'It's just how it is.' Her voice shook. 'You'll think about what I said, won't you?'

'Yes.' I paused. 'Is this why you don't want us to go to that band audition?'

'When I walked away from… all that stuff, it took me a long time to start enjoying music again. I mean, a very long time. Years. It was only when I met James and Dan that I started to think of myself as a musician again. I love what we have with the band. I love making music, playing the odd gig. But the thought of doing that on someone else's terms… it scares me. Like I'd be giving up my freedom. And I know it sounds bloody selfish, because there are other people involved, but I'm honestly afraid it would break me. Do you understand?'

'I think so.' In truth, I wasn't sure I did. It was so hard to make a career in music that we were taught to seize every opportunity. I knew I should say something supportive, something comforting, but I had no idea what. 'Wouldn't you ever consider playing the violin again? I'd love to hear you.'

'You're missing the point again, Matthew.'

'Sorry. It's just... on the video, you look *transported*, as if you really love playing. Wouldn't you try it again now that the pressure's off?'

She was quiet for a moment, as if considering. 'I don't think so. It's been so long. I think I would disappoint myself. I'm not the girl in that video anymore.'

'But maybe if you just tried? Like I did with the karaoke... and the harmonies—'

'It's different.'

'Why?'

Silence.

'Lucy?'

'Do you think this Dave's going to show up soon?'

'I'll try him again.'

I brought up Dave's number and was just about to dial when I heard the auditorium door slam.

'That'll be him,' I said, standing up.

'Wow, it's dark in here,' said a voice.

I froze.

It wasn't Dave.

Lucy tugged my sleeve. 'Matthew?'

'Shush!'

'What's wrong?' she whispered.

A torch beam danced around the aisle.

'Wait a minute... I'll just get the lights,' said the voice. A pause. 'Damn. Must be another power cut.'

'It's Richard,' I hissed. 'Hide.'

I took Lucy's hand, and we crept backstage and into the wings. We tucked ourselves into the prompt corner just as the lights chose to come on again.

'Bugger,' I muttered.

'Who's Richard?' Lucy whispered.

'The owner. He hates me.'

'Sorry about that,' said Richard's voice. 'This place has a mind of its own.'

'Wow,' said a second, unfamiliar male voice.

'Ugly, isn't it? I've been saying to Charlotte for years that we need to lose the place. It isn't earning its keep.'

'I'm sure it isn't,' said the stranger.

'There's just too much competition out there. She wants to refurbish it, but I think it's a pipe dream. Much better to sell. Develop the land.'

My heart leapt into my throat.

'It is a prime spot,' said the other.

'I'd be grateful if you didn't mention this to Charlotte. At least not yet. I need to talk to her myself. But if you could get the valuation to me, that would be helpful.'

So Charlotte didn't know about this. That was why they were creeping around the place at night.

'That won't be a problem,' said the stranger.

'It's all a bit sad, really,' said Richard. 'She's organised this ridiculous variety show to raise funds, like something out of the 1950s. And they're pretending this singing phantom is haunting the place, and that he might perform on the night. As if that's going to save the place.'

He laughed. The stranger laughed, too.

I shook with rage.

Richard had no interest in saving the theatre. He wanted it razed to the ground.

'It'll be gone by next Christmas,' said Richard. He raised his voice. 'You hear that, Phantom? You'll have to move out!'

I felt my blood boil. *Yes, you evil bastard. The Phantom hears you, and the Phantom is fucking furious...*

I stepped forward, suddenly compelled to reveal myself and show Richard that I had heard every word.

Lucy grasped my arm, holding me back. The stage creaked beneath my foot.

'What was that?'

Footsteps stomped up the steps and onto the stage. I almost stopped breathing.

'Is there someone here?' said Richard, sounding less sure of himself.

The footsteps were coming closer. We huddled further into the prompt corner.

They stopped just short of our hiding place.

'Nobody there,' said Richard. 'It must have been the stupid old floorboards. God, this place gives me the creeps.'

The footsteps started to recede. The lights went out. I heard the auditorium door creak and slam.

I let out a choking breath and dived out of the wings, followed by Lucy.

She switched on her torch. 'Are you all right?'

'No. I'm not. I've never been so angry.'

'So that guy owns the theatre?'

'Co-owns it. He's going over his partner's head.' I clenched my fists. 'I have to do something.'

'What are you going to do?'

'I don't know yet.' But in truth, an idea was already forming in my mind.

Perhaps it was time for the Phantom to step out of the shadows.

\*

We walked home in silence. I said a hurried goodbye to Lucy, who looked at me worriedly.

'Don't do anything rash, Matthew.'

'I won't,' I said, and went into my flat.

Once alone, I switched on my laptop and opened the Phantom's Twitter account. Jess had done well: our ghost now had over 5000 followers. She was still posting regularly. I read her latest tweet:

@PhantomOfTheMoonAndStars: *Very excited about our big All-Star Gala! Have you got your tickets yet?*

I clicked through to the login screen and typed in the password Jess had given me in case I wanted to contribute.

I hesitated for just a moment, then started to type.

@PhantomOfTheMoonAndStars: *Hello. This is the Phantom speaking. My theatre desperately needs your help. I hear distressing rumours of demolition! Please buy tickets to our concert. Donate to our fundraiser, and I'll give a live performance on the night. #SaveTheMoonAndStars*

I stared at the tweet. I knew if I pressed send there was a strong possibility I would get sacked. Then again, if Richard got his way, we would all lose our jobs anyway.

I clicked send.

By this time, I was shaking so much that I decided to make myself a calming cup of tea. I drank it in the kitchenette, and tried to ignore the computer, which I was now strongly tempted to throw into the Thames.

Five minutes later, I risked a peek.

There were already dozens of replies, most of which expressed horror at the situation.

A familiar name caught my eye.

@AngelaNilssonOfficial had quoted the tweet, adding: *Horrible news. An old friend works there. Please let me know if there's anything I can do to help!*

My fingers hovered over the keys.

@PhantomOfTheMoonAndStars: *We would be delighted to welcome you as a guest star.*

I waited for a reply. There was none. I began to regret the message. She probably thought I was a creep. Meanwhile, my reply acquired lots of 'likes'.

There was a little ping from the computer. I stared at the screen.

@AngelaNilssonOfficial: *I'll see what I can do! Please contact my management with details.*

She'd tagged Chris's Twitter account. Oh God. This was going to be interesting.

I was trying to work out how I should approach Chris when my mobile rang.

Angela.

'The Phantom, I presume?' she said, when I answered.

'You knew it was me?'

'Of course I did, you weirdo.'

'Er... how did you know?'

'I recognised your voice from the YouTube video. And you work there. I'm not entirely stupid.'

'Oh.' Was she angry? I couldn't tell.

'Why didn't you tell me your theatre was in trouble?'

'Well, we haven't exactly talked very much over the last couple of months...'

A pause.

'We haven't, have we?' There was something odd in her tone. A hint of guilt? 'Sorry. I'd love to sing at your concert.'

'Oh... great! Thank you.'

'I'll talk to Ralph. Make sure he's up for it.'

My shoulders slumped slightly. I had been envisioning singing with Angela as myself, on the stage of my own theatre. 'Of course. Ralph.'

'That way, we can sing a duet. It'll be lovely.'

'Yes, yes. It will.'

'I'll have to explain this whole Phantom thing to Chris, of course. But it'll be good publicity for all of us.'

'Yes. I'm sure.'

'I'll call him right away.' She paused. 'Oh, and by the way, Matthew?'

'Yes?'

'We're having a little party next Friday to celebrate the success of the album. I know it's short notice, but I'd love to see you there.'

Her tone was warm, and my heart sped up. Angela was inviting me to her party. She was inviting me *personally*.

'Thanks. I'd love to.'

'Great! It's at Masquerade! on Piccadilly. Black tie dress code. I'll text you the address.'

'I'll be there.'

'Wonderful. I couldn't have done any of this without you.'

Warmth pulsed through me. Could all this mean that she actually returned my feelings? Did I dare tell her how I felt, right now, on the phone? She couldn't see me, so it might be the ideal opportunity.

'Angela, I just want to say...' I paused, flustered. 'I'm so glad we found each other again.'

'Me too.' I could hear the smile in her voice. 'Goodnight, Phantom.'

'Goodnight.'

# Sharp

I went into work the next morning with a great feeling of trepidation.

The first person I encountered was Dave, who was inspecting the fuse box.

'I take it you had no more trouble last night,' he said.

It took me a moment to realise what he was talking about. 'Oh. You mean the lights.'

'Yes.'

'No, no... they came back on in the end.'

Dave gave me a slightly odd look, and then turned his attention back to the fuse box.

Maybe no one from the theatre had looked at Twitter yet. In the cold light of day, I was wondering if I had acted too hastily. Perhaps I should delete the tweet before anyone else saw it.

I reached the office I shared with Jess. I grasped the door handle but stopped when I heard a raised voice.

'What on earth were you thinking?' It was Richard's voice. And Richard sounded furious.

I felt cold. It hadn't even occurred to me that Jess might take the blame for my actions.

'But I didn't... it wasn't—' Jess was obviously in tears.

'Do you think I'm stupid? I know you look after the Twitter account.'

I took a deep breath and opened the door.

Jess was sitting at her desk, her cheeks blotched with tears. Richard was glaring down at her.

'What's going on?' I said, as calmly as I could.

Richard turned his glower upon me. 'Oh, your wonderful assistant wrote some rubbish on Twitter saying the theatre's going to be demolished.'

'Yes? So what?'

'*So what?* For a start, it's not true.'

'Isn't it? I thought we were threatened with closure.'

Richard looked slightly uneasy. 'Well... even if it is, she had no right to go public. It's not her decision.'

'Matthew.' Jess sniffed. 'I swear I didn't write those things.'

'Who else could it have been?' Richard shook his head. 'You stupid girl.'

Jess gave another sob. I stared at Richard and realised I would have absolutely no regrets about exposing him.

'I won't tolerate you talking to my staff in that manner.'

Richard blinked. 'I beg your pardon?'

'You'll apologise to Jess at once.'

'Why should I? Don't you realise what she's done?'

'She hasn't done anything.' I looked him straight in the eye. 'It was me. I posted the message.'

'Matthew!' Jess gasped.

'You...' Richard turned towards the door. 'Just wait until I tell Charlotte about this.'

'Yes, tell Charlotte. Why not? I'm sure she'd be very interested to know what I overheard in the auditorium last night.'

'What?'

'I was there. I heard everything.'

Richard went red, his features contorting with rage. 'Get out!'

'What's going on?' Charlotte poked her head into the office. The three of us froze.

'Charlotte!' said Richard. 'I'm sorry, I didn't realise you were here.'

'Yes, that's obvious,' said Charlotte. 'What's all the shouting about?'

'Your precious "Matty" has been lurking around in the theatre after dark, without our permission.'

Charlotte looked at him levelly. 'I know, darling. Is that a problem?'

I stared at her in astonishment.

'You knew?' said Richard.

'Yes. He's been rehearsing late. He's been bringing his band. They're quite talented, but a bit loud for my taste.'

Richard opened his mouth, then closed it.

'What's going on?' said Charlotte again.

'Nothing,' said Richard.

'Matty?'

I looked at the floor. 'I posted something on Twitter as the Phantom. I said the theatre was under threat of demolition and asked for help.'

'I see,' said Charlotte. She turned to Richard. 'And is the theatre under threat of demolition? Is there something you're not telling me, Richard, darling?'

Richard seemed to shrivel under her sharp gaze.

'Look, it was just the one viewing,' he spluttered. 'I only wanted advice, to see how much the land would be worth, that's all...'

Charlotte blanched. She raised a shaking hand to her heart and clutched her gold necklace. 'You've been talking to buyers without my permission?'

'Not even a buyer, just a surveyor.'

Charlotte's face twisted in pain, her mouth falling open. She looked like the tragic half of a pair of theatrical masks.

'Oh, Richard,' she wailed. 'How *could* you?'

Richard threw up his hands. 'For God's sake, Charlotte! Do you really think there's any hope for this place? All you do is swan around in a dream, wearing your stupid costumes and talking about *handbaaags*. Some of us have to live in the real world.'

Anger flashed across Charlotte's face. 'I think you should leave. We can discuss this later.'

'Leave?' Richard looked confused. 'But this is my theatre, too.'

'You heard me,' said Charlotte. 'Get out!'

I watched in fascination as she seized my favourite stress ball, the one that wasn't actually a ball at all, but shaped like a banana. She hurled it at Richard. It bounced off his shoulder.

'*Get out!*'

'Okay, okay, I'm going. But don't come crying to me when you run out of money.'

Charlotte held up the stapler.

Richard made a swift exit.

Charlotte lowered the stapler and turned to look at me and Jess.

'So, darlings, I think it's about time you filled me in.'

# Waltz

It was the night of Angela's party.

Parties weren't exactly my favourite social events, but I had come up with an excellent plan to use the evening to my advantage.

1. I would dress in full evening wear, so Angela knew I was taking the dress code seriously.
2. At the very first opportunity I would ask to speak to Angela alone.
3. I would confess my feelings for her.
4. I would present her with the love song and ask if she would sing it with me at the Moon and Stars.
5. I would tell her I no longer wished to hide behind Ralph and explain that I felt confident singing as myself after my success at the rock gig.
6. I would find Ralph, buy him a beer, and thank him for all his help. This would free him to pursue his own career as a singer-songwriter.
7. I would find Chris and demand full credit for my work from now on.

It was going to be great.

\*

My confidence wavered the moment my taxi drew up outside the club.

I hadn't been to a club since I was at the Conservatoire, and something told me that Masquerade! (despite the unfortunate exclamation mark) was a completely different type of club from the one I had last visited when I was a student.

I had a horrible feeling it was going to be 'trendy'.

This was partly due to the people heading inside. The men were wearing suit jackets, of course, but some of them had their shirts partly unbuttoned; others were wearing jeans, and some actually had trainers on.

I hesitated on the pavement, wearing my evening suit complete with black bow tie and tailcoat. For a moment, I considered diving back into the taxi and going straight home. No one would ever know I had been there.

I took a deep breath. Running away was something the old Matthew would do. Not this new, assertive Matthew who played rock gigs. I was not going to run away. Not on such an important night. Not when Angela had invited me.

I straightened my shoulders and walked over to the entrance.

A large, suited bouncer was standing guard at the door, holding a clipboard and wearing an earpiece. I approached him with a smile.

'Name, please?'

'Matthew Capes.'

He scanned the printout on the clipboard.

'You're not on the list.'

'I'm a friend of Angela's. She invited me.'

'Sorry, sir. I can't let you in.'

'There must be a mistake…'

'Matthew?'

I looked up. Angela had appeared in the doorway. She was wearing a long silver evening gown, her hair held up with diamante grips. She looked like a star, in both senses: talent and astronomy. My heart gave a nervous thump.

'Hello,' I said.

Angela turned to the bouncer. 'Is everything okay?'

'This gentleman's name isn't on the list.'

'That's all right. He's a friend. You can let him in.'

The bouncer stepped to one side.

'I'm really sorry about that,' said Angela. 'Bloody Chris. I told him to put you on the list.'

'That's okay. No harm done.'

Angela smiled at me. 'Nice suit.'

'Thanks.' I tugged at my waistcoat, which was a little tight. I had bought the suit for my recitals at the Conservatoire, a long time ago now.

'I thought you weren't coming.'

'Traffic was bad.'

'Well, never mind – you're here now. Come on in.' Angela placed her hand lightly on my shoulder and guided me through another door.

I found myself in a bar with black chandeliers and leather seats. Instead of classical music, or even tasteful pop music, there was this awful pulsing dance beat which barely qualified as music at all. The place was crammed with people. I thought I vaguely recognised a few faces from the studio, and some people who might be slightly famous, but I couldn't be sure.

'Help yourself to a drink.' Angela pointed to the bar, which had been laid out with flutes of champagne. 'The label's paying.'

'Thanks.'

Angela picked up a glass. 'I've spoken to Ralph and Chris. We're so excited for your Phantom concert.'

'Great. Me, too.'

'It's good to see you.' Angela ran a finger around the rim of her glass. 'How have you been?'

'Okay, thanks. Apart from the stage fright thing, but I think I'm finally getting on top of that.'

*Confident. Assertive. Good.*

'I'm so glad. I was worried about you.' Angela's expression was warm, a slight smile on her lips. Perhaps this was the moment.

The song was in my jacket pocket. Best just to give it to her and wait for a reaction. I reached for the envelope.

'Angela, there's something—'

'Matthew. Great to see you.'

My hand left my pocket, and I forced a smile. I'd known he'd be here, of course. I'd just hoped to avoid him for a little while; long enough for me to have a private conversation with Angela.

'Hello, Ralph.'

There was something different about Ralph. He was as polished as ever, dressed in a very smart grey suit, although I noted he also hadn't bothered to wear a tie. But his posture had a strange sort of tension I had never seen before. He almost looked suspicious.

Then he smiled, and suddenly the old Ralph was back. 'Thanks for coming.'

'No problem.' I wondered why Ralph was thanking me for coming. After all, we were celebrating the album, and I had as much right to be there as him, if not more.

'It really means a lot,' said Ralph. 'Doesn't it, Angie?'

He put his arm around her.

'Yes,' said Angela. 'It does.'

She leaned into his embrace, putting her own arm around his waist.

I stared at them both.

I had the sensation of something opening up inside me, a cold hollow at my centre, a wound without heat.

'The stage is set, if you want to do it now,' said Ralph.

'Are you sure you're okay with this?' said Angela. 'You're ready?'

'Yes,' said Ralph, giving her a look of such softness that my breath caught in my throat.

'Great,' said Angela. She gave me a polite smile, the sort of smile reserved for acquaintances, or work colleagues. 'You'll have to excuse us, Matthew. It's lovely to see you. Maybe we can catch up later?'

'Yes,' I said dully. 'Lovely to see you, too.'

I watched them walk away, looking like a glossy celebrity couple from the front page of *Hello!* magazine. *Of course.*

I turned away and took a glass of champagne from the bar.

'Of course,' I said aloud.

The barman gave me an odd look. 'Pardon me?'

'Nothing.'

I stood at the bar, my back to the rest of the room. I drank my champagne but didn't enjoy the taste.

I knew I should leave. There was no longer any point in staying. Not if Angela was going to spend the entire evening with Ralph.

Placing my empty glass on the bar, I turned to go and came face to face with Chris. Much to my surprise, he was also wearing an evening suit, complete with dinner jacket and black bow tie. He even had a golden waistcoat.

He stared at me and blinked, his forehead creasing in a frown. 'Matthew. I didn't know you were coming.'

This was all the proof I needed to know that he didn't want me there. Hadn't he been asked to put my name on the guest list? I was embarrassed but determined not to show it.

'Hello, Chris.'

'Angie invite you, did she?'

'Yes.'

'She's great like that, Angie. Anyway, good you could make it.'

'Thanks. I'd better go.'

'So soon? Aren't you going to stay for the speech?'

'Speech?'

'Angela's going to say a few words, a few thank yous.'

'Sorry, but I really have to go—'

'I want to say something, too.' His voice was wistful. 'There are lots of things I want to say. But I learned a long time ago that I'm not exactly at home in the spotlight.' He looked at me, and I noticed his eyes were bloodshot, as if he had been drinking heavily, or crying, or both. 'We're two of a kind, you and me. We do all the work and spend our lives standing in other people's shadows.' He raised his champagne glass. 'Here's to us!'

Drunk. Definitely drunk.

'Yes, well... I didn't feel I had much choice, Chris.'

'Nor me, Matt, mate. Nor me. Ah! Here we go. Showtime!'

Someone turned off the background music, and the lights came up. The club suddenly looked stark, and a little too bright, like a gymnasium. The intimate atmosphere evaporated.

'Ladies and gentlemen, may I have your attention, please?'

The rumble of conversation died down, and people started turning towards the stage.

Angela had taken her place at the microphone. Her gown sparkled. Ralph stood on the stage, too, a little to one side.

Angela smiled out at the audience.

'Hi, everyone. Thank you so much for coming here tonight. I've made some great friends since I embarked on this adventure, and I'm so grateful for all your support. So thank you.'

A few people started to clap. Chris raised his champagne glass and whooped. Angela nodded and smiled and held up her hands, asking for quiet.

'Thank you so much. Tonight we're here to celebrate the new album, which has been more successful than I could ever have hoped.' She paused and glanced at Ralph. 'And there's another reason why we've asked you all here. Ralph?'

She beckoned to Ralph, who came forward to join her. She took his hand.

'As some of you know, Ralph and I have become very close over the past few months. And tonight there's something we'd like to share with you all.'

She turned and looked into Ralph's eyes. In return, he gave her a look of pure, uninhibited adoration. I had never seen him look so *open* before.

My heart was racing. What the hell was going on? Whatever it was, I knew I didn't like it.

'We want you all to know that we're engaged!' said Angela. She gave a bright laugh.

There were cheers, whoops and several *awww*s from the assembled guests. Angela looked at Ralph with that same besotted expression on her own face.

And they kissed.

And the cold hollow inside me broke open until I feared I would be sucked into it.

I watched as Ralph swept Angela up into his arms and spun her around, twice, while they both laughed.

There was a movement at my shoulder. I turned and saw Chris. His face was a picture of astonishment.

A new sound found its way into my shocked brain. Someone had turned the music back on, but this time it was no generic dance beat. Instead, a familiar piano introduction began, augmented by strings.

And then Angela started to sing, and then I started to sing. Or rather, my voice did. It sang outside of me.

It was the single. *My* single. The first song Angela and I had recorded together.

They were playing our song.

Our voices rang out, entwining in harmony. I felt my face start to burn. Sweat broke out on my forehead. My tenor was clear and passionate and I sounded like a man in love.

There was another sound, too. A sort of gasping. Angela broke away from Ralph and looked straight at me.

Then I realised it wasn't only Angela who was staring at me, but Ralph, too, and most of the other guests.

There was a moment of stillness while my voice crooned away in the background. My heart was thudding so hard I could feel it in my head. I touched my cheek. It was wet.

'Are you all right, mate?' asked Ralph, from the stage.

'Fine,' I said. 'I'm fine. I just… need some fresh air.'

I turned and ran. The guests parted to let me through. I reached the front door and dived onto the street. I couldn't stand the exposure beneath the bright lights of the Masquerade! club. And most of all, I couldn't stand the sound of my own voice, imprisoned on a recording, singing of a love I would never have.

# Crescendo

'Matthew!'

Angela's voice brought me to a halt. I turned and saw her framed in the doorway. A confused-looking Ralph peered over her shoulder.

'What do you want?' I sounded tired.

She took a tentative step towards me. 'Are you okay?'

'Yes, Angela, of course I'm okay. I'm more than okay. I'm hunky-bloody-dory.'

'Hey! Don't talk to her like that.' Ralph laid a hand on Angela's shoulder.

'Oh, I'm sorry, Ralph. Have I upset you?'

He glared at me. 'Yes, you have, a little.'

'Didn't you stop to think how that little stunt might have upset me?'

'What little stunt?' asked Angela.

'Oh, I don't know – using our song as emotional underscoring for your engagement announcement?'

'It's our party,' said Ralph. 'We can do what we like.'

'Yes. You always do, don't you?'

Angela stepped forward. 'What's wrong with you? I don't understand why you're being like this.'

I was silent.

Ralph's eyes went wide. 'Matthew... are you jealous?'

I folded my arms. 'No.'

'You are! You're jealous. You're too much of a coward to even go *onstage* yourself, so you make everyone else's lives miserable instead.'

Angela shot him a glare. 'Ralph, that's enough.'

'What? It's true, isn't it?'

I stared at Ralph, with his self-confidence and good looks and utter lack of integrity.

'How *dare* you? You wouldn't even be here if it wasn't for me. You've got everything you want, haven't you? Fame, admiration, a ready-made career. And you haven't had to work for any of it! I gave you my *voice*, and you dare to accuse *me* of making *your* life miserable!'

Ralph's face hardened. 'You know nothing about me. Not one fucking thing.'

'I've known you since school!'

'So bloody what? People change! You've changed. The Matthew I knew at school wouldn't dream of ruining his best friend's engagement party, because he wasn't a selfish bastard.'

'I'm not selfish.'

Ralph laughed. 'That's not what the evidence suggests, mate. You're currently having a hissy fit over some stupid song.'

I clenched my fists. 'What do you know? You don't care about music. You just care about fame, about getting your face splashed around on pretty posters. As long as you're handsome and can strike dramatic poses in front of a camera, who cares if you've got no talent?'

Angela gasped. 'Matthew!'

Ralph was silent. There was hurt in his eyes. Then his face hardened again. He shook his head and gave a harsh laugh.

'You think I don't care about music? I've spent years – *years* – busking on the streets. I've played in bands; I've gone to auditions.

And you think because you've got some fancy certificate from some fancy college you're better than me?'

I didn't know how to answer that because, honestly, I didn't feel better than anyone. I felt like shit.

'No,' I said finally.

Ralph snorted and turned away.

'Matthew.' Angela's voice was unexpectedly soft. 'What Ralph said... is it true? Are you jealous?'

I couldn't look at her, but I nodded. Why deny it?

'Why?' she asked.

I gave a short laugh. 'I thought it was obvious.'

'Well, it isn't.'

I felt my anger drain away, leaving only that awful, tugging coldness in my chest.

'I thought, when you contacted me, that there might be a chance,' I mumbled.

'A chance of what?'

'Us.'

'What do you mean?'

'I hoped we could try again.'

There was a long silence. Then Angela shook her head. 'God, Matthew. You really pick your moments, don't you?'

'Woah,' said Ralph. 'Hang on. You told me you were never with Matthew.'

'What?' My voice was soft.

'I wasn't,' said Angela. 'Not like that.'

'So what *was* it like? Do you still have feelings for him?'

Angela had gone very pale. She gripped Ralph's hand. 'There's nothing going on. I promise. There never has been. We *work* together. Do you really think I would lie about a thing like this?' She turned to me. 'Matthew, tell him!'

There was nothing to lose now.

I might as well admit it.

'I loved you,' I said. 'I still love you.'

Angela and Ralph both stared at me. The anger had vanished from Angela's face, to be replaced by something much worse. She looked hurt.

'No, you didn't,' she said. 'You don't.'

'I do.'

Ralph looked at me as if he had never seen me before.

'I can't believe this,' he said. 'You self-centred little...'

I stared down at the paving stones. 'I'm sorry, Ralph.'

'Sorry? *Sorry?* Have you any idea what you've done?' He turned towards the door.

'Ralph, wait...' Angela grasped his hand again, but he shook her off.

'I'm going to make sure our guests are all right,' he said. 'I think you and Matthew should have an honest talk, and then maybe you'll be able to tell me how you really feel.'

His voice broke, and he rushed back into the club.

Angela glared at me. 'Happy now?'

I dropped my gaze to the pavement again. 'I'm... sorry. I just wanted you to know the truth.'

'The truth? Matthew, you walked out on me. At the showcase. And then I never heard from you, not for years. And now you think it's appropriate to tell me you love me? What's *wrong* with you?'

I jerked my head back. 'I didn't walk out on you. You just went ahead and sang with someone else.'

'I tried to explain, and you just stormed off—'

'You said you couldn't sing with me.'

'You were obsessed with what that judge said. You wouldn't listen to reason. What was I supposed to do? I had to have a back-up.'

'But...' My voice sounded far away. 'You were my closest friend. We were practically dating—'

'Are you serious? Matthew, we were not *dating*. You never wanted to go out with me. You only ever liked me for my voice.'

'That's not true.'

'Isn't it?' She paused. 'I can't remember us ever having a proper conversation that wasn't about music. Music, music, music, all the bloody time. Have you any idea how *boring* that is? How boring *you* are?'

And there it was.

The truth.

Of course Angela didn't care about me. Why should she? I was the ugly, music-obsessed freak who she tolerated because he was good at something.

God. What had I been thinking?

'Right.' I was still staring at the pavement, wishing that I could just dissolve into a puddle among the chewing gum and cigarette stubs. 'I... see. I thought we were at least friends. But I guess not.'

Light spilled onto the paving stones.

'Hey... guys?'

Chris was standing in the doorway. The top two buttons of his shirt were undone, his bow tie hung loose around his neck and his forehead shone with sweat. He held a champagne bottle in one hand.

'What is it, Chris?' snapped Angela.

Chris swayed slightly. 'Everyone's waiting for you. The press are here.'

'You invited the *press* to my party? Are you insane?'

'Yeah. And some bloggers. Thought it might be good whatsit. PE.'

'You mean PR?'

'That's the one. I said you'd sing.'

'What?'

'I said you'd sing so they could film it. I thought it would be good promo for the next album. Matt can sing from behind the bar.'

'For God's sake, Chris. What were you thinking?'

Chris staggered, splaying his hand against the wall. 'Sorry, Angie.'

She folded her arms. 'No way. I'm not doing it.'

'Oh, come on, Angie, where's the harm?'

'I'm going to find Ralph,' said Angela. 'And I want both of you to leave us alone.'

She marched back into the club.

Chris blinked at me blearily. 'Can you talk her into it?'

I shook my head. 'I'd better go.'

'No, Matt, my man... don't go. Stay and get drunk with me.' Without warning, he lurched towards me, lost his balance, and fell forward. I caught his arms just in time.

'You're already drunk.'

'Am I? What a pity... Where's Angie?'

'She's gone inside.'

'Oh, yes. To find *him*. She's going to marry... *him*.'

'I know.'

Chris pulled away from me, sank to his knees and burst into dramatic tears.

I stared down at him, unable to believe what I was seeing. I wanted to walk away, to leave the insufferable bully to wallow, but I was frozen to the spot.

He looked up at me with red eyes. 'You understand, Matt, don't you? You get where I'm coming from?'

'Get up, Chris.' My tone was flat.

'It was great when it was just me and Angie... but I wasn't enough. Sad thing is, I always knew that. You get it, don't you?'

My mouth had gone dry. 'I think we should get you inside.'

I offered my hand to Chris. Shakily, he rose to his feet, and leaned on me for support.

'I'm so glad you understand... I'm so glad... someone does...'

'Okay...'

I managed to steer him inside the nightclub. The harsh, bright lights had been turned down again, and someone had put the dance music back on. I looked around for Angela and Ralph, but they were nowhere to be seen.

A few curious guests glanced in our direction, but Chris seemed oblivious, continuing his nonsensical litany.

'It's like I said... we're not so different. We're very much... what do you call it? The same.'

I pushed Chris into a dim booth at the very back of the club.

'I'm nothing like you, Chris. I don't know why you keep saying that.'

He grasped my sleeve. 'They'll take all your music... whatever they want... then throw you away.'

'Who? You're not making any sense.'

'People like me!'

'Right.'

'I wasn't always... like me. I was going to be a composer.'

'Okaaaay...'

'All gone. All of it... gone.' He covered his face with his hands.

'I have to go,' I said.

'No, stay,' he sniffed. 'Please. Stay and have a drink.'

'I think you've had enough. So have I.'

'C'mon. Just one more. What's the harm?'

I looked at Chris and thought: *Fuck it. Why not?*

I fetched more champagne.

# Solo

I awoke with a terrible headache, as if someone was banging a timpani drum behind my eyes.

I glanced at the clock; it was a little before noon. For a moment I couldn't think why I had slept in so late. Then I saw the empty champagne bottle on my bedside table, and memories of the party came rushing back.

I slumped against the pillows and spent the next half hour reliving my argument with Angela.

*You only ever liked me for my voice.*

*You were obsessed with what that judge said.*

*You walked out on me...*

This was the part that made no sense. It was Angela who had turned away. I remembered the rejection. I had left the Conservatoire the next day and returned home, where I had stayed ensconced in my bedroom for almost two weeks. Clara had diagnosed a broken heart.

Angela had remembered it all wrong... hadn't she?

I fixed my eyes on the ceiling and forced my mind to return to that day in 2008.

*

The student showcase was the most important event before graduation. I knew there would be talent scouts there, and agents. Many previous students had been given their first professional opportunity because of their performance at the showcase. But the words of the judge at the talent contest kept echoing in my mind. He was a professional. What if there was some truth in what he said?

So I had taken decisive action. I had gone to a hairdresser and asked them to cut my long, thick hair. Then I had paid a visit to the makeup counter at Boots and left with a tube of concealer to cover the last of my teenage blemishes.

I thought I had my nerves under control, but on the night of the performance, I found myself unable to leave the dressing room. The other students had already left to wait in the dance studio adjacent to the theatre, to chat and warm up. I was alone.

I looked at myself in the mirror, smoothing my tuxedo with shaking hands. I leaned forward and peered at my face. The concealer hadn't been hard to apply. It was no different from wearing any other stage makeup. The bulbs around the mirror glared at me, illuminating every inch of my face with their unforgiving light.

Grasping the edge of my dressing table, I took a breath, and berated myself. 'Come on. Get a grip.'

A hand touched my shoulder. I looked up and saw Angela's face next to mine in the mirror.

'Are you ready?' she asked.

'Just… give me a few minutes.'

Her brow furrowed. 'They're starting in fifteen. Are you okay?'

My breath was rapid and shallow. Angela's face crumpled in concern.

'What's the matter?'

'I don't think I can do this.'

'What?'

'I'm too nervous...'

A long pause.

'Okay... well... come out when you're ready.' She started to turn away.

Angela was my friend. My only real friend at the Conservatoire. Panic flared inside me: I didn't want her to go.

'Wait...' I said.

She turned to look at me.

'What?'

'It's just... I can't... I'm not...'

The words swirled in my head. I couldn't make them fit together. My legs felt weak. I didn't think I would be able to walk out of the dressing room, never mind reach the stage.

She frowned. 'I have to go. Come and find me if you think you can go on. Okay?'

My bottom lip was trembling. I bit it to make it stop. 'Okay.'

She hesitated a moment, then left me.

I remained at the dressing table, taking gulps of sour air. A loud electric bell tore through the dressing room. Our ten-minute call.

I forced myself to straighten my shoulders. I could do this. I was a singer. This was who I was.

I shakily made my way out of the dressing room and reached the dance studio. The room was packed with students. Some of them stood alone, intense with concentration, clearly 'in the zone' as my singing teacher liked to call it. Others stood in pairs or in small groups, practising. The air was filled with chatter and song. The walls were lined with mirrors, so it seemed like there were twice as many students as there should be, their voices bouncing off the glass. I felt deeply peculiar, as if I was trapped in a mirror maze at a fairground. Disorientated. I stumbled slightly and put my hand against a mirror for support. I stood there for a moment, trying to catch my breath and to stop my head spinning.

Feeling slightly better, I looked around for Angela, but I couldn't see her, so I closed my eyes and searched for her voice. The cacophony in the room made it hard to concentrate, but after a moment I caught a snatch of our chosen song, delivered in a familiar soprano. I opened my eyes and followed the voice like an audible thread, weaving my way between the students.

Angela was standing in the far corner. Her back was to me, but I recognised her blonde hair and long golden evening gown. She let out a trill of silvery notes. I opened my mouth, ready to sing the next phrase and prove to her that I could do this. But before I could sing, another voice swooped into the gap: a light, lyrical tenor.

I could see him now, the other singer. He was handsome. And tall. I recognised him from last year's production of *Oklahoma!* He had played Curly, the male lead. His voice wasn't as good as mine, though. I hadn't realised that Angela knew him. Maybe he was helping her rehearse while she waited for me to arrive.

I tapped her on the shoulder. She jumped and spun around.

'Matthew! Hi.'

'Sorry about that. I'm not sure what came over me.'

'That's okay.' She indicated her friend. There was something a bit sheepish in her expression. 'This is Harry.'

'Hello, Harry,' I said.

'Harry, this is *Matthew*.'

'Ah,' said Harry. 'Right. Yes. Of course. Hi, Matthew.'

He was very posh, like a stereotypical Shakespearean actor. Weird choice for Curly.

The three of us stood there for a moment, looking at each other and not saying anything. I was expecting Harry to leave us alone to rehearse, but he didn't.

I looked at Angela. 'Do you want to run through the song?'

'I think I'm okay.'

'I'd feel better if we ran through it.'

There was a pause.

'So,' said Harry, looking at Angela. 'Are we doing this?'

'Doing what?' I asked. 'What's going on?'

'You're nervous. You were hiding in the dressing room...' Angela sounded near to tears.

'What's wrong?'

'I'm sorry. It's just... tonight's too important. I can't risk getting it wrong. There are agents out there. I... asked Harry to stand in for you.'

I stared at Harry, unable to speak.

Then understanding dawned, and a terrible ache bloomed across my chest.

'This is because of that judge, isn't it? Because of what he said.'

Angela's eyes widened. 'No! Of course not!'

Her protest was too strong. I wasn't at all convinced.

'It is, isn't it?' I looked down at the floor. 'You're ashamed to be seen with me—'

'It's not like that at all.'

'Oh, yes? Then what is it like?' I looked up, met her eyes. 'You think I'm ugly. You're worried I'm going to show you up. Just like at the contest.'

'That's not true.'

'No? Look at me and tell me I'm wrong.'

Angela was silent. She couldn't meet my eyes. Her gaze slid down to her feet.

Another loud bell tore through the theatre. The five-minute call.

'Angela?' Harry touched her arm. 'Are we doing this?'

I looked at them both. I couldn't deny that Angela had made a good choice. They looked right together. Something inside me wilted, my anger dying.

'Oh, just sing with him. See if I care.' My voice broke on a sob. I whirled around.

'Matthew—'

'I don't want to hear it.'

'Please don't leave.'

'What do you expect me to do?'

Ignoring the curious glances of the other students, I stormed towards the exit.

'Wait! You've got it all wrong... Matthew, stop...'

*

My eyes flew open.

Oh, no...

Angela was *right*.

I could draw several conclusions from this:

1. Angela's rejection hadn't been personal. It had been born of self-preservation. She had been genuinely worried that I wouldn't be able to sing.
2. On the plus side, this meant she hadn't rejected me because she thought I was ugly.
3. But also: I hadn't been dumped, because we had never been a couple.
4. Her friendship with me had been entirely professional.
5. Our thwarted student romance had occurred entirely in my head.
6. What had I been thinking?

I groaned and turned over in bed, burying my right cheek in the pillow and pulling the duvet over my head. I wanted to hide from the world and everyone in it, especially Angela.

I had even written her a love song. Who the hell did I think I was? The guy in *Moulin Rouge*?

At least I hadn't actually given her the song. That had saved me one extra humiliation. Now that I really thought about it, it wasn't even a particularly *good* song. Well, it could go straight in the bin.

I hauled myself out of bed.

My tailcoat and evening trousers were lying in a forlorn pile on the bedroom floor. I picked up the coat and reached into the inside pocket.

I froze.

The envelope was gone.

I searched the other pockets in both my coat and my trousers. I turned each one inside out. There was no sign of the song.

I began to pace frantically around the room, trying to remember what had happened.

Almost everything after my first drink with Chris was now lost in a haze of cheap champagne. I could only recall flashes: the pair of us staggering out of the club after almost everyone else had gone; trying to hail a taxi while Chris sang 'Sweet Caroline' at the top of his lungs; Chris saying he fancied a kebab and abruptly disappearing; creeping upstairs to my flat and almost falling over in the dark. But no memories of the song.

I thought back further, to when I had last seen the song. I had been about to give it to Angela. It had been in my hand. Ralph had come over. Then I had gone to prop up the bar...

I must have left it on the bar.

I tensed with horror. Somewhere in a club on Piccadilly, there was an envelope with Angela's name on it. And inside the envelope, there was a handwritten love song, and a little note that said: *With love from Matthew.*

And I had left it at her engagement party.

Oh, shit.

I grabbed my phone and began to search for a number for the club. Maybe the song was still there. I could ask them to throw it away.

It only took me a moment to find their contact details. A woman answered the phone.

'Hello, Masquerade! Piccadilly. How can I help you?'

'Hello. I was at your club last night, and I think I left something. An envelope.'

'Like, a letter?'

'Yes.'

'Please hold. I'll check lost property.'

I waited, my heart hammering.

She returned a minute later. 'No envelopes. I'm sorry.'

'Do you think it could have been thrown away?'

'I think there's a good chance. Sorry.'

'No, that's okay. Thank you.'

I ended the call.

So it wasn't at the club. What if that meant Ralph had found it? What if he had broken up with Angela because of me?

There was only one thing for it. I would have to call Ralph, apologise and make sure he hadn't found the song.

I took a deep breath and dialled his number. The phone rang and rang, and eventually went to voicemail. I didn't dare leave a message.

*

I pulled on a pair of jogging bottoms to complement my wrinkled white evening shirt and spent the next couple of hours on the sofa, watching television and eating. I ate a whole packet of Haribo, and later I had a banana to balance things out.

I watched a show about people looking at houses I would never be able to afford, followed by another show about people attending interviews for high-powered jobs, and then a final show about big, expensive weddings. After a while, I decided the television was deliberately trying to torment me and turned it off.

Why had everyone apart from me managed to get their lives sorted? First my sister, and now Angela and Ralph. How had they managed to achieve all these things, while I was forever blundering about in the dark?

Occasionally my phone would ping, and there would be a text from Angela.

12.58pm: *Please call me.*
1.16pm: *We need to talk.*
2.30pm: *Where are you?*

I ignored them, because what was there to say?

At 3pm someone started knocking on my front door. Then a voice called out: 'Matthew? Are you there?'

'Leave me alone.'

'Matthew, it's Lucy.'

Sighing, I put on my dressing gown to hide the evening-shirt-and-jogging-bottom combo and opened the door.

'Yes?'

Unlike me, Lucy was fully dressed. She was also carrying her guitar case.

She wrinkled her nose at me. 'What happened to you?'

'I was at a party last night. It... didn't go well.'

She frowned. 'Are you still coming?'

'Coming where?'

'We have a rehearsal. Remember?'

I had forgotten, but now the plans for the afternoon came back to me. I had promised the band access to the theatre, so we could run through the set for the fundraising concert.

I stared at the floor. 'I can't, Lucy. I'm sorry.'

'Because of a hangover?'

'It's not that.'

'Then what is it?'

'I… can't tell you. But you can still rehearse.' I unhooked my theatre keys from their place by the door. 'Here.'

'Matthew. The gig's tomorrow. What could possibly be so important?'

Tears pricked my eyes.

'I won't be playing the gig,' I said.

'What?'

'I'm sorry, Lucy.'

'Why? What's happened?'

I shook my head and turned away. Lucy followed me into the flat.

'Matthew?'

'I'd like to be alone, if you don't mind.'

'I think, after all the time we've spent rehearsing for this concert, that you owe me an explanation—'

'Angela's getting married.' I slumped onto the sofa. 'She's engaged to Ralph.'

A silence.

'Oh,' Lucy said finally. 'And that's stopping you from playing the gig because…?'

'You don't understand. I told her how I feel about her.'

Another silence.

'And how do you feel about her?'

'I…' I hesitated. That was a very good question. I loved Angela. Of course I did. Didn't I? 'I suppose I thought we had some sort of… connection. But it turns out she hates me. She thinks I'm some boring loner who only cares about music.'

Lucy sat down next to me. 'She said that?'

'Not in so many words, but that's what she meant. I don't know why I'm surprised. It's what everyone else thinks.'

Lucy sighed.

'Matthew, that is self-pitying bullshit of the highest order.'

'But Angela said—'

'Right. And this is the same Angela who was quite content to let her fiancé take all the credit for your singing?'

'He wasn't her fiancé then. And that's not what happened. It was my idea.'

'Uh-huh. It still seems a bit shallow.'

'Angela's not shallow. She's... She's...' I tailed off. What was Angela like? 'She has a beautiful voice. I don't blame her for putting that first.'

'Uh-huh.'

'Will you stop saying that? It's all right for you. You don't have to put up with this nonsense. You're not a professional musician anymore—'

'*What?*' The anger in her voice made me freeze. 'What did you just say?'

'I only meant that you can't possibly understand. Angela and I... we're both singers. Proper, professional singers—'

'Yeah. And I'm just a singer in a crap pub band.'

'You're twisting my words.'

'Am I? Are you quite sure about that?'

I was silent.

Lucy stared at me for a moment. The look of anger fell from her face, to reveal hurt underneath.

'You know what, Matthew?' Her voice was weary. 'I'm *done* here. I've tried again and again to get through to you. I thought we were friends. But you're so *obsessed* with pleasing these people that you're neglecting the people who are actually there. The people who actually care about you. If you just took the time to look around occasionally, you might see that you're not alone. But I'm not going to play second fiddle anymore. So come to the rehearsal or stay here and wallow. It's entirely your choice. But I'm *done* with you.'

Then she was gone. The door closed behind her, and I heard her thumping down the stairs.

I realised I was shaking.

Lucy was wrong. I couldn't go to the rehearsal.

It would be much better for everyone involved if she found someone else.

If I tried to perform, I would only let her down, just like I had let everyone down at the student showcase.

*

After my confrontation with Angela and Harry, I'd locked myself in the dressing room and tried to stop crying. I wiped my eyes on my sleeve, leaving streaks of makeup on the velvet cuffs of my evening suit.

I took several ragged breaths and told myself that I was being ridiculous. I needed to calm down, and quickly. The duets were only one element of the showcase. There were solo slots for the students, too. If I missed my slot I might never have such a good opportunity again, and it would be a major flaw on my spotless record of achievement at the Conservatoire.

I touched up the concealer as best I could, straightened my jacket, and left the dressing room.

Angela was waiting outside. 'Matthew—'

'I hope your duet went well,' I said, without looking at her.

'Matthew, wait, you don't have to do this…'

I ignored her and carried on walking. I reached the wings and waited, trembling, in the darkness.

When my turn came, I listened to my singing teacher praising my voice.

I took my position onstage, a place I had always felt at home.

But not anymore.

My voice emerged as a faint echo of its former self, fading away into nothing.

*

'What happened out there, Matthew?'

The student showcase was almost over, but I was not in the theatre. I was sitting in my singing teacher's office. The professor had been responsible for training my voice during my three years at the Conservatoire. I hated to disappoint her.

The office was elegant, with dark wooden furniture and burgundy leather armchairs. I had sat in this same chair for my entrance interview. On that day, the professor had seemed kind, and the surroundings were impressive and special, affording me a glimpse into an exclusive world which I longed to join. Now, the room just felt intimidating.

I stared at the polished wood floor. 'I don't know.'

'Is this about the talent contest?'

I flinched. 'How do you know about that?'

'Angela told me.'

I shrank further into the chair, curling my arms around myself in shame.

The professor sighed. 'Come on, Matthew. You're one of our best students, but you really need to toughen up.'

'I'm sorry.'

'I've spoken to my colleagues, and to some of the guests. They've agreed to stay an extra five minutes so you can sing again.'

I looked up at her. 'Wh-what?'

'It's all arranged.' She smiled.

I clutched the arms of the chair, my fingers digging into the leather. 'I... can't.'

She blinked. 'I'm sorry?'

My throat felt as if it was full of glue. I kept picturing myself onstage, frozen and unable to make a sound.

'I can't sing for them.'

'Are you serious?' Impatience had crept into her voice. 'There's a representative from the Royal Opera House out there. He's agreed to stay back just to hear you.'

I was silent, staring at my clenched hands. My knuckles had gone white.

'I... can't do it,' I choked.

'Do you really want to throw away all your hard work?'

'N-no.'

'Then I suggest you go out there and sing. You want to be a professional? Get out there and behave like one.'

'I can't!'

She shook her head. 'You know, at your audition, some of my colleagues didn't see your potential. They thought this environment would be too... *aggressive* for you. Do you want to prove them right?'

A tear slid down my cheek.

'Matthew...'

I shakily rose to my feet. 'I'm so sorry. I... can't... I have to go.' I left the office.

My tutor's voice followed me down the corridor.

'Matthew, you're not just letting yourself down. You're letting everyone else down, too.'

I didn't look back.

The next morning, I caught the train home to Newcastle. The professor's words echoed in my mind for the whole of the journey.

# Lament

It was the day of the Moon and Stars concert, but the thought of rehearsing left me cold. I had hardly slept the previous night. My mind had treated me to an endless montage of the talent contest and the student showcase and the Masquerade! club, concluding with Lucy closing the door in my face.

It was strange, not wanting to think about music. Perhaps giving it up would be liberating. Maybe I would find other hobbies, other interests to occupy my time.

I forced myself to take a shower and dress. At least I would start my new, music-less existence with a certain amount of dignity.

At ten my doorbell rang. For one ridiculous moment, I thought it might be Lucy, and rushed downstairs to answer. Then I remembered she lived in the flat next door and would have no need to ring.

I wrenched the door open to reveal Angela. She had obviously been crying; the skin around her eyes was red and swollen.

'What are you doing here?' I sounded harsher than I'd intended.

'I'm sorry.' She sniffed. 'I didn't know where else to go. Can I come in?'

I moved aside, and she stepped into the hallway. I was suddenly painfully aware that I hadn't applied the concealer. This served to irritate me even more. 'How did you get my address?'

'From Ralph. It was in the back of his diary. He's not here, is he?'

'Why would he be here?'

She gave a muffled sob. 'He's gone.'

'Gone?'

'I think he's left me.'

She covered her face with her hands and started to sob.

Guilt knifed through me. 'You'd better come upstairs.'

We went up to the flat, and I made us both a cup of coffee simply to give myself something to do and delay the actual conversation. I wondered why she had called on me, after everything she had said outside the club.

I put the coffees on the table and sat down opposite her.

'Thanks,' she sniffed.

'What happened with Ralph?'

'We had a massive row about... about the other night. Then he walked out.'

*Shit.*

'I thought he might have gone home. To his mum's, I mean. But he's not there. And he's not answering his phone.' Her voice broke. 'I thought he might have got in touch with you.' She reached into her coat pocket. Time seemed to slow as she produced a familiar envelope, now crumpled. 'He found this at the club.'

I looked down at the floor, cheeks ablaze. 'I was going to give it to you at the party. As a gift. I didn't know about the engagement. If I had, I wouldn't have brought it with me. I must have dropped it. I'm so sorry. I don't know what I was thinking.' I shrugged helplessly. 'It's only a song.'

'Except it's not, is it? Nothing's "only a song" to you.' Angela's eyes had filled with tears again. 'Ralph knows that, too, and now he thinks we have feelings for each other. He said he didn't want to get in the way. But I love him, Matthew. I love him...'

Ralph had been my closest friend for so many years. And now I had completely messed things up. Maybe what he'd said was true. Perhaps I really was selfish.

'I see,' I said, in a flat tone. 'I'm sorry.'

'Please stop apologising.' Angela wiped her eyes with the cuff of her jacket. 'I should have known this was never going to last.'

'What do you mean?'

'Ralph is... *amazing*.' She gave a forced laugh. 'He's kind and supportive and completely without ego. And he's so *talented*, but in a really natural way, whereas I feel like I always have to transform into someone else whenever I set foot on a stage. Sometimes I feel like this ridiculous singing doll. Everything has to be perfect. Perfect voice, perfect hair, perfect dress sense, perfect, perfect, perfect—'

I couldn't believe what I was hearing. 'But... your voice *is* perfect. It's beautiful.'

Angela rubbed her eyes again. 'I find performing really stressful sometimes. There's so much pressure, so much expectation, and Chris can be a bloody *nightmare*. Ralph taught me how to have fun again. It was nice not to have to go through it alone for once.' She met my gaze. 'You always compliment my voice, Matthew. Whenever you say anything nice to me, it's always about music. Do you realise that? It was the same at the Conservatoire. But I don't always want to be a *voice*. Sometimes I just want to be a *person*. Do you understand?'

I blinked. 'Yes. Yes, actually, I think I do.'

I thought of all the times I had watched Angela onstage, the enchantment I felt whenever I sang with her. Had she felt this nervous, this insecure, all along? The thought made me sad.

'I'm sorry,' I said. 'I didn't know.'

Angela shrugged. 'No one does. That's the thing about faking it. You have to keep people at a distance. But I think you know that.'

I nodded.

'Ralph treats me like a person,' Angela continued. 'He doesn't care about popularity, or wealth, or fame, or any of that stupid stuff. And now I've pushed him away.'

'I'm sure you haven't.' I hesitated, wondering if I should elaborate further. I decided to take the chance. 'I've known Ralph a long time. He's a good person, but he does get cold feet sometimes. Maybe he's just gone somewhere to work things out. In his own way.'

She sniffed. 'I really hope so.'

I forced a smile. 'I used to think that he didn't take things seriously, that he wouldn't commit to anything, but maybe he just feels insecure, too.' I tried to focus. 'Did he give you any idea where he might have gone?'

'No. Only that he wanted to get back to his music. That he missed it. What do you think he meant by that?'

'I don't...' I trailed off, because suddenly an old conversation was echoing in my mind: *I really miss busking. Covent Garden. Trafalgar Square. I wish I was there right now... my music... my songs...*

'Busking,' I said.

'What?'

'It's just a thought, but he might have gone busking.'

Angela frowned. 'When he's upset?'

'He's an angsty singer-songwriter.'

Angela tried to smile. 'You may have a point.'

'He mentioned that he liked to busk in Trafalgar Square and Covent Garden. Maybe we could get the Tube into the West End, and split up and look for him?'

Angela sniffed and nodded. 'Okay.'

*

It was strange to see Angela do something as ordinary as ride the Tube.

I realised I had never really thought about her everyday life outside her singing career. She was right when she said we had never had a conversation that wasn't about music. As we sat opposite each other on the train, whizzing through darkness, it occurred to me that I didn't really know her at all.

I had placed her on a pedestal. And while I was gazing up at her, I had neglected to learn who she really was.

We would never be together. I could see that now. But I was determined to make things up to her. Maybe I could be a better friend.

'So,' I said, feeling a responsibility to break the silence, 'what are you going to do after you and Ralph... get married?'

She sighed. 'You mean *if* we get married? I'm not sure.'

'You hate working with Chris, right? Would you like to do something different? Apart from singing, I mean?'

She was silent for a moment, gazing out at the blank tunnel walls. 'Well, I would quite like to travel. Not tour as a singer. Just explore.' She smiled wistfully. 'I feel like I've seen very little of the world outside of theatres and hotel rooms. Hiking would be fun. Camping, maybe.'

I tried to picture Angela clomping around in hiking boots with a load of camping gear on her back. It was a surprising picture. I smiled.

'Where would you go?' I asked.

'I'm not sure. Somewhere with mountains. And I'd like to see the Northern Lights. Norway first, maybe?' She shook her head. 'I know it sounds silly.'

'I think it sounds nice.' I gave her a mock-serious look. 'And there'd be no Chris.'

She smiled. 'No Chris.'

Angela stood up when we reached Covent Garden. 'I'll get off here. You check Trafalgar Square, and we'll meet in Piccadilly in two hours. Ring me if you find Ralph.'

\*

Trafalgar Square was thronged with people.

I walked around the periphery of the square and then searched between the fountains in the middle. I passed three buskers, two mime artists and someone reproducing Van Gogh's Sunflowers on the pavement in chalk.

But there was no sign of Ralph.

I walked around the square a second time, just to be sure. But I still couldn't see him.

Maybe I'd been wrong.

I was sitting on the rim of a fountain, wondering whether to phone Angela and ask if she was having any luck in Covent Garden, when music broke into my thoughts.

Someone was playing acoustic guitar – classical guitar – with a skill I had not heard since music school. This wasn't Ralph's usual style, but I decided to take a look.

I followed the sound.

The music led me to the steps of the National Gallery. A busker stood with a guitar case open at his feet. He was wearing a black beanie hat and dark sunglasses. Half a dozen listeners stood a few feet away.

As I approached, he shifted from classical instrumental to a more contemporary sound. After a short intro, he started to sing.

*I want to reach out, to have the courage to love you...*

I stood a short distance away and listened. The lyrics were quite banal, but the song was delivered with a sort of rough passion, the melody was strong, and the guitar playing was virtuosic.

It was very impressive.

*I want to reach out, to have the courage to love you...*
*But I'm just a loser eating toast and Pot Noo-dles.*
*Ooooo-ooooh! Noodles on toast!*
*I'm eating noodles on toast!*
*Nooodles... onnn... toooaaast...*

I stared at him. He hadn't just sung that. He hadn't.
'*Ralph?*'
No response. I moved closer, close enough to see the familiar shape of his jaw and nose, and some tufts of dark hair poking out from beneath his woollen hat. His shoulders tensed for a second, but he carried on playing and singing as if he didn't know me. He reached the end of his ode to love and snack food. His audience clapped and whooped and dropped coins into the guitar case, before moving away to watch a levitating Darth Vader.

'Ralph?' My instinct had been right, but I still couldn't quite believe what I was seeing. 'What are you doing?'

He crouched down and began to scoop up the coins. 'What does it look like?'

'You're *busking*.'

He looked up at me. 'Well, *duh.*'

'What if someone recognises you?'

'That's why I'm wearing these.' Ralph indicated his glasses and hat. 'I find that people only see what they expect to see. And no one's expecting to see me here.'

'Angela's looking for you. She's worried sick.'

Ralph glanced towards Piccadilly, in the direction of the studios. 'I needed to get away from everything for a bit. I needed to play and sing again. Just to remind myself that I've got *some* talent.' He glared at me, and I flinched. 'You told me I'd have all

333

these opportunities, that this job would open all these doors. But all I do is stand there and look pretty.'

'There's a bit more to it than that.'

'Is there? I'm not so sure.' He sat down on the steps leading to the gallery. 'I've let Chris use me as a walking advert. And I'm sick of it. I'm tired of pretending to be something I'm not.'

I sat down beside him. 'I thought you enjoyed that stuff.'

'What stuff?'

'The clothes… the photo shoots… the videos.' I thought of him hiding from the press in my booth, and hesitated. 'Don't you?'

Ralph glared at a passing pigeon. 'Actually, I don't. I hate it. I've been doing it for years now – too long. It makes me feel like I'm being… scrutinised. That my appearance is the only thing that matters.'

I gave a short laugh. 'With respect, I don't think you really know how that feels.'

'I think I do. I can't get a zit without being whisked into makeup for two hours. Or at least it feels that way.'

Ralph took off the sunglasses and rubbed his eyes. I saw they were red-rimmed.

'Ralph?'

He slipped his sunglasses back on. I wondered if this was because he was afraid of being recognised, or because he was embarrassed that I had seen him crying.

'It's all happened so fast,' he said. 'I never wanted any of this, not really. I just wanted to play music and write moody profound songs and be a bit successful at it. But there was Angela…' He gave a wistful smile, and then his face grew sad again. 'I thought I'd found a person I could really talk to, who saw me for who I was and not just some good-looking guy in a designer suit.' He gave a shuddering sigh. 'Now I'm not so sure. I'm constantly on edge, terrified I'm going to let her down somehow.'

I thought of his strange, wary attitude at the party. 'But you love her, don't you?'

'Of course I do. But this is her world. And I'm not sure I fit into it. Maybe we should just call it off.'

'The concert?'

'The engagement.'

The sights and sounds of Trafalgar Square faded into the background. I looked at Ralph and felt that I was truly seeing him for the first time in years. I saw the uncertainty and tension emanating from him. He was still the same arty, kind young man who had befriended me at school. Who had bunked off PE with me, and hidden from bullies behind the canteen with me.

I swallowed hard. 'But you want to marry her, right?'

'I don't know. I just don't know anymore.' He put his head in his hands. 'I can't stand this. This isn't me. I'm so tired of pretending to be someone I'm not. I've been unhappy about it for weeks. But Angela was there, and I loved being with her. I thought, once we got engaged, that things might be different. But then the other night happened.'

He looked miserable. I felt cold.

'I'm sorry, Ralph. I never meant... it just slipped out.'

Ralph gave a bitter laugh. 'I'm sort of glad it did.'

'What do you mean?'

'Why would Angela want me, when she's got this master musician who sings like no one else and writes love songs for her? She said she wanted to keep the engagement a secret. Because of the press. But actually, I wonder if she was a little bit embarrassed by me. Or maybe she's really in love with you. I mean, you're both singers, and you're both clever and talented. And what am I? All I do is parade around and wear nice clothes.'

'That's not true. Angela loves you.' I closed my eyes on tears. 'She told me. You can't just run away.'

'Then what am I going to do?'

'Tell her the truth. Tell her how you feel about this whole thing. Please. I... I think she feels exactly the same way.'

'How can you possibly know that?'

'Because she told me. *She* feels like she's faking it most of the time. You have to talk to her.'

Ralph raised his eyebrows. 'Why do you care? I would have thought you'd be glad to see the back of me. You love her, right?'

I took a breath. 'It was a long time ago. We didn't even date... not really. And I thought – wrongly – that we could just start again where we had left off. I always regretted not telling her how I felt.'

'You weren't honest with her.'

'No. I wasn't. And I regret it.' More tears crept to my eyes. I blinked them away. 'She loves you, Ralph. Come and talk to her. Please. We can do the concert. Then, afterwards, we can go our separate ways.'

'But what about you? You'll still want to work with Angela, won't you?'

I stared out across the square. 'I'm through with singing.'

'Oh, mate, no. Don't say that. You've got a great voice. You could sing on your own, as yourself. You don't need me.'

I forced a smile. 'I do tonight, and so does Angela. So does the theatre. Please. One last gig, and then you can do what you like.'

Ralph was silent for a moment. Then he bent over and put his guitar in its case. He closed the case slowly, as if buying time to think.

'Ralph?'

'Okay. I'll do the gig.'

I closed my eyes. I felt as if I'd both won and lost at the same time.

'Thank you. Now please, please call Angela.'

*

I travelled home alone, trying not to think about the tearful reunion currently taking place outside Fortnum & Mason.

My email pinged. I looked at my phone, worried that Angela and Ralph had decided to miss the concert and elope to Gretna Green instead.

But the message was from Dave.

*Hi mate,*

*Looking forward to the concert and finally hearing our Ghost sing in public!*

*I thought you might like to see this. Somebody made a petition to help the theatre.*

*Dave*

*P.S. I've removed all the Haribo from the bar so you won't be tempted.*

He had included a link to the petition. It already had more than 3000 signatures, despite only being launched a few days before.

The author was LucyGothGirl.

There was a blurb about the theatre, including a potted history that she must have lifted from our website. There were also several photos of the theatre from its glory days, and a more recent photo showing its unassuming blue door. Lucy had also included a link to the crowdfunding page Jess had set up.

I blinked back a tear.

I couldn't believe she'd gone to all this trouble.

I had to thank her.

I knocked on her door as soon as I got home, but there was no reply. She was either out, or still angry with me.

Perhaps it wasn't too late to make things right with her.

I wrote a text.

*Hi Lucy, I'm really sorry about yesterday. I didn't mean what I said. You're a great musician. Thank you so much for launching the petition. I'm assuming it was you? It was a really lovely thought. Best regards, Matthew.*

I stared at this for a moment, deleted the last line, put *Love from Matthew xxx* instead, and pressed send.

# Finale

I arrived at the Moon and Stars just before 4pm. The concert didn't start until 7.30pm, but there was a lot of preparation work to be done, including two hours of soundchecks. I wasn't looking forward to this. I still had a dreadful headache, and I was grateful for the cool darkness of the auditorium.

'Matthew!' Jess waved at me from the front row. I cursed inwardly; I was in no mood to talk. I wanted nothing more than to slip into the shadows backstage.

'Hello, Jess.'

'This is so exciting!' Jess pointed towards the stage. 'What do you think?'

I looked up. There was a new backdrop dotted with stars, and a great silver moon hanging from the flies, a mirror image of the chandelier. Everything sparkled.

'Quite spectacular,' I muttered.

'Good, isn't it?' Jess grinned. 'So, are you all ready to unmask the Phantom?'

I hadn't told Jess that Ralph would be miming to my voice. She would no doubt have a million questions for me after the show, but I had no intention of hanging around to answer them. I intended to leave the theatre as soon as I had played my part.

'Absolutely.' I forced a smile. 'Excuse me. I'm needed backstage.'

I was desperately in need of a distraction, so I assigned myself the task of greeting the performers at the stage door.

Angela and Ralph arrived together, much to my relief. I directed them to their dressing rooms.

'I'll be along in a minute,' said Angela.

Ralph nodded and set off down the corridor.

'I wanted to return this.' Angela held out the envelope containing my song.

I looked at it sadly. 'It was a gift. You're welcome to keep it.'

'It doesn't feel right, after everything.' She gave a tiny smile. 'But I did play it when I got home.'

'Oh?' My mouth was as dry as dust. 'What did you think?'

'It's lovely.' She didn't look too sure.

'What's wrong with it?'

'Nothing. It's great. There's just this small mistake in the last verse, when they both sing together...'

'What?'

'Well, the line for the female singer... you wrote it for an alto.'

I stared at her. 'No, I didn't.'

'I'm afraid you did.'

'But you're a soprano.'

'Yes. Interesting, that. Take a look. You'll see what I mean.'

I read the music and saw she was right.

I was an accomplished musician. How had I managed to make a mistake like that? Her voice had been in my head while I was writing it. I remembered it well. It had been just after my first gig with the band.

*With Lucy.*

Oh, no. No. I couldn't have got their voices confused. That was just ridiculous.

'I think it might suit someone else better,' said Angela. 'Unless you want to transpose the last part?'

'I'll take a look.'

She patted my arm. 'Have a good show, Matthew.'

'Thanks. You, too.'

I slipped the song into my jacket pocket and watched Angela walk away. Then I turned my attention back to the stage door.

Lucy and the band were the last performers to arrive.

I stepped forward. 'Welcome to the Moon and Stars Theatre. The fire exits are—'

Lucy waved a hand. 'Yes, all right, Matthew. We've been here before.'

She strode on ahead, down the corridor. Dan gave me a sympathetic grimace, but James followed Lucy without looking at me.

I hurried after them. I had to keep Lucy talking.

'Lucy, please wait...'

She stopped and whirled around, pinning me in place with a glare. '*What?*'

I didn't think it was possible to literally quake in one's boots. But I actually felt it happen at that moment.

'I... I have to tell you about the fire assembly point.'

Lucy sighed.

'All right, Matthew. Tell us about the bloody assembly point.'

'It's... outside the Rose and Crown pub... next door... God, Lucy, I'm so sorry—'

'Where do you want us?'

'Well, er... there aren't enough dressing rooms, sorry, so I've assigned you the green room. Follow me.'

I led them behind the stage and down a passage into our small green room. It had seen better days: the green wallpaper was peeling at the corners, and it had the ugliest brown sofas in existence.

Dan's face lit up. 'Hey, cool! An actual green room!'

'Yes,' I said.

'I mean, like, the walls are actually green!'

'Yeah, we see it, Dan,' said Lucy. She sounded tired.

I took a step towards her. 'Can we talk in private?'

She hesitated, then nodded. 'Fine. But please make it quick.'

We stepped back into the passage and closed the door.

'Did you get my message?'

'Yes.' Lucy folded her arms. 'And?'

'I just wanted to say I'm sorry.'

'You've said that already.'

'That thing about you not being a professional musician... I didn't mean it.'

'Didn't you? Are you sure about that?'

I flinched. 'I'm sorry about tonight, too. I just can't face it... I understand if you don't want me in the band anymore.'

Lucy frowned. 'Do you really think that's why I'm upset?'

'You needed a keyboardist, and I let you down, so—'

'For God's sake, Matthew, do you honestly think I want to perform with you because you can get a tune out of a keyboard?'

'Um... yes? Isn't that how it generally works?'

'I can't believe I need to spell this out.' She shook her head. 'Matthew, I want to perform with you because I *like* you.'

I blinked. 'You... like me?'

'Yes.' She fiddled with the strap of her guitar case.

'But... why?'

'Right now? God knows.' She shrugged. 'I guess... when you play music, you get this look of joy on your face. I like that. And I like the way you always listen to me and try and say something comforting, even if it's usually the wrong thing. I like that you care about things so intensely. I even liked it when you brought mini quiches to a band rehearsal. It's not about your voice or your songs. I just... I like *you*, Matthew.' She stopped, blushing.

I stared at her. 'I... don't know what to say.'

'You don't have to say anything. Just listen.' She held my gaze. 'You know what I *don't* like? In fact, you know what I hate? I hate the way you cut yourself off, the way you push people away. Is it honestly so hard to believe that people want to spend time with you?'

I was stunned. I searched for a reply, but before I could say anything, a shadow fell across the passageway.

I turned to see a very tall young man, handsome in a floppy-haired sort of way, dressed rather incongruously in a tweed jacket with leather patches on the elbows.

'Hey, Lucy.' He grinned at her. The expression wasn't entirely pleasant.

She lowered her gaze. 'Oh. Hi, Mark.'

Mark. *Keyboardist* Mark? What on earth was he doing here?

Tall and Handsome Mark wrinkled his small and handsome nose. 'God, this place is the pits, isn't it? Where do you want me?'

Lucy nodded towards the green-room door. 'The guys are just in there.'

'Fab.' He seemed to notice me for the first time. 'Hello. I don't think we've met?'

'This is Matthew,' said Lucy. 'He's the manager of the Moon and Stars.'

'Oh.' His mouth twisted. 'Sorry, I didn't mean anything by that "pits" comment. No offence, yeah?'

'None taken,' I said.

'Good, good. Oh, Lucy! I'm sorry about this get-up. I came straight from work. I don't suppose you have some crazy Goth garb I can wear, do you?'

'We might have something going spare,' said Lucy.

'Great. See you in a bit. See you, Matt, mate.'

He went into the green room and closed the door.

I stared at Lucy. 'What's going on?'

'I'm sorry, Matthew. You did say you didn't want to play the gig.'

'But... Mark? I thought you all hated him.'

'Yeah.' Lucy winced. 'But... we didn't think we had much choice, under the circumstances. He knows most of the material. The old material, anyway. And the thing about Mark is he'll play if he's guaranteed a decent audience. Big ego.'

'I see.'

She met my eyes. 'Listen. If you really don't want to perform, none of us can make you. I know what it's like to be pressurised; I shouldn't have put that sort of pressure on you. So I guess I'm sorry, too.'

I tried to think of something to say, something that would make things better, but I couldn't.

'I see,' I said. 'Right. I... hope it goes well.'

Her expression softened. 'Matthew—'

'I've got to go.'

I turned away from her and headed to the wings, where my curtained booth awaited me like a fabric cage.

*

The soundchecks seemed to last forever.

I stayed in my booth, too caught up in my own thoughts to fully concentrate on what was happening onstage. When Angela and I tried our duet, I sang without hearing the words, without even really hearing myself.

Shattered Chandelier's soundcheck was more eventful.

They played one verse and a chorus. The keyboard stopped. A brief discussion followed – I caught the words 'sloppy' and 'rhythm' from Mark. Then there was a discordant *crash* of symbols, followed by the thump of feet. I poked my head out of the prompt corner in time to see Dan storm off into the wings, pursued by James.

Worried they would see me, I quickly hid behind my curtain again. But I could still hear their voices.

'Dan, wait!'

'I can't *stand* that man! Why the hell did you ask him back?'

I blinked. I had never heard Dan sound angry before.

'It was an emergency... You know that.'

'He makes my blood boil. Sloppy rhythm?! I would like to shove this drumstick—'

'Okay. I get the picture.'

'Where's Matthew?'

'Indisposed.'

'Why should we have to suffer just because he had a fight with Lucy?'

'It's... more complicated than that.'

'It always is. I hate bloody musicians sometimes. You're all insane...'

His voice faded as they headed back in the direction of the green room.

I peered out of the prompt corner again to see Lucy standing on the edge of the stage. She looked towards the tech booth at the rear of the auditorium.

'Sorry about that.' She sounded tired. 'The sound's good.' She gave the technician a thumbs-up.

Guilt gnawed at my insides. Perhaps it wasn't too late to join them. But no... It would be much better this way.

A pause. A lull onstage. The blue velvet curtains glided shut. And then there was a low rumble of voices as the auditorium started to fill up.

I sat in my chair, staring at my clasped hands, wishing the performance was over.

'Matthew?' I jumped and looked up to see Jess standing onstage. 'Your family are here. Your parents and sister.'

I stared at her in horror. I had completely forgotten that I had sent Clara the date of the fundraising gala. She would be expecting to see me play with Shattered Chandelier. Could this night get any worse?

Jess smiled. 'Would you like to pop out front and say hello?'

'Er... no, not right now.'

Jess nodded. 'Your mum said you might say that. She asked me to give you this.'

She handed me an envelope.

'Thanks.'

I waited until Jess had gone before I opened it. It was a greeting card, with *Good Luck! You Rock!* printed in shiny green letters, and a cartoonish drawing of black cats playing musical instruments. I smiled involuntarily. It was exactly the sort of cheesy thing my mum would buy.

Inside there was a message in Mum's handwriting:

*Dear Matthew,*

*We've come to see your band and support the theatre. We're so excited to hear you play!*

*Clara showed me the video of you singing as the theatre Ghost, and I read that you might sing a song tonight. I really hope that's true. But I want you to know that we're all very proud of you, regardless of what you do.*

*Love, Mum, Dad and Clara xx*

My eyes were stinging. I wiped them on the cuff of my jacket and placed the card on the little shelf next to my desk lamp.

A bell sounded. Then another bell, five minutes later. The murmur of the audience faded to nothing, and there was a whirr as the curtains slid open.

Shattered Chandelier opened the show with a song I recognised from my early rehearsals with them. Mark had apparently turned the keyboard up to max and was plonking away at the keys, while Dan pummelled the drum kit in a way which suggested he was trying to drown Mark out. Between them, there was little space for Lucy's excellent vocals.

It struck me just how much we had developed as a band over the last few months, but I shook the thought away. There was no 'we' anymore.

'Okay,' said Lucy, when the song was over. 'Let's try something different.'

This time, they played one of Lucy's own songs. Mark's playing was lacklustre – it was obvious that he didn't know the new material – but Lucy was superb. I could tell that even from the wings. It was as if she was singing to the theatre itself, her voice a rallying cry for the place to be saved, preserved.

*Loved.*

She loved the theatre as much as I did.

The song ended to applause. I realised I was on my feet. I was applauding, too.

The band were leaving the stage, but Lucy lingered. She turned towards the wings and met my eyes.

And I knew then I had been wrong.

So, so wrong.

I looked at Mark and knew how much I wanted to be in his place.

And more than that, I wanted to sing with the band.

I wanted to sing with Lucy.

But I couldn't do that while I was hiding behind a mask, pretending my voice belonged to someone else. And the thought of stepping out of the shadows and into the spotlight was terrifying.

And yet, maybe there was a way…

A moment later, I had left the booth and was hurrying towards my office.

# Forte

I stared at the coat.

It was hanging on my office door where I had left it after our last rehearsal, inky black, a dark temptation.

The perfect garment for a theatre ghost.

I took it from the hanger and wrapped myself in it. Once again, it felt perfectly natural, as if it had been made just for me, a second skin.

Then I put on the black lace-up boots.

I brushed the gel out of my hair, allowing it to fall in dark locks around my face.

Finally, I found some makeup wipes in the desk drawer, and carefully removed the concealer.

There was no mirror in the office, and the dressing rooms were all occupied, so I slipped down the backstage passage and into the costume store. A naked lightbulb provided the only illumination in this room full of ghosts from past productions. I stood between racks of empty crinoline dresses and evening suits, and looked at my reflection in the old, full-length mirror.

The Phantom of the Moon and Stars stared back at me.

\*

I left the costume store and crept towards the wings. I could hear recorded music: the finale of Tchaikovsky's *Swan Lake*, indicating that the local ballet troupe were now onstage.

This meant Angela and Ralph were next.

I quickened my pace.

I reached my booth in the wings and waited, a shadow within shadows.

The music swelled and ended, and the ballet troupe glided offstage, white glaring against darkness.

A pause.

Angela entered from upstage, sweeping forward in her long silver gown. She sparkled and smiled at the audience, who were already applauding, because here was the big star of the evening.

She began her set with a rendition of 'I Could Have Danced All Night' from *My Fair Lady*. It was charming, but I was too focused on my own nerves to enjoy it.

The song ended to enthusiastic applause.

I saw Ralph take up his position in the opposite wing.

Angela smiled again. 'Welcome, ladies and gentlemen, and thank you for joining us in this magnificent theatre. It's such an honour to sing here tonight. For my next number, I'll be joined by a special guest. I think you know who!'

There was a cheer from the audience.

'I'm delighted to introduce the man behind the mask, the Phantom of the Moon and Stars... Ralph!'

I took another step forward, still in the wings, but far enough for Ralph to see me. He met my eyes.

I placed a hand on my throat, and then gestured towards the stage, hoping he would understand.

His eyes widened, and he mouthed something which looked like 'You sure?'

I nodded.

The music began.

Angela sang the first verse of the song, her voice lovelier than I had ever heard it.

I took several deep, calming breaths and tried to get my thoughts in order.

*Okay.*

*You've sung on this stage many times. True, there was no one watching, but it's still the same stage, still the same theatre.*

*You are an accomplished singer and performer.*

*You can do this.*

*You can do this.*

*You can...*

It was time for the second verse. Time for me to sing.

I stepped forward, into the light.

There were gasps from the audience.

Angela turned and saw the dark figure of the Phantom of the Moon and Stars.

Surprise and confusion flitted across her face.

'Matthew? What are you doing?' Her voice was a stage whisper, drowned by the music but audible to me.

'Will you sing with me?' I asked.

She hesitated for a moment. Then, to my vast relief, she nodded.

I turned towards the audience and stood in the full glare of the stage lights.

A sea of darkness stretched out before me. The darkness was made up of one thousand shadowy heads and two thousand invisible eyes, all fixed on me. The heat from the lights was incredible, like a row of twelve suns beating down on me from the lighting rig. It made me want to flee, to hide from this glare which exposed me to the world.

And suddenly I wasn't the Phantom anymore.

I wasn't playing a role, because this was me.

I stood before the audience, myself at last. Matthew Capes, ugly singer.

The small orchestra faltered. I was tempted to flee.

Then I heard the chanting.

'*Phan-tom, Phan-tom, Phan-tom.*'

It started at the back of the auditorium, where I knew the theatre staff would be sitting, and quickly spread around the audience.

'*Phan-tom, Phan-tom, Phan-tom.*'

I knew I had to do this. I nodded to the musical director, and the small orchestra began to play once again.

I took a breath, and I sang.

When we reached the chorus, I heard Angela join me.

We sang together, Angela and I, and for a moment it was just like old times, just like our days in a rehearsal room at the Conservatoire when we would sing for each other alone. But so much had changed since then, and I knew in my heart this would be the last time.

We launched into a final chorus, voices ringing around the theatre.

Our song came to an end. The last note vibrated into nothingness.

There was a beat of silence. I wondered if something was wrong. Had we performed badly?

Then the tension broke, and the audience erupted into applause. Some of them got to their feet, clapping and whistling.

Angela's hand slipped into mine. We bowed low.

The applause slowed and became a rhythmic clapping. The chant started up again – '*Phan-tom, Phan-tom, Phan-tom*' – accompanied by shouts of 'More!'

I looked at Angela.

She smiled. 'Solo?'

My heart lurched. 'Really?'

'Yes!'

'What should I sing? I haven't rehearsed anything.'

'It's okay. I have an idea.'

She raised her arms, asking the audience for quiet, and then stepped up to the mic stand.

'Thank you so much, everyone. I would like to take this opportunity to introduce Matthew. He wrote this next song many years ago, and you may recognise it from my latest album.'

I stared at Angela. I couldn't believe she was doing this for me.

She locked eyes with me for a moment, and then turned back to the audience.

'Matthew has never received the credit he deserves. His name was even left off the sleeve notes of the CD. But not any longer. Tonight, I want you all to know that this is his music. And the voice on my album is his voice.'

There were some confused murmurs from the audience, but also quite a few cheers.

Angela stepped to one side and gestured towards the mic stand. The orchestra began to play the single from our album. My song. *Our* song.

The audience quietened.

I sang. My anxiety faded, and I began to enjoy the music. There was complete silence from the audience. I could feel their collective attention like electricity in the atmosphere.

I had almost finished the second verse when I saw movement out of the corner of my eye. Then a figure dashed on from the wings and barrelled into me, making a grab for the microphone.

'*Shit*,' said Chris, his face a mask of horror. 'What are you doing? Get off the stage!'

I continued to sing, avoiding Chris's lunges for the microphone. My voice quavered.

Chris finally managed to seize the mic.

He turned towards the audience. The music died.

'Ladies and gentlemen, I'm sorry about this... change to the advertised programme. We're experiencing some slight... technical difficulties.' Chris's voice faltered. 'We're going to take a short interval now.'

There was an awkward pause, during which Chris stared at the audience with his fake Cheshire Cat smile.

'Now!' said Chris, clearly hoping the assistant stage manager would take the hint.

The curtains whizzed closed.

Chris rounded on me, holding the microphone aloft like a weapon.

'What the hell do you think you're doing?'

'Singing,' I said.

'No, you're not! We had an agreement!' He turned to Angela. 'And you! What do you think you're playing at?'

'Hey!' Ralph stepped out from the wings. 'Don't talk to her like that.'

Angela's face twisted in anger. 'We're all fed up pretending, Chris. Matthew deserves credit.'

Chris shook his head. 'I don't believe this. After everything I've done for you both.'

There was a commotion in the wings, and Dan and James rushed onto the stage.

'Bloody hell, Matthew,' said James. He laughed. 'I can't believe you just did that.'

'I can't either,' I said, glancing nervously at the glowering Chris.

'Good for you, mate,' said Dan, thumping me on the back with such force that I almost lost my footing.

'I knew you'd conquer your stage fright,' said James. 'It's amazing what a decent coat can do.' He noticed Chris. 'Why does that man look so angry?'

'Long story,' I said.

'Matthew.' Angela was suddenly at my side. 'Who are these people?'

I smiled. 'They're my band.'

'Your... band?'

'Yes. This is Dan and James.'

'Okay,' said Chris. 'I don't know what's going on, but you lot have to leave. Right now. Angela needs to sing again. She was promised four songs tonight. Matthew, get back in the wings.'

'I don't think so.'

'Get back in the wings right now, or I'll see to it that you never record anything again.'

I stared at him.

Then I started to laugh.

Chris flinched. 'Why are you laughing?'

'Well, firstly, I don't believe you have that sort of power. And secondly, I don't actually care.'

'Look... just... get back in the wings, you ugly sod, or there'll be consequences.' He was spluttering, shrinking before my eyes. 'Do you hear me?'

'What's going on here?' A voice like cut glass rang around the stage. I turned to see Charlotte, decked out like a 1920s movie star in a green velvet gown and strings of pearls, feathers quivering magnificently on her tiny hat. 'I will not have shouting on my stage.'

Chris leered at her. 'And who are you? Norma bloody Desmond?'

I clenched my fists. 'Don't you dare speak to her like that.'

Charlotte placed a gloved hand on my arm. 'It's all right, darling, I'll deal with this.'

She marched up to Chris until she was almost nose to nose with him.

'I'm the owner of the Moon and Stars Theatre,' she said, in a voice of unnerving calmness. 'And I would like to know why you're disrupting my show.'

'I'm not disrupting anything.' He pointed at me. 'It was him! This wannabe. He's ruined everything.'

Charlotte glanced at me. The corner of her mouth twitched in a smile. 'Ah. It would appear our theatre manager has finally taken his turn in the spotlight.'

'He doesn't belong in the spotlight.'

'That's not for you to decide,' said Charlotte. 'Now would you kindly bugger off and let us get on with the show?'

'Fine,' said Chris. 'That's fine. I don't want to stay in this dump anyway. Come on, Angela. We should never have agreed to this.'

Angela hesitated. She looked from Chris to Ralph, and back again.

Ralph took her hand. 'You don't have to follow him.'

Angela looked at me, and I saw there were tears on her cheeks. I gave her a nod of encouragement.

She turned back to Chris. 'No. I'm staying here. I'm finishing the show.'

'What?' Chris gave an ugly bark of laughter. 'But you're better than all these people!'

'I don't think I am,' said Angela softly. 'I'm tired, Chris. Tired of lying, tired of seeing you treat people like dirt and pretending it's for my benefit.'

'But it *is* for your benefit!' Chris's eyes were wild.

'Chris.' Angela straightened her shoulders and took a step towards him. 'I think it's time we parted ways.'

He stared at her. 'What do you mean?'

'I mean you're fired.'

'What?' Chris's jaw went slack. 'But it was all for you! I made you a star! Are you seriously going to throw it all back in my face? I gave you everything. Is this really how you're going to repay me?'

I looked at Chris. And I understood, for the first time, what it meant to be truly ugly.

'I don't think it works like that,' I said. 'You know, Chris, just the other night you told me how alike we are.'

Chris gave a harsh laugh. 'You're nothing like me.'

'Maybe not... but I think I realised that just in time.' I kept my voice steady and sympathetic. 'Maybe you should join a band. You might be a bit happier.'

'I don't know what you're talking about.' Sadness flashed in his eyes. 'Angela, please.'

Angela shook her head. Chris's face hardened.

'Fine,' he said. 'If you want to stay here with these losers, that's your prerogative. See if I care. You're nothing.' He looked at me. 'And you're less than nothing.'

I straightened, drawing myself up to my full height. I found myself moving towards Chris, the long coat swirling around my ankles.

I towered over him and fixed him with a glare.

'*Get out of my theatre!*'

My voice boomed around the stage, bouncing off the flats.

Chris's mouth fell open. Then he turned on his heel and scarpered into the wings.

I looked at Angela. 'Are you okay?'

'I think so.' She mopped her eyes with the sleeve of her gown.

'You don't need him. He's poison.'

'I know.' Angela took a deep breath, and summoned a smile, the mask of professionalism falling over her features once again. 'Shall we get on with the show?'

I turned to Charlotte. 'How are things out front?'

Charlotte beamed at me. 'Amazing, darling! Everyone's talking about the Phantom. They keep asking if you're going to sing again.'

'They're not angry?'

'Of course not. Why should they be?'

'Well, for a start, the show's been interrupted, and then there's this whole fraud, false advertising... thing.'

'They're fine,' said Charlotte. 'They love your voice. And besides, they all have Prosecco. Jess is supervising things in the foyer.'

I sighed with relief. 'That's good to hear.' I turned back to Angela. 'I think we can carry on.'

Angela smiled weakly. 'What would you like to sing? How about "Somewhere"? That's always a crowd pleaser.'

I was silent for a moment, looking at her.

'I'm sorry, Angela. I can't.'

'What?' Her eyes widened. 'Why?'

'It's just...' I hesitated. I knew what I had to say would sound absurd, and possibly insane. After all, it was just singing.

'It doesn't feel right,' I finished.

Angela stared at me. Then she said, 'Oh.'

'There's someone else I think I'd like to sing with.'

'Oh. I... see.'

'Do you mind?'

She looked at the floor. 'No. No, I understand.'

Ralph looked thoroughly confused. 'You musicians are all bonkers.'

'You're a musician, too,' I said.

Ralph smiled. 'It's only taken fifteen years for you to acknowledge that.' He pressed his hand to his heart. 'I'm touched, really.'

'Would you like to sing? As yourself, I mean?'

He went a bit pale. 'Won't they want to tear me limb from limb?'

'Apparently not. Apparently they're too busy raving about the Phantom. You could open the second act. Sing your Pot Noodle song. I suppose you've got your guitar with you?'

His mouth twitched. 'Always.'

'Excellent.'

'So,' said Angela. She forced a smile. 'Is your duet partner here?'

I looked around the stage, but there was no sign of Lucy. I really hoped she hadn't left the theatre.

'I need to find her,' I said. 'Will you sing again? A solo? You could close the show.'

She was quiet for a moment. I might have been mistaken, but I thought she looked a bit sad. But then she smiled. 'I would be honoured, Matthew.'

I bowed my head. 'Thank you.'

James and Dan were still standing upstage. I walked over. 'Do you know where Lucy is?'

'She went back to the green room,' said James. 'Just after you sang. She said she had a headache.'

'Oh. Right.'

'I don't think she really has a headache,' said Dan. 'I think she's pissed off with you, Matthew.'

James glared at him. 'Yes, cheers for that, Dan.'

'She said she wanted to be on her own,' said Dan.

Oh God.

I had revealed my identity so I could finally sing as myself, finally perform with the band, but maybe Lucy had got the wrong end of the stick.

Maybe she had watched the duet and assumed that Angela and I were deeply in love, and that I had no interest in singing with anyone else. This was something that happened with alarming frequency in musicals.

I had to find her.

I reached inside my coat and drew Angela's former song from my pocket. I held it out to James.

'Do you think you could play this?'

James looked at it and pulled a face. 'Bit sentimental for us, isn't it?'

'I was thinking you could... er... rockify it a bit more?'

He raised an eyebrow. 'Rockify?'

'Yes. Or something. Please. Is your friend Mark still here?'

'Nah,' said Dan. 'He buggered off as soon as we'd played. That's what he always does. He never listens to other people. Just not interested.'

I knew a moment of intense relief. 'Good.'

*

I knocked on the door of the green room, but there was no answer, so I pushed it open tentatively.

Lucy was sitting on one of the brown sofas, staring at a small rectangle of card.

I approached cautiously. 'Hey, Lucy?'

'Oh.' She turned to look at me, and I noticed her black eyeliner was all smudged, as if she had been crying. 'Hi.'

'Are you okay?'

'Fine, just... thinking about stuff.'

'Ah. Okay.' I sat down on the other end of the sofa. 'Lucy, I just wanted to tell you that I messed up. I can see that now. I got everything wrong, and I'm so sorry.'

'Hmm.'

'And I was just wondering if, maybe, you could give me another chance?'

She was silent, still staring at the business card, turning it over and over in her hands.

'Would you like me to go?' I asked. 'Because I will, if you want me to. But I just want you to know that... my feelings for Angela aren't what I thought they were.'

She scowled. 'Good to know, Matthew. And what would you like me to do with this crucial piece of information?'

'I would really like to sing with you.'

'Right. And I should be pleased about this because...?'

'Lucy.' I twisted my hands in the folds of my coat. 'I'm sorry if I hurt you. What you said to me the other day, about not noticing the people around me... about taking them for granted... you were right. I've been a fool.'

'Yes. You have.'

I cleared my throat. This was it. 'I thought I knew what I wanted, but I didn't. But now I finally think I do. I... love the band, Lucy. I love everything about it. And I want to join you again, if you'll have me. You made me remember who I am and why I love music. I'm so, so sorry. And... I like you, too. You mean the world to me.'

Lucy was silent. She did not look at me.

I felt like I'd been dismissed.

'That's all I wanted to say.' I stood up. 'I'll go now.'

'Wait.' Lucy's voice stopped me. I turned around again. 'Matthew, what you did tonight... I thought it was very brave.'

'Oh,' I said, surprised. 'Thank you.'

She reached for my hand. 'I know what it took for you to stand on a stage and sing, and while I still think you're an idiot, I also think you're sort of amazing.'

'Er... thank you very much.'

Her face broke into a smile then. 'You're also an enormous dork.'

'Right.'

'And I'd love to sing with you.'

'You would?'

'Yes.'

I met her eyes and smiled. 'That's wonderful.'

She stood up and wiped her eyes on her sleeve. The business card had disappeared.

'So, maestro. What are we going to sing?'

# Duet

We took our positions onstage: Dan on drums, James on bass, Lucy with her guitar.

Unable to keep still, I smoothed down my coat and paced around the stage. I remembered this feeling, these strange warm butterflies in my stomach. This was the *good* sort of excited, the enjoyable pre-show nerves. I went to the keyboard and played a few chords, eager to get started.

Dan and James had come up with a few ideas to give the love duet more of a rock sound, but we were still going to keep it more stripped back than our other material. I remembered when Lucy and I had performed the song in my flat, and I wanted to preserve some of that subtlety and rawness.

The curtains slid open.

It was time.

I stepped up to the microphone.

The audience cheered, and for a moment I was worried they would start up the Phantom chant again. I raised a hand, asking for quiet.

'Good evening,' I said. 'I'm Matthew. I'm the manager of the Moon and Stars Theatre. If you would indulge me, there are a few things I'd like to say. Firstly, I would like to thank you for coming tonight, and for supporting this wonderful theatre. We wouldn't be here without our fantastic audiences.' I paused as the crowd applauded. 'The second thing I would like to tell you is a bit more personal. A few weeks back, Dave, our head technician, recorded me singing here in the theatre. He put it on YouTube as proof that the building was haunted by a singing Phantom.'

There were a few titters from the audience.

'Apparently, people liked it. They liked the idea of a singing ghost. But I didn't realise I was being recorded. I didn't want anyone to know about my rehearsals in the theatre.

'As you may have realised, thanks to the earlier chaos, I'm Angela Nilsson's duet partner on her latest album. The vocals are mine. It was all my idea. I did it because I felt... ugly. I felt that I wasn't right for the stage. I used to sing here, alone, because I thought that was the only way I could: in the shadows, without an audience. But now I know that isn't true.' I took a breath. 'I'd like to introduce Dan and James and, especially, Lucy, who helped me find my voice again.'

There was another round of applause from the audience.

Lucy stepped forward and smiled. Something glittered on her cheek. 'And now Matthew is finished with his soppy stuff, here's our latest song. We hope you like it.'

*

In the eight years since I left the Conservatoire, there had been few times when I'd felt really, truly swept up in music. I was usually too self-aware to get lost in it. But that night, standing on that scuffed, worn stage in that small, shabby, glorious theatre, surrounded by my friends, I finally gave myself up to it.

The three-minute rock ballad passed in a wonderful blur of gentle piano and fiery guitar riffs and moody, pulsing drums. I wondered how I had ever doubted the quality of Lucy's voice, the raw, uninhibited emotion of it. I loved it when we sang together,

her sultry alto contrasting with my dark tenor which was perhaps not as smooth as it had once been but was more expressive for it. I found I didn't care that I sounded rough sometimes. I had sacrificed perfection for emotion, and, in that moment, I was glad of it.

Afterwards, I was brought back to reality by applause. Loud, enthusiastic applause. Remembering the etiquette, I stepped out from behind the keyboard and folded into a bow. Lucy took my hand and raised it high, and we stood there, in the spotlight, for what felt like a very long time.

I looked at Lucy, who was smiling at me. I smiled back. And I realised that although the response from the audience was nice, what I really wanted was to return to the music, to sing with Lucy and the band again, and to keep doing that forever.

*

As soon as I left the stage, Lucy grabbed my arm and pulled me behind the backdrop.

'Matthew, that was amazing! *You* were amazing!'

I felt myself blush. 'Thank you. You were, too.'

'I loved your song.'

'I loved singing it with you.'

She rolled her eyes, but her expression was gentle. 'You're so soft.'

I did my best to look affronted. 'I beg your pardon?'

'You. Soft.' She smiled. 'I'm supposed to be an edgy rock singer. You're going to cramp my style, big time. You do know that, don't you?'

'Yes.'

Lucy laughed. Then she kissed me. And this time, I didn't pull away.

We stood against the back wall of the stage, between two papier-mâché trees left over from last year's pantomime. Lucy was in my arms, meaning that she was almost completely encircled by my coat.

'I've been thinking...' she said. 'About that talent scout.'

'Oh?'

'I think we should ring him.'

'Are you sure?'

'It's just... after tonight, I'm not sure we've got anything to lose. I think we might have something good here. I mean, really good. What do you think?'

'I think so, too,' I said.

'Would you be up for going to an audition? If we had the chance?'

I didn't hesitate. 'Yes. Yes, I think I would. But why the change of heart?'

Lucy reached up and cupped my cheek, brushing a few strands of hair out of my face. 'You. The way you went out there tonight, when I was so convinced you wouldn't. It made me realise I've been making my own excuses. I've also been hiding for too long.'

'I see.'

She smiled. 'I've started to play my violin again. Just a bit. And I've realised I still enjoy it. I didn't abandon it because of the music. It was the pressure. The feeling that I'd failed. But I know that doesn't have to happen with the band. Even if the audition doesn't lead anywhere, we can still play for fun, can't we?'

'Of course.'

'Matthew?'

'Yes?'

She shifted slightly in my arms. 'Your coat's bloody warm.'

I lowered my arms. 'It really is. I think it's wool.'

'Shall we go and get a drink?'

We found the other half of the band in the rehearsal room, where, in my role as manager, I had arranged for drinks to be left out for the performers. Dan and James had already made a start on the Prosecco, but I didn't care. They deserved it, and I decided the Phantom was allowed some guests.

Fifteen minutes later, the show was over and the room was crowded with the various acts. Charlotte was in her element, handing out more glasses of Prosecco and congratulating everybody. At one point, several large pizzas arrived, having been delivered to the stage door. I assumed Dan was the culprit.

Someone tapped me on the shoulder.

I turned to see Angela and Ralph. They were holding hands and smiling.

'Hi,' said Angela.

'Hello.'

'Congratulations, mate,' said Ralph. 'Great show.'

'Thank you.'

They shared a strange, secretive glance.

'What's going on?' I asked.

'We wanted you to be the first to know,' said Angela.

Oh, God. What now?

'We've decided *not* to get married,' said Ralph. And his face broke into a huge grin.

'Oh,' I said. 'I'm sorry. I mean... what? Am I supposed to be pleased?'

Angela squeezed Ralph's hand. 'We talked about it, and decided we were rushing things.'

'Okay. Well, that's probably a wise decision.'

'We've decided we both need a break from the spotlight for a while,' said Ralph.

'So we're going travelling,' said Angela. She smiled. 'Norway first, then Italy, then who knows?'

'That sounds great,' I said.

'You'll be all right, won't you, mate?' said Ralph. 'You can sing without me now.'

'I'll be fine.'

'We'll send you a postcard.'

'Great... Well, congratulations on not getting married yet.'

'Thanks,' said Angela. 'And congratulations on your impending rock stardom.'

'Oh, I don't know about that...'

'I do,' said Ralph. 'Let us know when the first stadium tour happens.'

We said our goodbyes, and then Angela and Ralph slipped out of the rehearsal room, laughing.

Honestly. And people thought I was weird.

'Matthew!' My mum appeared in the doorway, with my dad and Clara close behind.

Jess sidled up to me. 'I said they could come back to see you. I hope that's okay.'

I nodded. 'That's fine.'

Mum stepped forward and encircled me in a hug. 'I'm so proud of you. Congratulations.'

I smiled. 'Thank you.'

My dad patted me on the back, looked around worriedly at the assembled performers, and went to take refuge by the refreshment table.

Clara looked me up and down and raised her eyebrows. 'Is this the new rock image?'

'Yes.' I swirled my coat a bit. 'Do you like it?'

She laughed. 'It suits you.'

There was the bright ringing sound of someone tapping the edge of a wine glass. The room quietened, and a circle formed around Charlotte.

'Sorry to interrupt the party, everyone, but I would like to say a few words.' She smiled at the performers. 'Tonight's show was a sell-out. And what's more, donations are still coming in via our crowdfunding campaign. I would like to thank you all for taking part tonight.' Her gaze rested on me. 'And I would especially like to thank Matthew, whose ghostly exploits seem to have inspired most of the donations.'

The guests clapped, and I blushed.

Charlotte's face broke into a huge grin. 'I'm delighted to announce that, thanks to the generosity of your good selves, our audience, and our supporters around the world, we are able to secure the future of the Moon and Stars Theatre for the next year, and hopefully many more to come.'

There were cheers. I looked at Jess.

'We saved it?' I asked.

She nodded.

A weight lifted from my shoulders. The room went blurry, and I blinked back tears. Lucy swam into my line of vision.

'We saved it!' I exclaimed.

She laughed and hugged me. 'I heard.'

# Coda

'You've missed your vocation,' said Lucy, nudging me in the ribs. 'You should have been a wedding singer.'

I glared at her, then laughed. 'Get lost.'

She chuckled. 'Still the same old music snob.'

I was wearing a smart grey suit, with a carnation in the buttonhole, and we were walking from the church to the golf club. Twenty minutes earlier, I had stood up at my sister's wedding and sung 'Some Enchanted Evening' in front of a tearful congregation of friends and relatives. Lucy swore she hadn't been crying, but I'd seen her reach for a tissue.

It was one of the most mortifying experiences of my life, while simultaneously being one of the nicest.

As we took our seats at the top table, a hand fell on my shoulder. I turned and saw Clara in her elegant, plain satin wedding dress.

'Thank you for the song,' she said. 'It's good to see you looking like yourself again.'

I knew she wasn't referring to the grey suit, and I smiled.

*

There had been a moment, a few weeks after our concert at the Moon and Stars, when I'd realised I didn't feel ugly anymore.

It was the weekend, and we had spent the afternoon at the theatre, rehearsing with the band. Afterwards, Lucy and I had gone back to my flat for a glass of wine. She had played a beautiful piece on her violin for me: something she had done several times in the weeks since the concert. At one point, I went into the bedroom to fetch something – a piece of sheet music, I think – and I caught my reflection in the mirror on my wardrobe door.

There had been no dramatic change in my appearance. My hair was a bit longer, and I thought I would continue to grow it. I wasn't wearing the concealer so often – now I only wore it when I felt like it, and on that particular occasion, I didn't have any on at all. But that night, as I looked in the mirror, I realised that although my face hadn't changed, my perception of it had.

I didn't see the flaws anymore.

I just looked at myself in the mirror, and I thought *That's me.*

And then I went back into the living room.

*

My sister had hired a karaoke machine. Or, rather, it had come with the golf club, so it was inevitable that we use it.

I sipped white wine and listened as my new brother-in-law threw himself, heart and soul, into a spectacularly awful yet passionate rendition of 'I'm Gonna Be (500 Miles)' by The Proclaimers. I was proud of him. I glanced at Clara and saw her laughing and cringing.

Lucy tapped me on the shoulder. 'Will you sing?'

'I'll sing if you will.'

'I'll go afterwards.' She smiled. 'Headline act.'

I went up to the mic and selected a rock ballad.

It wasn't perfect – I had consumed a lot of food and wine since the church – but that didn't matter.

As the music swept around me, I thought about all the things I could do:

1. Perform with the band.
2. Join an operatic society.
3. Record my own songs.
4. Audition for musicals.

But for now, I would just sing.

# Acknowledgements

Thank you to...

My lecturers on the Creative Writing MA at Teesside University for their support and belief in my work.

James and Laura at Writers' Block North East for your mentoring while I was developing early drafts of this story. The idea for this novel came from one of your wonderful workshops.

Catherine, fellow *Phantom* fan, for encouraging me to share my early stories.

Em, for reading my first chapter and synopsis and giving me lovely, writerly advice over coffee.

Louise Walters, for longlisting a page from this novel in your fabulous 'Page 100' writing competition. The page in question is now gone, but such is the nature of redrafting! Thanks for giving me a confidence boost when I really needed it.

The community of writers I met on Zoom courses in 2020/2021 for your positivity and words of encouragement.

All at Saltburn Writers for cheering me on and being such a lovely, supportive group. Special thanks to Helen for your feedback on my first three chapters and the dreaded synopsis.

Janet, my first reader, who read through two entire drafts of this book and gave such wonderful, helpful feedback.

Carmen, who also read through successive drafts and helped me shape this novel into something I'm truly proud of. I couldn't have asked for a more insightful mentor.

Daniela, Laura and all at Fairlight Books for being such brilliant editors, understanding Matthew and his theatrical world, and giving me the opportunity to share this novel with readers. It's a dream come true. Thanks also to Laura Barrett for designing the most beautiful cover an author could wish for.

Special thanks to Mam and Dad for all your love and support.

# About the Author

Jenna Warren was born in Middlesbrough and grew up in Saltburn-by-the-Sea. She studied Theatre at the University of Hull, and completed an MA in Creative Writing at Teesside University. Her stories have featured in the anthologies *Whitby Abbey: Pure Inspiration* and *Through the Cracks: The Teesside Literary Society's Inaugural Anthology*. After she worked for several years as an assistant in an art gallery, her passion for books led her to open Book Corner, an independent bookshop in Saltburn. *The Moon and Stars* is her debut novel.

DEBORAH JENKINS

# Braver

Hazel has never felt normal. Struggling with OCD and anxiety, she isolates herself from others and sticks to rigid routines in order to cope with everyday life. But when she forms an unlikely friendship with Virginia, a church minister, Hazel begins to venture outside her comfort zone.

Having rebuilt her own life after a traumatic loss, Virginia has become the backbone of her community, caring for those in need and mentoring disadvantaged young people. Yet a shock accusation threatens to unravel everything she has worked for. Told with warmth, compassion and gentle humour, *Braver* is an uplifting story about the strength that can be drawn from friendship and community.

'A heart-warming book ... Jenkins shows us the world through the eyes of someone who blossoms in the company of new friends she literally crashes into'
—Debbi Voisey, author of *Only About Love*

'Wonderfully uplifting, utterly human and deeply compassionate'
—Loree Westron, author of *Missing Words*

AMI RAO

# David and Ameena

MODERN-DAY NEW YORK, A SUBWAY TRAIN.

David, an American-Jewish jazz musician, torn between his dreams and his parents' expectations, sees a woman across the carriage. Ameena, a British-Pakistani artist who left Manchester to escape the pressure from her conservative family, sees David.

When a moment of sublime beauty occurs unexpectedly, the two connect. But as David and Ameena navigate their relationship, their ambitions and the city they love, they discover the external world is not so easy to keep at bay.

Ami Rao's masterful debut novel picks apart the lives of two people, stripping them of their collective identities and, in doing so, facing up to the challenge of today: can love give us the freedom to accept our differences?

*'Exquisite. Beautiful. Provocative. I love her writing'*
—Jim Lawless, author of *Taming Tigers*

*'Ami Rao intricately weaves threads of love, family, politics and identity to create a beautiful, and very real, modern love story that sparkles beneath a New York skyline'*
—Huma Qureshi, author of *How We Met*